First Published in Great Britain in 2023 by
Fish Bananas Publishing

ISBN 978-1-3999-5510-2

Titling & cover font Nina by Studio Margot Lévêque.
Body font Monotype Bembo

Design & Layout by Kate & Martin McCully | draftdesign.co.uk

Many thanks for advice and support to

Kay Williams

John Kittle

Heather Martin

Dawn Dowding

Kate McCully

Martin McCully

Ian Dowding

FISH FARCE

SEX, DRUGS & ELVIS

Justin comes to Cocklebury-on-Sea to find his real father – his only lead – a photograph.

Councillor's daughter, Jo, has lied about her age to take a part time modelling job.

Club owner, Ray wants to open an amusement arcade but the land he wants is not for sale and Ray doesn't like things getting in his way.

After a misspent youth Ben just wants to settle down and paint but his past keeps catching up with him.

FARCE: (n) a comic dramatic work using buffoonery and horseplay and typically including crude characterisation and ludicrously awkward situations.

THE OFFERING

{ CHAPTER 01 }

The road up to the church, flanked by banks of wild flowers and grasses in the summer, this winter's day was wet and muddy. What little traffic there was had splashed the grass at the verge making it drab and dirty. It spattered the wheel arches, back and sides of the white vehicle as it drove up the lane. The church at Tidwick was on a raised plateau and it looked down across the marshes. On a clear day you could see the sea.

A light dusting of snow had fallen in the night. The vehicle pulled up by the low wall left of the lych gate and a man got out. He put his collar up against the cold and pulled the knitted hat down over his ears. He held a flat, crudely wrapped parcel in his hand. There was no one about as he went through the gate. Old gravestones leant against the inside of the wall where the man had parked his vehicle. The grass was longish and matted, woven with weeds and studded with the remaining leaves of autumn. He took a path to the left that skirted the church on the seaward side. Snow decorated the tops of the gravestones in precarious little pillars and odd shapes. It lay on the ground in patches copying the rectangles that were a feature of some plots – as if they were blankets keeping the dead warm.

He left the path and wound his way between the graves as if making for the edge to look out over the view to the sea. But he wasn't going to look out to sea. He reached a gravestone that was relatively new compared to the worn and pitted stones of the older graves. There was a small angel, cherubic looking, carved into the top and he wiped the snow from it with a gloved hand before removing the glove and touching the name on the inscription with his fingertips like a man reading Braille.

He knelt like that for a moment and then as if it was an afterthought he remembered the parcel. He folded back the edges of the white paper to reveal a small flat fish. The skin shone in the weak sunlight, the red spots evident against the dark skin. He lifted the fish away from the paper and placed it on the grave where the grey shape of it stood out against the starkness of the snow. After a while he stood, gathered up the paper and walked slowly back to the vehicle.

Two yellow eyes blinked in the shadows of a yew tree as the sound of the motor became fainter in the distance. A cat, its black fur, camouflaged by the cloak of the tree's foliage, sniffed the air. With caution it moved out from the cove of the tree and moved towards the smell, high stepping like a show horse through the grass. It stood by the grave looking at the fish, sniffing it tentatively at first as if it too found the idea of a fish in a graveyard incongruous. The cat then touched it with a paw, inverting it to lift the head of the fish and sniffed again. Then, as if making up his mind of a sudden he took the head in his jaws, turned and made his way back to the cover of the tree, the fish jutting out of his mouth.

THE HANGOVER

{ CHAPTER 02 }

Ben rolled off the sofa onto the rug landing on all fours.

'Fuck,' he said softly and waited until the hammer inside his skull calmed to a steadier beat.

He had woken up in the room he called his office. It was at the back of the studio come gallery and was many things as well as an office, in the same way the sofa was more than just a sofa. It was big enough to seat four people comfortably which meant that Ben could stretch out on it and sleep when that was more convenient than any alternative.

A large Victorian, mahogany, beast of a desk stood in the middle of the room, daring anyone who thought they were strong enough to budge it an inch in any direction. The wood and leather surface, once lovingly and often cared for by servants, and lavished with unguents to keep its surface agleam, was now home to a chaos of art books, sketch pads, unpaid bills, unwashed cups and plates, paintbrushes, catalogues, flyers and near empty tubes of paint.

A sink and draining board were fixed in a corner of the room and like the other facilities was multi-functional. It was spattered with the results of brush cleaning and used for the washing of cups and plates when Ben either had a fit of domesticity or he ran out of space on the desk. An electric kettle stood to one side for the making of tea and coffee and a small shelf held the accoutrements for carrying out this task. At the end was a tooth mug that held a toothbrush and a tube of toothpaste, kept far enough away from the dangerous confusion of other tubes in the room.

A bookcase held more art books – Cezanne, Monet, Hopper etc that Ben had either come across in charity shops or bought new when his finances were at a peak rather than in a trough. Two chairs in the room held the sum total of Ben's wardrobe; jeans, t-shirts and various jumpers for the winter months, decorated with holes and spattered with paint.

A solitary window shed light into this space. A bush of valerian grew outside it, the pink flowers peeping over the sill in summer. Beyond it was the beach and the sea. Ben was lax about security and in summer it was more often open than closed, but as there was little of interest to thieves unless they were into art books it hardly mattered.

Ben stood up slowly, careful not to make any sudden movements, flicked the switch at the base of the kettle and lit a cigarette. The first light of morning was filtering through the window. He went through to the main part of the building, opened the back door and looked out over the shingle, down to the beach. The sea, mostly grey blue was waiting for the sun to improve its colour, but this being England there would always be a hint of battleship about it. The air was still damp and chill from the night but the clear sky promised another hot day. The tide that came up in the night had cleared the litter and oddments left on the beach; a jelly shoe, a child's vest, and had demolished the sand castles where there was sand, tidied, rearranged and cleaned the shingle further up and left its signature wavy line of black weed at the limit of its reach.

Ben made coffee and took the cup outside with him. It was still early. Only the gulls were up, shrieking and swooping, looking for anything that might resemble food. Too early for the joggers, dog walkers and cyclists; even the fishermen had left with the receding tide, their boats smudges in the distance, the chug of their engines too far out to hear.

Several commercial enterprises, mostly converted net sheds, dotted this no-man's-land between the petering out promenade and the coast road east of the main town. In the centre was a small car park, made of sand and shingle and deeply rutted. Between this and the sea was a boat repair shop, and next to that a fishmongers called Dean's Plaice with a sign painted on a placard the shape of the eponymous fish. To the left of the car park a converted caravan stood. It sold burgers, hot dogs and bacon sandwiches along with soft drinks, tea, coffee and ice cream. A sign above the serving hatch announced 'Toddy's Bacon Crematorium'. The caravan had settled over the years and now sat as if embedded in the ground, a patch of rough grass and nettles at its back and behind it two tennis courts, run down, unloved and uncared for.

The Fish Works Art Gallery was a long, low, single storey building. The front part facing the road was the main gallery. The entrance at the side opened onto the reception area and the back part of it, close to the beach path and the sea, was the office, though bedsit might have been more accurate. This arrangement, though strictly illegal as far as the local council would be concerned if they were ever to find out, suited Ben. He liked living where he worked, he liked being close to the sea and it was cheap. Any conventional housing that looked out onto the beach would carry a price tag well out of Ben's reach. The arrangement also afforded him a certain autonomy. His relationship with Wendy, the owner of a guest house a hundred yards along the seafront was unconventional by default. In summer when the guest house was full Wendy was always busy and they saw each other one or two nights a week. In winter Ben stayed over more often. They had both had conventional relationships previously that hadn't worked out so this loose arrangement suited them both.

Ben had painted the rendered exterior of the building a Farrow and Ball colour named 'Dead Salmon' which he thought was fitting, with a logo painted by Ben of three fish heads. The fishy signs tended to confuse people looking for the fish shop and this often meant redirecting people who came into the gallery asking for two ounces of coley or a wing of skate.

Ben took a towel from the office and walked across the shingle to the edge of the water. The sun was now over the horizon, burning off the last wisps of mist remaining from the night and casting a honeyed glow over the beach and seafront. He hung the towel over a breakwater, took off his jeans and t-shirt and walked into the shallows. When the water was up to his knees he launched himself into the sea and started swimming away from the beach. It was a ritual he carried out most mornings with few exceptions. It was both invigorating and cleansing and never failed to shake off a hangover. He struck out till he reached the yellow buoy, and then turned on his back, floating and looking at the sky. When his breathing had slowed he rolled over on to his front again and started a lazy crawl back to the beach.

THE REVELATION

{ CHAPTER 03 }

Justin made his way down the corridor, used now to the strange squelch the soles of his shoes made on the polished linoleum. He had resolved to visit every day since his mother had been brought here so the nurses all knew him well enough to nod and sometimes smile as he passed. One of them was by the bed as he went in.

'How is she today?' he asked in a whisper.

'Not too bad.'

He sat down in the chair by the bed and looked at his mother's face, made older than it should by the illness. Her eyes fluttered open and she smiled. 'Hello darling.'

He took her hand that lay on the covers. Her eyes closed

again. He didn't speak in case she wanted to sleep; besides over the last fortnight they had said all there was to say from practical things like dealing with the house and the funeral to the personal things, making sure they made all the emotional declarations that create regrets if left unsaid.

'I'm not asleep,' she said.

'I don't want to tire you,' he told her.

'You won't tire me; tell me something, anything, your voice is a comfort to me. Tell me about Amy.'

Justin smiled. 'Amy's fine. She's at work today.'

'You are going to marry her, aren't you? I want to know you are settled before I pop off.'

'No chance of escape with Amy's mother organising things.'

'Good, best thing for a man, marriage.'

'Is that what you told Dad?'

'I didn't need to; he was that keen.'

'Lucky you.'

'In a lot of ways yes, though he was a lot older. I knew I would be a young widow.'

'You were happy though?'

'Ye-es. A look of wistfulness crossed her face. I wanted to go back; see if I could..' She paused as if memories were coming back to her. '..but it was water under the bridge. It would have been wrong.'

'Go back where?' Justin asked.

'Oh take no notice of me. I don't know what I'm saying sometimes.'

A few days later the nurse intercepted Justin on his way to see his mother.

'She's not good today,' the nurse said. 'She had a bad night. It won't matter if you miss it today.'

'No, I'd like to,' Justin said.

The nurse was right. His mother looked distressed. She

didn't give her usual greeting and Justin wasn't even sure if she knew it was him.

'They've been visiting again,' she said, 'in the night.'

'Who, who's been visiting in the night?' Justin asked.

'Eileen and Carol,' His mother said in a stage whisper.

Justin knew these were his aunts; sisters of his father. Eileen had died several year's earlier and Carol was in a home for dementia. 'That was nice then,' said Justin hoping it was the best way to humour her.

'I think they know.'

'Know what?' Justin asked.

'You know.' His mother sounded cross. Justin didn't reply.

'I had to do it; you do understand don't you?'

Justin was lost. He wondered what was going on in her mind and what was causing this latest confusion. She looked at him and there was fear in her eyes. She beckoned him to come closer as if she was about to reveal some terrible secret. He leaned in.

'I was already pregnant when Dad and I married.'

Justin smiled. 'So what Mum; it was the nineteen eighties; it wasn't the dark ages. I would imagine that was pretty normal.'

'You don't understand, Dad didn't know.'

'What, you mean you didn't tell him?'

'No, I mean he couldn't have known.'

Justin felt a creeping sense of unease. 'Hang on; I'm not sure I get this.'

'I was on holiday with a friend called Janet, and you see I met someone.'

'Are you trying to tell me there was someone else before Dad,' said Justin.

'You knew that.' Her voice had gone dreamy as if she was drifting off. 'I told you before.'

'No you didn't.'

'Of course I did.'

'Well tell me again.' His voice was insistent; he needed to know more before she slept again.

'It all gets mixed up in my head.'

'Are you telling me you got pregnant on holiday before you married Dad?' Justin asked.

The image he had of his parents as solid and middle class, even a bit boring, to the point he often wondered if sex was ever on the cards, and now his mother was admitting to a holiday romance, getting pregnant by someone else before marrying his dad. It all seemed too far-fetched.

'I was young, innocent, confused. I didn't know what to do. My parents would never have understood. You see I knew Lionel, knew he wanted to marry me – it seemed an obvious solution.'

'You mean, he never knew at all?'

'Of course not; he wouldn't have married me if he'd known.'

'Christ Mother.'

'I'm sorry,' she said and started weeping. Justin put a hand on her arm just as the nurse looked into the room.

'Everything alright?' she asked

'Yeah,' Justin said, 'Mum's just got a bit upset.'

'Better leave it for today then,' the nurse said.

Justin got up, kissed his mother on the forehead and ushered the nurse out of the room with him.

'She's saying a lot of really weird stuff in there,' Justin said.

'Oh, that'll be the morphine,' the nurse said smiling.

'Really?' Justin looked at her to see if she was just trying to palm him off.

'Yes, she's on a really high dose right now, for the pain; it induces hallucinations.'

'Has she been saying strange stuff to you as well?' Justin asked.

The nurse smiled. 'She said how handsome your dad looked in his naval cap. But I suppose that's not really that strange is it?'

'It bloody well is,' Justin replied.

A SPLIFF ON THE BEACH

{ CHAPTER 04 }

Kevin took a drag on the joint making the end glow red in the dark and sucked the smoke deep into his lungs. He felt his eyeballs pricking as he handed it to Bo without looking in her direction. Breath watched intently the progression of the joint from Kevin to Bo, eager for his turn. Bo took a half-hearted puff and passed it on. Breath giggled.

'Who's that speccy kid?' Kevin asked when he opened his eyes.

'Some kid from year nine.' Bo answered. 'He's called Spig.'

Further down the beach nearer the sea Edward Spiggot sat hunched. Every now and then he produced a flare as he lit a match and watched it burn, holding it as long as he could, sometimes wetting his fingers so he could hold the burnt end and char the complete match.

'Woss he want?' Kevin asked.

'I dunno,' said Bo.

Breath threw a pebble that hit Spig in the middle of his back.

'Eff off,' called Spig without turning round.

'Come on, don't hog it,' Kevin said holding out his hand to Breath. Breath gave the joint back to Kevin who blew on the end. It had gone out. Kevin reached into his pocket for a lighter. It clicked a few times but it did not produce a flame.

'Take an ember from the fire,' Breath suggested watching Kevin trying to relight the joint.

The fire which had been burning brightly an hour ago from the dry drift wood they had found above the tide line, was reduced now to ash and a few red embers. Kevin found a twig poking out of the fire and held it against a piece of wood that was still glowing. He held it to the end of the joint and took a few trial puffs.

'Nah,' he said throwing the stick back in the fire.

'Here kid,' he called out to Spig.

'What?' Spig replied without turning round.

'Give us a light.'

Spig got up slowly as if old or world weary and trudged up the shingle. He handed the matches to Kevin who lit the joint and handed the matches back to Spig who sat down, a little apart but facing the fire. 'Give us a drag then,' he said.

'You're too young,' Breath pointed out.

'Smokin' that stuff 's not exactly legal is it?' Spig argued. Breath snorted.

'You're that kid who set light to the science block, aren't you?' Bo said.

Spig lit another match and watched it flare before answering.

'It was only the bench.'

'Whatever,' said Bo.

'I remember ole Simmons,' Breath recalled. 'He used to smell.'

'You can talk,' said Bo.

A pained expression replaced the grin on Breath's face but he didn't respond. Kevin got up from his sitting position on the shingle.

'Mr Simmons went ape,' Spig offered.

'My arse has gone numb,' Kevin complained and walked down the shingle towards the sea.

The long overcoat he wore summer and winter reached down almost to his trainers and with his long hair he almost disappeared in the darkness. He stood looking out over the slowly heaving ocean. The waves broke on the shore; the thin line of foam lit by the moon.

Only when Kevin held his arms above his head, fingers outstretched, could they see where he was from his pale hands.

'We gonna sleep on the beach then?' said Breath.

'Not likely,' said Bo.

'Can we crash at yours then?'

'No you can't.'

Spig wanted to go home but it wasn't safe yet. Not while Dad was in his present mood. Spig had made a quick exit. Avoidance was always the best policy. If only Mum didn't wind him up so much, it was almost as if she wanted to get bashed. It would start with something small and escalate from there. He knew better than to side with his Mum, that's when Dad would really start lashing out. The confusion of someone you loved not just hitting you but actually punching you, was not something Spig had managed to understand yet. All he knew was that lighting matches and watching them flare calmed and fascinated him in equal measure. He had slipped out of the back door this evening. He always had a door key and a box of matches in his pocket. No one would go looking for him. That he knew.

It was getting dark when he had approached the seafront. There were a few people around taking a stroll, residents from the hotels some just walking to or from the pub. A few foreign students were hanging around the entrance to the pier. Nobody took any notice of him and the proximity of people around only seemed to make him feel more isolated. He had wandered away from the town, along the seafront watching the glow of a fire in the distance, keeping it as a focal point and destination. He didn't know the group he found sitting around the bonfire but he had seen them around. They always seemed to hang out together; Kevin in his long black coat and greasy hair could be recognised easily. The police had picked him up so many times for suspected theft and possession they had now ceased to bother. The long hair and hunched attitude meant his face was rarely seen, which was preferable. A diet of chips, cheap cider and cannabis gave him a pallid complexion that was shiny and decorated with pustules of acne.

Kevin made his way back up the beach towards the group. Bo was relieved. She didn't like being left alone with Breath. She didn't count Spig because of his age. Breath often made a move on her when Kevin was not around or too stoned to care. Kevin had found another piece of wood on his brief trip to the shoreline and he threw it on the fire as he came level with it. A shower of red sparks cascaded into the darkness above the fire.

'That won't burn, it's too wet,' Breath commented.

'Don't matter,' said Kevin. 'It's going out anyway.'

Bo moved a bit closer to Kevin as he sat down. She was a short, dumpy girl who rarely spent time at home because of the constant rows with her mother, usually over the latest hair colour she had chosen, another piercing on her face, which were the only ones her mother knew about, or a tattoo. She hung out with Kevin partly because he never commented on these things so she didn't feel judged. Breath earned his nickname from the ever present problem of halitosis. He hung out with them partly because he thought there was a chance Bo might let him shag her (there wasn't), and partly to share Kevin's smokes. He never bought any dope himself and Kevin only shared his when he was feeling generous or when he had scored a larger than usual quantity.

Bo tolerated Breath so she could be near Kevin. They were in a sort of relationship but as neither of them ever discussed it they were not sure what sort of relationship it was. Sex was a tricky subject. Neither of them were organised enough to arrange any form of contraception so most sexual congress stopped short of actual penetration. On occasions when desire or drugs had got the better of her sense of control she would go to the local drop-in clinic and get a morning-after pill, but she tended to try and avoid that, only because she felt the friendly dishing out of advice was only another version of her mother's disapproval and was altogether too patronising. Sometimes if they were very stoned she had been known to get it on with Breath, usually sticking to oral sex on account of his halitosis, but mostly she was ambivalent about sex.

'I might be getting a place,' said Kevin poking the ashes with a stick.

'Cool,' said Breath.

'You'll have to give me something towards it,' Kevin told them.

'Like what?' said Bo.

'Like rent,' said Kevin sarcastically.

They fell silent.

'Is it a squat?' Bo asked.

'No-o,' answered Kevin in the same tone. 'You don't pay rent in squats. I got this guy, he owes me a favour.'

'Sounds OK,' Breath said.

'I'll come,' said Spig.

'You're too young,' Kevin replied.

THE MAN IN THE GOLD LEXUS

{ CHAPTER 05 }

Ben had lived in Cocklebury-on-Sea for most of his life apart from a brief sojourn to Morocco and another period when he had had to go away. It wasn't so much that he loved the town but, as he argued, there could be worst places to live. His education at the local school had been as brief as was legally possible. He left believing himself a failure but later on realised he was not quite as dumb as school had made him think he was. A series of jobs followed, none of which seemed to satisfy or stimulate him. He knew he was not destined to end up as a desk jockey, shelf filler or an automaton in a factory. The job hopping was a means of looking for something although he wasn't sure what, but he knew he would recognise it when he saw it.

The epiphany, when it came, arrived sideways when he took a job as assistant to a local picture framer. The owner was an old misanthropist who hated art, the framing business and most of the customers who walked through the door. With Ben he was fussy, pedantic and nagging; hating him for his youth and optimism. But he reserved his greatest scorn for his best customer, a large, florid, flamboyant painter called Max who brought in surreal works of great detail and complexity. Ben liked Max immediately, partly because his boss hated him, partly because Max couldn't care less what he thought, but mainly because he represented freedom, an alternative lifestyle and a different attitude. He also loved the paintings. It was as if they were a graphic portrayal of the man himself, which of course they were.

Working on framing the pictures Ben was able to study them in detail, while his boss kept up a diatribe on his view of them which was not complimentary. Max, seeing a potential acolyte in Ben that pleased his ego, befriended him. Ben became a regular visitor to Max's studio where he was introduced to a heady Bohemian lifestyle of marijuana, gin and lax attitudes to sex and nudity. He soon found out that the rest of the town shared Ben's boss's opinion of Max but by now Max's personality was beginning to rub off on Ben, something that he found excitingly rebellious. For all his anti-establishment posturing Max encouraged Ben to go to college and learn the basics and the history of art.

After his swim Ben went back to the gallery to get dressed and make more coffee. People were starting their morning rituals whether going to work or walking the dog. The man with the Doberman was always first. He raised an arm in greeting to Ben. Next would be the fat jogger. Ben lit another cigarette. Before he was half way through it he heard the familiar slap slap of labouring trainers getting closer. The fat jogger always wore a white T-shirt and shorts and every inch of exposed flesh, face, arms, legs and the expanse of belly where the T-shirt didn't quite meet the waist band of the shorts, was bright red. The man sweated profusely, his whole body uncoordinated in effort. It always made Ben check that his phone was in his pocket as he was certain that one day he was going to have to call the emergency services.

More people went by; the woman with the two Dachshunds, a pair of joggers, a husband and wife team, fit and lean and the man in the motorised wheel chair who struggled to lean over and clean up after his dog as it looked on fondly at this strange human activity; then the girl who ran without making a sound, as if her running shoes weren't touching the ground. She wore tight pedal pushers revealing golden calves and slim ankles, white socks and trainers; her smooth, shiny ponytail, protruding through the gap in her baseball cap, bounced up and down with each step.

Ben had left the picture-framers and enrolled at art school in a town twenty miles away. Now education had a purpose more meaningful than algebra and Ben, having tasted the jobs market unlike some of his fellow students, worked with alacrity and a desire for achievement. He also had to leave the comfort of the parental home as his parents disapproved of his chosen career, his lifestyle, and his involvement with Max, but mostly because he was now unable to pay for his keep. To complete the course Ben shared rooms and flats where he could and worked bars and hotels in the evenings to provide some income.

Max's lifestyle should also have been a warning to Ben of the financial vagaries of an artist's life. If Max had sold a painting or received a commission it would be open house, parties, restaurant visits and cases of gin. But at times when money was short the friends that helped him share the good times were strangely absent and the only people who came knocking were those to whom he owed money. By the time Ben left art school Max was long gone but Ben was a different person and any shortfall in art income was supplemented by odd jobs.

He was moderately successful but knew that staying in Cocklebury-on-Sea he was never going to become well known or be able to sell works for thousands of pounds. He painted dramatic landscapes of local places that sold reasonably well but the money was sporadic and never enough to persuade a bank or building society to offer him a mortgage. He made enough to rent a small studio, smaller than the one he rented now, not pleasantly positioned near the beach and with no room for a gallery space. In summer he worked out of doors catching the fleeting atmosphere of light over the surrounding hills, the sea and the beach. It was a free and easy lifestyle especially in summer when the town was filled with holidaymakers and visiting students, and when the heat made flimsy clothing almost obligatory. Ben had not been averse to obliging girls looking for a holiday romance. In winter it was different, the seafront shuttered and windswept and Ben worked in his studio in boots, thick socks, two jumpers and fingerless gloves to save money on heating.

Finishing his coffee Ben went back inside to do the chores necessary to opening up for business. After opening the blinds He swept the floor then went outside to check the exterior. The plain walls were a magnet to every graffiti artist with a spray paint can in the area so Ben kept a pot of paint in his store so he could cover up any latest attempt at local notoriety. As an artist he didn't mind the principle behind the need to decorate such a temptingly blank area, it was just that the tags that seemed to appear were so formulaic, repetitive, and dull. They were no challenge to Banksy that was certain. It was even a change when someone decided to decorate the walls with the more traditional FUCK or SHIT. Unfortunately it seemed that this particular graffiti artist was also dyslexic and words such as WHANKER would appear, and on one occasion the legend WAYNE IS A CNUT.

Ben once decided to put his own graffiti up to beat the locals at their own game and painted a jagged hole in the wall that looked out over a reasonable pastiche of Monet's garden, but all this seemed to do was attract the attention of the local planning officials who, with an irony that Ben found perplexing, informed him it was illegal and had to be removed. Today there was only a splash from one of the gulls and Ben went back inside to put the lights on.

The main part of the gallery was a plain white square with a divider down the centre on which to hang more pictures. This was removable should Ben ever want to open up the space or display 3D work or sculpture in the centre. Between the office and the gallery was an area that Ben used as his studio. It was not large but the light was good and he could work there but also keep an eye on the gallery area during opening times. Working in this space with the door open he could hear the children's voices from the beach mingled with the occasional wail of a gull and the mumble of activity from the immediate vicinity. The painting that stood on the easel at the moment was a half-finished beach scene with a boat in the foreground and the fishermen unloading boxes of fish. It was the sort of scene Ben had painted a lot in varying ways but they sold well and it was pointless painting disjointed faces or squares of colour if your clientele were more in the market for landscapes. A lot of tourists wanted something that reminded them of their holiday not something avant-garde.

The swim had sharpened Ben's appetite and the smell of griddled bacon wafting over from Toddy's burger van was telling him it was time for breakfast. He wandered across the car park. Arthur Todman was a middle aged man with an air of resignation about him. He wore a chef's jacket that was off-white verging on grey, and a red spotted bandanna around his neck that, with his stubble, made him look piratical. Ben leant on the counter.

'I'll have the pastrami on rye with gherkins, micro herbs and mustard salsa.

'One bacon sandwich coming up,' Toddy replied. 'You want ketchup?'

'Undoubtedly. How's things?'

'Oh, you know,' said Toddy. 'I had the Environmental Health here yesterday.'

'Yeah?'

'He said I had to have three sinks, one for hand washing, one for washing up and one for preparing vegetables.'

'What did you say?'

'I said I don't do vegetables.'

'Good answer.' Ben lit up a cigarette.

'At least they can't stop my customers smoking,' Toddy said indicating the outdoor area of tables and chairs.

Ben picked up his plate. 'I'll bring the plate back,' he told Toddy as he walked away.

'Make sure you do. How many have you got over there already?'

'Loads.'

Ben took his sandwich and sat back down in his deck chair at the back of the gallery where he could watch the promenade and the beach. The day was warming up and looked like it was going to be a continuation of the good weather enjoyed over the last few days. There was now a continuous flow along the promenade of walkers, dogs, joggers, skaters and cyclists. The sun, getting higher in the sky was warming the beach and reflecting on the sea with a glare that required dark glasses. It bounced off the domes of the pier visible in the distance.

The pier divided the town in half. To the west were the posh hotels, the gardens with their regulation patches of colour and benches dedicated to dead relatives. Here also was the bowling green, the tea rooms and the golf club. At the far end, slightly apart, as if it had its nose in the air was the De Montfort hotel looking like a wedding cake, grandly presiding over the more select beaches and boasting a semi-circular gravel drive and a two star Michelin restaurant. East of the pier was the less salubrious part of town, the smaller hotels giving way to the B&Bs. Parallel to the seafront ran the road out of town. Here were the cafes, the Polish and Asian food stores, the tattoo parlours and second hand shops; the shops that sold lettered rock, cheap sweets, buckets and spades, dangerous inflatables and lewd postcards.

The days of McGill's double entendre saucy postcards, that the town council had once tried to ban, had given way to a more blatant sexual humour. 'Kiss-me-quick' hats were an outdated anachronism that could no longer compete with baseball caps and T-shirts announcing 'Pornstar' and 'Shit happens'. Dotted amongst these were the fish and chip shops and cheap take-aways, where the ever hungry gulls lined up on lime streaked roofs ready to swoop on anything remotely edible. They had been known to snatch ice creams from children or the sandwiches from the hands of dozing pensioners. They attacked discarded fish and chip papers still redolent with the tang of greasy fish and cleaned up the discarded waste from late night, post pub, munchie-induced kebab suppers.

Ben wandered back to Toddy's with a small stack of borrowed plates still decorated with smudges of ketchup reminiscent of an early Jackson Pollock. As he crossed the parking lot a car pulled in scuffing gravel under its wheels and sending up plumes of dust.

'Flash 'git,' murmured Toddy as Ben handed him the plates. Ben turned and looked not having taken much notice of the car or its occupant. The car was a gold Lexus and the middle aged man that emerged from it was wearing a suit and had perfectly combed, almost sculpted hair like the models in a Grecian 2000 advertisement. The number plate of the car spelt RAY 100J

'Who is he?' Ben asked.

'Dunno,' said Toddy. 'I'd take a guess that his first name is Raymond though.'

The man leaned on the roof of his car holding a mobile phone to his ear.

'I think we're meant to be impressed,' observed Ben.

The man was now walking in small circles, hand in pocket and looking down at his feet. He eventually took the phone from his ear and held it up in front of his face.

'Well, he's not taking holiday snaps, that's for sure,' said Toddy. 'Looks like an estate agent.'

'There's not much to sell around here. You haven't put your cafe on the market have you?'

Toddy scoffed. 'Don't make me laugh, a caravan and a few tables.' The man turned and pointed his camera phone towards the cafe but then thought better of it when he saw Ben and Toddy looking at him. He put the phone away and got back inside the car. Ben wandered back across to the gallery as the man left the car park, leaving behind another small cloud of dust. Ben went inside and came out with the A board that said the gallery was open, and set it at the corner of the building where it could be seen from the road and the promenade. Cars started arriving, mainly families going to the beach. It was cooler in the gallery now than outside where it was starting to get hot. Ben stared at his painting on the easel and picked up his palette.

JUSTIN AND AMY

{ CHAPTER 06 }

'What do you mean, not your Dad?' Amy asked.

'Just that.' Justin told her about the conversation he had last had with his mother. They were in Justin's flat. Amy sat on a stool at the kitchen work-top while Justin opened a pack of fresh pasta and tipped it into the water simmering on the stove.

'I can't imagine your mother doing something like that,' Amy told him, a smile spreading across her face.

'Neither can I,' Justin replied.

'A dark secret in the Parker family; how exciting,' Amy continued.

'I don't quite see it like that,' Justin said.

Amy, realizing that Justin had not joined her in seeing

the lighter side of the revelation put her matter-of-fact face on. 'Your Dad is still your Dad; nothing changes that fact regardless of blood.'

'It changes everything,' Justin argued. 'Am I what I am because of my upbringing or because of the genes I inherited?'

Amy watched the steam from the pan curl up to the ceiling. 'You think too much Justin. It doesn't matter that much; you are what you are.'

Justin tipped the pasta into a colander over the sink wondering if Amy just didn't have the imagination to understand how he felt or whether she was right and it really didn't matter.

'Well, it hasn't happened to you, has it?' he replied eventually.

Amy made a face as Justin transferred the pasta into a bowl and spooned the sauce over it.

She went to a drawer and got out cutlery. 'Here, or at the table?' she asked.

'Here,' Justin said dividing the contents of the bowl between two plates.

'What are you going to do about it?' Amy asked.

Justin took a mouthful of wine while he thought. 'Ask Mother for more details when I next go and see her. She got a bit agitated telling me so I didn't push her any further.'

'Do you have any other clues?'

'None.'

'Can't you ask relatives?'

Justin thought for a moment. 'She had no brothers or sisters, a couple of friends who I doubt she would have confided in because of the circumstances, and it is unlikely she told anyone on Dad's side of the family seeing as she kept the secret from him.'

Supper over and Justin cleared up as Amy stacked the dishwasher. The telephone rang and Justin answered.

'Speaking,' he said.

Amy stood and watched his face as he listened. She watched as the frown on his face deepened.

'Thank you for letting me know,' he said at last.

Amy went over and stood beside him as he put the phone down. 'That was the hospice,' he said looking at the wall opposite.

'I thought it was,' Amy said. 'Are you OK?'

'I'll be fine,' Justin answered. 'It's funny; you do all the grieving beforehand when you know what is inevitable. Now, it's a sort of relief.'

Amy put her arms around him. 'I'll stay with you tonight,' she said.

HANNAH'S BRAINWAVE

{ CHAPTER 07 }

Ben was putting some finishing touches to the painting on the easel. He could hear distant voices coming from the beach through the open door of the gallery.

'Had many in?' Hannah asked.

'Not so far, one or two,' Ben replied.

Hannah was Ben's assistant and receptionist. She took charge if Ben had to be somewhere else, dealt with customers and enquiries and tidied up. Although Ben had never asked her she also did the paperwork. She took this upon herself when she found several cheques in a drawer that Ben had failed to bank along with a number of unpaid bills. Receipts seemed to have been stuffed into a filing cabinet and proper accounts did not exist. She had never even been officially recruited. She came in one day and started chatting to Ben. After a few more visits she got to making coffee and sometimes talked to customers. She didn't do it for money which was just as well although she sometimes told Ben she was paying herself something if she knew he could afford it but in total it didn't amount to much. She also knew that Ben appreciated what a muddle he would be in if she wasn't there to help out.

'Is it time for coffee?' she asked.

'It's always time for coffee,' Ben replied.

Hannah rattled as she walked. She liked chunky jewellery and she wore lots of it, necklaces, bangles, rings and earrings. Ben hadn't looked up from the canvas when she came in but Hannah was used to this and she didn't mind. She would pop in most days, make coffee, chat and do some office work. She came back with two mugs of coffee and put one on the table by the easel amongst the tubes of paint and jars of brushes.

'That easel is a work of art in itself,' Hannah commented.

Ben took his eyes from the painting and looked at the easel as if for the first time.

'Where did you get it?' she asked.

Ben thought. 'In an auction,' he said. The easel, made of a dark wood was battered and aged with time and use and encrusted with years of paint.

'Did it have provenance?' she asked.

'I shouldn't think so.'

'You never know it might have belonged to someone famous.'

'It's French, I know that. It's got a makers badge on it somewhere.

'There you are then,' said Hannah sipping her coffee.

'Not all French artists were famous.' Ben observed.

'Don't be so unimaginative.'

'I'm pragmatic,' Ben replied squeezing some titanium white onto his palette.

'Those blue splashes could be Monet.

'Yeah yeah.'

'That yellow dribble could be from Van Gogh's sunflowers.'

'Van Gogh was Dutch.'

Hannah sighed. Ben stood back from the painting, put the paintbrush down, picked up his coffee and looked at Hannah for the first time that morning. Hannah made most of her own clothes. She not only made them but had spun the yarn, woven the fabric, and dyed the material herself in natural vegetable dyes. The effect was not unpleasant. They were mostly shades of brown. If there were colours there they were muted and subtle. The overall effect was that of a rather lovely moth. With a professional eye Ben was thinking raw sienna, burnt umber.

'Did you sell anything yesterday?' Hannah asked.

'A small print and a few cards,' Ben told her. 'I'm thinking of jacking it in.'

Hannah looked shocked. 'I hope you don't,' she said.

A woman put her head around the door. 'Can we come in?'

'Of course you can,' Ben told her.

The woman stepped inside as if she were entering a church. A man followed her looking reluctant. They were an older couple. The man wore a sports jacket and combat trousers with a white flat cap and equally brilliant trainers.

'We like art,' the woman said. Ben smiled then flashed a look at Hannah as the woman turned away.

'Trouble is,' Ben said carrying on the conversation with Hannah in a lowered tone. 'There are more pictures about than there are walls to hang them on.'

'Yes but a lot of that is cheap, mass produced stuff.'

'People don't know the difference.'

'Really?' Hannah sounded surprised.

Ben kept an eye on the couple looking around in case they wanted his assistance. The woman was studying each picture thoughtfully. The man looked bored.

'Then you've got the brigade that wants something to match the curtains.'

Hannah laughed.

'And that's before we get onto amateur artists.'

'What's wrong with amateur artists?'

'Nothing,' said Ben. 'But they come in here get a few ideas from what they see and never buy anything because they've got so much of their own stuff on the walls at home.'

The couple decided at last it was time to leave.

'But you wouldn't know if someone was an amateur artist when they came in though would you?'

'I can spot them a mile off,' Ben said.

'How?' Hannah challenged him.

'I'll let you know when I spot one.'

Hannah gave him a dubious look.

A few more people came and went. Some asked Ben about the paintings, some bought cards, some came just to look. Ben treated them all in the same easy going way. A young woman came in and spent a long time looking at the pictures. Ben tapped Hannah on the arm and nodded at the woman. Eventually she picked up a couple of the cards from the display and came to the desk with them.

'Hi,' said Ben, taking her money. 'Have you been in before?'

'No,' she smiled at Ben. 'I only moved here a month ago and spotted you as I was driving along; you've got some really nice work in here.'

'Thanks,' said Ben. 'Do you paint yourself?'

'I do actually.' She looked faintly surprised. 'I only dabble, water colours mostly.'

'Well, you'll get a lot of inspiration now you've moved here,' Ben said.

'I will won't I? Thank you. Hope to see you again.'

Ben looked at Hannah after the woman had left. 'There you are,' he said.

'There you are what?' Hannah replied.

'I spotted she was an artist.'

'You asked her.'

'Only to prove my point. I didn't ask any of the others did I?'

'That's true,' Hannah said. 'Well, go on mastermind, how could you tell?'

'I'll show you.' Ben got up and walked into the main part of the gallery where Hannah could still see him and stood looking at one of the pictures from a few feet away, resting his chin in a cupped hand. Then he stepped forward and looked closely at the canvas. He turned and looked at Hannah.

'What, that?' said Hannah.

'Yep,' said Ben

'Just that?'

'They're looking at the brush work, all artists do it, checking out the technique.'

'I bet she had paint on her hands.'

Ben sighed, 'You try it next time.' He took the painting that was on the easel and took it out to the office. He had finished working on it.

'I've got it,' Hannah exclaimed when he came back.

'Got what?' Ben asked.

'A way for you to make more money.'

'I'm all ears,' Ben said wearily.

'Art classes.'

Ben groaned.

'No really,' said Hannah. 'As you have said, there are loads of amateur artists around. They all want to learn more. The Fish Works Art Club.' She gesticulated as if presenting a large sign. 'I can see it now. Two or three times a week you take a group and you set them something to paint, er, still life or go down to the beach, and you charge them so much a lesson; cheaper if they book a whole course.'

'Whoa, whoa,' said Ben. 'Don't get carried away. You can't teach people how to paint. You just have to get on with it. Just do it, as Nike says.'

'You know that, but they don't. All you have to do is go round and offer advice. They're not going to blame you if what they do is rubbish.'

'I hate still life,' said Ben.

'If amateur artists aren't buying pictures get them to spend their money another way.'

'I don't know,' said Ben. 'I'll think about it.'

'Okay,' said Hannah not wishing the subject to rest. 'If you reckon you can't teach people how to paint, why did you go to art school?'

'That's different.'

'How?'

'That's about learning technique.'

'I rest my case,' said Hannah. They were silent for a moment.

'It'll just be full of old women wanting to paint their pet dog,' complained Ben.

'You could get a life model.'

'Then it would be full of dirty old men.'

''Full' is probably the most important word in that sentence,' Hannah concluded.

A few more people came and went. A woman asked Ben if he had 'that sea picture'.

'I have quite a few with sea in them,' said Ben.

'No, I mean that one with the waves breaking.'

'I'm not sure what you mean by 'that one',' Ben replied.

'You know, the one with the sea and the waves and the white horses coming out of the waves.'

Ben twigged. 'I see, no I'm sorry, you need to go to a print shop or you can order it online.'

'On what?' she asked.

'You know, from the internet.'

'Oh right.'

'Another disappointed customer,' Ben observed after she had left. 'Your idea is growing on me Hannah.'

'I've been thinking about it,' Hannah said. 'You wouldn't even have to spend a lot of money to set it up because everybody would bring their own equipment or you could supply certain items and make a small profit on that.'

'The trouble with amateur artists is they always want to tackle the most difficult subjects.'

'I suppose it's natural to want to paint something that inspires you.'

'I suppose that's true but what is it about tigers?'

'What about tigers?'

'You go to amateur art shows and there's always a tiger's face amongst them. I'd put money on it. You need loads of practice to get graphic skills right. You can't just pick up a pencil or brush and do a tiger's face straight off.'

'Give them a choice,' said Hannah. 'Offer different levels, beginners and then more advanced,'

'If only people would start with something simpler. I mean painting sea, sand and sky is much easier than a tiger, because they're amorphous, you don't need graphic skills; you can have a lot of fun and get a reasonably good result.'

Hannah looked at him thoughtfully. 'I think I've just had my first art lesson.'

UP AT THE LIGHTHOUSE

{ CHAPTER 08 }

Jo laced up a trainer, her foot perched on the glass coffee table in the conservatory, she then clipped an iPod to the waist of her shorts and did a test run on the spot. Her mother, leaning on the breakfast bar in a pink fluffy dressing gown, watched her.

'It makes me tired just looking at you,' she complained.

'That's because you're out of condition,' Jo replied. 'You need some exercise.'

'Do me a favour.'

Jo shrugged.

'Bit later than usual aren't you?' her mother asked.

'I'm meeting up with Maddy at the Lighthouse.'

'You two,' her mother observed.

'What's that supposed to mean?'

'Thick as thieves.'

'We're just mates,' Jo said.

Bob Elliot, Jo's father walked into the room and looked at his daughter. 'No need to ask what you're doing today.'

Jo ignored him.

'Any coffee going?' he asked.

Jo's mother stood up and poured some coffee into a cup from a pot near the stove. 'You can ask me what I'm doing today if you like,' she said to her husband.

'Go on,' he said. 'Surprise me.'

She laughed.

The kitchen, like the conservatory that adjoined it was immaculate. Magazines like Coast and Homes and Gardens were in neat piles on the coffee table. Cushions on the conservatory furniture were placed as if a photographer from one of these magazines was about to arrive for a photo shoot. Every leaf of every plant shone. The kitchen, equally buffed and sparkly, looked that way because it was rarely used. Bob, a Conservative councillor, owned a car hire company, and had interest in several other businesses. He claimed that it was his old-fashioned sensibilities that persuaded his wife not to work, but the real reason was that Bob liked to know she was at home when he got there to pour his whisky and soda. He entertained his business associates at home and like the Mercedes in the drive, the house was meant to reflect that Bob was a successful business man. Clare, an ex-local beauty queen was another of what Bob thought of as one of his assets, though lately the gin she had been getting through was making her face a little puffy.

He idolised Jo, who took after her mother in looks, and was proud of his son Tom, younger than Jo at ten and doing well at a local public school. He would have preferred Jo to be more amenable to his success and values, and harboured a desire for her to attend public functions with him instead of Clare so he could feel proud showing her off, but Jo seemed reluctant to take on these roles. Her reaction to her father's pomposity was a barely concealed scorn and by turns a criticism of his political leanings and the people he associated with, which although highly irritating he put down to teenage angst and naivety.

'I've organised a little holiday job for you Jo.' He tried to avoid sounding smug as he said it but failed. It came out as if he was bestowing a great favour on her. Jo didn't answer but looked at him without expression waiting to hear the rest, knowing she was not going to be impressed.

'My secretary has set aside a desk in the registrar's office so you can get some work experience.'

'What, that mausoleum?' protested Jo.

Bob felt his ire rising. 'It could be very useful for you in your career prospects.' He was still under the impression that no matter how clever his daughter was, she ought to be thinking about becoming either a nurse or a secretary until she got married and started having children.

'I'm not planning to sit in some office getting a fat arse if that's what you think,' Jo pointed out.

'Don't be vulgar, there are lots of young people who work at the council offices, they have discos and things like that.'

Jo sighed. 'The reason I'm meeting Maddy today is that we are going to work out what we are going to do in the holidays and sitting at a desk in the council offices is not on the agenda.'

'Well I don't want you working in some burger joint or worse still as a barmaid.'

'I've got my sights set a bit higher than that,' Jo retorted.

'Oh you talk to her,' Bob said to his wife. 'She won't listen to me.'

Clare gave him a 'why me' look. Jo put her I-pod ear plugs in and allowed Beyonce to end the conversation with her parents.

'Bye all,' she said, her voice louder than she intended. She slammed the front door after her and started jogging down the road.

'I don't know why she has to be so bloody difficult,' Bob said to his wife as he bit into a piece of toast.

'It's just her age,' Clare replied.

'You weren't like that at your age, were you?'

'Probably, I can't remember.'

'Well she doesn't get it from me.'

'Good little boy were you?'

'I wasn't bolshy like that if that's what you mean.'

'Have you seen my glasses?' Clare asked picking up the Daily Mail.

It took fifteen minutes to reach the seafront and by the time she got there she had worked up a sweat. She had run harder than usual owing to the frustrating argument with her father and as a result was breathing faster than usual. She slowed her pace and ran up the short slope where the pavement joined a short detour to the start of the promenade. As she mounted the steep little path the sea came into view and that always made her feel good. It was as if the sea, being so vast, dwarfed any minor problems or worries. Shingle had been thrown up on the promenade from the high tide the night before but Jo nimbly stepped around it without breaking her stride.

She jogged past the bandstand where a brass band was playing favourite marching tunes to a meagre audience of elderly holiday makers. Two hundred yards further on was the Lighthouse Cafe. It had a semi-circular open seating area at the front arranged with tables and chairs that looked out over the beach and sea. In the winter these were stacked away as the sea and rain lashed the area and scattered pebbles over it. Maddy sat at a table close to the railing that cordoned it off from the beach. She was engrossed in the screen of her smart phone and didn't see Jo approach. Jo went into the cafe and took a bottle of mineral water from the refrigerated display, ignored the queue at the till and put the money on the counter.

'I gotta scan that,' the girl at the counter shouted at Jo.

'Scan another one then,' Jo shouted back. She had worked in the cafe briefly at Easter, telling her parents she was at a friend's house revising for exams, so she knew how the system worked and how long it took to serve a queue of pensioners. She went back outside and sat down opposite Maddy, swung her legs so her feet were on the railings and took a swig from the bottle.

Maddy looked up. 'Hi'.

'What you got?' Jo asked.

'Nothing much,' Maddy answered.

'My dad wanted me to work in the council offices for the summer.'

Maddy laughed. 'What did you say?'

'I said I'm not dead yet.'

'Well there isn't much online unless you fancy a job as a carer.'

'Do me a favour.'

A group of people got up from the table next to them. A gull landed on the railings ready to help clear the table. A light breeze ruffled its feathers and blew the newspaper they had left behind on the table to the ground. Jo got up and started to retrieve it.

'You forgot your paper,' she called after them.

'We don't want it love, you can have it.'

Jo shrugged and put the paper back on the table picking up the teapot to hold it down. She stopped as something in the paper caught her interest. She put the teapot down and sat back opposite Maddy with the paper. Maddy looked up from her phone. 'What's that?'

'Local paper,' Jo replied.

'Oh that rag,' Maddy said.

'It's got jobs in it,' Jo said studying the page. She looked up.

'Don't look now but that creep Elmore is just over there.'

'Where?' Maddy said looking around.

'I said don't look now,' said Jo raising her eyes as she saw Elmore spot them.

He approached grinning, pushing a hank of hair away from his face.

'Hello girls, fancy running into you.'

'Hello Elmore,' Maddy said. Jo ignored him.

'I'm just going to the bathing station to apply to be a life guard.'

'Cool,' said Maddy.

'You know you have to be able to swim don't you?' Jo said. Her intention had been to ignore him but she couldn't resist the jibe.

'I can swim,' Elmore retorted.

'Doggy paddle doesn't count,' Jo shot back.

Maddy grinned up at Elmore. She was quite struck with him; he was good looking in that floppy sort of way; wore fashionable clothes and had wealthy parents. 'We're looking for a job too,' she told him. Jo sighed impatiently.

'I could talk to my Dad about crewing on his yacht,' he said.

'If you're looking for a job why don't you do it?' Jo countered.

Elmore took some time to reply, looking pained as he formed the answer. 'Dad won't let me near the yacht at the moment.'

They both looked at him waiting for an explanation.

'Not since I marooned it on a sand bank.'

Jo laughed.

'It wasn't funny,' Elmore replied. He stood for a while not knowing how to continue. Jo looked at him hoping he was going to go away.

'Is it just your knob holding up your trousers?' Jo asked.

Elmore looked down. His trousers were half way down his hips showing an expanse of Calvin Klein underwear.

'Probably,' said Elmore grinning. 'You noticed then.'

'I could hardly miss it when it's virtually in my face.'

'Would you like me to stand somewhere else?' he asked suddenly feeling self-conscious.

'Yes,' said Jo. 'How about the other side of the bandstand.'

'Thanks very much,' Elmore replied. 'Only trying to be friendly.' He walked away.

Maddy and Jo giggled.

'He's sweet really,' said Maddy.

'Oh get off it, he's a plonker,' Jo said and handed Maddy a page of the Situations Vacant from the local paper. They both scanned the pages.

'Get this one Jo. Model Portfolio, Flash Studios. We will create your model portfolio. Our team of experts will create a dynamic profile of your potential. Essential for any girl starting out in the glamorous world of modelling. Initial photo session and consultation free. Maddy looked up at Jo, a gleam in her eye.

'Sounds like a con,' Jo said.

'Yeah but you've got to have a portfolio before you can get anywhere.'

'And, it's not even a job. We're supposed to be looking for a summer job.'

'It's a first step,' said Maddy.

Jo carried on reading. 'How about this. Model required for

art classes, good rates of pay.'

'Yeah, but you might have to get your kit off for that,' Maddy pointed out.

'So,' Jo countered. 'That doesn't bother me.'

'What, and all those dirty old men ogling you.'

'They can ogle all they like as long as they don't touch.'

'You've probably got to be eighteen or something.'

'Then I'll lie,' said Jo. 'It sounds a better option than carer, crewing on Elmore's dad's yacht, which was bollocks anyway, or sitting at a desk in the council offices. They have discos you know.'

'I don't know how you can resist.' Maddy laughed. 'Where are these art classes anyway, at the college?'

Jo looked at the paper again. 'Fish Works Art Gallery', I pass that when I jog along the front.

HOUSE CLEARANCE

{ CHAPTER 09 }

Justin reversed into a parking space in the street near his mother's house. He could never visit this row of solid suburban houses without the mixed feelings connected with the nostalgia of childhood. He had been brought up in this house, played in the street and gone to school two streets away. Moving away from Bamford and nearer the city had been a gesture, a way of becoming more independent.

'Is this going to take long?' Amy asked. She sat in the passenger seat looking at the screen of her phone.

'Shouldn't do,' Justin replied getting out of the car. He opened one of the rear doors and took out two plastic boxes. Amy followed him up the short path to the front door. Weeds had grown in the small front garden but it was still possible to see that not long ago it had been carefully tended; properly edged beds and clipped rose bushes. It had been six weeks since Justin's mother's death and he had been putting off the job of sorting out her things until it got to the stage where the only way to stop the niggling worry that it had to be done was to do it. He put the key in the door and pushed. A build-up of mail stopped the door opening easily. They squeezed in.

'It smells in here,' Amy said and although it wasn't his fault Justin found himself taking offence.

'It's just a bit musty,' he said. 'I emptied the fridge and the rubbish when Mum went in to the hospice. We just need to open some windows, that's all.' He picked up the stack of mail from the door mat sorting them as he made his way through to the kitchen. He dropped the offers for double glazing, insurance quotes and the garish advertising of local takeaways into the bin. He felt a pang of guilt over the overdue bills, something his Mother would never have allowed to happen.

Amy had wandered into the living room. 'What do you want me to do?' she called out. Justin put his head around the door.

'You could have a look around and see if there is anything we might want to keep.'

Amy wrinkled her nose.

'Or you could go through her jewellery if you wanted to. See if there is anything of value. I wouldn't have a clue.'

Amy brightened up a little. 'OK,' she said. 'Where is it?'

'There's a box on the dressing table in the bedroom.'

Justin caught sight of himself in the hall mirror as Amy went upstairs and stopped to look at his reflection. It was something he had been doing a lot since his mother had died. He knew it was irrational and wouldn't tell him anything new, but he couldn't seem to help it. He could never quite fathom if he was anything other than ordinary. This in itself didn't bother him and he didn't dwell on it, but the times when he delved into his personality there just wasn't anything there that was offbeat or even marginally peculiar. He was clever without being brilliant, he had had a very straightforward upbringing by unremarkable parents and the face that looked back at him from the mirror was mildly pleasant and unthreatening with no features that stood out as being particularly attractive or ugly. Even his job would be considered ordinary; a travelling salesman for a firm that made security devices for homes and shops, and he drove an ordinary sales rep type car.

Thoughts like these had now been upstaged by his mother's confession. Was he ordinary because of his upbringing when in fact there lurked in his genetic make-up a wild, romantic character waiting to spring to the surface, or was his blood father as down to earth and practical as his surrogate father had been?

Perhaps that's why Amy likes me, he thought, solid, conventional – dull. Again there was nothing in their relationship that would have made it to the pages of a romantic novel. No social or religious conventions stood in their way. They had met at a friend's party, started going out, slept together after their fourth date and at some point had decided to get married. He had liked her dry wit and soft voice, unlike so many other girls who seemed to screech and say nothing of importance. She was good company, and ticked the boxes Justin felt were important; she was attractive, intelligent and kind and she had a sense of humour, so what if she was a little self-absorbed, four out of five wasn't bad. In the end it came down to that mystery called 'chemistry', that indefinable thing that has baffled poets and scientists alike for centuries. They had both had relationships before and were mature enough at twenty eight (Amy), thirty one (Justin) to feel they were ready to commit.

After Amy had gone upstairs Justin looked around the living room. Everything was so familiar but at the same time alien, belonging to another world, another era, another time in his life. With a sigh he started to place things into the boxes he had brought; the books, the magazines on the coffee table, and the photographs along the mantelpiece, most of them of him at different stages of growing up. The bureau against the wall he decided to leave until later.

Since his mother's confession he had started to think about the man he had called Dad in a different light, examining their relationship and his characteristics in a more analytical way. He still thought of Lionel as his father. Thirty years didn't change in an instant because of one opposing fact. He had been older than his mother and had died some five years earlier. He had been an easy going, undemonstrative, dependable sort of father that Justin had taken for granted in the way that sons do when they have easy going, dependable sort of fathers. Dad was Dad - that was it. He hadn't beaten, abused or threatened him or demanded impossible feats from him.

The weeks following his mother's death had been difficult enough, dealing with the hospice, the funeral directors and solicitors and because nearly all of it was about family, subtle feelings of connection and belonging now seemed inappropriate and at times strange. He was aware of feelings of anger, that he had in effect been lied to over so many years, but this was countered by an understanding that despite the loosening of strict moral codes over the past decades his mother had been old-fashioned in her outlook. Rationally he knew he was the same person but those simple lines that are taken for granted connecting people on family trees, did not seem so simple now. Random lines could twist and turn like tangled string or a broken spider's web till it was impossible to trace where you came from.

There was an unrecognised satisfaction in knowing who your dad was, a feeling that by knowing him you could know yourself better even if it did make you want to kick against it and rebel at age seventeen. Now that had been taken away from him. Who was the mystery man who had sired him, was he some bad character whom his mother had slept with in a moment of madness or some dashing naval captain irresistible to women? That was the trouble, there was just no way of telling.

Justin could hear Amy upstairs opening cupboards and drawers. He had arranged for a house clearance firm to come and take away the furniture but wanted to make sure all the personal effects were removed first. He had once been in a second hand shop where there were still letters, diaries and photographs in the drawers of a bureau. The bits of someone's life had ended up in a place where the public could browse; it was like catching a stranger in their underwear.

He took a roll of black plastic bags from one of the boxes he had brought with him and went upstairs to see how Amy was getting on. She had the contents of his mother's jewellery box laid out on the bedspread. Justin was sure that there would be little of any real value amongst it but he also knew he would not be able to tell if there was.

'How's it going?' he asked.

'I've separated it into costume stuff and any that might be more precious.'

'We can take the precious pieces to a jewellers and let them value it. Is there anything you would like?'

Amy made a face. 'It's all very seventies isn't it?'

She tried on one of Justin's Mother's rings and looked at it. 'Do you think we should get Petal Power or Rosebuds to do the flowers?' Amy asked.

'What?' asked Justin only able to think that the funeral had been five weeks ago.

'The flowers for the wedding,' Amy said.

'Crikey Amy, it's another year yet.'

'You have to plan these things, there's a lot to think about.'

'Look, can we just get this sorted first. I've got all this stuff to deal with and the selling of the house.'

Amy made a little moué with her mouth and didn't reply.

'I've brought up some bags. Do you think you could put the clothes in them?'

'OK,' said Amy.

Justin went to the room that used to be his, and surveyed it from the doorway. He had long ago taken away anything he wanted to keep. The times he had visited his parents since leaving home had been few but more frequent after Dad died and Mum was by herself. Dad, an image popped into his head; the thinning sandy hair, the half tortoiseshell glasses, the cardigan that seemed welded to him from the day he retired, whether he was in the garden or the shed or his armchair. The man he had always thought of as Dad and now wasn't. If he had been delayed in getting to the hospice on that day he would never have known and perhaps it would have been better like that. What a burden knowledge can be. He remembered her getting the words out, struggling; a death bed confession with him as the priest.

Justin went back downstairs to the living room. Amy followed with two black bags full of clothes and placed the box containing the jewellery in with the other things.

'Is that it now?' she asked sitting heavily in one of the armchairs as if to point out she was both tired and bored.

'I've still got the bureau to go through,' Justin said.

Amy exhaled through puffed lips.

The bureau was really a sideboard; a dark oak affair on barley twist legs that Justin could remember having been there forever. The drawers and cupboards were full of the minutiae of his parent's lives: keepsakes, important letters, certificates and photographs. Justin pulled the drawers out and put them on the floor then sat down and opened the cupboards. He started putting things into two piles, one to throw and one to keep. He resented feeling he had to deal with the task quickly because of Amy's boredom but when she saw some family photographs she seemed to become more interested and sat down on the floor with him. Photographs were more interesting than other memorabilia as they seemed to bring things alive. Looking at the eyes and faces of people, a moment caught in time from decades before; whether they were smiling or looking uncomfortable, how the clothes and background detail informed you of the times. Justin picked up a photograph of a cat from the top of the pile.

'That was Scally,' he said handing it to Amy. She studied it smiling.

'Dad took up photography. Every now and then he would take up a hobby, and if Dad took up a hobby it would be done properly.'

Justin sorted down the pile finding more photographs; himself as a toddler; his parent's wedding pictures with his dad in a wide lapelled suit and his mother in white. He looked closely at his father's face thinking, she was already pregnant with another man's child and no one there knew her secret and a sudden wave of sorrow for the man who had brought him up swept through him.

Justin peered into the dark interior of the sideboard and swept his hand around it. To make sure there was nothing left. Amy was getting up from sitting cross legged on the floor.

'When are the house clearance people coming?' she asked.

'Day after tomorrow,' Justin replied as he closed the doors of the bureau and picked up the box. Together they took the boxes and bags of clothes out to the car.

LIFE'S TRIALS AND HAIRSTYLES

{ CHAPTER 10 }

Raymond James Collins was six feet two inches tall and had to bend his knees to see properly in the mirror which his wife had set to suit her own height of five feet five inches. Combing his hair was an operation for Ray of great care and precision. He felt lucky that at fifty five his hair was still as thick and luxurious as it had been when he was twenty two. All the new hair preparations that were on the market for the more fashionable spiky hair styles, were eschewed by Ray for his favourite Brylcreem, that he had been using ever since he had first put on a drape jacket and crepe soled shoes and fashioned his hair into an impossibly elevated quiff. The style of his hair these days still bore the echoes of that wave but was more subdued.

With knees bent and arms raised Ray combed his hair back from his forehead, still unable to resist the action of pulling it forward slightly with his left hand to create a cliff shape at the front. He patted and preened the finished result, turned a bit left then a bit right to check his three quarter profile from both sides, and tried out a couple of his more winning expressions. Satisfied he left the room and went downstairs.

Sylvia was sitting in an armchair with a copy of Chat magazine on her lap. The TV was on but with the sound down low. The programme, some sort of variety show, all glitter and garish colours, reflected in her pale face and glasses so that to a casual observer she might resemble a chameleon going through several mood changes, one after the other.

'Where are my shoes?' Ray asked.

'Which ones?' Sylvia asked without looking up.

'The fackin' Italian ones of course.'

Sylvia looked up. 'They're in the closet where I put them after I cleaned them for you.'

'Oh, right, thank you.'

Ray collected his shoes and sat on the edge of the sofa to put them on.

'Who is it tonight?' Sylvia asked.

Ray looked up. 'What? Oh. Toby Tyrone.'

'And who's he when he's at home?'

'Singer,' Ray replied.

'Any good?' Sylvia asked.

'Oh yeah, consummate performer, consummate performer.' Ray was apt to repeat words or phrases when he liked them. 'Sounds of the sixties but sung properly, not like them long haired gits.'

'Has he got a backing band?' Sylvia asked.

'I've got the Three Tones.'

'Oh them.'

'There's nothing wrong with the Three Tones.'

'Except their age.'

'And they're cheap.'

'That's more like it,' Sylvia pointed out.

'Phil, I'll have you know, is a brilliant guitarist.'

'Who says?'

'I'll tell you who says. I had that impresario chap in the other week and he said he was as good as Eric Clapton, and he auditioned for Wings once.'

'Didn't get it though did he?'

'Anyway, they can bang out a tune well enough for Toby Tyrone. People like Toby, he's a crooner. The ladies love him. You should come.'

The last bit was said somewhat half-heartedly in case she took him up on his offer.

'Can't, I've got Reeny coming round; we're going to watch 'strictly'.'

'Strictly what?'

'Strictly Come Dancing,' Sylvia replied as if to a child.

Ray watched the flashing colours on the TV for a bit.

'That builder guy rang up while you were out the other day,' Sylvia said.

Ray raised his eyes. 'Now she tells me.'

'I forgot.'

'What did he say?'

'He wants to know when he can start.'

'Oh, right, I'll ring him in the morning.'

'What's that all about then?'

'Just those flats in Earls Road. We've got to get them done up but we can't start the renovation while there are still residents in them.'

'He says he might have to start another job.'

'He always says that.'

Ray stood up. 'OK, showtime.'

'Go on then,' Sylvia said.

'See you later.'

Ray patted his pockets for keys, wallet and phone, slammed the front door behind him and got into the gold Lexus in the drive. He put his hand out of the window and pressed a gadget he was holding. The gates at the end of the drive opened silently. Ray smiled and turned the ignition.

The club 'RayJays' was in a square, squat building on the outskirts of town. Originally it had been a warehouse, but as Ray correctly surmised it didn't really matter what it looked like from outside. He had tarted it up with some paint, smart signs and neon but it still wasn't Vegas, and as customers rarely saw it during the day the rest didn't matter. Ray had bought it cheap in an auction when the previous owners went bankrupt. Business rates were cheap being out of town and it had a large car park. The inside was spacious and it had been divided up into several bars, a dance floor with a small stage, a dining area and kitchen. The food part of it was a joke but necessary for the licence.

Ray also had an office there and the bit he was most pleased with was a section of wall that concealed a pull-down double bed. This was used mostly by Ray to show off to other men he was trying to impress. He would mention it casually when he was showing off the rest of his office; the leather topped desk, green leather button backed office chair that tilted and swivelled. 'Oh and look at this.' Pulling a lever would result in the bed slowly lowering, complete with faux wolf skin throw. A lot of nudging and winking would follow but Ray had rarely used it in the way that fuelled his fantasies.

He parked in his reserved space by the entrance. He liked

the car to be right outside, firstly to impress and secondly it was under the canopy of the entrance so his hair didn't get wet if it was raining.

'Evening Dave.'

Dave nodded. Dave was a nineteen stone ex policeman and his neck was the same girth as his head. Dave's size wasn't necessarily all muscle but nobody got past Dave if Dave didn't want them to. Dave always dressed in black.

The club had been a hit from the first day it opened. It certainly wasn't anything to do with stylish location. It wasn't much to do either with the interior décor which was somewhere between gin palace and brothel. It wasn't the price of the drinks, the looks of the staff or the stylishness of the clientele, but it did have a lot to do with the fact that on the opening night, which had been invitation only, booze, food and entertainment were free and those invitees were not local grandees, the heads of important firms or local characters, Ray had invited every taxi driver and every hotelier in town, given them a good time and schmoozed them like only Ray could schmooze.

The car park was satisfyingly full and there were bursts of laughter coming from the performance area. The stand-up act was warming them up. Ray stood and looked over at the people crowding the bar. He knew most of the faces. Three bar staff were kept busy; Neville who was gay, Stella and Hermione. Hermione a tall willowy blonde had been recruited entirely on her looks, she had never pulled a pint before but she was learning fast. There was a band of red-faced business men at the bar, fat chins wobbling over collars and ties. Even on an evening out they were still in uniform.

Ray went and stood at the edge of the bar. He liked to watch what was going on quietly before anyone spotted him, as it changed the dynamic and he liked to see how everything worked without him. He could have gone to his office and looked on the CCTV to see who was there but it wasn't the same. He caught Hermione's eye. 'Half a lager,' he said to her. She was pleased to be interrupted as it gave her an excuse to get away from a guy who had been talking to her. Ray looked to see who it was and groaned inwardly, Cyril Granger was a local photographer and owner of Flash Studios.

'Hello Ray; got a few in tonight then I see,' he said rounding off the comment with a chuckle, which was a characteristic of Cyril whether out of self-consciousness or the fact that life amused him no-one was sure. Hermione brought over Ray's half of lager.

'I was just saying to your very lovely employee here that that comedian you've got, he's a bit near, a bit risqué if you know what I mean.'

'This is the twenty first century Cyril; you can hear worse stuff on the telly.'

'I know, but still,' Cyril said.

'I think he's very funny,' Hermione commented.

Cyril gave Ray what he hoped was a knowing glance. It was hard not to look at Cyril without one's gaze constantly being drawn to his hair. It was worn in the style commonly referred to as the comb over. Unlike Ray, Cyril had not done so well in the follicle department. Thinning and eventual baldness had left the top of his head clear and shiny, which was unfair as the rest of it grew thick and luxurious around the sides and back. Cyril had tried several methods of evening up the disparity. He had grown it long at the back and tried combing it forward but this proved as uncomfortable as it was impractical as the natural direction for the hair to grow at the back was downwards. The best solution Cyril decided was the side comb over which required careful nurture of the hair on the left side of his head until it was long enough to cover the crown. It did mean having a parting about one inch above his ear but the effect in the mirror pleased Cyril more than any other alternative. Another drawback with Cyril's hair was the fact that it was very wavy, which was a great bonus when he was younger but now used for its latest incarnation had a rippling effect across the top of his head. He had tried plastering it down with gel and even tucking the ends under the side bar of his spectacles but it seemed to have a mind of its own. Seen from above, which admittedly was rare except from high up CCTV cameras, it looked like seaweed stretched across a rock as the tide goes out. Cyril had been going to the same barbers for many years and the subject of the comb over was always politely avoided. Ron would ask if Cyril would like 'the same as usual' then trim around the edges, carefully keeping the striated strands meticulously in place. Cyril never went out when it was windy.

Ray spotted Bob Elliot, who he knew to be a councillor, standing in a group who he assumed were all connected with the council. Ray had seen this trio before at the Golf Club; another favourite watering hole. Ray inclined his head to Stella. She came over. Unlike Hermione, Stella was street wise, knowing and down to earth. She always reminded Ray of a joke another of the stand-up comics at the club had made about his mother-in-law; 'I wouldn't say she were 'ard but she could crack diamonds in her teeth'.

'Evening Ray.' She refused to call him Mr Collins as the other staff did.

'Alright Stella, just wanted to say, you see those guys over there by the fountain, look after them, know what I mean?'

Stella looked him in the eye. 'No, I don't know what you mean.'

Ray exhaled. 'Be nice to them.'

'What like give them free drinks.'

'No-o, just, you know, chat them up, give them a bit of banter.'

Stella put her forearms on the bar and leant forward. 'Flirting was not in my job description,' she said to Ray.

'Christ in heaven,' Ray moaned. 'No-one's asking you to take your knickers off.'

'Better not,' said Stella.

The comedian had finished his stint and Adele was playing on the music system as coloured lights swept around the room. Ray suddenly realised he was hungry and made his way to the kitchen. He pushed his way through the swing doors to find the kitchen empty except for Mildred stacking the dishwasher. Ray looked over the hot plate at the empty kitchen.

'Where's Barry?' Ray asked.

'Dunno,' said Mildred. 'Out back I expect.'

'Barry,' Ray shouted. No answer. 'Fackin' chef,' Ray said and shouted again. 'Barry.'

A thin lad came scurrying into the kitchen.

'Where've you been?' Ray asked.

'I had to go to the toilet Mr Collins.'

Ray looked him up and down. The chef's jacket, grey from many launderings, hung from his shoulders as if it was still on a hanger. He had facial hair, sand coloured and patchy, and a greasy skin from eating too much fried food.

'Make me a chicken sandwich, with chips. And wash your fackin' hands.'

'Yes Mr Collins.'

Ray sniffed as Barry went past him and had a sudden intuition. So as not to arouse suspicion he put his hands in his pockets and walked to and fro a couple of times, waited till Barry turned his back to get the bread, and went around the corner to the back door. He peered outside keeping just inside the doorway. It was dark but as his eyes got used to the darkness, he spotted a figure skulking by the bins. Ray stepped back, took out his phone and sent a message. He waited two minutes until his phone pinged and looked out again to see if the figure was still there.

'Oi, what's your game?' he barked.

The figure sprang to life and made a run for it. He didn't see Dave coming around the corner in the darkness and running into him at full tilt was like running into a mattress backed by a brick wall. Dave grabbed the collar of the guy's coat and marched him over to Ray. Ray was looking pleased.

'Get off, I ain't done nuffin,' the guy complained.

'Loitering with intent, wouldn't you say Dave?'

'Definitely,' Dave replied.

'You smell very, how shall I put it, herbal,' Ray said. 'A bit like Barry, he smelt herbal.

Can you detect a herbal smell Dave?'

'I think I can Mr Collins.'

'OK, my office,' Ray said.

Barry came over to see what was happening.

'You, get back in the kitchen,' Ray told him. 'I'll deal with you later.'

Dave grabbed the guy by the upper arm.

'Get off, you can't keep me here.'

Ray snarled in his face, 'Listen sonny, you're in big trouble. You do as I say or I'm going to get Dave here to give you a smack.' Ray, by now seeing how young the guy was, knew he could intimidate him, especially when he had Dave to back him up. Once in his office he told the kid to empty his pockets.

'You can't make me do that.' The kid was trying to act hard but it was just a show and it wasn't fooling Ray or Dave.

'No I can't,' said Ray. 'But Dave here can pick you up by

your ankles and shake out every bit of substance you've got hidden in your greasy little pockets.

Slowly the kid started to place the contents of his pockets onto Ray's desk. Dave and Ray watched as he took out pocket-worn bits of paper, sweet wrappers, a squashed packet of ten cheap cigarettes with two still in the packet and some rolling papers. He stopped. Dave delved into the pocket of the kid's coat and fetched out some small packets wrapped in tin foil and a small plastic bag with dried weed in it.

'Right, what's your name kid?' Ray said when Dave had finished helping him empty his pockets.

'John Smith.'

Ray's right hand shot out and cuffed him on the side of his head. 'Listen kid, this stuff here,' and he picked up one of the packets of foil. 'Might be of interest to the police.'

'They don't bother with small amounts for personal use.'

'Personal use?' shouted Ray. 'I caught you red handed selling your waccy baccy to my chef. No wonder he's so slow all the time, he's stoned out of his fackin' head. Now give me your name.'

'Kevin Malone.'

'Right, now we're getting somewhere. Address?'

'No fixed abode,' Kevin mumbled. This time Dave cuffed him, thinking it was about time he joined in.

Kevin turned to look at Dave. 'S'true, I don't live nowhere.'

Ray sat down in his chair and leaned back. 'Make much money selling that stuff do you?'

'Yeah loads,' Kevin said.

Ray laughed. 'You look like you do. I expect you live in a palace too.'

Kevin didn't reply.

'What if I could find you somewhere to live?' Ray inclined his head to let Dave know he could go.

'What's the catch?' Kevin said.

'No catch. You can live in a flat I've got to let, rent free for a given amount of time. And, I'll give you a small stipend for expenses.'

'Where?' Kevin asked. Ray wrote down an address on a piece of paper and slid it across the desk to Kevin. He picked it up and looked at it.

'I'll even take you there for a private viewing.'

'Is it a set up?' Kevin asked, still suspicious.

'You can bring some mates; I assume you've got mates.'

Kevin nodded.

'Is it a deal or do I ring the local constabulary now?'

'It's a deal,' Kevin mumbled.

'Good,' said Ray. 'Now what sort of music do you like?'

THE PHOTOGRAPH

{ CHAPTER 11 }

Justin drove to the centre of the town to drop the clothes and other items to one of the charity shops. Amy sat in the passenger seat, thumbs dancing over the screen of her phone. 'Just got a text from Mum saying Rockfords do a whole package with fifty guests for one thousand nine hundred and ninety nine pounds. Oh, and she wants to know if we've done a wedding list.'

'OK,' Justin said.

Amy looked up at him. 'Is that all you can say?'

'Yes, OK,' said Justin. 'Your Mum seems to have everything under control. What more do you want me to say?'

'You could at least be a bit more enthusiastic. Mum's

working very hard on this.'

'But she enjoys doing it. It gives her something to do.'

'That's not fair,' Amy said. Her phone pinged and she looked back down at it. 'You're such a grouch sometimes.'

Justin wanted to remind her that firstly his Mother had recently died, he was still reeling from the truth about his parentage and he was trying to deal with winding up her affairs, but she knew all that and still seemed to think about nothing other than the wedding. A wedding, that when he thought about it, and how Amy and her mother were planning it like a military campaign, made him feel as if he was being bamboozled into something he barely remembered agreeing to.

'It just seems to me,' Justin said. 'That sometimes the actual wedding has become more important to you and your Mother than the idea of getting married, as if the groom i.e. me is a bit of an afterthought and could well be anybody.'

'Well perhaps you ought to try and get a bit more involved.'

Justin pulled up at the red light of a pedestrian crossing. 'Nearer the time I will, but at the moment all I keep hearing about from you is wedding this and wedding that, wedding cakes, wedding outfits, flowers, bridesmaids, pages, dresses, venues, guest lists, invitations, champagne, buffets, bloody sodding Moss Bros and Uncle Tom Cobbly and all.'

Somehow, spilling out this list, allowed Justin to vent the anger that had been building up for a long time. A horn sounded from the car behind and he realised the lights had turned green. He put the car in gear and moved off again. Amy sat with her head down and her silence started the slow creep of Justin's guilt as his anger ebbed. He pulled into a parking space, got out of the car and got the two bags of clothes out. Justin took the stuff from his mother's house into the charity shop.

When he got back to the car Amy had gone. Sitting in the middle of the driver's seat was the engagement ring that Amy several months previously had suggested they go out and buy. Guilt mixed with a certain amount of relief touched Justin as he sat in the car mulling over the situation. Should he go and apologise; resurrect the status quo which would then mean that everything would be back on track? Or should he let Amy sulk for a bit and get used to the idea he wasn't going to be like some dog wagging his tail at everything her and her mother organized? In reality he quite liked the idea of getting married and he did love Amy, it was just this all-consuming organisation that made him cross.

Amy had been brought up as the only daughter in the family. Her two brothers, rumbustious and sporty, had been Daddy's boys. Amy's mother had made her a project and thus spoilt her. The upbringing, education, and the coming marriage were stage managed by her mother. All this had made Amy self-centred. Justin thought Amy might be different if he could shake off her mother's influence. It had happened before, this running back to Mum when things became difficult. Justin sighed and turned the key in the ignition.

Back at the flat he took the final box from the car, the one with all the personal things that needed to be destroyed, such as bank statements and the things he wanted to keep, which were mainly the photographs. He picked up a diary of his mother's. It was dated 1982 and thinking this might hold some clue he leafed through it. There was little of interest in it; dentist's appointments, notes on the weather and reminders for birthdays. He was about to consign it to the pile for disposal when something fell out of it – a photograph. Justin picked it up and studied it. It was a group of three young people sitting on a beach, a young woman flanked by two men. They were all roughly the same age. It dawned on him that the young woman in the centre in a swim suit was his mother. The young man on her right had a mop of light brown hair and pale eyes. She was leaning close to him, their upper bodies touching with her arm loosely through his, her hand on his forearm. The man on her left had darker hair and wore a moustache. He was leaning back slightly apart from the other two and grinning at the camera. Perhaps this was a clue thought Justin. The two men in the picture were unfamiliar. His mother had said it was a holiday romance and it was apparent they were sitting on a beach. Their ages seemed about right. Could that be his real father? It wasn't much, and it could be nothing to do with the mystery, but it was all he had to go on. He fetched a magnifying glass and scrutinised the picture for clues.

The quality of the photograph was not good, it was a holiday snap taken on a cheap camera and it had faded over the years. He realised that as clues go this one was pretty slim but it was all he had. Even with this there was only a remote chance he might be able to track down the man in the photograph, and even if he could there were so many other ifs. There was no evidence that this was the man of his mother's holiday romance and therefore his biological father. He may be impossible to trace after thirty odd years. He may be dead. He might have emigrated.

The photograph had been taken looking inland. The beach was strewn with rocks that were obviously chalk, so it was most likely the south coast, but Justin didn't fancy trekking along several hundred miles of beach to try and spot the scene in the photograph. Behind them a rocky wall rose dotted with scrub and hardy bushes. The sky was visible as a thin strip of blue at the top. In the top right of the picture he could make out the corner of a white building. There was lettering on the front but it was too small and hazy to make out. He went to his desk and placed the photograph into the scanner of the printer. He increased the size and opened photoshop on his laptop. Enlarging the image made everything seem more hazy and indistinct.

He tried sharpening the image. Eventually he could make out the letters MONTF. He put the letters into the search box of Google and came up with a lot of Montfords, Montforts and Mountfields but none of these seemed to fit. Thinking it was most probably a hotel he next put in 'Hotel Montf'. There was a Hotel Montford but that was in Austria. Maybe she had gone abroad but everything about the picture said 'English seaside' He typed UK in the box after it and De Montfort Hotel came up in a resort called Cocklebury-on-Sea. That had to be it. Justin clicked on it and there it was; a white building with a drive. It looked similar to the one in the photograph but taken from another angle and up closer. Thirty one years also separated the two images but there was no doubt.

A FISH SUPPER

{ CHAPTER 12 }

Ben turned out the gallery lights, locked the door and picked up the battered cool box that had been sitting outside. He scrunched along the shingle eastwards. The promenade ended just past the gallery so there were no skaters or cyclists to dodge and only the occasional dog walker. This was where nature ruled more than man, no sea wall, smart gardens or benches, just shingle, the odd patch of sea cabbage and fishing boats. If anyone came to the beach here it was to get away from the crowds that massed on the beaches nearer the centre of the town. It smelt different here; you got the iodine tang where the air met the sea, a whiff of oily fish and diesel rather than the smell of fish and chips. This was the best time of day, Ben thought, especially in summer when there was still daylight at six o'clock and the warm light of the sun touched the phosphorescent glow of the sea.

The few boats along this patch each had a winch and a rope that snaked off into the sea. The winches were housed in squat boxes sitting on the shingle and looking like so many garden sheds that could belong to dwarves. Most of these were covered in tarred paper or with plastic sheeting lashed with rope and looking like badly wrapped gifts. There were proper size sheds too that the fishermen kept their stuff in. Nothing here was smart, not like the gaily painted beach huts of the well-to-do at the western end of the beach, or the elegant white yachts in the marina. There was workaday debris around here; it wasn't pretty but unlike the litter of the tourists it belonged – the ropes, lobster pots, nets, buoys and tyres.

Ben reached the spot where Wilf's shed stood. The Tupelo Honey, Wilf's boat, named because it always smelled so sweet, had already been winched up onto the beach where it sat at an angle a few metres in front of the shed. This was Wilf's patch, between the shed and the boat, as sacrosanct as any fenced off area, garden or home turf, where the shingle was tamped down from constant use. Wilf was down on the shore line in the shallows scrubbing out plastic fish boxes with a broom. He spotted Ben and raised a hand in greeting. Ben put the cool box down by the shed and took a bottle of beer from amongst the ice in the box. He opened it and took a long drink from the bottle, his throat rippling as he swallowed. All the tourists had gone home and the only other person around was a guy fishing from the beach.

Ben put the bottle on a rickety table outside the shed and went to help Wilf bring the boxes back up.

'Good day?' he asked.

'So so,' said Wilf as he chucked the boxes up onto the deck

of the boat. He then threw the broom in the shed and took a beer from the box.

'Cheers,' he said to Ben.

When he had drunk about half of the bottle he reached inside the shed and brought out a bag of coal. On the shingle stood a converted pot-bellied stove - converted meant that at some point Wilf had cut the top off it. He tipped some coal into it and it started smoking. Like most things that Wilf owned it had either been found on the beach or dragged up in one of his nets. It was the ultimate in re-cycling. The shed also owed its existence to this method, constructed from driftwood, old doors, tarred paper, sheets of corrugated iron, rope, and bits of plastic. Wilf climbed a short ladder at the side of the boat and reached over the side. He retrieved a cool box, even more battered and old than Ben's, and took out of it two fat fish with bright silver sides.

On the rickety table he deftly gutted the two fish throwing the contents over his shoulder. The fish guts never hit the ground. Four seagulls who knew the routine had been perched on the shed and the prow of the boat watching Wilf with their sharp yellow eyes. The fastest one swooped, swiped the fish innards and swept away from the scene, the other three in angry pursuit. Wilf went back to the shed and brought out a wooden box rattling with bottled condiments. He smeared some oil on the sides of the fish then, after sorting through the other bottles, picked one and held it up.

'Cajun spice?'

'Sounds good to me,' Ben replied.

Wilf sprinkled some over the fish, opened up the gut cavity to douse that as well. He shook some salt over them and transferred them to a grid over the fire in the pot-bellied stove. They waited, drinking beer as the fish sizzled.

Ben and Wilf had known each other from as far back as

school, from conkers and scraped knees, through to beer and girls and onto careers and marriage and other disasters. Their lives had crossed and re-crossed, losing touch and re-kindling. Unlike Ben, Wilf had never been away. For as long as he could remember he had fished, helping his father on the boat as soon as he was old enough to pull on a rope. Fishing was in his blood. Career choices hadn't concerned him at school. At sixteen he spent the summer holidays as he always did – fishing with Dad. The only difference that year was that he never went back to school. As his dad had got older and less spry their roles slowly reversed until Wilf was doing most of the work and running the business and Dad was just helping. But Wilf's dad had made a shrewd move and in the seventies when property had been cheap and development less frenetic than in subsequent decades, he had purchased a patch of scrub land with a motley selection of net sheds and boat houses. It was like buying Whitechapel and The Old Kent Road on the Monopoly board, and although today it was still not Park Lane or Mayfair, it brought in enough rent, now Wilf had inherited it, to make a reasonable income. Wilf didn't need to go out fishing any more but he was at a loss to think of other things he might do if he didn't. Besides it was in his blood.

'What is it about this town Wilf?' Ben said after a while.

'How do you mean?' Wilf asked.

Ben thought. 'We could be in any seaside town around the coast; I mean would it be any different?'

'I don't know,' Wilf replied not sure what Ben was trying to say.

'There's nothing particularly wonderful about this actual town.'

'S'pose not.'

'But it gets under your skin, even the crappy bits.'

'When you're out at sea, it looks very pleasant,' Wilf observed hoping this was along the lines of what Ben was getting at.

'But does it look any better than any other town seen from the sea.'

'I don't know, I've never fished off any other town.' Wilf got up and turned the fish over.

'When I'm out there,' he waved a hand in the general direction of the sea. 'I know where everything is.'

Now it was Ben's turn to puzzle at what was meant.

'Underneath,' Wilf expanded. 'Under the sea.'

Ben nodded.

'There are wrecks down there, gulleys, flat beds of sand, big rocks, and I mean big, deep holes, ledges. I know the terrain. In here.' Wilf tapped his head with a forefinger.

Ben was beginning to understand. Wilf continued. 'I know these modern gadgets, the echo sounders, the GPS but there's no substitute for knowledge.'

'That's very profound,' Ben observed. Wilf didn't think he'd said anything particularly clever.

'There's a wreck out there,' he continued. 'Well, there are a lot of wrecks, but this one, some divers have told me it's an old U-boat; the bass love it. Bass are the wiliest fish in the sea, they're hunters and they're clever. They lurk, using the wreck to hide, to conceal themselves. Bass fetch a good price.' Wilf grinned and got up to see to the fish. The skin was blackened and crisp. He took a pair of tongs and a couple of chipped plates. He handed one of the plates to Ben.

'Could you do anything else?' Ben asked lifting the skin away from the fish to reveal the creamy white flesh underneath.

'Not now. There was a time.' He stopped to take a mouthful of steaming fish. Ben looked over at him. 'I've never had a proper job,' Wilf continued.

'Neither have I,' Ben countered, then laughed.

They were silent for a while as they picked the delicate steaming fish from the bones.

'Not thinking of selling up, are you?' Ben asked.

Wilf looked at him and shook his head.

'Only there was a guy hanging around the other day, looked a bit like an estate agent. Which reminds me, I owe you a bit of rent.'

'Don't worry about it,' said Wilf taking another slug of beer.

There were two subjects that Ben found difficult to talk to Wilf about. One was the rent he owed for the gallery. In lean times he had trouble paying Wilf anything. It was a gentleman's agreement for a start with no official documents involved. Wilf never pressed Ben for the rent, although he sometimes took a picture in lieu, pressed on him by Ben because of the embarrassment of being in debt. Wilf had some very nice pictures on his walls – and quite a lot of them.

'I get rent from Dean's Plaice and the Beach Shop but they get a more regular income. I'm very pleased to be supporting the cultural advancement of Cocklebury; you don't get a lottery grant that you haven't told me about do you?'

'Not likely,' Ben grinned. 'Do you get any rent off Toddy?'

Wilf spluttered. 'Let's put it this way. I know where I can get a sausage roll or a bacon sandwich if I'm short of change.'

The other area of Wilf's life that Ben picked around carefully was his failed marriage to Eileen. They had seemed an unlikely couple from the start. Eileen had been delicate, almost bird-like, Ben thought, pretty and slim with long sensitive hands, the skin almost translucent with a visible blue tracery of veins beneath. Wilf on the other hand was like a tree; weathered, wind-blown and ruddy. His hands, blunt, etched with work and coarsened by salt water, could have enveloped one of Eileen's and made it disappear. Ben couldn't help wondering about this contrast when it came to sex, more in a mechanical sense than for prurient reasons. He had mentioned it once and Wilf had smiled indulgently; 'She likes it. Must be something to do with opposites attracting.'

At their wedding it was more than noticeable. Eileen looking slim and elegant, and Wilf obviously not at ease in a suit, his beard and hair trimmed, still looked wild, moving his head awkwardly, not used to a collar and tie. At one point in the ceremony, Ben, watching from three rows back, saw Eileen's head turn to look up at Wilf. Ben had noticed she was wide-eyed, happy. Of course she would be, but there was something else in that look; neediness and a frailty that wasn't physical.

Five years later Eileen had left. Wilf only mentioned it once but Ben could see it pained him so much he started avoiding the subject from then on. After the break up Wilf plunged himself into work, partly as a way of forgetting but as he now seemed to go out in any weather, he could have been wishing for something to happen to him. There didn't seem to be a complex story to Eileen leaving and Ben heard through others that knew him, she had plain and simply gone off with another bloke.

'Daft isn't it? I've never made any money, not real money,' Wilf said.

'Do you regret it?' Ben asked.

'Not a bit,' said Wilf. 'You don't have any regrets do you.'

'Of course not, I'm the same as you. I can only live like I do because I have no commitments. A few paintings a month wouldn't pay a mortgage.'

'If you'd been stuck behind the till in a supermarket or behind a little window in the post office you would never have had such a good time. Remember the deck chair?'

'Oh Christ, that deck chair,' Ben laughed throwing his head back.

Wilf opened another bottle of beer chuckling to himself.

Flashback Summer 1983

The sun beats down on Cocklebury-on-Sea and the season is in full swing. People throng the esplanade. All ages – all sorts. The beach and the sun have no prejudices, all are equal, they all share. Roughly in the middle is the entrance to the pier. This is the meeting point, east meets west, land meets sea, town meets beach. Buskers strum and sing and are moved on or drowned out by the brass band further down. Pseudo gypsies sell charms. A man with a camera takes photographs of couples and groups and gives them a card pointing towards the town.

Wilfred Finchley sits in a crow's nest on the top of a painted steel structure watching bathers out at sea, mainly kids in the shallows, splashing and bouncing on inflatables. Two girls walk by, flimsy blouses over bikinis, flip flops, sun hats, straw bags, towels. Loose limbed like puppies their skin shiny from sun cream. Wilf can't take his eyes from them, hoping as he glances back to the sea and his responsibility, that they won't disappear in the throng. They are looking for a place on the beach and Wilf hopes it will be near. The girls stop and lean on the railings. Wilf chances a glance over to Ben. He knows Ben has spotted them too as he keeps glancing up towards them whilst giving a man a ticket for his deck chair and taking the money. When Ben has completed the transaction he looks up at Wilf and grins. He walks over to the girls.

Wilf watches. It's a good line to start talking to the girls; 'would you like to hire deck chairs ladies? Wilf can't hear above the noises of the beach and promenade but he watches Ben smiling and talking, engaging the girls, keeping them there even though he knows they won't want deck chairs. The girls' body language and smiles tell Wilf they are flirting with Ben. It looks promising, Ben points down to the beach and the girls look to where Ben is pointing. He moves to leave, the girls wave. Their blouses flutter in the breeze as they descend the steps to the beach. They select a spot and unroll towels. Wilf looks over at Ben and raises a thumb. Ben grins back at him.

An hour later a guy raps on the metal structure of the crow's nest to get Wilf's attention. Wilf gets up and climbs down the ladder.

'Anything happening?' the guy asks.

'Nothing much,' Wilf replies. 'Keep an eye on the bloke swimming out to the buoy.'

'Will do,' he says climbing the ladder.

Wilf doesn't mention the girls. Pete will spot them anyway.

'Been bird watching then?' Wilf asks Ben ambling over to him.

'A pair of lesser spotted crested finches with very nice plumage.'

'I saw,' Wilf replies.

Ben was sitting outside his official hut. His uniform was a pair of shorts and a naval cap that gave him at least an air of authority. On a leather strap around his neck was the ticket machine which got hot if the sun was on it. Ben wasn't sure if he always collected all the money he was supposed to, but the council never seemed to challenge him on it. Some people would come and pay him before taking a deck chair, others took the chair not knowing you had to pay for it so Ben would go and ask for the money. Sometimes when people vacated the chairs other people came and sat in them. It was an inexact science and if Ben couldn't remember if someone had paid or not he tended to leave it.

'Third one down on the left,' Ben said to Wilf.

'Oh right,' Wilf replied grinning. 'We going for a beer later?'

Two people came and took deck chairs. Ben got up to take their money. When he came back Wilf nodded to the stack of deck chairs. Third one down was now on top and a man was getting ready to take it. He was about fifty, had long military looking khaki shorts and a sandy moustache. He took the deck chair. This chair, marked with a yellow spot had been put together incorrectly and was impossible to erect. It looked normal as if all you had to do was swing one of the bars over the top to the other side and fix it on the lower bar, but there seemed to be another bar in the way. There were several potential possibilities for setting up the deck chair but none of them worked. Also it wasn't obvious there was anything wrong with the chair itself. Ben and Wilf slightly embarrassed by this childish prank still enjoyed hours of amusement watching people trying to solve this Chinese puzzle of a deck chair. Most fun were the groups who, when one of them got the marked chair and started having problems, another member of the group would take over with a 'come here let me have a go' attitude. Or there were the husbands thinking their wives were inept, trying to show off their superior skill with predictable results. The man with the deck chair had by now tried three combinations of assembly and was looking at the flattened chair scratching his head. Wilf had already gone into the hut to hide his mirth, Ben was chuckling into his chest.

'Why don't you go and help him?' a voice next to Ben said.

Ben looked up; it was one of the girls from the beach. She saw Ben was laughing and looked cross.

'That's horrible,' she told him. Ben was laughing so much he couldn't explain.

She stalked off and approached the man with the deck chair. He looked up unsure about being helped by a young woman. The man stood back and the girl took the wooden bar of the deck chair and lifted it, trying to secure it on the lower bar. Then she flipped the other bar over and saw that wasn't going to work either. She looked up hearing a howl of laughter from Wilf watching from inside the hut, and seeing Ben doubled over in his seat, she marched over to them.

'I think you're both despicable,' she said. 'Give the man another deck chair; that one is faulty.'

Ben stood up and went to fetch another chair but she could see from his back he was still laughing. He took the chair over to the man and, trying to keep a straight face, handed it to him taking the other one away. The girl put the deck chair into position and the man thanked her. She turned around and approached Ben and Wilf.

'You should be ashamed of yourselves,' she said. 'Behaving like children.' She turned and went to join her friend who had been standing watching the scenario.

'I don't think you've pulled,' said Wilf and they started laughing again.

Ben thought twice about putting the dodgy deck chair out again, suitably scolded by the girl in the yellow bikini.

'I thought that was going to be a possibility,' Wilf said later over a beer in the Pirate's Rest.

'Yeah, they were nice,' said Ben. 'But I think we blew it.'

'I'll say, probably won't see them again anyway,' Wilf commented.

'I liked her,' said Ben. 'Yours wasn't bad either.'

'Oh I thought of it the other way round actually,' said Wilf.

'Hardly matters now does it?'

The following day Ben was collecting up the deck chairs as the day cooled down and people started to go home, folding them and stacking them. It had gone six o'clock, and was still warm but the sun was sinking. He stacked the last one up and returned to the hut to lock up for the night. She was waiting for him. She had on a short, pale blue dress and she had put on Ben's naval cap he had left on his seat.

'Hello, have you come to tell me off again?' he asked

'No,' she said. 'I've come to apologise.'

'No need for that.' Ben was strangely humbled by the apology.

'I was over the top, high handed. I'm sorry.'

'I understand,' Ben said. 'You were right.'

'No I wasn't, I was being a stuck up little bitch.'

Ben put his hand out and touched her shoulder. 'No you weren't.'

She seemed to melt under his hand and then Ben understood. She took the hat off and handed it back to him. He put it back on her head. 'It looks better on you,' he said. 'Look I'm finishing here in five minutes do you want to go for a drink?'

'Okay, why not?'

'Where's your friend?'

'Janet went back to the chalet, a bit of heat stroke I think. I'm Rose by the way'

'Have you got a boyfriend? Ben asked as he put the drinks on the table.

'Sort of,' she replied.

'That's a strange answer.'

'Well,' she looked down and watched the bubbles break on the surface of her drink, 'there's a guy at work. I've been out with him a couple of times.'

'That doesn't make him a boyfriend.'

'No.' She paused. 'He's very nice.'

'But you don't love him?'

'No, he's just, I don't know.'

'Just what?'

'He's so eager all the time.'

'I see.'

'That's why I was a bit moody see. I'd come away with Janet to sort my head out. He's a good person. I might fancy him a bit more if he wasn't quite so keen. Enough about me what about you?'

'Me? I haven't got a boyfriend either.'

She punched him on the arm. 'Stop avoiding the question.'

'Nothing serious, the job makes it difficult.' This was true but could be taken two ways.

'Too much temptation, is that it?

'There is that,' Ben admitted.

'Lots of notches on your bed post are there?

'You give me more credit than I deserve.' Ben said hoping she wasn't going to think she might just be one more conquest.

Shadows were lengthening but the evening was still warm as the sun continued its trajectory towards the horizon.

'Do you want to stroll; it's cooler now, less people around?'

'Come on then,' she said getting up.

They walked along the promenade, watching the sun get redder as it dipped towards the horizon. Their arms brushed now and then and made more than accidental contact, but they didn't hold hands. Further away from the pier there were smarter gardens and the hotels looked more expensive. Ben jumped down onto the beach and held out his hand to her. She took it and he caught her waist to steady her as she jumped. There was a bank of fine shingle, still warm from the sun and they sat down.

'I don't see horizons where I come from just the tops of houses,' she said.

'That's also a horizon,' Ben countered.

'Not like that,' she nodded towards the sun, now a ball of red flushing the sky with colour.

'If you watch, in a minute you'll see the sun kiss the sea,' Ben said. It was a tried and tested line. He turned and looked at her and leaning forward he kissed her gently on the lips.

She opened her mouth slightly and he increased the pressure. They stopped only when the sun was just a crescent above the sea.

'You made me miss that now,' she said putting her arm through his.

'It'll do it again in twenty four hours,' he replied.

They walked back along the beach, sometimes arm in arm. Every so often they stopped to kiss again.

'Do you want to do something tomorrow?' Ben asked.

'Like what?'

'I dunno, spend the day together, take a picnic. What about your friend?'

'Janet?'

'Yeah, Janet.'

'And your friend, would he come?'

'Wilf? Yeah, he was quite taken with Janet.'

When Ben got home he rang Wilf. 'Guess what?' he said.

Wilf chucked the heads and bones of the fish on the stones and the gulls swiftly cleared it up.

'I don't remember all that well,' said Wilf. 'There were a lot of girls. You were terrible.'

'You didn't do so bad yourself.'

'It was the perfect set up.' Wilf smiled at some recollection. 'I wouldn't do so well now, look at me.' He patted his stomach. 'And I stink of fish.'

'You're still a fine figure of a man Wilf.'

'Fuck off,' Wilf responded as he took another beer.

There was a cove. You had to climb over some rocks to get to it and you had to keep an eye on the tide. Ben and Wilf helped the girls scramble over the rocks, flip flops not being ideal for rock climbing.

'Where are you taking us?' Janet complained.

'You'll see, believe me, it'll be worth it,' Ben said.

As they came to the top of the rock fall they could see the beach below. Unlike the shingle of the other beaches this was smooth sand.

'See,' Wilf said.

Rose kicked off her flip flops and ran across the sand, then did a twirl to face them.

'To dance beneath a diamond sky with one hand waving free,' she sang and they all laughed.

They laid down towels on dry sand, further up where the tide didn't reach, in front of a great rock of chalk.

'Is it safe to swim Mr. Lifeguard?,' Janet asked.

'It is with him around,' Ben said.

'Come on then.' Janet held out a hand to Wilf.

'I'm afraid of the water,' Wilf joked.

'I'll have to pretend I'm drowning then,' she said and ran towards the sea.

'I'm going to catch some sun before I swim,' Rose said.

'Me too,' said Ben pleased they had been left alone together. They

laid back on the towels and Ben reached across and took her hand. After a while she turned over, supporting herself on her elbows and looked down at Ben.

'I couldn't stop thinking about you last night,' she said.

'Be careful,' Ben replied. 'Holidays always make you feel more romantic.' He didn't know why he had said that. It was something he was aware of and often used to his advantage, not to warn girls off with.

'That's a strange thing to say,' she said.

'It happens,' said Ben. 'Like wine tasting better when you are abroad.'

'I don't care,' she said and kissed him.

They spent most of the day on the beach. They swam. Ben smoothed sun cream on her now golden limbs. He had brought lunch of sorts, some rolls from a bakery, beers and a bottle of fizzy wine. By mid-afternoon, and still hot, Wilf said the tide had turned and they had better be making their way back.

'Wait a minute,' Janet said and delved into her bag bringing out a small camera.

Ben and Wilf stood looking sheepish as their photograph was taken.

'Your turn now,' said Wilf, and took the camera from her. Rose and Janet linked arms and posed for the camera.

'Now you three together,' Wilf said. 'Ben, get in the middle.' Ben obliged.

'Move that way.' Wilf waved his free arm.

'Now you three,' Janet said taking the camera. Wilf went and stood the other side of Rose.

'Sit down,' Janet said. 'You all look like you're standing to attention.'

They sat down; Rose put her arm through Ben's, their upper arms touching. Wilf leaned back on his hands. Janet knelt to take the picture. The camera clicked.

'That's it,' she said. 'End of the film.'

They packed up their stuff and scrambled back over the rocks.

THE SEARCH FOR CLUES

{ CHAPTER 13 }

Justin stood on the seafront looking down at the beach. He had driven to Cocklebury-on-Sea that morning after booking into the Falkirk Hotel online the day before. Most of the things to deal with his mother's effects had been put into action; a house clearance firm had taken away the furniture and a 'for sale' sign had gone up outside the house.

He had felt strangely unsentimental about the process but wasn't sure whether this was down to a lack of feeling or a suppression of emotion. In some ways the break with Amy had made him feel calmer by taking some of the pressure off him. It was a battle of wills, Justin knew, to see who would make contact first. He didn't see it as a complete break and he knew Amy was unlikely to either. He could just hear her sitting at the kitchen table with her mum saying something like: 'He'll come back, I know Justin, give him a few days and he'll get in touch and want us to get back together.' Well, he thought, two could play at that game. But in case she came around to his flat in person and was worried about his whereabouts, he sent her an email that just said he was going away for a few days. He didn't say why, and it was carefully worded to be non-committal about the row they had had and how he felt.

In the inside pocket of his jacket was the photograph. Justin turned his gaze to the headland on his right and could see the De Montfort Hotel in the distance. He hadn't been able to find out much about the town or at least nothing that might help him in his quest. He had hardly anything to go on except the photograph so it was all a bit of a shot in the dark. The information was tenuous to say the least. He didn't even know which of the guys in the photograph was supposed to be the one his Mother had had the fling with; it could have been someone else completely. The men in the picture might have been holidaying as well and were by now completely untraceable. He had made the excuse to himself that a break would do him good, he had holiday owing to him and a little detective work could make it all a bit more interesting.

He argued that even if he did track down the guys in the photograph, and even if one of them was his biological father, he might deny it or might not remember anything about it, and even if he did might not want to be reminded. He could even be a total arse thought Justin.

The Falkirk was a mid-priced hotel along the seafront. He had decided against the De Montfort hotel as it was a little out of the main town on the headland and very expensive, but the Falkirk seemed very pleasant from their website with comfortable rooms, good facilities and a dining room. Justin had taken a room that looked out over the sea.

He decided to take a walk westwards towards the De Montfort Hotel. He was aware that nothing much could be gained by visiting the hotel or even working out the position and angle the photograph had been taken from, but he was curious all the same. As he got further away from the town the land started to rise and the main road swung inland. The drive of the De Montfort hotel started on this bend and Justin made his way along it till he was standing outside the hotel. The beach was now several metres below and the steep slope down was planted with shrubs. There was a path with a sign that said 'to the beach'. The path took him down the incline in a zigzag pattern that made the descent gentler. The beach, when he got there, was sandy. It was not an exclusive beach for the hotel but was far enough away from the town to seem so. There were a few groups of holiday makers and judging by their beach wear and paraphernalia they were probably residents of the De Montfort. Justin looked back up at the hotel and compared the scene in front of him to the one in the photograph.

He walked along the beach a little further west and looked again. He took several paces back. This had to be the spot more or less. He turned and surveyed the environment, looked at the sea and the rocks. It was not earth shatteringly meaningful but he felt it was an important starting point for his investigation, and even though it would tell him very little, he wanted to feel the spirit of the place. Had his mother been here thirty five years ago and met someone? It was almost impossible to think of his mother doing something rash like having a holiday romance – sex with a virtual stranger, but Justin was aware enough of human weaknesses to know it could happen to anyone in a fit of madness or emotional turmoil.

Instead of retracing his steps back up the path to the De Montfort Hotel Justin scrambled over the rocks that separated the beach from the rest of the seafront. He went back to his hotel, had a shower and went down to dinner in the hotel dining room. He was given a table by the window overlooking the sea. The season being at its height meant the dining room was full with tables of twos and fours with a couple of larger parties. Justin was suddenly aware of his single status and wondered, as the waitress handed him a menu and smiled, whether she was smiling because she felt sorry for him being on his own, but he dismissed the thought. When she had taken his order she asked: 'Are you on business?'

'Er, sort of,' he replied.

'Oh, right,' she said, unable to find a suitable next question.

Justin expanded: 'I'm doing some research, locally, but having a bit of a break at the same time.

'Lovely,' she said.

Justin smiled and handed back the menu. She was pretty and probably in her early twenties. There was little chance of her being able to help him in his quest. Older people, Justin thought, old timers who have lived in the town most of their lives. He knew he was going to have to check out the pubs in the town and ask around.

In the morning, with the sun shining, Justin was slightly disappointed he had booked in at the library to look at the archives of the local paper. He could see the beach from the window in his room with the sea gently lapping at the shingle. Seagulls wheeled in the sky and it looked idyllic. He doubted the local paper archive would give him any concrete evidence or any leads but it might just give him a flavour of the times, to see what sort of thing was going on in the town the year before his birth, and one never knew, he may just see something that could give him a lead. After breakfast he put on a light jacket and started the short walk into the main town. The library was a tall building opposite the railway station. It was already busy with older people poring over the daily newspapers in the reading room and what looked like a mother and toddler group in the central bit of the library. So much for silence, thought Justin as he approached the enquiries desk.

'I have an appointment in the newspaper archive department,' he said to the woman behind the counter.

'One moment,' she said, and left her post. Justin waited. She came back with a nervous looking young man.

'Peter here will take you up,' she said.

'Sorry, it's a bit of a trek,' Peter apologised, holding the door open for Justin.

They went up three flights of stairs and then into a room. Along one side were computers with people working at some of them and on the other some large grey desk top machines that looked like old fashioned photographic enlargers. Peter went to a filing cabinet in the middle of the room.

'What year were you looking for?' he asked.

'Nineteen eighty-two,' Justin answered.

Peter opened a drawer, 'Month?'

'June.'

Peter took out a white box and went over to one of the machines. We are still using micro film I'm afraid – it should all be computerised soon. He took a roll of film out of the box and placed it on a wheel to the left of the machine and threaded it across to a spool on the other side. He pressed a switch and the screen came to life. He showed Justin how to scroll through the film and how to adjust the size of the image.

'I'll leave you to it then,' he said cheerfully. 'Just give me a shout if you get stuck.'

Justin thanked him and sat down. The first headline

said: 'Residents fury over planned housing estate'. Well, nothing much changes thought Justin. Petty crime and small time events seemed to dominate the pages dotted with advertisements for restaurants, car dealerships and local shops. The local cinemas were showing 'Dawn of the Dead' and 'Jaws 2'. The town theatre had a holiday show featuring Val Doonican as its star performer. There were pages of classified advertisements, followed by the births, deaths and marriages. After scanning through four consecutive weeks of local news Justin got a sinking feeling that it was not really going to help him. Peter was at a desk by the door.

'Would you like me to put anything away?' Justin asked.

'Don't worry, I can do that,' Peter smiled. 'Did you find what you were looking for?'

'Not really,' Justin replied. 'It was a bit of a long shot.'

'Do you mind if I ask?' Peter said.

'No, not at all.' Justin reached into his inside pocket. 'I'm just trying to trace someone.' He handed the photograph to Peter. 'The guy on the left,' he explained.

Peter scrutinised the photograph. 'Well at least you've got the right town, that's definitely the De Montfort Hotel. I wasn't even born in nineteen eighty-two. I can't think what to suggest.' He handed back the photograph. 'Sorry I can't help,' he said.

Justin took a roundabout route through the town looking at the shops. The local paper archives had been like getting in a time machine and going back, with their brand new cars looking outdated, old films at the cinema and fashions from another era. If only he could really go back, he thought.

Coaches lined the seafront, cars stopped and started at the zebra crossings for pedestrians in holiday gear, families and parents gathering children together like shepherds with their sheep. Justin walked further away from the town in the opposite direction from the evening before. He could see the arm of the bay sweep around in the distance and the small houses dotted along its shore.

A MODEL INTERVIEW

{ CHAPTER 14 }

'I love it,' said Freda putting her hand on Ken's arm.

'It's very striking,' he replied.

'The way the sun reflects on the sea, makes you want to squint, it's so realistic.'

'There is something about it,' Ken mused. 'Like one of the impressionists.'

'Go on, how much is it? No don't tell me,' Freda said.

Ken leaned forward and peered at the card on the wall.

'Not that bad really.'

'I like the figures in it.'

'It's four fifty,' Ken said.

'That's not bad for an original,' Freda said. 'Nicely framed too,'

'We can always make an offer.'

'No you can't,' Freda chided.

They wandered around looking at the other pictures but seemed to keep drifting back to 'Day on the Beach'. Hannah watched them, recognising them as potential buyers even though she could not hear their conversation. They weren't the sort that came in to kill ten minutes or the ones that might say, 'Alright if we come and have a look at your photos'. Those ones drove Ben mad. Hannah thought it might be useful to chat to them. Ken moved nearer to the desk to look at another painting.

'Are you on holiday?' Hannah asked.

'Oh no,' said Ken. 'We live here; been here about five years now.'

'Nice town isn't it?' Hannah said.

'I'm afraid we are the classic retirees,' said Ken. 'Came on holiday here several years running and decided to move here when I retired.'

'Don't blame you,' Hannah said. 'Lots of people do.'

'We like the painting on the end wall,' Ken told her.

'That one, yes its lovely isn't it?' Hannah was pleased her hunch was proving correct.

'Is it a local artist?' Ken asked.

'Yes, that one is painted by the owner of the gallery. He's not here this morning.'

'My wife can't stop looking at it.'

'I know.' Hanna smiled. 'He does sea pictures well, he really captures it.'

The conversation seemed to peter out and a silence hung between them that Ken found embarrassing. It came out without him really realising what he was saying. 'Can I put a deposit on it?'

'Yes, of course,' said Hannah.

Freda came up behind Ken. 'What are you doing?'

'I think I've just bought a painting,' said Ken.

Freda looked at him.

'You do like it don't you?' he asked.

'Yes, but.'

'It's virtually the same price we paid for the living room carpet, and I know which I would rather look at. We'll get ten times more pleasure out of it.'

'Thank you,' said Freda quietly.

'I'll give you a hundred now,' Ken said to Hannah.

'That's fine,' Hannah replied.

Ken took out his wallet and counted out five twenty pound notes. Hannah opened the sales book on the desk.

'I'll just take your name and address and give you a receipt.'

'It's Ken and Freda Macmillan, Belvedere Heights, Earls Road.'

Hannah handed Ken a receipt. 'I shall go and put a nice red sticker on your painting then.'

'Thank you,' said Ken, and then to Freda, 'Shall we go and get a coffee to celebrate then?'

'You've sold 'Day on the Beach,' Hannah told Ben when he arrived back at the gallery.

'Fantastic,' said Ben looking pleased. 'That'll keep me going for a while.'

'And pay some bills,' Hannah suggested.

'Oh yeah, bills,' said Ben as he caught sight of a woman standing just outside the gallery door. She was taking one last, hard drag on a cigarette before she ground out the stub with the toe of her shoe on the concrete. She blew the smoke sideways before putting her head through the door.

'I've got an interview at twelve thirty,' she said to Ben.

Ben looked at Hannah who looked down at the book. 'Ah, you must be Mrs Calthrop.'

'That's right love.'

Hannah turned to Ben 'Mrs Calthrop has applied for the job of life model.' She mouthed 'sorry' to Ben. He smiled at the woman who was in her fifties with peroxide blonde hair and a lot of make-up. She wore a white blouse and red skirt that were both a little tight. The skirt showed her knees and sturdy calves. She was wearing white pointed shoes with stiletto heels.

'I think we had better go through to the office,' Ben said and stood back to let the woman pass. Ben mouthed 'thanks' at Hannah and followed Mrs Calthrop through to the office. He took a pile of books off a chair and positioned it opposite his desk. 'Sorry about the mess,' he said.

'Don't worry about that love,' Mrs Calthrop said. 'You should see my place,' and laughed. The laugh turned into a cough which settled down to a wheeze. She pulled her skirt down further towards her knees as she settled into the chair.

Ben knew some people had applied for the job of life model but as he had been out he had no idea about the interview. Hannah had obviously been keener to tell him about the sale of the picture and had yet to get around telling him of the interview.

'Now,' said Ben trying to sound business like. 'Have you done this sort of thing before?'

Mrs Calthrop thought for a moment, as if going through her memory banks, for the period in her life when she might have modelled in the nude for a group of art students, was something she might struggle to recall. 'Not exactly,' she said.

Ben was stumped by the answer. 'So you've done something similar but not exactly life modelling?'

'Yeah, that's it,' Mrs Calthrop replied.

'I see,' Ben said. There was a pause while he composed the next question.

'And this was a form of modelling was it?'

'That's right love.'

Ben was thinking it was becoming a bit like twenty questions. 'And did this modelling entail taking your clothes off?'

'Sometimes,' Mrs Calthrop said enigmatically.

'So you are aware of what life modelling entails?'

'Oh yes,' she replied. 'And this sort of thing will be much better for me now.'

'Yes, of course,' said Ben without having a clue what she meant. He wished he had got Hannah to do these interviews. Ben was not sure he was handling it all that well. Mrs Calthrop seemed to relax now the question of nudity had been touched upon; as if they now understood each other.

'See, I can't move as well as I used to, but I had some lovely moves.'

'I'm sure you did,' Ben replied.

'It was an art; I was quite sought after you know.'

'And where was this?' Ben asked politely.

'In the clubs, that was a while ago now love, but my speciality was Bolero. You know Ravel's Bolero.'

'I do,' said Ben.

'Tasteful it was, a slow dance while I, you know.'

'Yes,' interjected Ben quickly.

'Of course these days it's nothing like that, they all shimmy up poles and stuff and call themselves exotic dancers; that's not exotic and it's hardly dancing either, hanging upside down from a pole. No, I'm glad I'm out of it now. I've done a bit of photography and stuff, again very tasteful, magazines, that sort of stuff, but that's out now. The girls they get doing that, so young I doubt if it's legal, and now with the internet, no, it's all changed. Then I saw your ad and I wondered why I hadn't thought of that before. Just sitting there, couldn't be better, now that I don't move as well as I did.'

'Well that was just what I was going to mention,' said Ben. 'Sitting still for a long time can be very difficult and artists can get very put out if you move your pose.'

'Don't worry about that, it won't be a problem for me. I can sit still for hours, even without a telly.' Her voice cracked into a laugh at her own joke and again descended into a cough.

When she recovered she stood up. 'Well I expect you'll be wanting to...'

Ben inwardly relaxed thinking she was voluntarily bringing the interview to a close.

'...see the goods as it were.' She reached to the side of her skirt where the fastening was.

'A little sneak preview.' She smiled at Ben and winked.

'No, no that won't be necessary,' he responded quickly. 'Artists models are not meant to be the pinnacle of perfection.'

She looked a little crestfallen. 'As you wish,' she said rather haughtily.

'Well thanks a bunch for that,' said Ben to Hannah after Mrs Calthrop had left. Hannah laughed.

'She was about to strip off in there,' Ben complained.

'I thought you were going to weed out the worst ones on the phone.'

'I did, I did,' Hannah was still laughing. 'You can't always tell on the telephone, I thought she might be OK until I saw her. I've taken loads of calls this morning and believe me she was by no means the worst. I think the fact that you put 'good remuneration' might have something to do with it. I have had two who didn't realise they might be obliged to take their clothes off, a man in his nineties who was at pains to let me know he was exceptionally well endowed, a woman who wanted to know if we had a crèche for her children, oh, and a woman who wasn't interested in the job but wanted to tell us we were exploiting women even when I explained that the advertisement had not been gender specific.'

'So have I got anyone else to interview?'

Hannah looked at the book in front of her. 'There's Maud Caffrey at five thirty and Jo Elliot at six.'

'Jo as in Joseph or Josephine?'

'Josephine.'

'That'll do I think. Don't book any more interviews just take their names and a telephone number. And perhaps you had better be there for these other interviews.'

'What, in case they want to strip off for you.'

'No, it's just more professional, Ben said.

CYRIL

{ CHAPTER 15 }

Justin pushed through the doors and into the Merry Wives public house. He had done a short survey of the pubs in the town, avoiding any that looked as though they were just for the tourists, and the ones that seemed to be kitted out to appeal to a younger clientele. What he was looking for was an old style pub, tucked away somewhere, a place that might be frequented by older people and locals, people who might have lived in the town for thirty years or more.

He had chosen well, he immediately felt out of place. If it had been busier he might have expected all conversation to stop and everyone slowly turn and look at him. As it was, there were three guys sitting at a table in the corner with pints of mild. There was a man in his late sixties standing at the bar. He had a loud check jacket, military moustache and heavy black framed glasses. The barman who was talking to him was of a similar age and wearing a shirt that stretched uneasily over a large paunch.

'Morning,' said Justin to the barman.

'Good day sir,' the barman replied.

'Can I get half a lager?' Justin asked.

'You can indeed.' The barman picked up a glass and started pouring lager into it from a tap.

The man in the glasses looked resentful as if Justin had rudely interrupted his conversation with the barman. 'Harry been in?' he asked as if nothing had happened.

'On holiday,' the barman said.

'Ah,' the man replied.

The barman put the drink in front of Justin. 'One forty five please,' he said

Justin paid him

'Just passing through?' the barman asked.

Justin was beginning to think it was really turning into a Clint Eastwood movie.

'No, I'm here to do some research,' he replied.

'Historical?' the barman asked.

'Sort of,' said Justin. 'I'm trying to trace a relative.'

The man in the glasses pushed his glass over to the barman indicating a re-fill. The barman pressed the glass against the Grouse whisky optic and slid it back.

'Everyone's at it these days,' the man said.

'Sorry?' Justin asked.

The man stood up straight. 'Meet the ancestors, trace your family tree, Who Do You Think You Are?'

'I beg your pardon?' Justin was suddenly annoyed. The man had joined in the conversation unasked and was now being rude.

'Who was it last night, Jeremy Paxman wasn't it?

Justin then realised the man was referring to a television

programme.

'Alive or dead?' the barman asked.

'Who?' Justin said, worrying he was not following this three way conversation.

'The relative, alive or dead?'

'Oh, he could be alive, I don't know.'

'Have you got a name for this relative?' the whisky man asked.

'No, I haven't.'

The man gave Justin a look of mock surprise. 'He's a relative, you don't know his name or even whether he's still alive; you haven't got much to go on have you?'

'It's a bit complicated,' Justin said. 'My mother came to this town on holiday over thirty years ago and met this man. I may be the result of that liaison.'

The whisky man grinned, 'Well, it wasn't me.'

Justin ignored him. 'I've just got this photo,' he said taking it out of his pocket and handing it to the barman. 'The guy on the left,' he said.

The whisky man leaned in to have a look as well.

'He's got a moustache, Frank,' the barman said.

'That's not me,' he said, ignoring the barman's tease

'Here Tom,' the barman shouted over to the guys in the corner. 'You've lived around here for quite a while, do you recognise this guy.'

Justin took the photograph over to the man addressed as Tom. He squinted at it holding it close to his face. 'Turn the lights up a bit Jack; it's like a blinking coal mine in here.'

'Try putting your glasses on Tom,' one of the other guys suggested.

Tom reached into the pocket of his jacket, took out a spectacle case, and proceeded to put on a pair of very antiquated glasses. He squinted at the photograph again.

'These are the wrong ones,' he said.

Everyone else thought this was hugely funny but Justin was beginning to lose his patience.

'Here try these,' one of the other guys said to Tom, holding out another pair of glasses.

Eventually when they had all had a look, shaken their heads and handed the photograph back to Justin, he went back to the bar.

'You wanna see Harold,' the barman suggested. 'He comes in now and again, he knows everyone.'

Justin thanked him but the thought of hanging around the Merry Wives on the off chance that Harold might drop in, made him feel depressed. He drank his lager and left. He tried a couple of similar pubs in what he now realised was referred to as the old part of town but drew a blank at each one.

He got in his car to make his way back to the hotel and was travelling down a minor road in the town when he spotted something he recognised. He braked suddenly, earning a blast on the horn from the car behind, and pulled in to the side of the road. He got out of the car, walked back fifty metres and stood outside the premises called Flash Studios. One thing Justin had remembered from ploughing through those pages of the local paper the day before was Flash Studios. There had been a quarter page advertisement for this shop with a photograph of the exterior.

It hadn't changed much in all those years. The large 'F' and 'S' of the sign above the shop with a logo of a flash bulb were pure seventies. The shop seemed to have survived the changing years by adapting to new trends, even if the outside was stuck in the past. Flash studios sold cameras and accessories. It had a photograph printing service, passport photograph service and offered family portraits and model portfolios. What Justin hoped was that if this place was still run by the original owner he might be old enough to remember something of the period Justin was interested in. It seemed it might just be a slightly better bet than talking to old men in pubs.

Justin entered. There didn't seem to be anyone in attendance but he had heard a bell ring somewhere further back, so he waited while taking in the jumbled interior. A cabinet displayed a small selection of digital cameras and some older, obviously second hand ones. Shelves behind the counter held batteries, film and digital camera cards. There were books on how to 'do' photography, photograph albums and frames and a big yellow machine where you could print your own pictures.

'With you in a minute,' a disembodied voice called out.

Justin looked at the display of photographs from the local camera club, plenty of sunsets, pets, close-ups of flowers and family members posing like celebrities but still managing to look self-conscious. Cyril appeared from a doorway behind the counter.

'Sorry to keep you, how can I help?'

Justin looked at Cyril, his gaze inevitably being drawn to the top of Cyril's head. Out of politeness he dragged it back again to his face.

'I was wondering if I could get a couple of prints from my mobile.' He placed his phone on the counter. I don't live around here and I just need some prints to send to a relative.'

Cyril picked up the phone and looked at it. 'That machine,' he said nodding to the yellow contraption in the corner that looked a bit like a fruit machine. 'Only takes cards, but if you email them to me I can print them off for you.'

'That's great,' said Justin who only wanted a reason to chat to the guy.

'Here, email it to that address.' He showed Justin a card and turned to the computer behind the counter.

'Been here long?' Justin asked.

'For about as long as I can remember,' Cyril intoned.

'You've seen some changes then I expect.'

'I'll say,' Cyril replied. 'You couldn't do this sort of thing then.' Cyril indicated the screen of the computer where one of the photographs Justin had just emailed had appeared. Justin had chosen two photographs of Amy.

'When I first opened I used to sell a few Box Brownies, some film and send people's pictures off to a laboratory to be developed. That was when, ooh let me see, nineteen seventies.'

'You've always lived in the town then,' Justin asked realising he was only going to have to ask a few key questions to prompt Cyril's reminiscences.

'Born here, and I'll probably die here.' He grinned a gap-toothed grin at Justin.

Justin laughed.

'Every business was family owned when I started here. There were greengrocers, butcher's shops. Now they are all computer repair places and pound shops.'

'Have you always done photography,' Justin asked.

'Oh yes.' Cyril couldn't help chuckling; a willing ear to listen to him talking about himself.

'I started off as a street photographer. I used to stand outside the entrance of the pier and take peoples' photographs. I had a monkey once too, but he bit someone and I had to get rid of him. I used to put a selection of them in the window and people would come to see if their picture was there. Postcard size be OK for you?'

'That'll be fine,' said Justin.

'I used to freelance for the local paper, cover the bathing

beauty contest before they stopped all that. Political correctness eh.' Cyril tutted and grinned at Justin again. Justin mimicked his expression.

'You must know a lot of people then,' Justin said.

Cyril laughed. 'Just about everyone.'

'You might be able to help me with this then.' Justin reached into his inside pocket. I think this was taken here in about nineteen eighty-three. You can see the De Montfort Hotel in the background.' Cyril looked closely at the picture.

'I'm trying to trace a relative, the guy on the left.'

Cyril picked up a magnifying glass and studied the picture.

'Who's the girl?' Cyril asked.

'My mother,' Justin said.

Cyril carried on looking. Justin was unnerved by how long he was taking.

'The face is familiar,' Cyril said looking up at last.

'Is that all?' Justin said.

'I might be able to help you but I'll have to look through my files.'

'How's that going to help?' Justin asked.

Cyril made a face and pointed to a shelf behind the counter that held a row of twenty identical files.

'See that lot there?' Cyril said. Justin nodded.

'There's forty years of negatives and contact prints there. I have meticulously filed every photograph I ever took and recorded the date, event and names. The reason that guy seems familiar means I probably photographed him sometime in the past. If I find the negative, I can give you a name. With a name you have a chance of finding him.'

'I see,' said Justin. It sounded plausible.

'If I can take a copy?'

'Yeah, sure,' Justin said.

Cyril placed the photograph in a scanner and went back

to his computer. Justin's prints were just coming out of the printer. Cyril handed them to him. 'Is that what you wanted?'

'That's great, thank you.'

'How can I contact you?' Cyril asked. The printer started chattering again.

'I'm staying at The Falkirk, but you can have my mobile number.' Justin handed over a card.

'Give me a couple of days and I'll see what I can come up with,' Cyril said.

After Justin had left, Cyril leant across the counter on his elbows looking at the copy of the photograph and grinning.

'You dirty old bugger, Ben,' he said softly.

PIZZA, DOPE AND NIRVANA

{ CHAPTER 16 }

Kevin took a key out of the pocket of his coat and unlocked the door of the flat. Breath stood just behind him, hands in pockets, looking nervously up and down the corridor. Bo watched Kevin.

'Lock's a bit stiff,' Kevin explained. He looked up at Breath. 'Hey, why don't you chill, we are not doing anything illegal. This is like totally above board.'

'OK man.'

The door opened and Kevin led the way in. The hall was dark but when he opened the door to the living room the sun was coming in through the windows, making the spacious room look light and airy.

'Wow,' said Breath. 'This is cool.'

Kevin felt pleased by the response but tried to remain looking straight-faced.

'What d'ya think?' he asked Bo.

'It's alright, where did you get the furniture?'

'The dude said some of the people who had moved out of the other flats left some bits behind so he had them moved into here.'

'This sofa's a bit crummy.'

'Well, I know it's not the Ritz, but hey.'

Breath had wandered out into the kitchen. 'Hey it's got a kitchen an' all,' he said.

'Course it's got a kitchen,' Kevin said 'All flats have got kitchens, but check this out.'

Kevin stood to one side and made a flourish with his hand towards a huge sound system sitting on a low table by the far wall. Two massive speakers stood sentinel either side of the system. Breath looked out from the kitchen and his eyes widened. 'That is awesome,' he said.

Bo was unimpressed. 'What's the deal with this place?'

'It's sort of temporary,' Kevin answered.

'Who does it belong to?'

'Just this dude,' Kevin answered.

'Why did he let you have it?'

'Well, I done him a few favours, so he owes me like,' said Kevin.

'Hey, wow, Slayer!' said Breath who was going through a stack of CDs by the music system.

'Nirvana, Fields of Nephilim, this is cool stuff.'

'Check out the bedrooms,' Kevin said to Bo.

Breath was scrabbling on the floor trying to find a power point for the plug. Kevin sat down and fished some tobacco and rolling papers from his coat pocket. Bo came back into the room.

'There's no sheets or nuffin,' she said.

'I'm not bothered,' Kevin replied.

'Isn't there a telly?' Bo moaned.

'Christ Bo, aren't you ever happy? We get a gaff like this and all you can say is 'where's the telly'.'

Breath pressed a button on the stereo and a thunderous chord reverberated around the room. Bass and drums pulsed from the speakers. Breath rolled over onto his back bicycling his legs in the air with delight. Kevin continued rolling a joint oblivious to the noise. Bo sat in an armchair, arms folded, looking moody. Kevin twisted the paper at the end of the joint and lit it, inhaling deeply. Breath was now standing in front of the stereo, playing air guitar and banging his head up and down to the beat. The track ended and they became aware of someone banging on the front door. Kevin looked at Breath who looked back at Kevin.

'Well fuckin' answer it then.'

Breath went out into the hall and opened the front door.

'Who is it?' Kevin called out.

'Spig,' Breath called back.

'Oh shit,' Kevin said quietly, then: 'Tell him to sod off.'

Spig came into the room carrying a stack of pizza boxes that nearly came up to his chin.

'I've brought pizza,' he said to Kevin.

'How did you know we were here?' Kevin asked.

'I saw you coming in with that geezer,' Spig said, placing the pizza boxes on the coffee table. Kevin caught a whiff of the cheese mingled with hot cardboard and suddenly felt hungry.

'What are you, some sort of spy? Kevin asked. Spig grinned and pulled some cans of Coke out of his jacket pocket. Breath hovered. 'Is there any pepperoni?'

'There's all sorts,' said Spig. Bo leaned forward, took a slice of pizza and hunched back in the chair still looking moody.

'Nice pad,' Spig commented.

'You can't stay here,' Kevin told him.

'Didn't ask to did I?'

'Anyway, how did you know which flat we were in?' Kevin asked.

'The music, duh,' said Spig. 'It wouldn't be any of the other old duffers would it?'

'What old duffers?' said Kevin.

'The other people in the flats. Most of them are empty but there are three or four still occupied. They'll love your music.' Spig sniggered.

'Death Metal,' Breath shouted and made a fist salute.

They sat chewing the pizza silently for a while, Breath cramming whole slices in his mouth and wiping his fingers down his jeans. Kevin re-lit the joint when he had finished eating. Bo leaned forward in readiness. Kevin took a drag and handed it to her. He looked at Spig who was watching intently.

'Don't give him any,' Kevin said. Spig watched them passing the joint and picked up the box of matches that were sitting on the coffee table.

'Ever seen a match burn twice?' Spig asked grinning.

'What do you mean, burn twice?' Bo asked.

'I'll show you.' Spig took a match from the box and struck it. The match burned brightly.

'Burns once,' Spig said holding it upright. He then held the flame under Breath's forearm.

The hairs flared and crackled. 'Burns twice,' he said.

Breath jumped up, snatching his arm away from Spig, rubbing it and looking hurt.

'Ow, that fuckin' hurts,' Breath exclaimed.

Kevin started to giggle. Bo looked at him and started

laughing as well.

'It's not funny,' Breath said. Spig grinned, pleased that he had amused the others and started laughing as well. This, and Breath's hot anger, fed the situation until Kevin and Bo were laughing uncontrollably. Breath, realising he was the odd one out, got over his discomfort and let out a few guffaws. Kevin started rolling another joint, occasionally erupting into giggles which would start them all off again.

As they got steadily more stoned they ceased to take as much notice, and Spig if he put his hand out at the right moment got to take a few puffs. He had never smoked marijuana before and as his brain got the first hit of it, and he started to feel a bit light headed, he relaxed and felt for the first time that this was somewhere he really belonged. Kevin went to pass the joint to Bo and noticed she had fallen asleep. Breath was staring at the wall, mouthing words and obviously in some sort of private world. He suddenly had an overwhelming desire to listen to Nirvana. He stumbled over to the stereo, put the CD in the drawer and pressed play. Smells Like Teen Spirit started chugging out of the speakers and Kevin started to move around the room in a kind of dance to the music. It was three a.m.

EXPLOITING THE INNOCENT

{ CHAPTER 17 }

Maddy stood at the counter in Flash Studios and said, 'I rang up earlier about a model portfolio. You said you did them.' Now she was actually saying the words to a real person, she had a crisis of confidence as she looked at Cyril and waited for an answer. Cyril didn't answer straight away. He looked up and saw, as he had seen so many times before, a nervous, naïve teenager. His penetrating gaze was shadowed by overgrown eyebrows and the strange arrangement of hair on the top of his head. Would he laugh her out of the shop, thought Maddy, would he scoff and say something like 'You! A model?' The determination and ambition she felt inside that willed her to fulfil this goal, only just outweighed her lack of confidence and self-esteem.

'Oh yes,' Cyril said, his eyes roving over her face and upper torso like a mine sweeper.

'Madeleine Bright isn't it? Proust liked his madeleines,' he quipped. Maddy hadn't a clue what he was talking about.

'So, you'd like to be a model?' Cyril said.

'Yes,' Maddy agreed, beginning to feel even more awkward because of the way Cyril's eyes seemed to be all over her.

'And what sort of model would you like to be Madeleine?'

Maddy only knew of one sort of model, the ones that posed on the pages of Vogue; the ones that wore beautiful clothes and had fabulous hair and make-up, and of course the ones in the television advertisements, who not only looked wonderful but were sassy and confident and had teams of people doing their hair and make-up and nails, the ones that looked at the camera in that 'drop dead' gorgeous way and said 'because you're worth it'. Maddy knew with a passion that brooked no argument that this was what she was destined to do. A film ran through her head in which she is standing against the backdrop of a stylish room, she's holding a pose of nonchalant disdain, there are lights pointing into open umbrellas and a young guy - slim, designer stubble, Levis, white Yves-St-Laurent shirt, is holding a camera up to his eye and pointing it at her: 'More pout darling, hold your head up a bit more, that's it lovely, lovely' and with each click of the camera she sees a still of herself on the page of a magazine. This, and other scenarios that fed Maddy's dream, are stored away and screened in moments when something negative might cloud the vision, or just for the thrill of daydreaming it.

'Well, a model, model,' she replied lamely.

'Well, my dear there are quite a lot of different types of model, those that have beautiful hands or feet or perfect skin, they all have a place, a role as it were in advertising, magazines, newspapers. They're not all cat walk and fashion models you know. We have to find your hidden talents, your best attributes; your unique selling point. That's what this consultation is all about, that and a sort of little photo session.

'It said in your ad that there would be a team of experts.'

'Ah, yes, well, not for the initial consultation, not the free bit. That comes later if you decide to go ahead with the complete package and portfolio.'

Maddy had spent a long time prior to coming to Flash Studios doing her hair and make-up. Even though she thought there would be a team doing that for her she didn't want to go in looking as if she hadn't bothered. Maddy spent a long time with friends experimenting with different products and techniques so for this she had used what she thought was the best she knew. She had taken a long time looking at her wardrobe wondering whether to look cool and trendy or severe and sophisticated. She had compromised with something in between, a tunic dress from Topshop over a pleated skirt from Next. This had been her first decision but she had changed many times and tried lots of combinations before selecting the choice she had started out with.

'How much does the model portfolio cost?' Maddy asked.

'Well there are several options. Shall we go through to the studio and get started then we can discuss it while we work.' Cyril came around from behind the counter, turned the closed sign on the door and flicked the lock. 'After you,' Cyril said, ushering Maddy through to a room at the back. Maddy was feeling very apprehensive now that she knew it was just her and this creepy man, whose eyes she felt were penetrating the very fabric of her clothes. Cyril on the other hand was getting excited because of previous encounters that had started this way.

Cyril's studio bore little resemblance to the stylish sets that lived in Maddy's imagination. An old trolley stood in the corner, host to the paraphernalia for making hot drinks. Chipped mugs stood next to a carton of milk, angled slightly because it was sitting on several used and dried out tea bags. In the other corner was a bench that held cameras and other bits of photographic equipment. Over the wall at the end was a rail with a curtain pulled across it. The only thing that matched Maddy's fantasy of a professional photographic studio was a couple of lights on stands pointing into white umbrellas. In front of the curtain was a reasonably smart chaise longue and in front of that, on the floor, a fur rug. A short distance in front of the chaise longue was a camera on a tripod. That and the umbrellas at least gave it a semblance of professionalism.

'Just make yourself comfortable on the chaise longue while I get set up here.'

Maddy sat down holding her handbag on her lap. Cyril pressed a switch and the room flooded with light. He fiddled with the settings on the camera, bent down to look through the viewfinder and twisted the barrel of the lens. He stood up and smiled at Maddy.

'Now, you don't want me to photograph you looking like you are waiting for someone to ask you to dance at the local hop, do you?' Cyril flashed the gap-toothed grin at her.

Maddy felt out of her depth. This man said strange things she didn't really understand. She didn't know what a chaise longue or a hop was. She stared at him blankly.

'Put the handbag over there and relax a bit.'

Maddy did as he asked and when she sat down again she put her hands on the seat behind her and put her head up, a pose she had seen recently in Vogue. Cyril looked through the viewfinder again and sighed. He went over to her. 'Look, sit like this.' He pushed her knees to one side and angled her shoulders. 'Right, now put that leg up a bit; three quarter profile, clasp your hands around that knee.'

As Cyril touched her she shuddered and hoped he hadn't noticed.

'It's a bit cold in here. It'll warm up in a minute with the lights.' He went back behind the camera.

'That's better, now you're beginning to look a bit like a model.' The camera clicked several times. Cyril adjusted one of the lights. Perhaps this was it, thought Maddy. Perhaps you had to go through all this to get somewhere. Maybe all those women who were famous now started by doing something like this.

It was starting to get warm and Cyril was sweating, although it wasn't just the lights that were responsible. He pressed a switch by the door and the whirr of a fan started.

'Right, now try leaning back against the end of the chaise longue.' He went over to her again and lifted her legs by the ankles so they were stretched along the seat.

'I think we'll take those off shall we,' Cyril said slipping the shoes off her feet with clammy hands. Maddy attempted a smile.

'OK, now look at the camera,' Cyril told her. 'Give me that little smile you just gave me then, that's it.'

'You were going to tell me how much the portfolio costs,' Maddy said.

'Well, that depends,' Cyril replied.

'On what?'

'There are certain costs that have to be factored in. How many pictures you want done. What sort of market you're aiming at.'

'Yes, but how much does it cost?' Maddy didn't like all the prevaricating. She just wanted a figure. She had saved four hundred and sixty-three pounds and forty-four pence from pocket money and holiday jobs which was sitting waiting in her Halifax Building Society account and she was hoping that might cover it. Cyril sucked air through his teeth. 'Packages start at two thousand nine hundred pounds.'

Maddy felt physically sick. She felt her face begin to wobble and she tried to hold her feelings in check, hoping they wouldn't show or worse still that she might start crying. Cyril was changing a lens on the camera pretending he was oblivious to Maddy's emotions.

'Off course there are ways to offset some of those costs.'

'Like what?' asked Maddy but the words were catching in her throat.

'I have this friend who's a talent scout; now that might be a useful contact for you, he's always looking for pretty girls to do modelling.'

Maddy, innocent as she was, got a strange feeling that there might be some sort of catch.

'Just think,' said Cyril. 'There's a girl on Page Three of the Sun every single day of the week. That's three hundred and sixty-five girls needed every year. My friend said it's not easy trying to find girls for that. Mind you lots of girls want to do it but not all of them are suitable if you know what I mean. They haven't got good enough...' Cyril coughed as he said 'breasts'.

'I don't want to do that sort of modelling,' Maddy said.

'Everyone has to start somewhere,' Cyril said in a voice that sounded as reasonable as the smoothest politician's

Maddy felt hot and confused. Cyril sounded so professional, so credible, as if there was nothing to appearing topless in a national newspaper. Why was it that adults always had this ability to have the upper hand and leave her feeling helpless?

'I'm seeing him in a couple of days as a matter of fact,' Cyril continued. 'I've usually got some pictures to show him. He trusts my judgement. I know he's going to love you.'

Maddy wished Jo was there, she'd know what to do.

'But that's OK; I don't want you to do anything you're not comfortable with. I've got some good pictures of sexy girls to show my friend; they'll be up there in no time'

Maddy thought of other girls getting a job in modelling while she got left behind. Maybe it was that Cindy from school, she wanted to do modelling so did Belinda, perhaps they had already been here and had their portfolios done.

'Is it just topless?' Maddy asked.

'Yes, that's all dear, that's all we want.'

Cyril felt a little thrill in the pit of his stomach. She'd taken the bait. All he needed to do now was reel her in slowly.

'Can I come back in a couple of days?' Maddy asked.

''Fraid not,' said Cyril. 'I don't see the guy that often. It might be too late by then. Do you know how much Page Three girls make?'

Maddy didn't answer as she was sure Cyril was going to tell her.

'About two thousand pounds for that one picture, then of course there are the spin-offs. Being in a national newspaper can lead to some very exciting jobs.' Cyril waited while that sunk in.

'Alright then,' said Maddy.

Cyril suppressed a grin. 'Just whizz that top off then. At least it's nice and warm in here now,' he joked trying to sound friendly. She turned her back to him and Cyril took the opportunity to arrange his semi-erection into a more comfortable position. Maddy took the tunic top off over her head, and then took a quick look over her shoulder at Cyril who was now doing something else to the camera. Suddenly it seemed professional and normal; at least he wasn't watching her. She reached behind her, undid the clasp of her bra and took it off. She turned around. Cyril looked up.

'Very nice, very nice.'

She felt self-conscious again now that Cyril was appraising her breasts.

'I think the skirt is all wrong though.'

'What's wrong with it?' Maddy couldn't help her voice cracking.

'The waist band's a bit high and it's cinched in a bit. We don't want that little bit of puppy fat showing over the top now do we?'

Maddy wanted to cry but she undid the button and zip on the skirt and took it off. Cyril made a sound through his teeth again.

'Oh, no,' he said.

Maddy looked at him.

'Tights are so ugly aren't they?'

Maddy hesitated. Cyril was getting impatient.

'Take them off,' he said.

Cyril had done this many times before. He had had girls in this studio who couldn't wait to get their clothes off, girls he didn't have to cajole or persuade, but he liked these ones, the reluctant ones, the demure. It was more of a challenge, like a slow strip-tease. But he knew with this sort that once they took the bait he could be more commanding. Of course there were the failures, the ones who walked out or point blank refused. When he was younger it had, on occasions, got even more exciting when they let him touch them thinking pleasing him might increase their chances of success. Cyril was good at spinning tales about contacts with talent scouts and knowing the editors of magazines but the truth was he knew nobody like that.

Mostly the pictures were for Cyril's own use. He had persuaded girls before to pose much more erotically than just topless. Before the days of the Internet he had even been able to sell sets of pictures to punters on the seafront, lads and old men. It had been easy to do when he was a street photographer, a good side line.

Maddy was now standing in front of him in just a pair of white panties.

'Hardly worth keeping them on is it?' said Cyril.

Maddy looked down. 'I'm keeping these on,' she mumbled.

'As you wish,' Cyril said trying to sound as if he couldn't care less. 'We'll try a nice full on shot first. Good. You might want to try smiling a bit, look like you're enjoying yourself, like you're proud of those breasts – and so you should be, nice and firm.'

All the time Cyril was talking the camera was clicking. He stopped, stood up straight and looked at Maddy frowning a bit.

'What?' she asked.

'It's too warm in here now. We need to make those nipples stand out, like they do on cold days, like when your boyfriend's playing with them. You know, like this.' Cyril mimed, his hands at chest level, rubbing the thumb and forefinger together. 'I can do it for you if you like.'

'No,' Maddy said quickly and started massaging her nipples.

'That's better,' said Cyril. 'Nice little embonpoints.' There was another of those words that Maddy didn't understand.

'Turn to the side a little darling, lovely.' Cyril took the camera off the tripod and started moving around Maddy with the camera in front of his face. Maddy looked at his weird hair, the sheen of sweat on his forehead, the dreadful shiny suit trousers with the obvious bulge in the front, and for the third or fourth time in the last two hours wanted to cry.

After she had gone, Cyril, hands shaking, started to load the pictures into the computer along with the video he had been shooting secretly from another camera in the corner of the studio, so that later he could re-live every juicy second.

Cyril smiled, not like the old days when everything had to be developed and printed. But there had been a joy in the anticipation of that. The smell of fixer never failed to remind him of those days, watching the pictures in front of him in the developing fluid like a sort of magic strip show. He never made the connection as to why the darkroom had such a powerful effect on him, he thought it was just association. Even starting off taking innocent pictures of street scenes and portraits, the dark room had a strange hold over him, compounded further when he had taken the first nude pictures of a girlfriend. He did not understand that it was probably a childhood experience that had made him the pervert he was, when his mother would lock him in the cupboard under the stairs when he had been naughty and during the long wait to be let out, he would sit on a squashed cardboard box and relieve the feeling of misery by masturbating.

Maddy hurried away from Flash Studios walking fast and sometimes breaking into a run. She didn't want to go home straight away in case her parents saw her obvious distress. She tried Jo's number but her phone was switched off. She was walking in the direction of home that took her past the park. She went in, found a bench, put her head in her hands and burst into tears, letting out the emotion that she had been suppressing all afternoon.

A BUSINESS PLAN

{ CHAPTER 18 }

Ray watched the small screen on his desk, a finger poised over the switch in front of him. It was early evening and the view of the bar on the screen told Ray it was still quiet. He could see Bob Elliot leaning on the bar talking to Stella, and a few other groups and couples dotted around. Ray studied with interest the body language of Bob and Stella. Bob was leaning on the bar with both elbows and when Stella was talking to him she also was leaning across the bar, so their heads were quite close. He could see them laugh occasionally Stella saying something that they obviously both found amusing. Luckily he couldn't hear them as they were talking about him.

'Why do you think there are so many mirrors in the place?' she was saying.

Bob chuckled.

'He'd have one outside if he could,' she continued. 'So he could see himself getting out of that damn car.'

'I suppose he has to keep checking his hair is in place,' Bob offered.

Stella gave him a mock serious look. 'Don't mention the Barnet, every hair is insured I'll have you know.' Stella turned to get Bob another bottle of Peroni out of the chiller cabinet. Ray could only see a back view of Bob but could see from the angle of his head he was studying Stella's backside, the material of the black skirt stretched showing the outline as she bent over.

She poured the beer for Bob. 'That Hermione is only here as eye candy. I think he prefers blondes. She's half German you know. Doesn't know shit about bar work.'

'Not my type,' said Bob.

'I thought you were married,' she scolded him.

'I may have bought some goods but I can still look in the shop window,' Bob said.

'Naughty boy,' Stella admonished.

Ray thought he would let Bob get a few beers down him and be softened up a bit by Stella before he went and had a chat with him. He tapped the switch in front of him and the screen changed to a scene in the kitchen. The new chef was Polish and Ray was glad to see he seemed to be more industrious than his previous incumbent, Barry. At least he spent most of his time in the kitchen, chopping or stirring rather than slouching outside the back door smoking.

'She gets her words mixed up too,' Stella was telling Bob. 'Someone asked for a coffee the other day and she asked them if they wanted a catheter.'

Bob laughed mid swallow and spluttered beer across the bar. Stella leant forward.

'Anyway speak of the Devil; here he comes now – Mr Sheen.

'Hey Bob.'

'How're you doing?'

They shook hands.

'How's your drink?' Ray asked

'I'm fine thanks.'

'Get me half a lager,' Ray said to Stella

'Got a new chef I hear,' said Bob.

'Yeah, he's continental.'

'From Poland,' Stella offered. 'His name's Bogumil.'

Ray gave Stella a furious look. He knew Bob was affiliated to the UKIP party and spouted about immigration at every opportunity, mainly because he knew it won him votes. The last thing Ray wanted to shout about was having a Polish chef. He agreed with Bob on issues of foreign workers but sat on his principles when he realised how much Bogumil was happy to earn. But Ray needn't have worried. The politics that Bob expounded when electioneering held no conviction when it came to running his office cleaning business. The company was registered in the name of his business partner so he did not have to declare it as one of his business interests and secondly, as the business employed mainly Polish and Romanian workers he was keen that nobody found out he owned part of it.

'Business is business,' said Bob.

'Funny you should say that,' Ray declared because there was something I wanted to run past you. Just a little idea I've had, wanted to know what your thoughts were.'

'Fire away,' said Bob.

'Come and sit over here,' said Ray. 'I don't want anybody

ear-wigging on this one.'

Ray led Bob over to a table by the ornamental fountain, the gurgling noise of the water keeping their conversation private. Part of Ray's plan was to get someone on his side for this venture. To have someone on the inside of the council who had an interest in Ray's idea would smooth everything along, making it more likely to happen and a lot easier and quicker to negotiate.

'I've been thinking,' Ray started when they were sat down. 'What Cocklebury needs is an amusement arcade.'

'There's one on the pier,' Bob said.

'Yeah, but it's rubbish isn't it?' Ray countered.

'I don't know, I haven't been there for years.'

'What the town needs is something a bit more up to date. All you've got on the pier is a crane grab for cuddly toys, penny falls and pin ball machines.'

'What's wrong with that?' Bob asked.

'I think you're a bit out of touch, mate. Kids these days are more sophisticated, they want Space Invaders, video games, that sort of thing.'

'Don't they do that at home on their computer?'

'Yeah, that's why you have to go bigger and better, simulators for skiing, riding motorbikes and flying aeroplanes.'

'I see.'

'And in with that you put the gambling machines, the one arm bandits.' Ray looked at Bob intently hoping he was getting through.

'I went on this fact finding trip to the States, to see how they do it there.'

Bob was quite impressed that Ray had gone as far as that for research. What Ray had actually done was go on holiday and visit a few arcades near where he was staying in Florida.

Ray laughed. 'Do you know what they do there?'

Bob took a mouthful of lager. Ray continued. 'When the fruit machines are not being played they flash lights and make bleeping noises like, to attract attention.'

Bob nodded, this much he knew and he was hoping that Ray had found out more than this on a fact finding tour.

'But every now and then they have a recorded noise of cascading coins, like a big payout, so people think somebody in the hall has just won a big jackpot.'

Bob smiled – that was more like it.

'There's a motto among the cognoscenti about these machines. People don't lose money; they just keep failing to win.'

'Neat,' Bob said. 'Where are you thinking of having this place, here?'

'No, no,' said Ray. 'I had an idea. You know that place on the seafront, between the fish shop and that gallery. It's a car park, sort of.'

'Where the burger van is?'

'Yeah, that's it, now this is where you come in.'

'In what way?'

'I need to find out who owns that bit of land and who owns the freehold where the gallery is.'

'That shouldn't be a problem,' said Bob.'

'Then of course there will be planning permission for any buildings and permission to open an amusement arcade.'

'Well, you'll have to put in an outline planning application.'

'Yeah, but you see I don't want to piss around and waste a lot of time and money. I need someone on the inside who is with me on this, someone who is going to help it through. They could be a sort of sleeping partner. No names on anything, know what I mean? Just a little sweetener now and again.'

'I see,' said Bob. 'But why that spot Ray?'

'It's perfect see, the right end of the town, not too posh,

slightly out of town but not in it. On a main road, but further down going out of town. And think about it, what have you got down that end?'

Bob thought for a minute. 'Er Holbury holiday park?' he said.

'Exactly,' said Ray. 'Hundreds of families with hundreds of bored teenagers.'

A slow smile spread across Bob's face. 'That's genius,' he said.

Ray leaned back; pleased he had hooked Bob in.

'It won't be easy,' Bob said. 'There are people I know who will object.'

'Who could possibly object,' said Ray, who only ever really saw his own point of view.

'The conservationists, the lefties, the greens, the people who want to see the town kept smart with no riff raff,' Bob pointed out.

'You can't stand in the way of progress.'

'They don't see it like that,' Bob argued. 'We mustn't underestimate them.'

Ray liked the 'we' in that remark.

'Can I get you some more drinks?' Stella asked. She had come over from the bar and stood close to Bob. He looked up. His face was level with her waist and he could smell her perfume and under that a musky feminine scent.

'No thanks Stella, we're going through to my office.'

'OK, have fun boys.'

'Come with me.' Ray said getting up. 'I've got something you might like, something a bit special.'

'Not your barmaid is it?' Bob joked.

Ray grinned. 'If you get in there with Stella, my friend, you can have the use of my office and its facilities.'

Bob smiled. Ray went to the shelf unit in his office that displayed a few items, minor trophies, photos of Ray glad-handing minor celebrities who had visited the club, and a display of different malt whiskies. 'This,' he said. 'Is twenty year old McCallan, smooth as the inside of a virgin's thigh.' He took two large cut glass tumblers, put them on his desk and poured out two generous shots. He handed one to Bob.

'The way I see it,' Ray said after he and Bob had sat in the two leather arm chairs with their whisky. 'We need the tennis courts and the parking area. That fish shop and the beach shop aren't a problem being further back but that gallery, Fish Works or something, is right slap bang in the middle of where the arcade would go to get full visible effect from the road. Of course that burger van will have to go as well, it's a fackin' eyesore.'

'My guess is that the tennis courts and car park are probably council owned so that won't be a problem, neither will the burger van, we can revoke his licence to trade at any time, it's such a shit hole. The gallery might be a problem.'

'Any idea who owns it?' Ray asked.

'A guy called Ben Frampton runs it. He probably rents it, I doubt if he owns the freehold.'

'No? Why?'

'Ben Frampton?' Bob laughed. 'He's a beach bum, or was. An old hippie. Hasn't got a pot to piss in. He's got a couple of women on the go who give him money now and again. I can't see him owning any property.'

'I hate that sort,' said Ray

'So do I,' Bob agreed. 'He's been around for years. Bit of a Casanova by all accounts. He's a trained artist but they never make any money unless their name happens to be Damien Hirst. And he's got a bit of form.'

'Now that does sound interesting,' Ray said.

'Apparently at one time he had a scam going copying well known artists and selling them off as the real thing.'

Ray grinned. 'Yeah?'

'He was in partnership with this other guy. He painted pictures like Monet and Van Gogh, that sort of thing, and the other guy shipped them over to America and sold them at auction. They were doing quite well by all accounts. They got caught out eventually and they both went to prison for a stretch.'

'He had a nerve to come back here then.'

'That sort don't care.'

'I suppose there might be a bit of a lever there,' Ray said.

'He does anything dodgy now the law will be on him like a ton of bricks.' Bob grinned.

'Interesting,' Ray mused.

MORE MODEL INTERVIEWS

{ CHAPTER 19 }

'So you've done this sort of thing before?' Ben asked.

'Oh yes,' said Felicity with a condescending smile.

'For art students?' Hannah asked. Ben was taking no chances this time by insisting Hannah was present at the interviewing process.

'On no, not art students. I used to pose for George Franks.'

'I see,' said Ben.

'The George Franks,' Felicity said.

'Yes, yes, the sculptor,' Ben replied. Felicity sat back pleased that the famous name was not lost on him.

'You see, I was more than just a model to George. I was his muse, his inspiration.'

Felicity Bartlett was in her sixties, with long dark hair and heavy, black rimmed glasses. She was wearing an outfit that was difficult to discern where it began and ended. The material was flimsy and seemed to be made up of several parts, all diaphanous and floaty so she looked like a tropical fish, all rippling fins of camouflage against waving weeds of coral reefs. The job of the dress was probably based on the same idea, trying to camouflage, in this case, the fact that Felicity Bartlett was a rather large woman.

'His sculpture of me, 'Wood Nymph',' Felicity continued. 'Was commissioned for the fourth plinth in Trafalgar Square.'

'Did he not finish it?' Ben asked knowing that the sculptor had died recently.

'I'm afraid his wife destroyed it after he died,' Felicity said.

'That was unfortunate,' said Ben.

'The woman was a philistine,' Felicity replied. She got up rather awkwardly. 'This was the pose I created for Wood Nymph,' she said. She stood on her right leg pointing the left arm and leg backwards, her head and right arm raised, the hand cupped upwards as if ready to catch a ball.

'I see,' said Ben. 'That must have been hard to hold for a long time.'

'I am a professional,' Felicity said standing normally again.

'And were you clothed or unclothed for this pose?' Hannah asked.

'I wore a white chemise,' Felicity said. 'I still have it in fact. George, you know, was wonderful with fabric, especially folds. Tobias Trump, the art critic said he could tell a George Frank's sculpture from the folds of the clothing.'

'Really,' said Ben politely. 'But you understand that this job requires a life model?'

'Oh yes,' said Felicity. There was a pause and some instinct told Ben that Felicity was not going to be comfortable taking off her clothes in front of a bunch of strangers.

'In this case there could be as many as ten students.'

Felicity nodded.

'And you'll be happy posing nude in front of them?'

'Well,' said Felicity. 'I was thinking it would be more suitable to wear something simple like the chemise I mentioned earlier. It adds a bit of mystique to the whole process. More tasteful I feel.'

'Mrs Bartlett,' Ben began.

'Miss, actually,' she corrected him.

'Miss Bartlett,' he continued. 'The human form is one of the most demanding subjects for art students. The students who have enrolled for this course are expecting to work from a live nude model.'

'Mr Frampton,' Felicity said. 'You do not need to inform me on the finer points of artistic modelling. I, who have worked with the finest of the last century.' She stood up. 'You have my details. You can get in touch with me if you decide to employ a professional.' She swept out of the door.

'I didn't know it was going to be this difficult,' Ben said leaning back and rubbing his face with his hands.

'She was quite a character,' Hannah commented. 'Do you think that was true, all that bit about George Franks?'

'Probably,' said Ben. 'He had a reputation for seducing all his models. That was probably why his wife smashed the work. What a palaver this is turning out to be. I bet Picasso never had this much trouble. Who's next?'

'Jo Elliot,' Hannah said consulting the book. 'She sounded quite young on the phone.'

'We don't have a lot more choice,' Ben moaned. 'And the first class is next Wednesday. Bugger – well let's just hope she's OK.'

Jo arrived at five thirty as arranged and did not know whether to feel awkward or comfortable being interviewed by two people old enough to be her parents.

'Have you done this sort of modelling before,' Hannah asked.

'No,' said Jo thinking honesty as the best policy at this stage.

'But you know what the job entails?'

'Yes, I have to sit still while people draw or paint me.'

'And you realise you won't have any clothes on?' Hannah asked.

'Yeah, I'm cool with that,' she said.

'You're very fit,' Ben commented.

Jo gave Ben a sly look.

'What Mr Frampton means is that you seem to have a very well-toned body.' Hannah interjected to save any misunderstanding

'Oh yeah, I keep fit. I go jogging most days.'

'I think I've seen you,' Ben said. 'You jog along here don't you?'

'Yes, and I've seen you too, mostly smoking out the back here.' Jo countered.

Ben smiled. 'Not as fit as you then.'

'Is it a problem?' Jo asked. 'I mean me being slim and that. Were you looking for someone with a bit more flesh on them?'

'That's not an issue,' Ben said. 'It's the human form that is important.'

'But all the women in those old paintings, they were all fat.'

'Well that was the fashion of the time, it doesn't matter today. More important is the ability to hold the pose. It's not as easy as it sounds, just sitting still.'

'I can do that,' Jo told them.

'Everything will be carried out with the most professional decorum. There will always be a chaperone present. Students will not be allowed to touch or take photographs and there will be a changing room and a robe to put on when you are not posing.' Hannah told her.

'Sounds OK to me.'

'And you are comfortable posing without your clothes?'

'Yes.' said Jo.

Jo didn't have a problem with body image. She knew she had a good body and had no problem with being seen naked. It hadn't always been like that. At school she had been average at most things but she didn't shine at any one of them. She had always been small and being small she got picked on by bigger girls and teased by the boys. Her way of dealing with it was to keep a low profile, hang back, stay in the shadows. If she could have chosen a super power it would have been to be invisible. That all changed one sport's day when Jo was thirteen. She had been entered in several events at the school sports day and was expecting just to get her usual average results. She had been talking to her mother at the edge of the spectator's line when she heard a whistle being blown and a call for all those entered in the eight hundred metres to get to the starting point. Slightly day dreaming and with the sun in her eyes she lined up with the other contestants and only when the whistle blew for the start did she realise she was in the race for the year above her.

Too shy to draw attention to herself by dropping out she started with the others with a plan to just walk away at the end of the race hoping no one had noticed the mistake. After two hundred metres she realised she was in third place. There were five girls behind her and only two in front. As she passed the sport's mistress she could see the look of consternation on her face and wondered if she was in trouble. But she put her head down and ploughed on. She passed the girl in front of her, Sue Owen, with the thought that she was still not really trying. There was only one girl in front of her now, Beth Bartholemew, a legend in the school for being a sporting hero. Jo had never felt a competitive urge before, being average and shy it had never occurred to her to be competitive, but watching the image of Beth Bartholemew, sporting whiz, getting larger and nearer, in her view, changed all that. The thing that finally did it for her, the image that sent power to all her muscles, was the expression on Beth's face as she stole a glance over her shoulder and realised that she was being challenged for the race by a girl in the year below her.

That look sent Jo's legs into overdrive. They felt like pistons being driven by some force outside of her but she knew that wasn't possible. In some sort of state of Zen she passed Beth and could see from a glance the strain in her face, the sluggishness in her limbs and the sweat on her red face. Jo knew it was the face of defeat. As she passed Beth and ceased to worry about her, all she could see was a set of clear lines narrowing towards a tape at the end of the track. She was oblivious to the growing noise of cheering from the girls in her class, jumping up and down at the finishing line, and the teachers looking nonplussed. Only when she ran through the tape did her other senses kick in and she heard the crowd and felt hands on her back, wanting to be near her and touch, because now she was a winner. She heard Beth complain to a teacher that Jo should be disqualified for being in a race for the wrong year, but even the teachers were smiling now at Jo's triumph.

That day changed her. From then on she signed up for all the extra-curricular activities that were sports related. She was a regular at the school gym, taking up gymnastics and practising with weights to build up muscle. She pestered her mother into getting food and meals that would build her strength and stamina. She travelled with the school to sporting events against other schools and joined the girl's football team. Being at so many sporting events had made Jo completely blasé about nudity. Showering after events was desirable if not essential and at games played with teams from other schools almost certainly meant showering with strangers.

Some girls tried to hang on to a form of modesty by having a wrap or towel with them for all but the act of getting under the water, but it was a pointless exercise and Jo soon became nonchalant about walking around naked. She also started to wear her hair shorter for the obvious reason that it made it easier to get it dry after a shower. There was a down side to this in that it attracted attention from girls who had lesbian tendencies and drew comments about her own sexuality. Now with physical strength and mental confidence Jo was able to deal with both of these problems either with a sharp remark or an equally sharp elbow.

Both Jo and Maddy were in the same class at school and were acquainted but not friends at this stage. They were, however, the girls who the boys had sexual fantasies about. Jo, slim, pretty and tough now walked with a swagger owing to her new found confidence but she didn't have much time for make-up or trying ways to make herself more attractive. Maddy on the other hand, with obvious good looks, played up her best features with beauty products and make-up, but she was shy and lacked confidence. In Jo she saw the part of her that was missing, and the confidence she wished she could have. She also thought that Jo would benefit from a little help from her. All she had to do was to pluck up the confidence to tell her this.

Maddy took the opportunity one day when she saw Jo at lunch in the canteen and took the spare seat opposite her. She didn't say anything for a while.

'I watched you playing football the other day. Good penalty,' she said at last.

Jo looked up and grinned. 'Thanks. You should put your name down for the team'.

'Not my thing,' said Maddy. 'Too physical for me.'

Jo shrugged and they were silent while Maddy thought of what to say next.

'Do you ever wear make-up?' she asked eventually.

'Not really – too much faffing about.'

'You've got good bone structure.'

'That's enough then isn't it?'

'If you put some blusher on it would accentuate your cheek bones.'

'Yeah?' Jo looked at Maddy's face and saw that although she was wearing very little make up it was sensitively applied. 'What else?'

'Some eye liner would bring out the colour of your eyes'.

'I wouldn't know where to start,' Jo said.

'I'll help you,' said Maddy. 'The boys have got the hots for you already; if I get to work on you they'll be creaming their pants.'

Jo looked at her for a full five seconds and then burst out laughing.

'Do I really want that?' she asked.

'Doesn't hurt,' said Maddy grinning.

In the end they became friends, not because they saw anything in each other that was lacking in themselves, but because they made each other laugh. Before long Maddy had got Jo to grow her hair a bit longer and wear it in a ponytail and Jo got used to wearing a little bit of make-up. Maddy liked being with Jo, it made her feel more confident and she liked the respect she was afforded when in her company. Maddy tended to consider too much how people might perceive her looks whereas Jo didn't care that much. Little bits of character rubbed off from one to the other.

Alone in her bedroom with the door locked Jo stood naked in front of the mirror viewing dispassionately what she saw. She knew from a sporting point of view she had a good body but she wanted to assess herself as a sexual being. She was muscular without being muscle bound, lean without being skinny, rounded but not fat. She turned sideways, her breasts were small, but a good shape. She was pleased they weren't large for practical reasons, especially for jogging. She had a small waist and a flat stomach and her hips curved outwards giving her a pleasingly feminine look. The flesh of her thighs was rounded at the front tapering to the knees. She decided that even though she thought she was good looking and sexy, she still wasn't sure what boys thought. She had fended off a few gauche passes from the youths in her year whose testosterone levels outweighed any sophistication but had never thought there was anyone who might appreciate her for what she had to offer. The sporting jocks were too crude and obvious, she didn't like the so-called intellectuals and the rest were just wimps. Jo sighed and put her clothes back on.

'We just need to know you're over eighteen?' Hannah said.

'Yes,' Jo lied.

Hannah flashed a glance at Ben. 'Are you still living at home?' she continued

Jo nodded.

'Do your parents know about this?'

'It's not a problem,' Jo said.

'We have to cover ourselves against any possible litigation so would you mind getting one of your parents to sign a form to say they approve?'

Jo hesitated for a split second. 'Sure, I can do that.'

'I'll draw one up over the next couple of days, do you mind popping in to collect it.'

'I'll come in one day when I'm jogging,' said Jo.

'Great,' said Ben. 'In that case we would like to offer you the job pending the parental signature.'

'Cool,' said Jo.

MORE MODEL INTERVIEWS

WENDY

{ CHAPTER 20 }

Wendy put a plate of food down in front of Ben who looked at it with appreciation.

'Haven't seen you for a while,' said Wendy putting her own plate down and sitting opposite him.

'I've been busy preparing for these art courses,' said Ben. 'You've been busy too by all accounts. Have you been full every night?'

'More or less.'

They were sitting in the dining room of Wendy's guest house, overlooking the coast road and the sea beyond. It was only a short walk from the gallery. The residents had all eaten earlier and Wendy and Ben had the dining room to themselves. The muted sound of a television in another room was all they could hear along with the occasional passing car making its way along the coast road.

Wendy and her husband John had bought the guest house fifteen years earlier when he had been made redundant. They had sold their house and with John's redundancy money had managed to buy the guest house with only a small mortgage, and moved in with their son James, then aged ten. It had been named 'Philandor' by the previous owners, Philip and Dora, and they had hated the name from the start. The only reason they kept it was to avoid confusion for the bookings that were already in place. Phil and Dora were very pleased with what they thought was a highly original idea, and said they also liked it because it had a sort of 'Lord of the Rings' sound to it. Wendy and her husband had jokingly referred to it as 'The Philanderer' and even 'Dun Philandering'.

They found they could make a reasonable living from it even though it was hard work. But, five years after they had been trading, John left with no explanation. Wendy when called upon to explain what had happened, used to tell people: He went out for a walk one morning; it must have been a long walk because he hasn't come back yet. She carried on running the guest house single handedly with some help from hired staff. James, on his own initiative, did some research to find his father and discovered he was living in a town ten miles away with another woman. Perhaps the name of the guest house had been an omen.

Wendy, ever the pragmatist, decided after some thought that she had got the better deal. John had always been a bit lazy, allowing Wendy to do most of the work, so she was happy that the other woman got John but she got to keep the guest house.

Wendy was an excellent cook and most of the guests who returned usually booked the dinner, bed and breakfast option knowing they wouldn't get much better even in the posher restaurants in town. Ben, whose options for meals were 'al fresco' fish suppers with Wilf in the summer or a takeaway, jumped at every opportunity to dine with Wendy. When she found out that Ben mostly slept on the sofa in the office at the gallery, she allowed him to use a room at the guest house in winter when she wasn't busy. They became friends and eventually lovers, and the arrangement of not quite living together suited them both.

It was dark by the time they finished dinner. Wendy got up and pulled the curtains.

'How're the art lessons going?' she asked.

'Yes, good,' said Ben. 'We are all set up to start next week. 'Seascapes and landscapes' has got quite a few on it. Still Life not many, but full for 'Life Drawing and Painting'.'

'Hm, I wonder why that is so popular. Have you got a model yet?'

'Yes at last, I thought I was going to have to ask you at one point.'

Wendy laughed, 'There's only two people I would take my clothes off for.'

'Who's the other one?' Ben asked.

'George Clooney but he hasn't booked a room yet.'

The food, the wine and the company along with having the dining room to themselves had given Ben a feeling of contentment and he leaned back in his chair with his glass of wine as he entertained Wendy telling her of the interviews and the prospective models.

'And this Jo that you've chosen, are you going to draw or paint her?' Wendy asked.

'I probably won't get a chance. With eleven people booked I expect my time will be taken up going around and giving advice.'

'Can they work in any medium?'

'Yes, I'm going to encourage them to make lots of studies

in pencil and charcoal getting the shape right, then spend the last two or three sessions doing a painting and working from their drawings.'

'Sounds very professional. Will it be a steady income for you?'

'If they keep getting booked up, yes. I've got Hannah to thank, it was her idea. Apart from paying the model it is nearly all profit but we charge a bit more for that one anyway. I've had to spend a bit buying a few extra easels and chairs but the materials will be for sale. Not that there's much profit in that.'

'Are there a lot of men on the Life classes?' Wendy asked.

'A higher proportion than in the other classes but there are a few women doing it as well.'

'Men must still find it a turn on having a real live nude in front of them.'

'It's strangely rather cold and clinical in reality.'

'There must be a certain voyeuristic quality to it.'

'Maybe for some. It's different in a one to one situation, in a group there's safety in numbers.'

'Have you ever hired a model just for you to paint?' Wendy asked.

'Funnily enough I never have. It's not terribly commercial. Women don't buy paintings of nudes. Couples who buy paintings for the family home wouldn't buy a nude, so that leaves bachelors. We did studies like that at art school but they were mostly portly middle-aged women, so as art students we were not exactly turned on.'

'So if she had been young and attractive you would have found it a turn on.'

'Touché,' Ben smiled. 'Of course. Men are attracted by their eyes more than women are. You just have to be professional about it. If a doctor has to examine a woman that he might find attractive in other circumstances he has to be dispassionate.'

'Doesn't always work like that though does it?'

'It's bound to happen every so often.'

'So there's a grey area between art and porn then?'

'Yes, and there always has been. The Victorians were shocked by nudity but there was a huge underground porn scene, although we wouldn't consider it to be porn now – in fact it's rather tasteful, and artists still carried on painting nudes as they had before. There has always been a resistance to what polite society calls the lax morals of the art establishment.

Toulouse L'autrec, Van Gogh and many others found their models in brothels. How may Madonnas do you think are out there in classical art whose image has been based on a local prostitute? You can have a painting of a nude looking demure and chaste, change the pose and she becomes a siren or a temptress, the body is still the same. Sometimes the pose can be enigmatic so that the interpretation is down to the viewer.'

'Just be careful you don't shock the good burghers of Cocklebury, you don't want to start a campaign of moral outrage.'

'Oh, surely times have changed,' said Ben. 'Anyway it's all going to be very tasteful. Hannah will see to that.'

Wendy picked up their plates. 'You can go and have a bath if you like while I clear up; I expect it's been a while.'

'I have a bath every day courtesy of the English Channel,' Ben told her.

'Swimming in the sea is not the same,' Wendy said.

'Salt water is very cleansing,' Ben offered.

Ben had been married once but it was not a success. In his last year at college he had started going out with a first year student called Marilyn. Second year students always looked on the new influx as easy meat. They were usually young, nervous and flattered by the attention of older students. Marilyn came from a wealthy, middle class background and had become an art student mainly to annoy her parents. Having afternoon tea at the wrong hour would have annoyed Marilyn's parents but Marilyn didn't do things in half measures. Next she took Ben home. Ben at this time looked like the typical art student. His thick hair was quite long; he wore an earring and had stubble. When the encounter had produced the desired effect she told her parents they were getting married.

Because of the parental disapproval the marriage took place at a registry office, and only when they came to sign the official documents did Ben find out that Marilyn was not her real name. It was Constance. This was not the only thing that Ben didn't know about her. In the intoxicating combination of love, youth and rebellion he missed the fact that Constance / Marilyn had issues, represented by the fact that the name she chose was that of a victim. Her conscious reasons for choosing the name was that the original Marilyn was a beautiful free spirit, untamed and exotic, but deep down she identified with the manipulated, insecure plaything of moguls, magnates and mandarins. Too young to understand, they soon made each other unhappy, each laying the blame on the other. They parted company and put the experience down to – well experience.

The fall-out from this broken marriage was short lived for Ben. He never had any trouble getting girls. It wasn't just looks, although the unruly hair, pale eyes and bone structure were an advantage, it was mainly attitude. An insouciance born of a tendency to day dream gave him a sort of lost look, a powerful magnet to females who wanted to look after him or smooth his rough edges. Also he was an attentive listener and had an unlearned knack of listening in a way that convinced the person speaking that what they were saying was the most interesting thing he had ever heard in his life. There was no shortage of choice either, at art school or the beaches at Cocklebury in the summer when it thronged with students and holiday makers. The marriage to Constance made Ben wary of further commitment and he had managed to stay single since.

He had met Wendy through Wilf when she had been to see him to arrange a fishing trip for some guests. Wilf had introduced her to the gallery and Ben. A few weeks later she bought a couple of his paintings for the lounge downstairs and after Ben had hung them for her he did a couple of small maintenance jobs around the place. He had refused any money for the jobs so Wendy had invited him for dinner.

Wendy had a small bedsit she used when the guest house was full. There was a bathroom, bedroom and small sitting room. When Ben came out of the bathroom he found there was a glass of wine on the table in front of the sofa.

'If this takes off,' said Wendy. 'We could advertise painting holidays. Art lessons during the day and then dinner, bed and breakfast here.'

'I can't think of anything better.' Ben said taking Wendy's hand. 'In fact that's almost my lifestyle now.'

'You didn't mention sex,' Wendy said.

'I hope you won't be offering that to the guests as well.'

SLEIGHT OF HAND

{ CHAPTER 21 }

'Salade Niçoise anybody?' Clare announced from behind the kitchen bar. She snapped a pair of salad servers in the air. They were a souvenir from a holiday in Spain, made from olive wood and hinged in the middle like a lobster claw.

'What's Salade Nicoise?' asked Tom.

'Tuna salad,' said Jo, without looking up from the book she was reading.

'I wanted burgers,' Tom complained.

'We had burgers yesterday for dinner,' said Clare.

'I know, but I like burgers.'

Clare had opened a packet of mixed leaves from Waitrose,

shaken them into a bowl, opened a can of tuna and doused it all in Lloyd Grossman's special dressing. She poured herself another glass of wine from the fridge. Her philosophy for providing food for her family was that anything was OK as long as it didn't keep her in the kitchen any longer than five minutes. She felt that if she was shopping in Waitrose she was being the perfect mother / wife / hostess. With careful planning, she argued, one could provide a varied menu with the minimum of fuss. Salads, oven fish and chips, packets of fresh pasta, bottled sauces and microwave meals made up the bulk of the choice. Clare didn't see the point of buying a whole range of ingredients just to make one dish, and besides if you went in for all that cooking like they did on the telly, you gave yourself another job in that you then had to clean up the mess – that or pay the Polish woman extra to do it.

Jo came over and looked at the offering on the kitchen bar. 'Is there any bread Mum?' she asked. 'I need carbs.'

'Oh, hang on a minute.' Clare delved into the freezer and pulled out a stick of garlic bread.

'I'll put it in the oven,' she said.

'I don't like salad,' said Tom. 'It's for rabbits.'

'There's ice cream in the freezer for afters,' said Clare. Tom made a face.

'Aren't you having any Mum?' Jo asked.

'I'll have some a bit later; I'm not hungry at the moment.'

Jo served herself a bowl of the tuna salad, which took a while as the salad servers only seemed to be able to pick up one leaf at a time. Jo would usually be taking verbal pot shots at her mother over issues such as the supper provided, her drinking and occasionally her laziness. Today she was holding back, and all for a good reason. She had been back to the gallery and collected the form that Hannah had prepared; the form that she had to get one of her parents to sign before she could take the job as life model. There was no way she was going to present it to her father unless she fancied the idea of starting World War Three. She had considered forging the signature as no one would have any idea what either of her parents signatures would look like anyway, but decided she had better keep it above board in case there were any come backs. She had the form neatly folded in the pages of her book and had chosen a time when she knew her father would not be around.

Clare looked at the clock. 'Time for Emmerdale,' she said picking up her glass.

She went through to the living room, settled in the arm chair and put the TV on. Jo and Tom sat at the table in the conservatory. Tom picked out bits of tuna from the salad. The oven pinged. Jo got up from the table, took the garlic bread out of the oven and cut it up. She took a board and the bread to the table.

'That's better,' said Tom taking two pieces. Jo positioned herself so she could see her mother through the archway to the living room. She got up again, went to the fridge, took the bottle of white wine over to her mother and topped up her glass.

Clare looked up. 'That's very sweet of you darling, thank you.'

Jo smiled, and as her mother turned to look back at the TV screen, Jo picked up her mother's reading glasses that were in a case by the glass of wine and left the room. In the kitchen she slid the case onto the dining bar behind a vase of flowers. Tom watched her with curiosity but didn't say anything. Jo waited until she heard the advertisements come on in the middle of Emmerdale. She took the form from the pages of her book, grabbed a pen and went back into the living room.

'Mum. I just need you to sign this form.'

'What form?'

'I've applied to join the rowing club and they need a parental signature as I am under eighteen.'

'What more sport?' Clare said.

'It's just for the holidays; there's nothing much happening at school.'

'Give it here,' Clare said. 'As long as I'm not signing you away into white slavery.'

Jo laughed at her mother's joke.

'Where are my glasses,' she said looking down at the table.

'On your face Mother.'

'No, my reading glasses.'

'I don't know; when did you last have them?'

'I thought they were here.'

'Shall I read it to you?'

'Oh, go on then.'

'I, Clare Elliot, I've written your name in there already, give my consent for my daughter, Jo, to take part in the Cocklebury-on-Sea rowing club as a full and participating member,' Jo pretended to read out, making it up as she went along. 'The rest is just stuff about insurance and liability.'

The programme was coming back on and Clare looked anxiously at the TV screen. Jo picked up the Radio Times, put the form on it and handed it to her Mother with the pen.

'Just there,' Jo pointed. 'Down the bottom, along that line.'

Clare signed and Jo whipped the form away from her. 'Thanks Mum,' she said breathing a sigh of relief but also pleased with herself, not only for managing to get the form signed, but for pulling the wool over her mother's eyes so easily. She went back into the kitchen, poured herself a glass of juice from the fridge then went up to her room.

After about five minutes there was a soft knock on the door.

'Yes,' she called out. The door swung open and Tom

stood in the doorway. He was holding the form by the corner between thumb and forefinger, waving it gently and smiling at Jo. She looked around her, on the bed; sure she had brought it up with her.

'You left it in the kitchen,' Tom said, and then holding it up: 'Rowing club eh?'

'Give that here, it's private,' Jo said.

'Not any more it isn't.'

'You'd better not have read it.'

Tom held it up in front of him, made a theatrical cough and read out, 'The Fish Works art gallery...'

Jo jumped up and snatched it from him.

'Doesn't matter, I've already read it.' He made a face. 'Anyway who'd want to draw your scrawny body?'

'It's none of your business.'

'It is now,' Tom taunted.

'I'll tell Mum I caught you wanking in the shower,' Jo said.

'I was not,' said Tom going red.

'No, but she'll believe me if I tell her.' But they both knew that Tom held more of the aces.

Jo looked at him with steady gaze. 'If you tell Mum or Dad I'll make your life hell.'

'It'll be too late by then. You could of course buy my silence.' Tom waited.

'Go on then,' Jo said.

'Grand Theft Auto Three,' Tom said, getting enthusiastic and sitting on the bed next to Jo. 'It's awesome.'

'I'll think about it,' Jo said.

'When you get all that money you'll be rolling in it,' Tom said.

'It's just like any other job you get paid for,' Jo commented.

Tom thought for a bit. 'Do you have to show your tits and your bum?' he asked.

BRIBERY AND BLACKMAIL

{ CHAPTER 22 }

Cyril was a whistler. In idle moments when he was concentrating, walking or driving somewhere, Cyril would whistle. It could have been any tune, it didn't really matter. Cyril didn't know the tune and anybody listening certainly wouldn't be able to name it. It was just a tuneless whistle, something that Cyril did. If he had been married it would have been one of those things that could drive a wife to distraction, like a repetitive phrase or picking one's teeth. But Cyril didn't have a wife. Being married meant compromise, doing things he didn't particularly want to do and going on endless shopping trips. He argued, mostly to himself that what he lost in comfort and companionship was made up for with bucket loads of freedom.

Today was Cyril's official day off. Being self-employed also meant he was free to do what he wanted, when he wanted, so today was a day when Cyril could do all the things he wanted to do and nothing he didn't want to do. This was why he was ambling down the seafront, hands in pockets, whistling. He had already had coffee and a slice of cake at the Lighthouse Café, and read the paper, occasionally looking out over the flat calm sea. Now and then he got out the photograph that he had copied from Justin's original and chuckled to himself. He was making his way down to see Ben at the gallery and taking his time while he savoured every moment of the proposed meeting. He wasn't sure what he was going to say to Ben or how he would use the information that he had. But what Cyril liked was just being in possession of that secret and the power that it gave him.

Ben was sitting at the reception desk. It was quite early and he was alone. Cyril put his head around the door. 'Morning,' he said.

Ben looked up. 'Hi Cyril.'

Both men had lived in the town long enough to know each other to nod to and know a short potted history of each other and the salient points of their history. Cyril knew Ben to be a painter, with a chequered history of serial girlfriends, a failed marriage and a conviction for fraud. Ben knew Cyril had started off as a street photographer with a sideline in dirty pictures, who had become respectable via wedding photography, to own a shop and studio in the town and that he was unmarried with a prurient interest in young girls, whether legal or not Ben didn't really know.

'I was having a stroll so I thought I might just pop in,' said Cyril.

'Be my guest,' said Ben who sussed this was no idle visit

but could not think what Cyril might want. Cyril started to study the pictures on show.

'We should hook up,' Cyril said. 'After all, what we do is similar- it's all art.'

'I don't think so,' said Ben who was always irritated by Cyril whenever their paths crossed.

He felt he could never take Cyril seriously and found he had an irresistible urge to wind him up.

'You just click a shutter,' Ben continued. 'I have to work hours to create a painting.'

'There's more to what I do than just clicking a shutter,' Cyril said suppressing a desire to be ruder.

'A lot of original photographs are fetching quite a lot at auction. I see from the local paper you are having to put on art lessons.' Cyril could be just as barbed.

'Well, where there's a market,' Ben said. 'People kept asking if I did lessons so I thought I might as well give it try.'

'Got many booking have you?'

'Yes, it seems it's going to be very popular. How's business with you?'

'Very good, very good.'

'Not affected by the downturn?'

Cyril laughed. 'People don't stop getting married.'

'Must be boring doing wedding after wedding.'

'It's bread and butter, Ben, bread and butter.' He moved to another painting and leaned forward to look more closely.

'Is that Wilf?' he asked Ben.

'That's right.'

'Is he still fishing?'

'Wilf will never stop fishing,' Ben said. 'He could stop tomorrow if he wanted to but it's in his blood.'

'Ah, we go back a long way, don't we?' Cyril said.

'I suppose so,' Ben replied, not keen to agree too

wholeheartedly in case Cyril was having some idea that they were all friends, or had some sort of three musketeer camaraderie.

'Those were the days,' Cyril sighed.

Ben groaned inwardly.

'Which reminds me,' Cyril said. 'Someone's been looking for you.'

Ben looked up. 'Well I'm not hiding. I'm here most days.'

'The thing is,' Cyril said. 'He doesn't know your name.'

Ben wasn't sure what Cyril meant but he knew if he waited he would find out.

'He's looking for his dad and all he's got is this.' Cyril reached into his inside pocket, took out the photograph and laid it down in front of Ben.

Ben looked at it. An odd feeling came over him as if reality had got skewed or he had got a glimpse of something in a parallel universe. It was familiar but unfamiliar. As he studied it he recognised himself first, then slowly came to realise the other man in the photograph was Wilf. He peered closely the girl in the centre.

'Remember that?' Cyril said.

Ben felt a surge of anger. Not only had Cyril wrong footed him, it was now as if he was intruding on a private moment but not sure what the private moment was about.

'Sort of,' said Ben.

'Ah, so many girls, eh?' Cyril smiled. 'She looks keen on you.'

Ben was trying hard to remember. There had been a lot of girls but not as many as everybody seemed to think.

'So what you're trying to say is that somebody is looking for me and they think I am their father.'

'More or less.' Cyril was enjoying himself.

'So how come you get to hear about it first?' Ben asked.

'Co-incidence really. He came into the shop. Don't worry I haven't said anything yet.'

'The girl in the picture; what's her name?'

'I thought you'd be able to tell me that.'

'I don't remember,' said Ben.

'It must have been taken down at the other end of the sea front; you can just see the De Montfort Hotel in the background.' Cyril pointed unnecessarily at the hotel in the photograph.

'Ring any bells?'

'Not at the moment,' Ben said. 'So what's your angle on this?'

'Depends on you,' Cyril said. 'Whether you want to get in contact with a long lost son or would rather let sleeping dogs lie.'

'How come he's so sure I'm his father?' Ben asked.

'That I don't know but he's invested a lot of time and energy into this search.'

'So, if I want to meet him I have to ask you and if I don't you've got me cornered.'

'I'm just a go-between,' said Cyril shrugging.

'Well you're keeping your cards very close to your chest, Cyril. You must want something out of this, is it money?'

'That's very crudely put.'

'I can't find another way of putting it.'

'I said we should work together more closely,' said Cyril. 'I quite like the idea of your art lessons. I would quite like to come along. As you say art is more demanding than photography. I might learn something. I rather fancied your life drawing classes as a matter of fact.'

'They're full Cyril.'

'I'm sure you can squeeze another one in.'

Ben suddenly felt very angry. He didn't like the way Cyril

was trying to use a bit of information to hold the upper hand over him. It wasn't exactly blackmail but it wasn't far off. And besides there might not be anything in it at all, he might even have made the whole thing up and Ben could see that if he gave in to him it wouldn't end there, and Cyril would be back asking for more. Besides, Cyril didn't seem to know much about whoever was looking for him and was probably bluffing. Ben weighed all this up in his mind and decided he was fed up with being polite to Cyril.

'I would have thought you had plenty of opportunity to practice art from that stack of porno pictures you used to peddle.'

The colour drained from Cyril's face. 'If you knew anything about art you would know that those pictures were art.'

'Look Cyril, if you want to get off sketching a nude model in here, you can book a place on the next course and pay for it like everyone else. But I understand you've got your own methods of getting girls to undress for you.'

'How dare you, everything I do is completely above board and legal.'

'I'm sure it is, but that doesn't stop it being, smutty, sleazy and suspect.'

'Well if that's how you're going to treat someone trying to do you a favour...'

'You're not trying to do me a favour,' Ben interrupted. 'You've probably got this other guy dangling on a string to see who is going to benefit you more. No Cyril, you're not going to threaten me. Go and see this guy, tell him where I am, in fact better than that,' Ben jumped up and took a leaflet from the desk. 'Give him a leaflet; it's even got directions on the back.' He grabbed Cyril by the lapel and thrust the leaflet inside his jacket.

'Now piss off.'

NOCTURNAL COCKLEBURY

{ CHAPTER 23 }

Ben sleeps. He dreams he is in a studio, but as this is a dream it is a studio he is not familiar with. There are lots of people at easels all working with concentration. Ben looks in front of him and there is just a blank canvas sitting on his easel. He realises he had better make a start but, what is he supposed to be drawing. He can't see the subject as there are too many easels in the way. He moves forward to see what all the others are working on, and as the forest of easels parts, there sitting on a dais is Cyril, naked, posed and grinning at Ben seductively.

Ray sleeps but with troubled dreams. Bogumil has several large pots boiling on the stove. All are full of Golonka the national dish of Poland. It is grey and strands of cabbage trail from the dishes as waiting staff ferry plate after plate to the dining room. On the stage is another Bogumil telling jokes in Polish – he is the only one laughing. Ray tries to escape to his office where yet another Bogumil is engaged in vigorous sex with Hermione. He runs from the building only to find Bogumil again doing hand brake turns in the car park in his gold Lexus. He wakes, strained and damp, grateful it was all just a dream.

Cyril is not asleep or dreaming, he is sat up in bed. Everything in the room is as Cyril likes it. He has no need to compromise as he shares it with no one. The bed is a large double and next to Cyril on a tray are the remains of a chicken passanda, yellow rice and naan bread. The meal is mostly eaten except the bread which is only half gone. Cyril is wearing pyjamas and is propped up by several pillows. On the bedside table is an array of different medicines for his various afflictions, Bisodol, Imodium, Anusol, and Zantac, also tissues and a bottle of Johnson's baby lotion. The room is very tidy. All Cyril's clothes are hung up in the wardrobe or neatly folded in the tallboy in the corner. Against the wall opposite the bed is a low chest upon which sits a large flat screen TV. Cyril has already rigged up the video he secretly filmed of his photo session with Maddy, and is reliving every sordid moment of it.

Jo snores gently. She has gone to sleep on top of the covers. The biography of Mo Farrar has slid to her side, his expression on the cover looking as though finding himself on a bed next to a girl in pink pyjamas is a rather pleasant shock. The walls in her room are decorated with a mixture of posters, some of boy bands but mostly of sporting stars. Clare comes in quietly, takes the book from Jo's side and places it on the bedside table. She folds the duvet over her sleeping daughter, kisses her lightly on the forehead and turns out the light.

Ken and Freda Macmillan are lying side by side in their bed, on their backs, eyes wide open. It is dark but they both know the other is awake. If the light were on, the strain on their faces from sleepless nights and stress would show. There is the thud of a beat that not only reverberates through the fabric of the building, but can be seen by the slight vibration of the fringes on the matching bedside table lamp shades. They do not speak to each other mainly because they have examined every aspect of the problem and tried to deal with it in lots of different ways. They have even tried ignoring it. They know the reason for it because Ray Collins, the new landlord of the flats, has given them notice to leave. He has no legal right to do this and in law Ken and Freda have security of tenure. They know that Ray wishes to remove all the people renting flats in the block, renovate the flats and re-let them at a much higher price. He has offered them money to go, he has offered to help them find somewhere else to live, and he has offered them temporary accommodation with the promise of their old flat back when the renovations are done but they don't trust Ray and they are certain he would renege on the promise.

Their dilemma is that fighting Ray with solicitors will cost them and so would moving to another flat and they have very little in the way of savings. And besides they like their home and don't see why they should be forced to move. So they know that the tenants that have moved into one of the empty flats, the ones who look a bit dodgy when they meet them on the stairs and who play very loud music at all times of the day and night, have been planted by Ray with the express purpose of forcing Freda and Ken from their home. Ken has knocked on the door and asked them to turn it down on occasions and they have complied, but the next night it's the same again. They are not sure how many are living in the flat as Kevin and Bo have had many visitors since word got around that it was an open house. They are also afraid that if they call the police the occupants will exact some sort of revenge on them. It is a stalemate and Ken and Freda lie in bed with their options going round and round in their heads. They don't like living somewhere knowing they are not wanted but neither do they want to go or, indeed, afford to.

Kevin navigates his way across the room. It is like an obstacle course of ash trays, legs, pieces of uneaten pizza and other unidentifiable detritus. He is looking for Bo. He doesn't know a lot of the people in the flat and he would rather they weren't there, but to ask them to leave would be like un-cool and against his principles and it would be like he was the state and making rules like who could stay and who had to go and that would be like a very heavy scene, because, see, if you believe in anarchy you have to live like that or you'd be like some sort of hypocrite, but then it's a real bummer when you can't find your girlfriend and you look in every room and there are just people there you don't know and someone has put something on the stereo that is like majorly un-cool and you have to keep your stash in your pocket otherwise some dude will come along and half inch it, and even when you're asleep you have to be like aware; and nobody like pitches in and helps with getting food and stuff, like that bit in Animal Farm where no one knows who's in charge or who's responsible for food or cleaning the loo when someone has taken a dump and not cleaned up after themselves, and why is it always him who opens the door when that freaky old guy from the other flat asks him to turn the music down and he's like smiling but you know he's probably one of those old vigilante dudes that's probably got a machete under his dressing gown and you come back and it's a major downer because you turn the music down and everyone thinks your some sort of square.

Kevin moves from room to room looking for Bo. He feels cold and a bit panicky. There are three, or is that four people on the bed in what he thought was his bedroom. There is someone on the floor, they are in a sleeping bag and Kevin feels a wave of despair that they are now bringing sleeping bags in with them. He looks down the other side of the bed to see if Bo is on the floor down there but she isn't. He checks the other bedroom with the same result and goes back into the living room. He looks around and sees Breath. He is talking to someone who is obviously asleep. Kevin shakes him and Breath looks up. 'Where's Bo?' he asks. Breath cups a hand to his ear and makes an enquiring face. 'Where's Bo?' Kevin shouts above Queens of the Stone Age. Breath shrugs. Kevin returns to the sofa, plonks himself down, wraps his great coat tighter around himself and sinks his head into the collar.

On the promenade, not far from the pier, is a hut. It's bigger than a beach hut but not brightly coloured like the ice cream or coffee vending huts. This one is brown like a garden shed, and when open, displays decorations hung on string of beachcombing finds such as oyster shells, driftwood and cuttlefish bones. It is shut now, this being night, and the wind chimes of wood and bone have been put away and a shutter of brown wood hides the serving counter where Joseph Robbins sells fishy snacks to the tourists during the day. Whelks, fat and chewy, are dispensed in polystyrene cups with a cocktail stick. Likewise mussels and cockles, jellied eels, crab sticks and seafood cocktail, a dubious mix of sea creatures, salty and vinegary.

Most of what Joseph sells to the mainly elderly tourists, who remember such delights from their childhood, have been purchased in industrial sized tubs from the local cash and carry, and the English Channel but a few yards behind Joseph's emporium would be a foreign sea to the creatures now on display on his counter. One side of the hut Joseph has turned into a smokery. Fillets of mackerel and trout get smoked over smouldering beech and oak chips. This wafts a savoury smell of sweet, smoky fish around the hut and immediate area, that not only attracts hungry strollers but of course the ever present herring gulls. They perch on the roof of the hut and strut hopefully up and down the promenade, sometimes stopping and thrusting an exploratory beak under the gap at the base of the smokery where the fish oils sometimes drip. The combination of combustible oil soaked into wood makes it not unlike a larger than life firelighter or a stack primed for November the fifth. The regular presence of fire to make the smoke means one small mistake or a less than responsible shutting down of the process could mean the end of 'Smoky Joes'.

Spig is huddled in a shelter on the lower promenade. It is getting dark. He has tried going to the flat where Kevin and Bo live but a stranger opened the door. He had gone in and looked around. There were a lot of people there and some of them were frankly a bit scary. He couldn't see Bo and Kevin was huddled on the sofa in his coat and seemed asleep. He had gone there when things at home had started getting out of hand again. Spig wasn't sure whether to spend the night in the shelter or try and creep home when things might have settled down a bit. The problem with the shelter was that there was always the likelihood of an old tramp joining him for the night, smelling of meths, old socks and ripe farting, which did not appeal, even if they left him alone. Also, Spig's distress by now had reached crisis level. He knew this from his compulsive fingering of the box of matches in his pocket, which he sometimes got out to look at, open and fiddle with the matches, but on this occasion lighting them one after the other was not going to cut it or ease his distress; he was working up to something bigger, something that was going to calm him more than just the flare of the match.

Spig's night time perambulations had made him an expert on the back alleyways, twittens, wynds and cul-de-sacs of the town. He knew his way around like a surgeon knows every blood vessel in the human body and where it goes. He knew the secret ways through buildings, occupied or vacant, and not just at ground level either. If he could not get to where he wanted through the alleys he could get across rooftops, down fire escapes, and through windows. The police had often tried to detain him, not because they suspected him of any wrong doing, but because of his age and the lateness of the hour. But Spig had never been caught. By the time the Plods had stopped the car and got out, Spig had evaded them down some back street or over a garden wall. Once one reasonably fit and zealous copper had given chase and followed him down several interconnecting alleys, but had given up at the back of one of the hotels, and after looking in the bins had gone back to his car. Spig had watched him from his perch wedged between the hotel kitchen's extraction system and the wall, having climbed there first by standing on one of the bins and then on the brackets that held the galvanised steel of the duct work in place.

This was where Spig went, after putting a match to a handy discarded fish and chip paper and thrust it under the boards of Smoky Joe's. After clambering up the brackets of the extraction system he had got onto the roof of the hotel's staff accommodation, up a fire escape and across a parapet to get behind the human sized illuminated letters on the hotel's roof. He had predicted, with his knowledge of all things combustible, that the burn should be slow and concealed long enough for him to get to his seat in the gods before the blaze really got going and the fun started.

One of the letters of The Queen's Hotel, the H of Hotel to be precise, was awaiting repair of the lighting system and was therefore in darkness and Spig chose this spot where his outline would not be visible. He could see a glow under Smoky Joe's and a few wisps of smoke were beginning to appear through the overlapping boards of the exterior. Spig waited. The smoke started to become more noticeable and the glow from underneath brighter. Some flames licked out periodically through gaps in the shiplap boards as they creaked with the ever increasing heat.

A man walking his dog slowed down and looked at it possibly wondering if any fish was being smoked overnight. He was about to move on when there was a mini explosion as the temperature inside reached a critical point and something inside burst into flames. The man took a step backwards and fumbled to get his mobile phone out of his pocket whilst still trying to hold the dog's lead. It took ten minutes for the fire brigade to arrive, ten minutes in which a sizeable crowd had gathered, and in which Smoky Joe's turned into what a lot of people were now calling Flaming Joe's. It burned with a ferocity that makes one understand what people mean when they say that fire consumes or devours.

Sparks shot skyward, burning bright as if from a firework, and then disappearing into the night sky. The flames at the centre reached outwards, warping and crackling the boards at the outside. Small detonations could be heard as bottles of vinegar and condiments exploded and fed the fire with their volatile vapours. Cracks, sizzles, smacks and pistol shots rang out as the flames leapt up, all cadmium yellow and scarlet vermilion.

Spig felt the skin of his scrotum contract with the excitement of watching the shack go up like a torch, and the crowd it attracted. The feeling went up a notch as the fire brigade arrived and the crowd started cheering and applauding. A police car rolled up and the two officers watched as the firemen trained their hoses on the fire and put it out in seconds.

CYRIL SPILLS THE BEANS

{ CHAPTER 24 }

Justin unpacked his suitcase in another room at the Falkirk hotel. Having searched further around the town, following leads that went nowhere, and even calling at Flash Studios to find it closed, he decided that there was no way he was going to find the identity of the man in the photograph, let alone the man himself. He had settled his bill, packed his suitcase and was preparing to leave. Sitting outside the doors of the hotel on a bench reserved for residents to enjoy the view, was Cyril. Cyril was looking dapper and smart, if not a little old fashioned, in a light weight tan safari suit circa 1973 Marks and Sparks, and smiling smugly.

'I've got some news for you young man.'

Justin put his suitcase down. 'Well?' He thought it unlikely that Cyril knew anything that might be of use to him but thought he had better hear what he had to say, even though looking at Cyril's smug face made him want to punch it.

'Aren't you going to buy me a drink? I think you'll find this very interesting.'

Justin picked up his suitcase. 'Come on then,' he said, heading back to the foyer.

'I think I might indulge in a cocktail,' Cyril said as they settled in the bar. 'Mind you, I'm not so keen on all these concoctions with silly names. Give me the classical ones any day.'

Cyril ordered a Gimlet. Justin had a glass of wine.

'OK, Cyril, tell me what you've found out.'

'Ah yes, very interesting. Now this took some doing, and I might add some not inconsiderable investigating skills. There were times you know when I felt a bit like Philip Marlowe.'

Justin waited while Cyril twirled the stem of his glass. 'You know, the private detective in the Raymond Chandler novels.'

'I know who you mean, why don't you cut to the chase Cyril?'

'I'm getting there but it is quite involved. What's the food like here?' and then to the barman. 'Can I see a menu please?'

'Cyril,' Justin said.

'Ah yes, paternity,' Cyril said. 'I'm afraid you might be a teensy bit disappointed with what I have found out.'

'You mean he's dead?'

'No, no, far from it, but,' and here Cyril made a grimace. 'Not a nice man, I'm afraid, not nice. But look, they've got an à la carte and they've got lobster.'

Justin sighed.

Over dinner of Lobster Thermidor, Puligny Montrachet, followed by a concoction of fruit, cream and meringue, Cyril made sure he gave away the few bits of information he had at agonisingly slow intervals, to make sure he not only got a good dinner out of it, but was also able to interweave his own life and triumphs, told in a way that made him look like a hero and Ben the villain. From his early struggles as a penniless street photographer, overcoming all sorts of obstacles to reach success, how he had photographed minor celebrities and film stars, how grateful they had been and how much they had admired him; how many girls had been in love with him and wanted to marry him but how he couldn't because of his aged mother who had sadly died five years ago. Justin put up with the tedium politely trying, but not always succeeding, to steer the conversation back to getting the information.

'So, he's an artist,' Justin said at one point when he managed to get a snippet out of Cyril.

'A minor artist,' said Cyril making a face and a 'so-so' hand gesture. He had a blob of cream on his chin that Justin thought not only made him look foolish, but gross as well.

'Quite scruffy' 'completely without scruples' 'forger convicted of fraud' 'been to prison' 'known to be violent' were all phrases dropped into the conversation by Cyril, designed to give a bad impression of Ben after the treatment he had got on his last encounter with him. Justin thought it all made Ben sound dashing and roguish.

Over coffee and brandy, another of Cyril's suggestions, with Justin groaning inwardly at the idea of having to spend yet more time with him, Justin learned of the gallery and where it was located, with a warning to take care when approaching Ben on a sensitive subject such as the one in hand.

After Cyril had tottered from the hotel red faced and grinning, Justin had asked the hotel if he could extend his stay. His original room having now been let to other customers, he was offered a smaller room without a sea view. He unpacked his things again, mulling over the long conversation, teasing out the relevant bits from the indulgent ramblings of Cyril's career. He came to the conclusion that (a), Cyril knew who the person was from the first time he looked at the photograph and (b) he only really needed to give Justin the name and location of Ben and the gallery. The dinner he had screwed out of the situation was payment. Justin shrugged and hoped he was never going to have to see Cyril again, even less spend an evening with him.

STILL LIFE WITH AEROPLANES

{ CHAPTER 25 }

At nine a.m. the first car pulled into the car park. 'This is it' thought Ben with a feeling of apprehension. He had got up early to be ready to receive his first students, no slouching around with a hangover, smoking and drinking coffee this morning. He had swept the gallery floor and set out the extra chairs and easels he had bought for the lessons. There was a new coffee machine sitting in the corner hissing steam and gurgling, all chrome and taps and levers. Hannah was standing next to it holding the instruction manual with a puzzled expression on her face.

'So far I've just managed to make a cup of warm water,' she said.

FISH FARCE

'I'm sure you'll work it out,' said Ben absently as he watched a largish woman struggling up the path to the building. She made it to the door, out of breath and with a hank of hair falling in front of her face. She was carrying a fold-away easel, a canvas stool, a smart box that Ben guessed would hold a brand new set of paints, two canvases, a handbag and a basket.

'I made it,' she announced, stumbling through the doorway and looking around. 'Ooh, this is nice!' The easel fell to the floor with a clatter.

'Good morning and welcome,' said Ben.

'Hello,' she replied. 'I assume you are Mr Frampton?'

'Call me Ben, this is meant to be informal. And you are?'

'Mrs Hoskins, or Betty if you prefer.'

'Let me see now,' said Ben, looking down at a list on the desk and trying to look efficient and professional. He made a tick next to her name. 'If you would like to find a place,' he said to her. 'Then you can get set up.'

'I've brought all my own stuff,' she said.

'I can see,' Ben replied.

'Can I take your bags?' Hannah approached and Betty's face relaxed on seeing another female. Obviously a bit nervous, thought Ben.

'You can leave them just here, they'll be quite safe. Would you like a coffee?'

'Ooh, yes please, Cappuccino, and lots of that frothy milk.'

Hannah started leafing through the instruction manual.

A man entered. 'Is this the art lesson place?' he demanded. He was wearing a blazer and tie. There were two small badges on the lapel of the blazer and an embroidered emblem on the top pocket. He had neatly clipped white hair, a military moustache and was carrying a large art folder under his arm. He looked Ben up and down, took in the jeans and loose flowered shirt and did not smile.

'I do a bit already,' he said to Ben. 'I'm not a complete

novice; mainly technical drawing, aircraft, that sort of thing.

'Good,' said Ben. 'If you'd like to find yourself a place we'll start when everyone is here.'

'How many have you got coming in?' the man asked.

'Five,' Ben replied. 'Could I have your name please?'

'Major Harding,' the man replied. He hesitated. 'I've brought some of my work to show you.' He indicated the folder. Ben looked up from the desk and smiled. 'Yes, thank you, maybe we can have a look at them during the break.

'Quite so, quite so,' Major Harding replied.

A man and a woman were waiting at the door while Ben was dealing with Major Harding. They came forward as he turned away from the desk. 'Good morning,' Ben smiled.

'Hello, I'm Susan Shelley.'

'David Thorpe,' the man said.

'Are you together?' Ben asked. 'Or did you just arrive together?'

'Oh no, we're together,' the woman said.

'Fine, thank you for coming,' said Ben ticking off their names. 'Make yourselves comfortable, Hannah's on coffee duty if you would like one.' Hannah cast a desperate look in Ben's direction.

A young man arrived. He was wearing gold rimmed glasses and sported a wispy beard. Ben surmised this was a first growth and the young man had probably never shaved.

'Peter Potter,' the young man said in a low tone. 'I've booked quite a few of your courses.'

'Great,' said Ben. 'Let's hope you are going to like them.'

'Oh, I'm sure I will,' he replied. 'I want to be an artist.'

'That's excellent,' said Ben. The young man joined the group and nodded as a couple of them acknowledged him.

There was a loud hiss from the coffee machine and Hannah screamed. 'Sorry everyone, I'm still getting the hang of this.' Peter Potter went over to Hannah and the coffee machine, and without saying anything at first he looked over the machine and turned a couple of the knobs. Everybody watched. He unlocked the chrome cup with a lever from the machine and saw it was full of ground coffee. 'Ah good, you've got that right,' he said. 'Now just turn this lever, remember to place your cup under here, turn this and, what was the first one Cappuccino?' Hannah nodded. 'Then the milk, voila, one Cappuccino.'

'Thank you so much,' Hannah said. 'How do you know all that?'

'Oh, I service the machines,' Peter replied and took his place with the group.

Ben stood in front of them feeling nervous. 'Good morning everyone, thank you for coming. This is our first art session, and as you know this subject is 'Still Life'. Some of you, I see, have brought equipment with you, but we have easels and seating for those who haven't. Again, with materials, if you haven't brought any or need some more they can be purchased from us at not unreasonable prices.'

Ben had arranged three white pots on a table, placed a white sheet over the window behind to take the glare out of the light, and placed a lamp to one side to create some shadow. The white pots were a tall vase in white glass, a plain white china pot and a squat alabaster dish with a lid.

'Today's session is about form. I've kept it simple so it is not too confusing. This exercise will not only look at form but also perspective, light and shadow. You can take paper from the pile over there where there are also drawing materials, pencils, and charcoal etcetera. Have a go at getting an impression of the shapes, do it several times as you get your eye in. Ask any questions you like and I'll come around with individual help.'

Although sounding authoritative Ben was out of his

comfort zone, never having spoken to a group before. People busied themselves selecting paper and materials and positioning themselves in front of the subject. He looked over at Hannah who smiled with encouragement. Ben surveyed the group, trying to spot who looked confident and who seemed tentative.

'I'm not sure I'm getting this right,' Betty Hoskins said to nobody in particular. Ben went over and looked at her paper. She had drawn the three pots very small in the centre of the page.

'It's not very good is it?' she said to Ben with a nervous laugh.

'Give yourself a chance; it's your first go.' Ben replied. 'You've got all this paper and don't worry about getting it right straight away. Draw it again here,' Ben indicated the top left hand corner of the paper. 'And here, just do quick sketches so you get the feel of the shape, like this.' He took the pencil from her hand and sketched some simple lines just showing the different curves of the pots.

'Oh, it's not fair,' Betty said. 'Look at that, why can't I do it like that?'

'You can with practice,' Ben said. He gave her the pencil back and went to look how the Major was getting on. His drawing was very precise.

'Technically very good,' Ben observed.

'But?' the Major enquired without looking up.

'I can't fault it.' Ben said. He walked over to where Susan and David were working side by side. Susan was making a bold charcoal sketch that filled the paper with bold lines and dark shading.

'She's good isn't she?' said David sheepishly.

'It is good,' said Ben turning to look at David's effort. He had got as far as drawing the neck of the tall vase and there was evidence of a lot of rubbing out.

David grinned. 'Sorry,' he said.

'Don't be sorry,' Ben replied. 'What you really need to do is to stop worrying about detail and just try and get the general shape down. And you don't need this,' he said picking up the rubber.

'Sorry,' David said.

Finally he looked at what Peter was doing. He had produced a reasonable drawing just using lines, although some of them were a bit out.

'Try having another go in a different medium,' Ben told him. 'And get a bit of light and shade in there.

After an hour and a half Ben told them to take a break for coffee. Peter went outside and lit a cigarette. Major Harding fished into his art folder and looked around to locate Ben. Betty had struck up conversation with David and Susan

'This one is of a Lancaster bomber that I did last summer,' Major Harding told Ben when he finally got his attention.

'It's excellent,' Ben responded. Major Harding pulled another one out of the pile.

'Ah yes, Spitfires in a dog fight with Messerschmitts over Beachy Head.'

Ben could see they had been done some while ago. 'It's really very impressive,' he told him.

'Thank you.' Major Harding sounded pleased.

'It just begs the question, with respect Major Harding, why are you here?'

Major Harding looked at Ben as if the question had been highly personal, and as he hadn't expected to be put on the spot he took a while to answer. 'I get a bit bored sometimes you know.'

'Yes,' said Ben as the Major paused thoughtfully.

'I need a bit of a kick start now and again.'

'I understand. Don't we all?' said Ben.

Major Harding looked at him. 'You can call me Terry if you like, no need for all this Major stuff.'

'Well, I think that all went very well except for the coffee machine, don't you?' Hannah said after they had all left.

'I'm not sure, I think so,' said Ben.

'Don't be negative, of course it went well. Betty struck up a friendship with that couple. I heard them arranging to meet up for lunch and you've made a friend in Major Harding,'

'Yes,' Ben laughed. 'I even get to call him Terry now, although I don't think he thought much of me when he first came in.'

'He just needed to get to know you that's all.'

'He can draw perfectly well you know.'

'People are going to come for all sorts of different reasons, he probably just wants some company,' Hannah observed.

'Do you think so? I found there was not a great deal I could do to actually help people.'

'I don't think they are really worried about that. They are here, doing it, with an expert giving them tips and encouragement, there's not much more you can do except draw it for them.'

'I suppose you're right.' Ben said.

'Drawing from life is fully booked with eight people now,' Hannah pointed out.

'Let's hope that girl turns up,' said Ben. 'Otherwise you'll have to do it.'

'There's only one person I'd take my clothes off for,' Hannah replied.

'Don't tell me, George Clooney,' said Ben

'How did you know that?'

ELVIS LIVES

{ CHAPTER 26 }

Pat had fallen in love the first moment she set eyes on Derek. Admittedly he didn't look anything like he would do in normal circumstances. The high collar, white rhinestone studded jump suit and wide belt might have had something to do with it, as did the atmosphere of the evening. And even though there were several men in similar gear, also with black quiffs and jutting triangular sideburns, it was Derek, when he came on stage, stood in front of the microphone and sang the first line of 'Love Me Tender', a strange physical sensation started in Pat. She felt it somewhere in her belly at first, then it moved upwards to make her heart beat faster, sending a rush of hot blood to her neck and cheeks. It went the other way as well, creating intense warmth that spread through her abdomen and reached a pitch that, if she had not been in company, would have had her squirming in her seat. As Derek's rendition of Love Me Tender came to a close Pat was besotted. The applause and whistles seemed to come from far away.

Pat had been an Elvis fan from the age of fifteen, a time when all her friends were fantasising about Bros and Wham. Pat had seen a documentary on television about Elvis and even though it had been ten years since his death, Pat was captivated by the images being shown. As soon as she saw the footage after he had dispensed with the guitar and sang 'Hound Dog' unencumbered, she realised that at last here was something meant for her, something she could identify with. And it wasn't to do with the provocative gyration of his hips that had so incensed middle America, although that may have been part of the appeal, it was the fluidity of that body, that snaking quality from his shoulders to his feet, and of course his beauty. Here was a man, a real man, not some skinny, hair-waxed adolescent or coiffed, cheeky boy-next-door; he was a man with raw sex appeal. She saw his decline and death like some Greek tragedy, a sweet, honest talented god brought down by the avarice of others and the grinding relentlessness of the entertainment industry.

Pat collected the records, videos of the films which she watched over and over and read about his life in the many books and biographies. At sixteen she got a job in a factory sewing clothing for a manufacturer of outsize women's wear. She didn't mention her Elvis obsession in case the other girls thought her strange. But eventually during coffee breaks she found some of the older women had been avid fans when they were younger, and at a time when Elvis had still been alive. Some of the girls the same age as Pat could see the appeal even if they weren't such avid fans. So when someone suggested an Elvis Impersonator gig in Birmingham for the staff outing it got the biggest vote.

That night was the night she first saw Derek. Pat knew he was the best; he had the looks, the charisma, the moves and the voice. When George Mulhooney, an overweight Irishman in a badly made white jump suit pipped Derek and won, Pat, before she was aware of what she was doing, had jumped up and shouted 'shame' at the lined up contestants and compère.

'It's all down to votes love,' the compère had said in his reasonable and smarmy voice. Pat would be teased about the outburst for the rest of the time she worked at the factory. At the end of the evening Pat lined up with the others to get back in the coach. Most of the women, worse for drink were being noisy, vulgar and raucous like only women can be in an all women group, but Pat felt strangely aloof from them as she waited at the back of the queue while the others navigated the steps to the coach, under the impassive gaze of the coach driver who had seen it all before. As she was waiting the flare of a lighter caught her eye, and she saw Derek across the car park light a cigarette as he stood by a Volvo estate car. She saw his face lit by the flame and glow red as he drew on the cigarette. He watched her as she approached him across the tarmac.

'Alright love?' he said while she was still a few yards away.

'You should have won,' Pat said.

'I know, I know,' Derek replied with a shrug and an open hand gesture.

'You were the best.'

'That's life innit.'

Pat got closer to him. There were still vestiges of stage make-up on his face, some powder on a cheek bone and a bit of mascara that only made him look more appealing, more decadent. Derek looked over Pat's shoulder before reaching into his inside pocket. He handed Pat a card.

'That's me, if you're, like, interested.' He gave her a devilish grin.

'Do you do this full time?' Pat asked.

'Nah, not at the moment but I aim to soon.'

Pat heard a clack clack of high heeled shoes approaching. 'Come on Derek, we've got a long way to go.'

Derek looked sheepishly at Pat and got in the car. 'See ya love,' he said.

The woman opened the passenger door and Pat heard her say 'Fuckin' groupies' as she got in and shut it. Pat ran for the coach which was by now pulling away.

Derek was apt to take full advantage of the second hand charisma that being an Elvis Impersonator granted him. The business cards he carried not only served their usual purpose but were a useful means of slipping girls he fancied his telephone number. Serial girlfriends and one night stands were part of the lifestyle which suited Derek. During the day he was a panel beater and kept his work mates amused by stories of life on the road and his style of low level show business, and the amount of sex he was offered though he tended to exaggerate this a bit. He vaguely remembered Pat when she rang him a week later.

'At the Stardust Club, y'know Birmingham, the car park, your girlfriend wasn't best pleased.'

'Oh yeah, yeah,' said Derek.

'I was wondering whether you were doing any more dates?'

'They're all on the web site love, you can look there,' he told her. Pat hadn't worked out anything else to say and there was a silence.

'If you wanted to go out for a drink, then of course that would be different,' he offered.

It wasn't far to go and over drinks in a down-at-heel hotel Derek told her of the moonlighting lifestyle of an Elvis Impersonator, making it sound more glamorous than it really was and leaving out the bits about groupies and one night stands. He told her how most of the impersonators knew each other and if they were not doing a job on their own would meet at competition evenings such as the one Pat had been to, and how they took it in turns to win and it was all decided before the audience had cast any votes. Pat in turn told him about her Elvis obsession and impressed him with her knowledge of the King.

Derek, too, started as a fan, miming to the records in his room as a teenager and eventually putting a band together called Elvis Lives. When Pat told him she was a seamstress and could make him a suit not only better than the one he wore but better than any of the other Elvis Impersonators, Derek was impressed. The partnership was sealed that night in a Travel Lodge at the Moto services on the M6 and their relationship began.

'There it is,' said Pat with an AA tourist map on her lap and pointing at a road sign. 'Cocklebury-on-Sea, left at the next roundabout. I wish you'd get a satnav.'

'Elvis wouldn't have used a satnav,' Derek replied, 'even if they had been invented.'

Pat didn't reply. They had this conversation often and it just got boring.

'Well it ain't Memphis and it certainly ain't Nashville,' Derek said as they sat in the car park looking at the squat ugly building that was Rayjay's night club.

Ray was in a rare mood of hyperactivity. He had spent a lot of money advertising and setting up the club for the Elvis Night. He had decided that if you're going to do something that is not entirely original you have to do it better than anyone else. The tickets included the Elvis buffet, a selection of all the King's favourite foods: foot long hot dogs, bacon peanut butter and strawberry jam rolls, double cheeseburgers and not a bit of salad in sight. The King didn't die to be remembered with salad was Ray's comment when asked.

'Have you got King and Barnes beer on?' he asked Stella.

'For the eleventh time this evening, yes,' she replied.

'I only asked.'

'Anyway, Elvis didn't drink, well only Pepsi.

'Yeah, but they don't know that. This has cost me a fackin' fortune and I need to make some money at the bar.'

Ray's mobile rang. 'Yeah, who? OK I'll deal with it.' Ray went to the entrance where an affronted Bob stood, his way barred by Dave. 'Let him through Dave.' Ray said.

Bob harrumphed, straightened his jacket and pushed past Dave.

'I should think so too. I only came in for a drink and that ape said tickets only.'

'Alright Bob, calm down, this has been a nightmare of logistics, what are you having?'

'I'll have my usual thanks Ray.' His face changed as he saw Stella. 'Hello darling,' he said.

'I didn't know you were an Elvis fan Bob.'

'I'm not; I came in to see you.'

'You know where flattery gets you.'

'I live in hopes Stella.'

'The acts are complaining,' Stella said to Ray.

'What about?'

'They say there are not enough dressing rooms.'

'Well tell them to share, we ain't the fackin' Albert Hall. Sort it out. I've got to check on chef.'

In the kitchen, Bogumil had opened an industrial size can

of Frankfurters in brine and was in the process of lifting one of the foot long sausages out of the tin.

'We have these in my country, they are called Kielbasa; we eat them with cabbage and potatoes.'

'Yeah, maybe, I am beginning to think you eat cornflakes with cabbage and potatoes over there, but Elvis didn't. Have you got the rolls for them?'

'Yes! And don't step on my blue suede shoes huh.' Bogumil laughed.

'Very funny,' Ray said and went back to the bar. It was filling up and Stella and Hermione were busy serving drinks. Bob tried to collar him. 'When you've got a minute I've got some news for you.'

'I'll be with you in a bit; I've just got to check on the band and the MC.'

The Three Tones, Ray's regular band, were already on stage and talking to Billy Baxter, the MC Ray had hired specially for the evening. He was checking the names of the acts and the songs they would be covering from a list he had been given. Ray was keeping his fingers crossed as he had never employed Billy Baxter before.

'Alright Billy?' Ray said and nodded to the band members, Frank on drums, Charlie on electric guitar and Neville on keyboards. 'You know all the numbers?' he asked.

'Are you kidding?' said Charlie.

'Just checking.'

'I could play Jail House Rock when I was in short trousers.'

'OK, OK sorry I asked.'

'You doing a bit of a warm up first?' he asked Billy.

'Oh yeah,' said Billy. 'I've got my routine worked out.'

'Good, I think we'll kick off soon, we've got a lot to get through and then there's the voting.

'It's all under control,' said Billy.

Frank started a quiet routine on the drums using just the brushes and the cymbal to create a bit of atmosphere and to let everyone know the show was starting soon.

'Ladies and gentlemen,' Billy announced, his lips close to the microphone. A few people that were left in the bar started to drift through. 'Welcome to the fabulous Rayjay's Elvis Night. Sadly the king of rock and roll is with us no more but his memory lives on. Tonight, to entertain you, we have an Elvis from each era of the King's career. We have a young Elvis, the Las Vegas Elvis and the mature Elvis.'

'Have you got a dead Elvis?' someone shouted.

The heckler unnerved Billy so he tried a joke hoping to bring the warm up back on track.

'I was in bed with my wife the other night,' he said sounding less confident.

There were some 'oohs' from the audience. Billy grinned. 'And I said, shall we do it the Elvis way, and she said, how's that? And I said.' Here Billy hunched his shoulders, struck a pose and said: 'A little less conversation.' There was some light laughter from the audience.

'Without any more ado,' Billy announced.

'Good,' shouted the heckler.

'Ladies and gentlemen, I give you all the way from Shepton Mallet in Somerset, Jeff West with his Elvis and 'Hound Dog.' Frank hit the drums as a slim youth jumped up on stage.

Ray went back to the bar which was mostly empty except for a few stragglers and Bob sipping his lager. He screwed his face up when he saw Ray. 'That compere's a bit rubbish; I could do a better job myself.'

'I'll bear that in mind for next time,' Ray told him.

'I've got some information that might interest you,' Bob said.

'Come and sit over here then,' said Ray. Bob followed,

giving a quick smile to Stella over his shoulder. She gave him a little wave.

'Your artist fellow, Ben whatsisname doesn't own the freehold of the gallery.'

'Interesting,' Ray mused. 'Do we know who does?'

'Well, I've been doing some scratching around and it seems the building is owned by a Wilfred Finchley, local fisherman.'

'Hmm, fisherman, he can't be that well off. He might be persuaded to sell.'

'Actually he is quite well off. His father was a fisherman before him and bought the bit of land with the net shops along there in the fifties when they were dirt cheap. The council bought some of the land off him years later to put in those tennis courts and he made a killing. He still owns the fish shop and the gallery.'

'What sort of lease is the gallery on?'

'That I couldn't find out but the rumour is it's a gentlemen's agreement. Apparently this guy and our Mr Frampton are friends.'

'I see, what about the parking lot?'

'That's no problem. It's owned by the council so I can probably wangle something for you especially if the other councillors can see it will raise some business rates.'

The rendition of 'Hound Dog' came to an end to applause from the crowd. Ray and Bob waited for it to subside. Billy Baxter took the microphone to a screech of feedback.

'Your voice has gone squeaky,' the heckler called out.

'Thank you. Now remember folks to mark your scorecard out of ten for that fabulous young man and 'Hound Dog'. Frank did a drum roll ending it with a thump on the floor tom-tom.

'And now from Burnley in Lancashire a young man

who has won the prestigious Elvis Impersonator title at the International Birmingham competition, Mister Derek Bradbury and his chosen Elvis song is 'Love Me Tender.'

There were whistles and applause. Pat was in one of the front seats, still with butterflies in her stomach even after thirty two similar competitions since she first met Derek who now appeared in the white jump suit that had been lovingly crafted by Pat; every sequin and every rhinestone sewn on by hand.

'What about the burger van,' Ray said.

Bob laughed. 'Toddy's Bacon Crematorium – yes, that's the least of our problems.' Ray waited for Bob to continue. 'He's got a license to trade but that can easily be revoked. I've only got to send in Environmental Health. He's got to be breaking every rule in the book.

'Good, so that leaves just the gallery then.'

The MC was back at the microphone. 'Knock knock,' he said as the applause died down. A few people called out

'Who's there?'

'Wurlitzer,' Billy shouted barely able to contain his mirth.

'Wurlitzer who?' someone obliged. Billy sang in a deepened voice,

'Wurlitzer one for the money, two for the show.' There were boos and cat calls as well as some laughter.

'Jesus, where did you get him?' Bob said to Ray.

'Actually, I thought that was rather funny,' Ray said. Bob tutted. 'So where were we?'

'The gallery,' Ray said.

'Yes,' said Bob. 'We could get a letter sent from a solicitor to see if this Wilfred guy wants to sell. That would be a good first step. In the meantime I'll go and have a sniff around to see what this Ben fellow gets up to. As I've said before, he's a bit of a dodgy character. I've got a friend in the Police, it might be worthwhile finding out if they still keep an eye on him to see if he's running any scams.

'I appreciate it Bob, as I said to you I'll see you all right. By the way, do you want to help yourself from the buffet?'

Bob hesitated. 'Er, I'll pass on that one.'

LIFE DRAWING

{ CHAPTER 27 }

'Very Cezanne,' said Hannah. Ben was draping a rug, with a pattern of oranges and reds, over the back and seat of a chair he had set up for the life model.

'Well we don't want to send the poor girl home with a Lloyd Loom pattern stamped on her rear end do we?'

'I can think of worse,' said Hannah. 'Which reminds me, we didn't ask her if she had any tattoos?'

'No,' said Ben. 'Would it matter?'

'I suppose not. It would be very modern if she did and a challenge for the students too.

'We have to make sure we do this very properly,' said Ben looking down at the chair and speaking his thoughts out loud.

'It will be less embarrassing for all concerned.' He started arranging the seats and easels in a semi-circle around the chair he had set out for the model, just as the students started arriving. Hannah was greeting them and ticking their names off the list as they entered. Only Betty and Peter Potter had been before, the rest were newcomers. Jo had cycled to the gallery and arrived as the students were coming in. Ben saw her standing at the desk talking to Hannah, and his first feeling was one of relief that she had turned up. The second emotion was one that took him by surprise and that feeling was one of concern. Looking at her form from that distance, her slight build, and slim almost boyish figure, he felt a wave of protectiveness and a slight queasy sensation about whether what they were doing was right. He pushed it out of his mind realising it was too late now for back pedalling. She came over to where Ben was standing and said 'hello'.

'We thought we'd give you an easy pose to start with, just a sitting pose so I set this up.' He gestured towards the chair.

'Shall I get undressed now?'

'Er not yet, we'll get the pose right first. Would you like to sit down?'

Jo sat in the chair.

'The rug should make it more comfortable and give them another element to draw. Would you put your legs out in front of you and cross your ankles?'

Jo did as Ben asked.

'Now if you put your right arm on the arm of the chair and the other arm just casually in your lap. And if you can, look at something, say over there so you're not looking at anyone directly. Great, now is that comfortable?'

'Yes,' said Jo.

'Hannah's got a robe for you to put on when you're not actually posing and you can get changed in the office over there. The front door will be locked so there will be no one just wandering in. Are you OK with all that?'

'Sounds fine,' said Jo.

'I think everyone is here now. Hannah will show you the office.'

When Hannah had taken Jo through to the office Ben spoke to the group explaining what they were going to do, much in the same way as he had spoken to the still life class.

'Just a few points of protocol,' he continued. 'I probably don't even need to say this but no photography and no touching. We will take two breaks rather than the usual one, more for the model's sake than yours, holding a pose even seated for any length of time can be quite hard.

Jo, left alone in the office looked at the green candlewick dressing gown that Hannah had given her and wondered whether she was more concerned about being seen in that than being completely naked. Now that the moment had arrived, where she had to sit in front of a bunch of strangers without any clothes on, the real impact of what she was doing hit her. She had liked the idea from the beginning because of the novelty of it being different, also the better than average remuneration, the fact that it was a little bit risqué and because her parents would not have approved.

Thinking about it after the interview and accepting the job, she had weighed up the good and the bad aspects of doing it, the emotional and moral issues, and come down on the side of rational, which was: It was only a human body, everyone had one, hers was better looking than average, sex was not an issue and it was not much different to being naked in the communal showers. Now, several other things she had not considered struck her: No one else would be naked, everyone would be studying her intimately and she might know someone in the class.

She looked at the slightly open window behind the desk and thought, if she wanted to, she could just slip out of there, but with resolve she pulled off her T-shirt, removed her trainers and took off her jeans and knickers. She looked at the green robe with disgust and put it on. Hannah accompanied her to the chair. All eyes were on her but she didn't look at them. She took off the robe, handed it to Hannah and sat down, arranging herself in the way Ben had asked.

'OK,' said Ben. 'This is our model, Jo.' There were some polite murmurs of greeting. 'Life drawing and painting, and by that we mean painting a nude figure from life, has been done for centuries by artists as it is the most challenging of all subjects. The subtle curves and contours, the colour and shade of skin, shape and form of the limbs, all require observation and skill. Take your time to look at the subject. Some of you will have a different view point from others. Work out the proportions of the model with the chair and the rug. Preliminary sketches are what we are after first. Do several, don't forget shadow and shading. Over the next few weeks we are going to work up to a finished painting so consider colour and make notes if you want. Ask any questions and I shall also be coming round to offer help and advice.' Ben stood aside so they could start and caught sight of Peter, easily the youngest in the group, his face as red as a chilli pepper.

After an hour Ben called for a break and Hannah took the robe back to Jo. Peter went outside for a cigarette. Hannah made coffees from the machine she had now mastered and Jo had a look at the works in progress. There were a few apologetic comments along the lines of them not doing her justice but Jo just laughed as she didn't really mind. She happened to be looking at Peter's when he came back from his cigarette break. His colour that had returned to normal from the effects of the cooler air and nicotine came back again when he saw Jo looking at his picture.

'That's good,' she said and smiled at him. Peter went back to chilli pepper and on to beetroot. 'Thanks,' he mumbled.

During the next hour Ben went around offering advice and improvements on the progress so far, pointing out discrepancies in proportions and perspective. Some of the students were quite proficient and only needed a little guidance, one or two were really struggling to get anything that looked like a human being and a couple, Peter being one of them, who were really quite good. Ben, aware he was going to have to get Jo back into roughly the same position the following week, and not wanting to take a photograph, placed a sheet of paper on one of the spare easels and did his own quick sketch of Jo in the chair. His practiced eye got the basic proportions down quickly and as it began to take shape he started to put in a few of the peripheral details and areas of shadow, especially around the folds of the rug. When the time was up he put the sketch aside and wound up the session.

'Take your drawings home and practice some more from those sketches. Next week you will need to bring in a canvas of your chosen size and shape; nothing too big please in case it gets in the way. You can work in oils or acrylic and we will lay down a sketch in paint.'

Jo went back into the office and got dressed. When she came out the last people were leaving. She looked at Ben's sketch and somehow felt more exposed than she had looking at the efforts of the students. He had captured something and Jo wasn't quite sure what it was. Eventually the door closed and left Ben, Hannah and Jo together.

'Were you OK with that? Ben asked Jo.

'Nothing to it really was there?' Jo replied.

'Exactly,' Ben said.

'It was all rather clinical and civilised,' Hannah commented.

'Well I am happy to call that a success,' Ben said.

'Did I do all right?' Jo asked.

'You were great,' Hannah told her, 'very professional.' She handed Jo an envelope.

'Same time next week?' she said to her.

'No problem,' Jo said. 'I'll be off then.'

'Thank you,' said Ben.

Jo was just going out of the door when she turned and said to Ben 'Yours was the best one.'

Ben looked up, not understanding at first what she meant; then he twigged.

'Oh, I see, yes, thank you. It's just so that we can repeat the pose accurately next week.'

'It's still good,' said Jo.

LIFE'S NOT FAIR

{ CHAPTER 28 }

When Maddy got home after her photo session with Cyril, she went straight upstairs and got in the shower. She scrubbed away at her skin with the soap as if Flash Studios and Cyril had left some sort of dirty layer, some slick effluvia like sweat, which could be washed off. She kept seeing his image looming into her consciousness, his blotchy red skin, gap toothed smile and that crazy hair. Even under the hot water of the shower she shuddered. She soon realised that the scrubbing of her skin was irrational and symbolic but it made her feel better, and as she stepped out of the shower and wrapped herself in a warm towel she started to recall and analyse everything that had happened at Flash Studios.

Disgust turned to anger realising she had been duped and cajoled into stripping off for a dirty old man. Some of the anger was with herself for being so easily fooled, but it hadn't detracted from her dream of becoming a model. How committed was she if one set back could put her off; these sort of things must have happened to Naomi Campbell and Kate Moss. She decided to let her anger subside and review the situation and how she felt after she had spoken to Jo. There was no way she was going to be able to tell her parents. They thought her dream was just a teenage fantasy that she would grow out of, so to add the 'I told you so' comments to the shame she already felt was just not on the cards.

She put the clothes she had worn into the laundry basket and put on all clean clothes. She felt a wave of emotion as she tossed the clothes into the basket, a mixture of misery, rage and impotence, but shook it off deciding tears were not going to help anything.

'So I hid her glasses and told her the form was for the rowing club, and she signed it,' Jo said grinning. Maddy laughed. 'But it cost me the price of Grand Theft Auto Three 'cos that little brother of mine saw the form and blackmailed me, the little shit.'

'How did it go, the first session, I mean?' Maddy was secretly hoping that Jo might have found the life-modelling humiliating so they could commiserate together.

'It was cool,' said Jo.

'It didn't bother you then?'

'Not a bit. I was nervous to begin with but it was strangely ordinary once it was happening.'

'You didn't feel dirty or ashamed then?'

'No,' said Jo wondering why Maddy should think like that. 'There was this guy, right, quite nice really, and he was like so embarrassed he couldn't really look at me, well not during the break and he was so red and he...' Jo stopped. Maddy had her head down and Jo realised she was sobbing.

'Hey, hey,' Jo said putting am arm around Maddy's shoulders. 'What's wrong?'

'I'm the one who wants to be a model, and you get a really nice job doing what I want to do and I get tricked into posing for some old guy's dirty pictures. I'm happy for you Jo, really I am, but I'm just so pissed off.' Maddy sniffed and wiped her eyes with a tissue.

'What happened?' asked Jo. Falteringly Maddy told her about the session with Cyril.

'The dirty old bastard,' Jo commented.

'But then you say it was nothing stripping off in front of ten or so strangers, am I just being silly?' She started crying again.

'No, it's completely different,' Jo said. 'I wasn't tricked it was all above board. This guy fed you with false promises and manipulated you.'

'I know, I know,' said Maddy. Jo thought for a moment.

'If, like he said, he could get you on Page Three would you do it?'

'Not for the money, only if it helped my career.'

'But then you'd just be a pin up model.'

'Perhaps I could change course when I became famous.' Maddy said hopefully.

'Mmm,' Jo said knowing it was highly unlikely, but not wanting to take away the straw Maddy was clutching.

'It's just that he's got these pictures of me and I don't know what he's going to do with them.'

'Nine people have got pictures of me starkers,' mused Jo. 'Mind you, in most of them you wouldn't recognise me, they're so rubbish.' Maddy laughed even though she didn't feel like laughing.

'What are you going to do next? I mean was it arranged for you to follow things up to see if this contact of his liked the pictures?'

'I don't know. I really don't want anything more to do with him. There's no way I can afford three thousand pounds for a portfolio and I hate to think what he might ask me to do to get the price down to something I can afford.'

'You could ask him about the Page Three guy, the talent scout he mentioned.'

'If he exists,' Maddy said.

'That way you only need to telephone and ask.'

'I suppose.'

'Go on. Ring him now.'

'Really?'

'Yes, come on, be positive.'

Maddy got her mobile out of her bag. 'It's ringing,' she said to Jo.

'Flash studios, Cyril speaking.'

'Hello it's Maddy.'

'Speak up dear, I can't hear you.'

'It's Madelaine Bright.'

'Oh hello.'

'I was wondering if you'd heard from the guy about the pictures.'

'What guy is that?'

'You know, you said you knew this talent scout...for Page Three...you were going to show him the pictures you took.'

'Oh yes.' There was a pause.

'Well have you heard anything?'

'Not as yet.'

'But you've given him the pictures.'

'Yes I have and he was very impressed but of course it's a long process, he has to have meetings, several in fact, then the approval of Rupert Murdoch. All sorts of things before anything happens.'

'How long does it take?'

'Oh it could be weeks, months more like.'

Maddy didn't know what to say next.

'Hello,' Cyril said. 'Look just give me a ring in about a month.'

'OK,' Maddy replied and cut the call.

'See, he's just playing me along,' Maddy said to Jo.

'What a bastard.'

'I want those pictures back; I don't believe he's given them to any talent scout.'

'We need to find out a bit more about this guy,' Jo said. 'Find out what he's up to. Did you have to sign anything?'

'No,' Maddy said.

'Well that might be technically illegal.'

'But it was just him and me. He's the one with the evidence. I've got nothing on him. He can just deny the whole thing ever happened.'

'Hmm,' Jo thought for a while. 'Leave it to me. I'll ask around a bit.'

'Don't say anything to your parents will you. I don't want any grown-ups making a fuss.'

'Of course not, they wouldn't be much help anyway.'

FISHING TRIP

{ CHAPTER 29 }

The prow of the boat cut through the water as if it were cream. Even though the sun was up it was still cold out at sea. Ben stood on the deck of the boat in a thick woolly jumper. Wisps of mist like wraiths were spiralling off the surface of the sea and disappearing in a flurry of activity as the boat swished through them. There were no actual waves, just a steady swell so the passage of the boat was smooth. Ben watched the town as it got smaller, the houses looking like so many match boxes and he understood why Wilf kept fishing. The chugging of the diesel motor stopped as Wilf cut the engine and the sudden silence made everything eerie.

'This is a good spot,' said Wilf as he came out of the

wheelhouse. 'We should be right over the Mary Ellen.'

'What happened to her?' Ben asked. He was already baiting some hooks.

'Big old converted dredger carrying tin ingots. Leaky as a colander they say, went down in a squall. Insurance job they reckon. I know some divers who have been down and they say there's nothing there.'

'Perhaps somebody got there before them.'

'That's possible, but more likely they had already off-loaded it. Common practice, leave port, pull in somewhere, unload, then sink her and claim the insurance, double your money. Anyway the bass like it.'

'Let's hope so,' said Ben as he cast a line over the side.'

'Did you see the smoke?' Wilf asked.

'Yeah, what was that all about?'

'Smoky Joe's.'

Ben smiled. 'That was an accident waiting to happen,'

'They reckon he hadn't put the fire out properly.'

'Easy done I suppose.'

Wilf was baiting several hooks and had three rods lined up along the opposite side of the boat. They were silent for a while watching the floats bobbing in the water. Ben remembered the photograph that Cyril had left behind on his desk, fished it out of his pocket and handed it to Wilf.

'Can you throw any light on this,' he asked.

Wilf took it and studied it. 'Christ where did you get this?

Ben told him about Cyril coming to the gallery, about the photograph and the conversation he had with Cyril. 'You mean dirty postcard Cyril?'

'The very same,' said Ben.

'Has this supposed progeny contacted you yet?'

'Not so far. That's if he exists of course. It might be just Cyril getting up to some sort of mischief.'

'Does it ring any bells for you?' Wilf asked.

'Unfortunately not,' said Ben. 'How about you?'

'No idea, she's very pretty though. I wouldn't blame you if you had.'

'Thing is Wilf, if I had, I'm pretty sure I would remember. I mean there weren't that many girls.'

'There were quite a few,' Wilf commented.

'What I mean is there were very few one night stands. I'm sure I would remember if it had been more than that.'

'That's the trouble then, you may not be able to recall it at all.' Wilf was still studying the photograph. 'That's got to be the posh end of town.'

'Yes, I think that's the De Montfort hotel on the edge there.'

'What are you going to say if this guy contacts you?'

'I'll just have to tell him I really don't remember.'

'And if he looks like you?'

'Well that's a game changer then isn't it?'

The sun was now coming up. It had sent the mist packing and the day was getting warm. Ben took his jumper off. A few yachts had appeared but there was not enough of a breeze to make sailing exciting. They watched the floats bobbing on the surface. Wilf had caught a couple of mackerel that were still twitching in a plastic box at their feet.

'How are the art lessons doing?' Wilf asked.

'They seem very popular,' Ben replied. 'I'd rather be painting. I'm not so sure I'm that good a teacher.

'As long as they keep coming back you must be doing something right.'

'We'll see. I'm not comfortable with it. I've never done anything like it before.'

'How did it go with the life model?'

'Yes, that was OK. She was good, totally natural.'

'And the students, any unnatural ogling or sniggering?'

'No nothing like that. They were all very polite and respectable.'

'And you, did you draw her?'

'I did actually; only so I could get her back in the same pose next week.'

'Are you sure?'

'Of course, although I have to say it is preferable, having a model that is attractive to look at. I mean art is about beauty after all.'

'You tell me,' said Wilf.

'Changing the subject I had a difficult situation the other day.'

'Tell me,' said Wilf.

'This couple bought a painting, well, I say bought, they put a deposit on one.'

'OK.'

'They came to see me the other day and said they couldn't complete the deal.'

'So they forfeit the deposit, yeah? Did you have anything in writing?'

'Paperwork? Me?' said Ben. Wilf laughed.

'Anyway, they were obviously distressed and I don't think they were going to tell me the full story just something about financial difficulties.'

'But they did in the end presumably?'

'Well she, the wife, started to cry, they both looked terrible as if they hadn't slept since Christmas and then it all came out. The owner of the flats where they live is trying to evict them but they won't budge. Then this bunch of youngsters move into one of the other flats and they're partying and playing loud music at all hours, a lot of undesirables coming and going, so they think this landlord has orchestrated it to get rid of them.'

'Sounds like a nice guy. So what did you say?'

'I said I'd keep the painting for them until things are sorted.'

'Did you give them back the deposit?'

'I did.'

'You have to be the world's worst business man, Ben.'

'I know, hopeless, aren't I?'

'You should go on The Apprentice,' Wilf said. 'Oh hello Mr Sugar, I'm Ben and I'm going to set up this business where I give everything away and lose all your money for you.'

'OK, OK,' said Ben.

Wilf pulled a line in with a squid thrashing around on the end of it. Black ink sprayed over the edge of the boat and Wilf held it there until it had dispensed most of it.

'Well there's lunch,' said Wilf, chucking the still writhing squid into the plastic box with the mackerel. 'Want to hear a funny story?'

'Go on then.'

'It's supposed to be true.'

'Yeah, yeah.'

'These two old guys, they go fishing together every so often.'

'Not me and you then?'

'No, listen. They're sitting in this small boat, back to back, lines over the side, and they're always messing about, joking and stuff.'

'It is you and me,' said Ben.

'Shut up and listen. One of them tells a joke and the other one laughs so hard his false teeth shoot out of his mouth and go overboard. So he's really pissed off about this as you can imagine, and after about twenty minutes go by the other guy decides to play a trick on him, attaches his own false teeth to his line and says to his friend 'Look at this, chance in a million of this happening' as he reels in the teeth. His mate takes them, has a look and says 'they're not mine' and chucks them over the side'.

JUSTIN MEETS BEN

{ CHAPTER 30 }

Jo returned the following week, recreating her pose using Ben's sketch as a reminder. The students had started roughing out the lines to start their painting. Everything seemed to be working out quite well. The curtain over the window behind where Jo was posing prevented anyone peering in casually and the door was kept locked with a note on it saying 'Lesson in progress'. If someone did knock it was possible to answer the door without the visitor being able to see the model. But word was getting round and Hannah and Ben had had to field a few phone calls enquiring about the life classes. This one being full they had started a list for when they ran it again and decided that they would only take students who had some experience, with the hope it might weed out any that were doing it for prurient reasons.

When the group had got started and Ben had been round with an initial perusal of the work, and given some advice or encouragement, he went back to his own study of Jo. He was finding a different subject matter, to his usual sea or landscapes, not only challenging but interesting as well. Hannah was making coffees when there was a knock on the door. Ben put his brush down and went to see who it was. The three teenage boys who stood there had hurriedly straightened their faces as the door opened but Ben could see there had been some amusement prior to this. One held a sketch pad as if this might make their intent seem more serious.

'We'd like to join your art class,' the chosen spokesman volunteered.

'Beginners class is on Tuesday,' Ben said, a smile twitching his lips.

'We want to do the life class,' he replied.

'I'm afraid that's full.'

The spokesman looked quickly at the others. 'When does it start again?'

'In six week's time.'

'Can we come back then?'

'Look, for life drawing, you need some experience; it's a very challenging subject. Why don't you practice then bring me what you've done and I'll see if you're good enough to join.'

One of the other lads spoke up. 'My girlfriend won't get her kit off for me.' The other two laughed which allowed Ben to smile at last.

'You could ask your Mum,' Ben said. This caused a lot of merriment and Ben sent them off with a leaflet. Hannah was looking at him as he shut the door. 'We're going to get a lot of that.'

'Oh, they were fairly harmless,' said Ben. 'I suppose it's the result of having a pretty model.'

Justin stood and read the notice 'Lesson in progress' as he was about to knock, and at that moment the enormity of what he might find out piqued. Several possible opening statements had been going around in his head as he walked down the seafront from his hotel. Even choosing to walk rather than drive meant that subconsciously he was putting off the meeting. He raised his knuckles to knock then changed his mind and paced up and down a bit. He stood outside the door again, wimped out again, walked across the shingle and down to the water's edge. He picked up a stone and skimmed it across the surface. After a few more stones, and mulling over the imaginary scenario several more times, he strode back up the beach and knocked on the door. Hannah looked at Ben.

'Your turn,' he said. Hannah opened the door.

'Can I help you?'

'I'm looking for Ben Frampton.'

'Can I ask who wants him?'

'He doesn't know me. Tell him it's Justin.'

'Wait here a moment, I'm afraid you can't come in.'

Ben came to the door. For a moment Justin couldn't find the right words to start. He was also scanning the face of the man who might be his father. He looked at the clear blue eyes, the weathered lines spreading from the corners, the mop of brown hair, still full but peppered with grey and the wide mouth.

'I'm doing some research,' Justin said. 'Er, into my family tree.'

Ben suddenly knew what it was about. 'Ah, you've been talking to Cyril,' he said.

'Mr Granger did help me to locate your whereabouts.'

'I bet he did. Did it cost you?' Ben grinned and then Justin knew that Ben was OK and friendly, not scary or angry.

Justin laughed. 'He got a slap up meal out of me before he gave anything away.'

'That sounds like Cyril. Look, I'm right in the middle of something here, could you come back?'

Justin hesitated for a moment thinking it might be a ploy to get rid of him.

'We've got an art lesson going on here, we'll be finished at three, could you come back then?'

'Who was that? Hannah asked.

'I'll tell you about it later,' Ben said.

To make sure he didn't miss Ben, Justin was back at three and stood outside the gallery. The door opened and the students started to leave carrying their various bits of equipment. Ben saw Justin and, realising Jo was now getting dressed, called out. 'Come on in.' Justin entered.

'This is Hannah, my assistant, Hannah, Justin.' Ben said.

The last student left and Jo came out of the office dressed in her usual attire of t-shirt, pedal pushers, trainers and baseball cap.

'I need to loosen up after all that sitting still,' she said to Ben. She saw Justin and said 'hi'. Justin smiled.

'You did well Jo,' Ben told her. 'I think everyone is making good progress, alright for next week?'

'Yeah, sure, same time?' Jo asked.

'Yes please,' Hannah said and passed Jo an envelope.

'Thanks, bye,' she said and jogged out of the door.

'I'm just finishing up here,' Ben told to Justin. 'Have a look around if you like.' He started to put the student's paintings away and move the easels and chairs. 'You can go if you like,' Ben said to Hannah. She frowned and asked quietly, 'Is everything all right?' nodding in Justin's direction.

'Yes, I'll tell you all about it tomorrow.' Ben saw Hannah to the door and when he turned he saw Justin was looking at his painting of Jo.

'Is that the girl in the baseball cap who just left?' Justin asked.

'Yes,' said Ben joining him at the easel. 'She's our life model.'

'She's um, very er, sort of ….'

'Yes she is, isn't she,' said Ben.

'The painting's pretty good too,' Justin said. 'Your students must be doing very well.'

'That's mine actually,' Ben said. 'It's only under painted at the moment.'

'It seems to be a good likeness from what I saw of her, although I never saw her quite like that.'

'You understand now why I can't let people just wander in.'

'Yes, of course,' Justin replied.

'Look, I've been stuck in here all day, do you want to get a drink? There's a pub across the road, it's not too bad.'

'Sounds good to me,' said Justin.

They settled into a corner table in the Crow's Nest and Justin told Ben about his Mother's dying confession, the finding of the photograph, his research in Cocklebury-On-Sea and his meeting with Cyril. Ben told him about Cyril's visit to the gallery.

'The problem is,' he told Justin. 'I just don't remember. I don't deny that is me in the photograph and you know that that is your Mother but you have to remember it was a long time ago.'

'Do you know who the other guy is?' Justin asked.

'That's Wilf, he's a friend and I still see him but he can't remember either. You see if something happened between me and your Mother I think I would remember.'

'You think you would?'

'Yes, I can't say for sure.'

'Does that mean there were a lot of similar situations?'

'You're asking me if I slept with a lot of girls.'

'I think what I'm asking is, are you less likely to remember if it was a one night stand?'

Ben thought for a moment. 'If you go unpicking the past, Justin, you may find out things you don't really want to know.'

'I think I already have,' Justin replied. 'Were there a lot of one night stands?'

'There were a few. Look I'll be honest with you. This is a seaside town, people come here on holiday; sometimes they're looking for romance, a bit of escapism. These days it's more open, it still happened back then but not in the same way. Does it bother you that you might be the result of a holiday romance?'

'It's confusing,' Justin said. 'My parents were so ordinary, so straight; I just can't imagine my Mother doing anything rash.'

'We tend to put our parents on a pedestal, but we're all human. Did your father know anything?'

'This is it, I just have no idea. If he did he hid it well, actually I don't think he did know.'

'Thirty years is a long time.' said Ben. 'I'd help you if I could and I will try and jog my memory...'

'You're not just saying that to fob me off are you?'

'No, I'm not. I am as intrigued as you are now having met you, but you have to agree we do not look alike.' Ben pointed to a mirror on the other side of the bar that reflected them both. Justin looked and laughed.

'We're nothing like each other, but that doesn't necessarily mean anything.'

'What did Cyril tell you about me?'

'Oh, he thinks you are a total charlatan, morally corrupt, untalented.'

'Coming from Cyril that's almost a compliment.'

'Would you be prepared to do a DNA test?' Justin asked.

Ben sighed.

'I don't want anything from you,' Justin answered quickly. 'I just need to know. To find out that the man you thought was your father wasn't, well, it sort of skews your identity. I know it's a hackneyed old phrase but I'm not sure I know who I am anymore.'

'I can understand that,' Ben admitted. 'Give me a couple of days, let me have a think and see what I can dredge up from the past. If I don't come up with anything then yes we'll do the test.'

'Thanks,' said Justin.

THUNDER AND LIGHTNING

{ CHAPTER 31 }

There had been a week of perfect days, the sky had been blue and the sun had shone. Every patch of earth not artificially watered became parched. Justin felt his shirt sticking to his back. The beer he had had with Ben hadn't helped. He walked along the promenade, his hands in his pockets recalling the words that had passed between them. On one hand it had been a relief that Ben was an agreeable person, but unfortunately Justin was no nearer the truth, and was Ben really telling the truth about not remembering? His mood was not helped by the weather, it was close and humid, the air felt thick and oppressive. Ben had been right, there was no physical resemblance between them and he felt no real connection with the man, but did that really make a difference?

The sky was darkening to the west. Justin could see clouds for the first time since he had been in Cocklebury-On-Sea coming in across the headland. A waft of air chilled his back where his shirt still clung to his skin. If they did a DNA test, what then? End of search really, whichever way the test came out. If Ben wasn't his father then there were no other leads, and if he was, what would that change? Would they go and have a beer now and again, exchange birthday cards?

A fat raindrop splashed on Justin's face close to his eye and a low rumble of thunder rolled across the town. Justin kept walking and could see dark spots on the concrete of the path as the raindrops began to fall. There was an eerie flash of light like the single flicker of a fluorescent tube. The rain fell harder. People began to move more hurriedly. Umbrellas went up, Pac-a-macs were shaken out and Justin pondered whether people knew it was going to rain or if they always came this prepared. He stepped inside a shelter. Two people, a couple, were already sat there. The woman had on a concertina type plastic rain hat and the man a flat cap. They both wore anoraks.

'Caught you out did it?' the man said, seeing Justin's shirt was now stuck to his body all over.

'Something like that,' Justin replied.

The three of them sat on the bench as the rain got fiercer. It was coming down at an angle and in waves. There was a deafening crack of thunder.

'Right let's make a run for it,' the man said, and then to Justin, 'Our car is just over there.'

'Good luck,' said Justin, and the couple ran out of the shelter with their heads down. Justin still had a way to go to the hotel so sat and waited. A jagged fork of lightning snaked across the sky, split and reached towards the sea.

There was squelch of rubber trainer sole on wet concrete and a figure turned into the shelter, stopping just inside the entrance and turning to look out. She was wearing a t-shirt which was as saturated as Justin's. He recognised her from the gallery. She kept looking out at the rain oblivious to Justin's presence. He looked at the outline of her slim waist, buttocks and thighs, accentuated by the wetness of her clothes, and then came the realisation that he had seen her naked, or at least an image of her naked. He recalled the classical pose, semi reclining on the rug, nonchalant, slightly aloof, her hand on her lap, curled round and hiding her pubic hair. He felt stirred.

'Oh hi,' said Jo seeing him for the first time. 'You were at the gallery weren't you?'

'That's right,' said Justin. 'I recognise you too.'

'Once seen never forgotten,' Jo said and Justin thought of the painting again.

'Booking up for a course were you?' Jo asked.

'Me? No, I just had some business with Mr. Frampton – Ben.'

'Right,' said Jo, knowing from experience that when she heard the word 'business' it was usually about something desperately boring like insurance, or council meeting minutes or local politics. She turned back to viewing the scene through the doorway of the shelter. There was another crack and boom of thunder and immediately everything was lit up by a display of lightning across the cloud dark sky, making it look like a map of rivers and tributaries.

'I love thunderstorms, don't you?' Jo asked.

'When I'm prepared,' said Justin.

'It's only water,' Jo protested.

'And electricity,' Justin pointed out.

'Did you know,' Jo said, turning round to face him again. 'That when one of those forks of lightning hits the sea it makes it boil.'

'Really?'

'Yes, I've seen it. I was in a dinghy with my Dad. I was much younger and this thunderstorm hit and we watched it. The lightening was hitting the sea at intervals around the boat.'

'It must have been dangerous.'

'I didn't know that at the time, it was just exciting.' She went and sat down next to him.

'We're both pretty wet aren't we?'

Justin laughed. 'You more than me.'

'Are you from round here?' Jo asked.

'No, I'm staying at the Falkirk.'

'Ooh posh.'

'Not really, it's sort of mid-priced.'

'It's posh to me.'

'I'm having a bit of a holiday.'

'You said you were on business.'

'Well, it's a bit of both.'

'Oh right.' Jo didn't want to delve further as the word 'business' had come up again.'

'You work at the gallery?' Justin asked.

'Receptionist,' Jo said, and Justin allowed her the small deception.

'Full time?'

'No, it's just a holiday job, I'm still at school.'

'Seriously?' Justin said.

'I know, I'm very mature for my age.'

A rumble of thunder echoed in the distance and Jo counted under her breath until the lightning flashed. 'It's two miles away now,' Jo said.

'It's stopped raining,' Justin pointed out.

'Come on let's go and get chips, I'm starving.'

'Where?' Justin said.

'I'll show you.' She led Justin across the road from the shelter and down an alleyway. It connected with another road and across the other side was a row of takeaways. Jo went towards the Chinese one.

'I thought you said chips,' Justin said.

'I did.'

'Well the fish and chip shop is over there.'

'You really are a bit naïve, how old are you?'

Justin was taken aback by the bold question. 'Older than you.'

'Then you should know that the Chinese make the best chips.'

'Really?'

'Yep, better than the chippy, better than Mcdonald's, better than any greasy spoon you care to mention.'

'Better than Heston Blumenthal's?'

'Well I wouldn't know about that would I?'

'I'll take you there one day.'

'Promises. Hello Wing. Two chips please.'

'Your friend innit?' Wing asked.

'Yeah, I don't know his name but I'm educating him.'

'Justin,' Justin said.

'Ha, you like Jo, she one fiery lady.' Wing said grinning.

'Yes?' Justin said politely.

'I have trouble here one time and she tell boys to piss off and they did.'

'He's exaggerating,' Jo said.

They went back to the promenade and sat back in the shelter eating hot, salty chips out of paper cones. The concrete outside was steaming, evaporating the rain away, even drying in patches.

'What do you do for a living then?' Jo asked, hoping it wasn't going to be one of those jobs where the person waffles on for ages and you still have no idea what they do at the end of it.

'I work for a firm that makes security equipment. A travelling salesman, I suppose.'

'Right,' said Jo.

'Dull isn't it? I know.'

'You gotta do something.'

'Where's home?' Justin asked.

'Over that way, past the gallery, a couple of miles.'

In the last few minutes as they sat side by side in the shelter Justin had sneaked several sideways looks at Jo. He had clocked the deep blue eyes framed by long lashes, her small white teeth and elfin tongue as she bit into another chip. He had already appraised her figure from when she had first entered the shelter with her clothes clinging to her. He was afraid she might just suddenly jump up, say 'goodbye' and be gone and he wanted this moment to last.

'I've got my car at the hotel if you want a lift.'

'I'm going to run home. I'll be dry by the time I get there.'

'OK,' said Justin. That hadn't worked. At least if she did just go he had the gallery as a point of contact. But the connection with her now was too good to lose. 'Look, can I see you again?' he asked.

Jo hadn't thought about this being anything more than just a chance encounter. She thought him to be reasonably attractive but older and had not considered he might be interested in her.

She looked down at her empty chip cone. 'I don't know,' she said.

'I don't mean anything heavy, it's just I like talking to you.'

Jo took off her baseball cap and shook her hair out. Some

strands of blonde hair were still stuck to the sides of her head making it look like she had sideburns. She flicked them behind her ears and looked at Justin more intently than she had up to now. She got up.

'Here, same time tomorrow,' she said and set off silently along the front.

SQUID GUTS

{ CHAPTER 32 }

Ben drove out to Wilf's house. It stood on the eastern side of the bay, a mile further from where he kept his boat and before one reached the estuary. Houses dotted this stretch of land in an uneven straggle; a town planner's nightmare of mixed houses of different ages and varied design. Wilf's grandfather had had the house built by a builder friend, from a design worked out on the back of a packet of Senior Service cigarettes. This was before planning permission and before anyone else had thought to build on this uninviting foreshore. Perhaps it had been something to do with the wildness of the weather in winter, not everyone likes shingle thrown up onto their back lawn, something that could happen when a gale was blowing in from the sea and the tide was high. The house had had bits added on since the original build and was therefore a hybrid of designs, but it stood solid and square defying anything the weather chose to throw at it.

Summer was a different matter. You could stroll to the end of the garden and be on the beach. From the windows the view was different every morning with the varying hues of the sea and the sky, the weather and light controlling it like some god was painting a picture, especially when he got carried away with yellow ochre and cadmium red at sunrise and sunset. Over the years others had seen the potential of the spot and more houses had been built, creating a rag-taggle line of dwellings as different from each other as scattered rocks on the beach, but more interesting than the serried ranks of bungalows on the estate two miles inland.

Wilf could be monosyllabic in the morning until three cups of coffee had got to work on his brain. Ben helped himself to coffee from the stove and sat down at the kitchen table without offering any conversational gambits. Wilf sat sipping coffee looking out across the garden, planted with salt and wind resisting shrubs, and down to the sea beyond. He had lived alone since Eileen had left and although the house was neither dirty nor untidy, it showed. Eileen hadn't liked the house much in the first place, most of the rooms were done out like the cabins in old ships, all wood and brass, which was not surprising in a house owned by three generations of seafaring men. Without looking in Ben's direction Wilf pushed a letter over to him that had been lying on the table. Ben ran his thumb over the raised print of the letter head that stated it was from Bollingbroke, Badger and Beale, solicitors, and was an offer from a client who was interested in buying the property and land where Ben's gallery was.

'It doesn't say who the client is,' Ben offered.

'It doesn't matter,' said Wilf. 'I'm not selling.'

'You know you can if you want to,' Ben said. 'I would understand.'

'It's not that, I just like it as it is. They can't want it for the rental potential so it means they probably want to develop it and build some big 'fuck off' mansion or a new Tesco's. No thanks.'

'I saw someone checking it out the other day,' Ben said.

'Checking what out?'

'I went over to Toddy's and there's this guy in the car park, smart guy, no holiday maker, taking pictures on his mobile phone. At first I thought he was an estate agent, but he was in a very smart car, one of those big things that look like a Bentley but isn't. There was something about the car. I can't remember what it was now.'

'Your memory,' laughed Wilf. 'Speaking of which, heard any more about the guy looking for his Dad?'

Ben told him the latest.

'DNA test, hmm,' Wilf commented. 'Serious stuff eh. Are you going to do it?'

'He's very keen. I suppose I wouldn't mind knowing for sure as well.'

Wilf stood up. 'Ready then?'

'As ready as ever.'

'OK, put this on.' Wilf picked up two boiler suits that had been hanging over the back of a chair and handed one to Ben.

'Where did you get these?'

'They were from a firm when I worked in the engine shop. The logos are fairly generic; no one will take any notice of us. And these, just in case.' He handed Ben an ID card on a lanyard. Ben looked at it.

'Not bad, I see I'm Thomas Hardy, who are you?'

'George Elliot.' Wilf grinned. 'I did them on the computer,

they look official enough don't you think?'

They put on the boiler suits.

'Grab that tool box, I'm just getting the stuff from the fridge,' said Wilf.

It was mid-morning so the traffic getting people to work had settled down. They drove into town in Wilf's white pick-up.

'This is it,' said Ben. Wilf parked and they got out.

'Number twenty-four, third floor,' Ben said as they entered the vestibule of the building.

They went up the stairs and Wilf knocked on the door of flat twenty four. They waited. Wilf knocked again. They could hear movement in the flat. Wilf knocked a third time.

'OK, OK,' a voice came from the inside. The door opened a crack.

'Who is it?'

'British Gas,' said Wilf

'What d'yer want?'

'Someone has reported a gas leak.'

'Not us,' and the door closed.

Wilf knocked again and spoke close to the door. 'We have to check all the flats.'

The door opened a crack again and Kevin looked out at them warily.

'It'll only take ten minutes,' Wilf said.

Kevin closed the door but they heard him undoing the chain. The door opened.

'I'm sorry man; I thought you were the pigs.' Kevin led them across the assault course of the living room and showed them the kitchen.

'Sorry about the mess, I haven't got my shit together yet.'

'Don't worry about us; we just want a quick look at the boiler.'

The boiler was above the sink but the sink was not visible, it being piled up with plates and cups and cutlery. All the surfaces were covered with bits of food, debris, crumbs, open jars of different spreads and open packets of bread. The bin overflowed onto the floor with food packaging, pizza boxes, pot noodle containers and McDonald's bags. Kevin leant on the door jamb. 'D'ya want a cup of tea?' he asked.

'No, we're fine thanks,' said Ben.

'I'll leave you to it then,' Kevin said.

Ben and Wilf looked at each other and Wilf bent down and opened the tool box. He took out a spanner and gave the housing on the boiler an exploratory tap. He handed Ben a jemmy and indicated the floor. Kevin was sitting on the sofa in the living room with his back to them rolling a joint. They heard other voices and bits of the conversation, 'gas board' and 'gas leak' as Kevin told them what was going on. Ben managed to prise up a floor board, enough to slide the plastic container that Wilf had taken from the fridge under it and remove the lid. He hammered the floor board back into place. Wilf made himself look busy doing nothing to the boiler. They packed up the tools. A few more people had joined Kevin in the living room as Ben and Wilf came out of the kitchen.

'All checked,' said Wilf. 'No gas leaks in there.'

'Cool,' said Kevin.

'We'll see ourselves out then.'

As they closed the door behind them they heard the beat and guitars of some music being played.

'Job done then,' said Wilf.

'Easier than I thought,' Ben said. 'What was in the box?'

'Squid guts.'

'Nice,' said Ben

'Nice and fresh now, but give it a couple of days for them to forget we were here and in this weather they'll begin to smell. And when squid guts go off, boy do they smell.'

Ben smiled.

FAILED MEMORY

{ CHAPTER 33 }

The storm had brought the wind with it which in turn had churned up the sea. The chalky deposits on the sea bed were stirred by this action and it looked as though someone had poured milk into it. Ben sat on a rock looking out at it thinking, ultramarine, viridian, and titanium white, lots of titanium white. His mind was wandering again, that was the trouble, always had been. He shook his head to get his mind back to why he was here and looked out across the expanse of smooth sand. The tide had recently gone out leaving it wet, glistening and sculpted in little wavelets. It was the perfect place to run about, kick a ball or play French cricket but he wasn't here to play games. When the sand dried you could lay out a towel with no shingle to dig into your ribs, but he wasn't thinking about sunbathing either.

He took the photograph that Cyril had left on his desk out of his pocket, and looked at it long and hard hoping something might trigger a memory. Climbing over the groynes to get here hadn't helped, neither had trying to imagine the girl in the picture sunbathing on a towel. Behind him the cliff rose steeply and where the cliff path ended rickety wooden steps allowed access to the beach. Below them the pebbles and rocks on the upper part of the beach were continually dry where the tide did not reach. The ones that bordered the sand were emerald green and slippery with weed, slowly drying in the sun.

He turned to judge roughly where the photograph had been taken, holding it up and comparing the view, but he felt no connection, no recollection of the day, the events, the taking of the photograph or a girl called Rose. She had a carefree smile, sun dappled her hair, her arm lay casually through his. He felt a pang of guilt that perhaps for a moment of pleasure her life had been changed irrevocably.

There was something, some distant feeling, like something that jogs the memory of a dream from the night before but only allows you a tantalising glimpse, a flavour almost, and nothing more. He couldn't understand why he didn't remember this particular day or what had happened around this time, the photograph was irrefutable evidence. He remembered a lot of the other ones, but how many had he forgotten. He remembered the Brazilian girl in the white swimsuit, the resting actress who he now saw occasionally on the television, the girl who had won the local beauty contest, but these had been more than one night stands even if they were only a week long holiday romance or a weekend. There were parties where events were hazy from the consumption of alcohol. He was sure that if he could just remember one small part of it, one single memory of the girl or the supposed fling, however short, he might be able to remember more, the day on the beach for instance that would bring it all flooding back.

He explained what had happened to Wendy over a glass of wine later in her neat back garden behind the guest house.

'Was this after your marriage broke up?' she asked.

'Oh yes,' said Ben. He didn't mind talking about it; he didn't mind talking to Wendy about anything. 'I was a teenager when I married Marilyn, far too young. It pains me to think about it, we were barely adolescents.'

'Where is she now?'

'In America, I think. Married to some big shot TV executive, last time I heard. Better off than still stuck with me I suppose.'

'I wouldn't say that,' Wendy smiled.

'People are funny really.'

'How's that?'

'Well, when you are young it's more difficult to talk about intimate things than it is to do intimate things. It's even difficult to talk about the intimate things you are doing.'

'Baring your body is easier than baring your soul.'

'In a nutshell I think,' said Ben.

'The human race would die out if the opposite was true,' Wendy observed.

'Can you imagine a world where thought was like speech? I mean if you thought it the other person would know what you'd thought.'

'Sounds worrying,' Wendy said.

'Not really, it would just change the dynamic, everyone would adapt, there could be no lies, no deceit, no secrets.'

'Would it work on TV? Would politicians still be able to lie?'

'That would be interesting.'

'There are some people who are brutally honest; if they think something they just say it. They don't make good diplomats but you know where you are with people like that. They will tell you if they don't like your hair or your jacket, say, but you feel more comfortable with people like that because you know they're unlikely to be lying to you.'

'There would be less crime I suppose,' Wendy offered.

'Yes, of course. You would know, if questioned, you would have to confess.'

'You wouldn't have had to go to prison.'

'None of it would have happened,' Ben said after some consideration.

'Is it OK to talk about it or shall I shut up?' asked Wendy.

'Better to talk,' said Ben. 'Nobody believes you are innocent when you've been convicted and served a prison sentence. It was impossible to prove my innocence. It was a non-evidence scenario, my word against somebody else's.'

'But you forged the paintings?'

'I never said I didn't do the paintings. Every art student copies the masters. If copying is a crime every art student would be in prison. Passing it off as an original is the crime.'

'And you didn't do that?'

'Call me naïve if you like but I was doing it in all innocence.'

'What happened?'

Ben took a mouthful of wine and swallowed it slowly. 'This guy came into my studio. I had a studio at the back of Preston Street then. Very smooth guy, well dressed. He said he had always admired Monet, but at several million apiece couldn't afford an original. Could I paint one for him? He was offering a lot of money, not Monet prices, but a lot to me at the time. He wanted something big, for a wall in his house, something to impress people, he said. He supplied the canvas, had it delivered to the studio. I should have known something was up then. The canvas was old, it had some highland scene on it but I was too caught up in my luck of having secured a good commission. I gessoed over the original and got to work. Monet is quite easy to copy really; he did little brush strokes in a circular motion.

Obviously I did water lilies. I didn't sign it, I wasn't that daft. He came back a few weeks later saying how pleased he was with it and how his wife loved it. Flattery is a very potent tool. He said she liked Gauguin. Well, the money was good so I painted the Gauguin, but he liked the Monets more, so I painted a couple more Monets and asked him where he was putting them all and he said he had given a couple to friends. I can't remember how many I did now, then one day the police came round. He must have got somebody else to sign them or did it himself. Anyway he had been shipping them over to America and selling them as the real thing. The police wouldn't believe me, firstly that I wasn't an equal partner in the business and secondly that I hadn't signed them. Of course the press had a field day. 'Easy Monet' was the headline. It's a bit like walking out of a shop accidentally without paying for something, technically you are guilty, but no one believes you were being absent minded and not intentionally shop lifting.'

'Are you still angry?' asked Wendy.

'A bit, but there is nothing I can do about it so I just have to move on.'

'And the guy who was selling them?'

'He got a similar sentence, and you won't believe this, he now owns an auction house.'

Wendy laughed. 'And this Justin guy, claiming to be your son. Does he know all of this?'

'You bet. Cyril fed him as much dirt as possible after I threw him out of the gallery.'

'Does it bother him?'

'I don't think so. I think he feels it's rather exciting having a dodgy dad.'

'Are you going to do the DNA test?'

'I promised I would if I couldn't remember what actually happened.'

FIRST DATE

{ CHAPTER 34 }

'You still here?' Jo asked as she arrived at the shelter the following day.

Justin just smiled, pleased to see her and pleased to see she was wearing normal clothes, not the jogging outfit.

'You look very nice,' he said to her.

'You're not so bad yourself.' She sat down next to him. 'Well, what would you like to do?' she asked. 'Shall I show you the stylish sights of Cocklebury-on-Sea, escort you to the illegal gambling dens, strip clubs and flesh pots or take you on a cultural tour of its many associations with art, literature and entertainment?'

'Not really,' said Justin.

FISH FARCE

'Good,' Jo replied, ''Cos it hasn't got any of those. We can go down to Scramble Beach if you like, it's about a mile east of here.'

'What's at Scramble Beach?'

'Nothing.'

'Sounds good to me,' said Justin.

'It's sort of interesting,' Jo told him when they set off in Justin's car. 'It's by the estuary, there are sand dunes, some abandoned boats and fishing huts. It's quite atmospheric.'

Jo directed him out of town, past the Fish Works Art Gallery and Toddy's Bacon Crematorium, past the arm of the bay where Wilf's house stood and then the caravan park until there was nothing but flat land on either side of the road.

'Turn right here,' said Jo.

Justin turned the car down a cinder track for a hundred yards until it opened out and the road ended. They got out of the car and Jo ran up the low bank and stood there while Justin locked the car. He joined her and found himself looking over a patch of dunes with their banks and tussocky grass, down to the sea. The tide was out and the flat, wet sand glistened with the sun shining on it, broken up by patches of water and the pebble dash of small stones embedded in it.

'We used to come here shrimping as children,' Jo said. 'We'd spend all day on the beach. It's great for shells and beachcombing.'

They walked along the beach towards the setting sun. Justin asked about her and Jo told him about her family and school and sporting ambitions for a while, until she became strangely uncomfortable talking about herself and felt the need to know more about Justin.

'I suppose you've got a girl friend at home, or even a wife?' Jo asked.

'Neither, I'm afraid.' And Justin told Jo about Amy, which led on to telling her about his Mother and the revelation he had recently encountered, but he stopped short of telling her that his search had led him to Ben knowing that she worked at the gallery.

'What about you, do you have a boyfriend?'

'No,' Jo replied and then because she thought it sounded somewhat pathetic she said:

'I'm a bit particular, me.'

'I would have thought you'd be spoilt for choice.'

'Yeah, but they're all schoolboys. Me and Maddy are in the final year so there are no older boys at school.'

'Who's Maddy?'

'My friend Maddy. I'm not going to introduce you. She's gorgeous. Going to be a model she is.'

It was the first thing apart from agreeing to meet again that Jo had said, that let Justin think she might be interested in him. They were walking on the lower edge of the beach next to where the sea ran up in little wavelets, depositing a line of foam on the sand. Each footstep squeezed away the water in the wet sand that then returned to fill the indent of their foot print, so looking back their steps shone in the fading light. Justin took her hand.

'You're a bit old for me,' Jo said.

'You said schoolboys were too young for you.'

'And you're on holiday, so if you're just looking for a bit of sex I'm not like that.'

'If I was looking for that, I'd pick up a girl on the beach.'

'Just like that eh?'

'OK, maybe I should have said 'try'.'

'Actually, that's exactly what you did do.'

'What?'

'Pick a girl up on the beach.'

'But I wasn't looking for a girl, it's just you happened to turn up.'

'Sounds a bit like your mother's story, history repeating

itself and all that.'

'I don't want to go home pregnant,' Justin said.

Jo pushed him. 'Be serious.'

They walked on for a while and then Justin said, 'I think we should walk back before the sun goes down.'

They turned around retracing their steps, the sun warming their backs. They walked further and turned into the estuary, past boats, tied up and keeled at angles like drunks, and fishermen's huts with coiled ropes, boxes and lobster pots stacked in front. Further on a longer shed sported lights and a hubbub of noise.

'What's that place?' Justin asked.

'That's the Lobster Shack,' said Jo.

They got nearer and the savoury smells of cooking drifted towards them.

'Are you hungry?' asked Justin.

'I'm always hungry,' Jo said.

'Do you want to have something here?'

'It's expensive,' Jo warned.

They went in. The place was heaving with people but they managed to get a table for two.

'This seems to be the place to come, judging by the numbers,' Justin commented.

'It's always full this place, the fish couldn't be fresher.'

The tables were scrubbed pine, the walls hung with fishing paraphernalia. The napkins were kitchen paper and the wine came in unmarked carafes. When the food came out it was on big platters, simply adorned and was the best seafood Justin had ever eaten. He had a whole grilled Dover sole that was hanging over the edges of the plate. Jo had a skillet of seared scallops.

'Dad brings us here sometimes,' Jo said. 'We like it but dad prefers the De Montfort Hotel because it's posh, you know, white table cloths and all that bowing and scraping from the wine waiter and poncy food.'

The kitchen, open to view with just a counter separating it from the dining room, showed industrious figures bent to their tasks. Steam and smoke emanated from pans and pots, spiralling around them and punctuated by the odd flame licking upwards. Waiting staff, aproned and purposeful, carried plates at head height whilst sashaying between chairs.

It was a short walk to the car afterwards and it was nearly dark. Jo shivered and Justin said, 'Hey wait, I've got a coat.' He opened the boot of the car.

'What's all that?' Jo said looking in the boot.

'It's just stuff I sell for work,' Justin said.

'Yeah, but what is it?'

'Surveillance stuff, CCTV, that sort of thing.'

'What, like for spying on people?'

'Yes, mostly businesses use it, hidden cameras in stores, over tills to stop fraud and prevent shoplifting.' He put a jacket around Jo's shoulders and opened the door for her. They drove back into town.

'Do you want to go home?' Justin asked.

'Not yet, let's park on the seafront.'

Justin parked the car and they sat looking out at the lights from the hotels and the pier sparkling in the dark sea. Jo laughed suddenly.

'What's funny?' Justin asked.

'There's a joke that during the day the cars park here and the windscreens steam up from the Thermos flasks on the dash board. At night they steam up but not from Thermos flasks.'

Justin took this as an invitation. He leaned across and kissed her.

'That was nice,' Jo said. 'You can do it again if you want to.'

Justin kissed her again and this time she responded, opening her mouth a little and kissing him back.

'I have this friend,' Jo told him when they sat back for a breather. Justin thought she was going to own up to having a boyfriend. 'You know Maddy, the one I told you about.'

'Oh yes, the model.'

'Something happened to her that wasn't very pleasant.' Jo told him about Cyril and the model portfolio scam.

'I've met this Cyril.' Justin told Jo of his own experience with Cyril leaving out any of the references to Ben, concluding, 'And what you tell me surprises me very little. A slimy character if ever there was one.'

'Where have you been?' Jo's father asked her as she opened the front door.

'I've been out with a friend,' Jo said.

'A boy?' he asked.

'A man actually,' Jo responded.

'You are only seventeen, you know,' he said.

'It was all very proper; he took me to the Lobster Shack.'

The emotions of anger, worry and helplessness in the face of his daughter conflicted in Bob, confounding any reasonable way of dealing with the situation. This made him shout even when he knew it was not helpful.

'Men don't take you out to expensive restaurants without expecting something in return,' he shouted.

'Don't judge others on your own standards,' Jo said to him. Bob felt like hitting her but knew he couldn't. He stood unable to form a suitable reply, his mouth opening and closing like a fish in a bowl. Jo continued. 'Wouldn't you rather I went out on a proper date than let boys grope me behind the bike sheds at school?'

'If anybody tried to grope you he'll need crutches after I've finished with him.'

'You'd have to find him first.' Jo smiled sweetly and went past him and up the stairs to her room. Bob watched her knowing he had not handled the situation well but was at a loss of how to do it better.

The confrontation with her father had not spoiled her feeling of elation. She was used to dealing with her father, and the evening with Justin had made her very happy. To be with someone who was mature, and knowing that he was attracted to her answered a lot of questions, and allayed a lot of doubts she had about her own feelings and concerns over her sexuality and appeal. There was a soft knock at the door and her mother came in. She sat down on the edge of the bed next to Jo. Her approach was much more considered.

'Don't take any notice of Dad,' she said. 'He doesn't understand these things.'

'I know,' Jo said, and her mother's obvious concern moved her more than her father's shouting.

'Do you want to tell me anything?' Clare asked. 'You don't have to if you don't want to.'

'I don't mind,' said Jo. 'I just met him and he asked me out. He's a bit older, twenty nine.'

She thought it sounded better than saying he was thirty two.'

'Men can be very persuasive when they want something,' Clare said.

'I know. I haven't done it with him if that's what you mean. We've only kissed so far.'

'Are you seeing him again?'

'I don't know. We didn't talk about it. He's got my number.'

Clare knew that any attempt at parental control would not work with Jo; she was too much of an independent spirit.

'As long as any decisions are yours. It doesn't matter what

he says, or what your friends are doing, only do what you want to do.'

'I'm still a virgin you know, probably about the only one in my year,' Jo said.

Clare put a hand on her arm, pleased that Jo could confide in her.

'You do it when you are ready and if you need any advice, practical or otherwise, you only have to ask, I won't judge you.'

'Thanks Mum,' Jo said.

WHO'S BEEN EATING TUNA?

{ CHAPTER 35 }

'Who's been eating tuna?' Kevin asked of no one in particular. No one answered.

Kevin stood in the doorway of the kitchen and surveyed the overflowing rubbish bin and the food debris on the worktops. He opened the fridge and peered inside. There was a carton of milk that had separated and turned to yoghurt, something on a plate now unrecognisable because of the grey green fur that was growing on it, and something that had dried and shrivelled in a plastic container.

Derek, one of uninvited guests to Kevin's flat, heard the fridge opening and came to see if anyone was organising some food. Kevin didn't know who Derek was, he just seemed to appear one day and everyone got used to seeing him around. He wore a beanie hat that he never seemed to take off and had a spider's web tattooed on his neck.

'Jesus, what's that smell?' he said to Kevin.

'I think someone's been eating tuna,' Kevin replied.

'The tin is probably amongst that lot.' Derek indicated the overflowing bin. 'You need to get rid of it.'

'Me?' said Kevin. 'Why is it always me?'

Derek shrugged.

'What do you do with rubbish anyway?' asked Kevin.

'There's probably some bins downstairs, you have to take it down there.'

'How?' said Kevin, suddenly feeling very tired.

'You put it in a bag.'

'What sort of bag?'

'A bin bag.'

'Where d'ya get those?'

'From a shop,' Derek offered, his voice going up a half tone at the end as if it was a question.

Breath came in. 'It really stinks in here, why doesn't someone do something about it?'

'Yeah, why doesn't someone do something about it?' said Kevin who was now getting fed up with the whole idea of having a place and the responsibility that went with it. 'Like for instance, everyone who's using this place like a campsite expecting me to clean up and supply stuff, and nobody's given me anything like for rent and such. I'm not the only one here.'

'Cool your socks Kev man,' said Derek.

'Yeah, let's not get into some heavy shit.' Breath concurred. 'It's easy to clear up.' He opened a drawer in one of the kitchen units and pulled out a roll of black bin bags.

'Where did ya get those?' said Kevin.

'Like, they were always there,' said Breath and he started

putting some of the overflowing garbage into it.

Kevin watched, amazed, as if Breath was performing some very complex task. He handed the bag to Kevin when it was full. 'There you are, done,' he said, even though there was still quite a lot of rubbish that needed picking up, and more in the bin. Bemused, Kevin went to take the bag out of the flat. He met Bo coming in. She sniffed in the hall.

'Has someone been eating fish?' she asked. Kevin sighed.

'I think a tin of tuna went off so I'm taking out the rubbish.' Bo made her way into the flat and Kevin went downstairs with the bag. He met Ken coming in the front doors of the flats.

They looked warily at each other and nodded.

'Er, where does the rubbish go?' Kevin asked.

'Go around the back and there are some bins. Don't forget to recycle.'

'OK,' said Kevin wondering what bicycles had to do with it.

At the angle where the wall met the ceiling in the Fish Works Gallery there was a chip in the plaster roughly the shape of Australia. At some point it had been filled in but the filler must have aged over the years and yellowed. Jo was familiar with this spot as this was the point where she fixed her gaze each time she posed at the gallery. For most of the students painting the figure of Jo, the direction of her gaze meant she was looking out of the frame towards the left. Ben realised that Jo's eyes were, or should be, the focal point of the picture and would add mystery and intrigue to it. To have the central character in a painting looking directly out at the observer changed everything. It meant the eyes looked at you even if viewed from an oblique angle, creating an intimacy, a relationship with the observer and if the subject was naked, promise and sexuality. The portrait of Jeanne Samary by

Renoir, Ben thought, was the sexiest look in art. The dark eyes looked at you from over the centuries and you were smitten. She must have loved Renoir. He was glad to have arranged that Jo would look away from the group as it might have been too unsettling to have her looking out at them.

Jo however was mainly thinking about Justin; when she would see him next, whether they would become lovers and the problem with her father. She wasn't sure about using the word 'love', after all she had only been out with him once and all they had done was kiss. All she knew was that whatever she felt it was pretty powerful even to the point of being concerned that her nakedness might give something away. So every now and then, when she found her thoughts straying towards Justin and causing the physical manifestation of those thoughts, she concentrated hard on 'Australia' and thought of her father standing in the hall, red in the face from too many whiskies and berating her for the things she might or might not have done.

Ben had been working on his own painting of Jo at times other than the life class lessons. He was excited by how painting something different from his usual subjects of sea and landscapes and fishermen made him work harder to reach what had always been considered the pinnacle of artistic achievement. To get the subtle contours of flesh, the tone, the colour and the way the shadows and light fell on skin, made Ben realise something he had always known but not necessarily acknowledged and what made the Impressionists so exciting, so fresh and alive, was that they were constantly experimenting. He saw this painting of his own as an experiment and could see the flaws and where his skill fell short of what he was aiming for. Only Hannah stopped Ben from putting the painting away from the view of the students.

'You need to show them how it should be done,' she told him. 'After all that is why they are here and why they are the students and you the teacher.'

His own learning from doing the study had helped Ben when advising the students how to improve their own work. The advice he offered students depended largely on their level of competence but he was at pains to be encouraging, pointing out that even Michelangelo didn't start painting the Sistine chapel on his first day at work. Peter by now had lost his embarrassment of Jo's nudity and was producing a dramatic interpretation with high contrast and accentuated angles. Few of them were recognisably Jo, except Ben's.

At the end of the lesson Jo seemed more than usually keen to get away and said goodbye to the students, Ben and Hannah and left. Ben didn't think anything of it, but ten minutes later when he went outside to have a cigarette he looked up the esplanade and saw Jo talking to Justin. Ben didn't realise it was Justin at first but as he looked he recognised him at the same time as they turned to walk on and Jo put her arm through his. Ben had already told Hannah about Justin after his first visit to the gallery, so Ben told her of the latest development when he went back inside.

'That was quick work,' Hannah observed.

'Yes,' said Ben. 'It gives him another reason to stick around I suppose.'

'When is he coming back to see you?'

'I'm not sure,' said Ben. 'Now he has other things on his mind it might not be quite as pressing.'

'I thought she looked a bit different today,' Hannah said.

'How different?' Ben asked.

'She was dressed differently for a start,' Hannah said. 'Not the usual jogging gear and she seemed to look more feminine and it wasn't just the clothes.'

'Amazing what a bit of romance can do,' Ben observed.

THE STING

{ CHAPTER 36 }

'Hi, I'm Jo, Jo Elliot. I rang about the model portfolio.'

'Jo, yes of course, that's right.' Cyril looked Jo over from his side of the counter. He couldn't believe his luck, two in the space of a fortnight, and what a bonus, she was just his type. For Jo, seeing Cyril for the first time, she could understand exactly why Maddy had been so repulsed and this was just the first impression, the treacly voice, the eyes that seemed to penetrate her clothes and the strange hair.

'So Jo, we're going to have a little photo session first, a sort of screen test,' Cyril said.

'If that's how it works,' Jo said. She was wondering if things would follow a similar pattern to the session Maddy had told her about. Would he use the same patter?

'Oh yes, we have to look at your potential, see what your good points are before we can decide what sort of marketing strategy we need to put together.'

'The portfolio, you mean,' Jo said.

'Exactly.'

Jo, even though she knew how Cyril worked, was acting as innocently as possible to let Cyril do what he had done to Maddy. It was Jo's idea and although she was nervous, once the idea had formed in her mind she knew she had to try and go ahead with it. She wanted to get Maddy's pictures out of Cyril's hands and to try and stop him doing this sort of thing again. It was obvious now that Cyril was unlikely to have any of the contacts he claimed to have so what he did with the pictures was anybody's guess. The idea had come to Jo when she had seen all the surveillance equipment in Justin's car and with his help, and the items he kept, she worked out how it could be done. Justin was concerned about Jo putting herself in danger but he was beginning to find out that when Jo decided to do something there was little anyone could do to change her mind.

'So you want to be part of the exciting world of fashion modelling do you Jo?' Cyril asked.

'That's right,' Jo replied.

'All those trips abroad to exotic locations.'

'If that's what it takes,' Jo said attempting a smile.

Even though she was playing the innocent, Cyril picked up that Jo was not going to be quite as malleable as some of the others. There was a fire in her eyes and a sort of insolence. He came around to her side of the counter.

'I can't see you properly from there,' he said. 'Ah, that's better; you've got a very trim little figure.'

'I like to keep fit,' Jo said, trying to sound demure.

'I can see that,' said Cyril his eyes not keeping still for a moment. He was getting excited.

The reservations he had about her character were not only a challenge but were outweighed by the fact that he liked slim girls with slightly boyish figures. He moved towards the front door still appraising Jo's form. She had chosen to wear a simple white blouse buttoned at the front and some plain black trousers. She had also applied a little make up the way Maddy had shown her.

'We don't want anybody disturbing us do we?' he said as he turned over the 'open' sign and clicked the latch. Jo knowing full well what happened now asked, 'What's next?'

'We'll go through to the studio and I'll just take a few pictures and we'll see if the camera likes you.'

Jo was holding a shoulder bag, perfectly innocent on the outside, but a small hole that looked like part of the design held a hidden video camera. This was pointing directly at Cyril as his eyes swept over her.

'Follow me,' Cyril said.

The studio smelt damp. Jo realised she was entering the monster's lair and there was no real way out of it now. Cyril pressed a switch and the photographic lights came on.

'You can put your bag over there by the drinks trolley.' Jo clocked the plastic trolley with the tea and coffee making stuff on it and placed the bag down so that the lens was pointing at the centre of the studio. The camera had a wide angle lens and with the experiments carried out with Justin's help she was confident the camera would get everything. She was just praying that Cyril didn't go and put something down in front of it. While she was putting her bag down Cyril had taken the opportunity to switch on his own secret video camera on the other side of the room, something that Maddy had not been aware of and so Jo would not know of either.

'Do you want me in front of the chaise longue?' Jo asked.

'Ah, the chaise longue,' Cyril grinned. 'The hurly burly of the chaise longue.'

'Pardon?' Jo said.

'Oh, take no notice of me,' Cyril said. 'It's just a saying. Sit down my dear, make yourself comfortable. I'm just going to get set up here.' He was holding a camera and screwing it to a tripod. Jo sat down and cast a nervous look at her bag, hoping nothing would go wrong. The hole where the camera lens was now looked larger and seemed to stand out from the pattern but Jo stopped worrying, realising she was probably just being paranoiac.

'Would you like to sit down?' Cyril said from behind the camera. Crouched as he was Jo could see the lines of his hair stretched across his bald head.

'That's nice dear,' Cyril said twisting the barrel of the lens. 'Have you done any modelling yet?'

'No, not yet,' Jo said.

He came around from behind the camera towards her and Jo felt a fluttering of fear in her guts. He put his hands on her shoulders and moved her upper torso so it was angled towards the camera.

'That's better,' he said. It was the first point of physical contact and Cyril liked to establish it early on. Jo could smell some sort of cosmetic on Cyril. It wasn't deodorant or aftershave, it was more like talcum powder and Jo thought it smelled of old ladies. Lavender. Yes, that was it with an underlying hint of TCP.

Cyril went back to the camera and Jo cast another look at her handbag.

'There are lots of opportunities for young ladies these days in the modelling world. This friend of mine, magazine editor, said there were a lot of openings for the right people. Hold your head up a bit, that's right. Can you put one foot up on the chaise longue and clasp your hands around the knee.

Jo started to do as he asked.

'Oh, take your shoes off, sweetheart, don't mark the fabric.'

'Sorry,' Jo said and took off her shoes. Cyril bent down to the camera again.

'Yes,' he said. 'There just aren't enough pretty girls each month for these magazines.'

'What magazines are those then?' Jo asked.

'You know, the lad's mags, Nuts and Zoo, that sort of thing.'

'I was hoping more for Vogue or Cosmopolitan.'

Cyril sucked air through his teeth. 'You've got to be well up the ladder before you can pitch for jobs like that. Lad's mags are a good place to start. The money's good and you get known.'

'Yeah, but it's not modelling clothes is it?' Jo said, knowing she didn't need to say much as Cyril would lead things in the direction he wanted.

'Oh, for sure,' he said as if concentrating on something else and not really bothered about where the conversation was going. Maddy had given Jo a detailed briefing of Cyril's 'modus operandi' so she was aware of the way he liked to get to touch. It was casual at first and seemingly innocent. Cyril used it believing he could gauge how far things were likely to go. He went over to Jo.

'I need a couple of reclining shots.' He reached down and picked up her ankles, lifting them onto the chaise longue. This forced Jo to lean back against the arm at the end.

'You've got nice slim ankles dear,' he observed.

Jo couldn't answer, her throat was dry. She knew she had to hold back enough to show Cyril doing his persuasive best to get her to undress, and to really get him involved, she was at some point going to have to take her top off. The plain white blouse she was wearing seemed to draw Cyril's eyes like a magnet. He went back to the camera, turned the barrel of the lens, took a few more shots and then said: 'It's nothing these days is it, they're everywhere.'

'What's everywhere?' Jo asked.

'Girls with their tops off. Everyday in the Sun, there's a different girl showing off her Mother Natures to anyone who cares to look.'

'I'm sure I am too small to be interesting for that sort of thing,' Jo said

'I think you'll find there's a market for all sorts. Certain men find small breasts very exciting.' Cyril found his voice going a little hoarse as he said this owing to his own predilection for pre-pubescent girls.

'Do you show these pictures to your friend?' Jo asked.

'Only in the strictest confidence and with the person's permission.' Cyril said speaking while he fiddled with the camera, pressing the shutter now and then and trying to sound like it was all just so much small talk. Quietly he was getting excited.

'Would you show these ones that you are taking now to him?' Jo asked

'Not these,' Cyril said taking several more shots of Jo reclining. 'We would have to show him what you've got wouldn't we. He won't be interested in these ones, would he? Not for a lad's mag.'

'You wouldn't show them to anyone else, would you?'

Cyril felt beads of sweat forming on his forehead. She seemed to be taking the bait. 'Of course not, it would be between you and me and the editor. You can make a lot of money doing glamour shots you know.

'Just topless is it?' Jo asked.

'If that's all you want to do, yes.'

Jo didn't say anything for a few moments, adding to Cyril's mounting tension

'Alright then,' she said at last, thinking she had kept things going long enough.

Cyril's semi erection swelled a notch. Jo stood up slowly and started unbuttoning her blouse. Cyril moved closer with anticipation, making sure he didn't block the view of his own video filming so he would be able to relive this part later on. His eyes watched greedily as she took off her blouse. Underneath she was wearing a simple bra. She turned around to remove it and at the same time took a swift look at her bag still on the floor. Cyril's hands twitched, 'Can I help you with that?'

'No, it's OK, I can manage,' Jo said, the thought of Cyril's hands touching her bare skin made her flesh crawl.

'That's the ticket,' Cyril said as she turned around and he could see her naked breasts.

Cyril was used to girls who were shy when they first revealed themselves; either that or they were the kind who needed little persuasion. But this one seemed to be neither. She looked at him with a sort of defiance.

'You'll need your camera,' Jo pointed out.

Cyril suddenly felt foolish; he was standing there with no camera gawping at her. He went back to the camera on the tripod and took several shots. 'Hold your head up, that's right, shoulders back a little, good. Now I'm just going to change the lens.'

He went over to his equipment table and selected another lens. As he turned back he saw Jo shoot another glance at her handbag. There was something about her that wasn't quite right. Nothing fitted the pattern of similar encounters. He felt wrong footed. Was he not reading the signs properly? Maybe that direct look was a come on.

'More fun if you took those trousers off,' Cyril suggested in a matter of fact voice.

'You said just topless,' Jo countered.

'As you like.' Cyril unscrewed the camera from the tripod. 'I'm just going to get some angle shots.'

'OK,' Jo said.

Cyril moved closer, the camera up to his eye. 'Look to your left a bit, that's it, head up.'

Snooty little bitch thought Cyril. He reached out with his hand and cupped one of her breasts. Jo moved back quickly pushing his hand away. 'That's enough,' she said.

'No need to get uppity, they're only tits,' he said. 'You won't get very far with that sort of attitude.'

Jo reached for her blouse. She wanted to get out as soon as was possible now that Cyril had touched her. She wondered what he might do next. Cyril felt angry and chastised by Jo's response and pretended he was doing something with the camera, knowing that the move to touch her had been the wrong thing to do, a miscalculation. He looked at the screen on the back of his camera and the last picture he had taken of her. It had been taken from the left, and at an angle that had included, in the bottom right hand corner, Jo's handbag. On the bag was a pinpoint of light. Cyril turned the control on the camera to zoom in on the spot. One of the studio lights, from the angle he had taken the last photograph, was reflected in the lens of the hidden camera. Suddenly everything about the whole session fell into place, his feeling of unease, the way she kept looking at her bag, her attitude, so difficult to fathom. Cyril was at that moment filled with a rage, made up of being caught out, being duped, and at her arrogance that she could come in here and try to trap him. He looked up.

'You little bitch.'

In that moment Jo knew she had been rumbled. She had

just managed to put the blouse back on. She hadn't bothered with the bra hoping she was going to be able to get out as soon as possible. She was about to button the blouse up when she saw Cyril stride towards her bag on the floor. She also sprang into action knowing she had to get out with the bag. Cyril crouched to snatch it and in that moment Jo pushed him hard in the chest. Cyril sprawled.

The crouching stance had caught him off balance. He fell backwards into the tea trolley, his head forced to one side by the impact, the comb-over unravelling leaving the hair hanging down on one side to his shoulder, his head as bald as a beach stone. The trolley crashed into the wall with the impact, knocking over a carton of milk that gurgled as it splashed out over Cyril's shirt.

Jo grabbed the bag and with the advantage of Cyril being incapacitated against the tea trolley, ran for the doorway. She skirted round the counter to the shop's front door, gripping the bag with one hand and trying to hold the two halves of her blouse together with the other. She grabbed for the latch that she had seen Cyril flick when he locked the door. She turned the catch downwards and tugged but the door wouldn't open. She could hear Cyril getting up from the floor. He was angry shouting, 'Bitch, little bitch.' She pulled the catch outwards and she felt the door give but it still would not open. There was another lock. She heard Cyril coming around the counter. She fumbled desperately at the door for another lock and saw a key lower down protruding from a dead lock. Her hands were shaking uncontrollably as she grabbed for the key and tried to turn it. She felt the bulk of Cyril's presence behind her, his smell and hot breath, and felt him grab the bag and try to tug it away from her. She managed to turn the key but the latch had closed again. She pulled it and felt the door open but Cyril still had hold of the bag and was trying to kick the door shut as she was struggling to get it open. Realising the only way she was going to escape was to let the bag go she slipped it off her shoulder. The momentum of her suddenly letting go of the bag caused Cyril to stagger backwards and in that split second she escaped.

Cyril was relieved she was gone but he was shaking with anger and the effort of the fight with Jo. He kicked the door shut and went and leant on the counter while he got his breath back, the bag in front of him. When his breathing eased he stood up and opened the zip on top of the bag. There it was, a little camera, still silently recording. It was a specialist spy camera and Cyril was not familiar with the make. He found the off switch and turned the camera over to inspect it, finding a catch and releasing the SD card. He held it in the palm of his hand, looking at it and every now and then saying the word 'bitch' under his breath. He closed his hand over the SD card and kissed his fist.

Jo ran out of the shop clutching the two sides of her unbuttoned blouse across her chest. She turned the corner at the end of the road and saw Justin standing anxiously by his car. She ran straight to him knowing she was now safe. Justin put his arms around her and held her. He could feel her heart pounding from fear and exertion against his chest. She refused to cry.

'Sorry,' Jo said when she could speak. 'He got the bag off me; it was the only way I could escape.'

'Don't worry; it's not important, as long as you're OK.'

LAZAŃKI AND GOŁOPSKI

{ CHAPTER 37 }

'Bob been in yet?' Ray asked Stella. Stella was polishing glasses in a lull between happy hour and when the evening was supposed to get busy at around eight-thirty.

'He came in, had two whisky and sodas but then he went again 'cos you weren't here.'

Ray nodded.

'Said he'd come back later. Got something going on you two, have you?'

Ray looked up at Stella. He was not always sure he liked her impertinent questions.

'I'd say that was a bit rich coming from you.'

Stella turned to put some glasses away. Ray smiled to

himself, pleased the remark seemed to have shut her up. When Stella turned around it was like she was starting a new conversation.

'You men are all the same,' she said.

'Don't include me unless you're going to say something nice.'

'Comes in here and flirts when he's all chipper and full of it, then when he's got a problem wants to unload all his frustrations like I was some sort of psychoanalyst.'

'What sort of problems was he unloading on you then?' Ray thought this was getting interesting. There was no harm in getting a bit of gossip that might help him in his dealings with Bob.

'Teenage daughter problems, that's what he's got.'

Ray grinned.

'Apparently she's started going out with an older guy.'

'And?'

'Exactly! He doesn't like it. He wants a Daddy's girl; a little princess that doesn't grow up. Apparently she's got a bit of an attitude and he can't handle it. This is what I mean you see, there he is chatting me up, I'm young enough to be his daughter, well nearly, and he'd shag me tomorrow if I let him.'

Ray looked around to see if they were in earshot of any customers. Stella was warming to her theme of indignation. 'And yet he expects his daughter to be some little ice queen virgin, talk about double standards.'

'OK keep your hair on.'

Stella turned to serve a couple who had just walked in. She altered her expression to her professional face and Ray went in the direction of his office, muttering to himself about staff problems. He checked the CCTV screens in his office. There was only a disco going on tonight and the sound system was playing a series of pop songs until the DJ arrived and the place started to fill up. He checked the kitchen to see what was going on there and it was empty.

'Fuck it,' he said under his breath hoping he wasn't going to start having trouble with Bogumil like he had with Barry. He walked out of the office and through the bar to the kitchen, kicking the swing door harder than was necessary. Bogumil wandered in from the other direction, carrying items from the storeroom.

'Ah, there you are,' Ray said.

'Mr Collins, I have idea.'

Ray waited.

'I put on special.'

'What is it this time?'

'It's called Lazanki.'

'And what's Lazanki?' Ray sounded weary.

'Is Polish.'

'I thought it might be. What's in it?'

'Pasta, cabbage and pork.'

Ray put his hand to his head like he was losing the will to live.

'Is very popular in my country,' Bogumil said.

Ray looked at him. 'The crucial thing in that statement, Bogumil, is the last three words.'

Bogumil thought back and reached 'in my country'. His eyes lit up 'That's right.'

'How many times do I have to tell you Bogumil, people come here to have something simple, burger and chips, chicken and chips, steak. Last time we put on one of your specials, Golopski or something, we had to throw most of it away.'

Bogumil looked crestfallen for a moment, then he seemed to brighten up. 'Perhaps they like Lazanki. I bought lots of cabbage.'

Ray felt like crying, he imagined the cold store piled high

with crates of cabbage.

'I don't want Lazanki, the staff don't want Lazanki, the customers don't want Lazanki. Understand Bogumil.'

'Yes Mr Collins.'

Ray left the kitchen kicking the swing door even harder than he had on the way in. In the bar he clocked Dave leaning on the bar drinking a pint of lager.

'Are you off duty?' he said to Dave.

Dave flinched, 'No Mr. Collins.'

'Well get back on the door then.'

'Yes, Mr Collins.' He put his glass down and moved hurriedly out of the bar. Dave's bulk had had a deleterious effect on Dave's feet, so watching him move was like watching someone walking on shingle. Ray stormed back into the office and poured himself a large measure of Scotch from the Macallan bottle, sat down and looked at the CCTV screen, then he looked at his watch. The car park had only half a dozen cars in it which was not good for the time. His intercom buzzed.

'Yes, what is it?' he barked.

Stella, in the bar, pulled the phone away from her ear.

'I'm not deaf,' she said. 'I just thought you might like to know Bob's here. I know you wanted to talk to him.'

'Alright Ray?' Bob said, shaking hands.

'Not really, this place is driving me round the twist,' Ray told him.

'Sorry to hear that, what's up?'

'Oh, you know, the trials of running a business. I hardly made a penny from that Elvis night. Friday night disco here and hardly anyone in. The chef's a fackin' liability and the staff think it's some kind of holiday camp. I tell you Bob, I've had it up to here. I've got a block of flats I can't develop 'cos there are still people living there and every day that goes by costs me a packet.'

'I know, it's a pain sometimes,' Bob commiserated.

'All I want,' Ray continued. 'Is to get that nice little amusement arcade up and running.'

'Yes, I was going to...'

'Do you know?' Ray interrupted. 'Those casino machines are highly addictive. People spend fortunes on them.'

'I did actually...' Bob tried again.

'Hardly any staff,' Ray continued. 'Captive audience. You can make thousands a day with a few of those machines. License to print money. I'm not getting any younger; this place is too stressful to run.'

'That's what I came in to tell you.'

'What?'

'The solicitor's letter I had sent to Wilfred Patten...'

'What happened?'

'He's not interested, doesn't want to sell.'

'Bollocks,' said Ray. 'What about a compulsory purchase order?'

'Can't do that, unless it's for something important like roads or restructuring, that sort of thing.'

'That's the trouble with having a weak government. It stands in the way of progress. Can't do this. Not allowed to do that. It's the bloody European Union.'

'It definitely puts the spanner in the works for your plan.' Bob concurred.

'Maybe we could lean on him a bit.' Ray said.

'I don't want to get into anything like that. I can't be associated with any rough stuff because of my position as a councillor.'

'I see your point, but Dave's very good at that sort of thing.'

'I am sure he is but I can't have anything to do with it if you go down that route.'

'OK, OK, stop worrying.'

'Give me time. I'll think of something. There have to be other ways.'

'Some lever under this Wilf guy. Do we know much about him, weaknesses and such?'

'Not that I know of.'

'Presumably if we can get this artist guy out of the gallery and he finds it difficult to rent out, he can't be getting that much for it, he might reconsider.'

'It's a possibility.'

'We need some more dirt on this Frampton fellow, see if he's running any current scams, something that might get him out.'

'I'll go and see him,' said Bob. 'Do some digging around; see if there's something we can get him on.'

THE PRIZE

{ CHAPTER 38 }

Justin took Jo back to his hotel room to recover from her ordeal of the photo session with Cyril. Her major concern in the aftermath was that she had not managed to get away with the bag and hidden camera, but Justin put her mind at rest saying he would get it back when he went to see Cyril. Having been watching the whole thing on his lap top in the car, he had been concerned after witnessing the first struggle and realising something was going wrong. He was in the process of making for the studio when Jo had come running round the corner.

'What would you have done?' Jo asked. 'The door was locked.'

'I'm not sure,' said Justin. 'I would have thought of something.'

'It will be interesting to watch it again and listen to all that tosh about magazine editors,' Jo observed. 'Do you think he uses those images, I mean sell them?'

'I doubt it,' Justin replied. 'There is far more extreme stuff on the Internet these days; I should think he just feeds his own fantasies with them. The ploy he uses is to see how far he can get the victims to go. I suppose there are some who will go further, even possibly have sex with him.'

'What a sad git, having to get it like that.'

'How do you feel now?' Justin asked.

'I feel fine actually; I've got a bit of an adrenalin rush after all that excitement. I wouldn't mind using your shower though.'

'Yes, go ahead,' said Justin. 'There are towels in there.'

While Jo was in the shower Justin went back to studying the video of Cyril and Jo, stopping, starting and sometimes rewinding. He studied Cyril's technique of casual indifference one moment, cajoling the next; the way he dropped stuff into the conversation about talent scouts, Page Three girls and the ability to fast track careers by going topless, and how he would establish physical contact, all the time gauging how far he could push his victim.

'This is interesting,' Justin said as he heard Jo come out of the bathroom. She had wrapped a towel around her and her hair was spiky from the shower. 'What's that?' she asked.

Justin was still studying the film intently.

'When you put your bag down in the studio, Cyril goes over to the table the other side where he keeps his camera equipment and does something. I think he's turning on his own video camera. I think he films it all as well.'

'Crafty bastard,' Jo said as Justin showed her the bit in the film. 'I hope you haven't been watching me take my top off while I've been in the shower.'

'Well, I watched it the first time in the car; mind you I couldn't see that well because of the sunlight.'

'It hardly matters now I'm so used to taking my clothes off in public.' And then she realised she had not told Justin about the life modelling.

'I know,' said Justin also realising too late he was not supposed to know.

'You know about that then?' she said looking at him intently.

'I saw Ben's picture of you when I visited the gallery,' Justin explained.

'Oh right,' said Jo. 'I didn't want to tell you at the time, we'd only just met.'

'I understand,' said Justin. 'So far I have seen an oil painting of you and some grainy footage of you taking your top off.'

'Doesn't matter, does it?' Jo asked. 'You don't think I'm a tart, do you?'

Justin was still seated at the dressing table where the lap top was set up. He half turned to look at Jo.

'No, of course not.'

'It's about time you saw the real thing then,' she said.

Justin's throat went dry. 'Yes,' he croaked.

Jo undid the towel where it was secured just above her breasts and let it fall. Underneath she was naked. Justin put his arms around her waist and his face between her breasts. She held him to her.

'You smell good,' Justin said brushing her breasts with his face and kissing them.

'Come on,' she said stepping back. 'You've still got your clothes on.'

'Are you sure you want to?'

'Better hurry up before I change my mind.'

'Excuse the cliché, but how was it for you?' Justin asked.

Jo thought for a moment. They were lying side by side on the rumpled bed. 'I didn't come if that's what you mean.'

When Justin didn't say anything Jo propped herself on one elbow and looked down at him. She smiled. 'It was very nice though, different to how I thought it would be.'

Justin looked at her, he was smiling. 'You make it sound like you were a virgin,' he said.

'I was,' she told him

Justin jerked his head up. 'What?'

Jo laughed. 'You, my friend have just had the enviable privilege of deflowering me.' She lay back down again. 'I like the word 'deflowering',' she said. 'It's sort of old fashioned and poetic isn't it? Better than all those terrible phrases like 'breaking in' or 'losing your cherry'. Makes it sound like a burglary or a fruit cocktail.'

'I thought it was supposed to hurt and you bled and stuff.' Justin said.

'Well, technically speaking I was a virgin but not in a practical sense.'

'I think I understand.'

'Are you sure?' Jo asked.

'Well just in case, you had better enlighten me.'

Jo thought for a moment before continuing. 'When you do sport, especially stuff like gymnastics and hurdles it tends to tear the hymen to put it bluntly.'

'OK.'

'I was advised by an older girl to do it for myself in the privacy of my room.'

'Why?'

'Well that way you get it over with and it doesn't happen in the middle of the four hundred metres hurdles wearing white shorts with everyone watching. So you, you lucky man are second only to a plastic vibrator.'

'Did you get a vibrator especially for that?' Justin asked.

Jo laughed. 'No, it was my Mother's.'

'Bloody hell,' Justin said, thinking this conversation was the strangest one he had ever had after sex.

'She didn't know, or anything like that,' Jo said.

'But you must have known she had one?'

'Oh yes. I found it once by accident in her underwear drawer. I was playing at dressing up in her clothes. I used to invite friends around and when Mother was out I took them up there and showed them, just for a giggle.'

Justin was stunned to silence while he absorbed Jo's frank explanation and her seemingly expert innocence. Jo lay back musing to herself on the situation that had just passed and its effect on her. Then thinking of another angle she propped herself up on her elbow again. 'The thing is, did you enjoy it?' she said.

'It was great,' Justin replied.

'I'm glad it was you,' Jo said. 'What I was trying to tell you was, I wanted the first time to be with someone I really liked. I was waiting for it to be special, that was why I was still a virgin.'

'One more question,' Justin asked.

'Go on then.'

'Did you come; I mean that time with the vibrator?'

Jo laughed and sank back into the pillows. 'You don't necessarily need a cock or a vibrator to have an orgasm. Look, I'll show you.' And she took his hand.

KEVIN QUITS

{ CHAPTER 39 }

Kevin took a packet of Doritos off the shelf of the local shop and then moved to the shelves further up, looking for the cheapest cider he could find. Two women were sorting through the chest freezer behind him.

'Can you smell fish?' one of them said.

'It's either that or something has crawled away and died somewhere in here,' the other one replied. Kevin, self-consciously picked hold of the lapel of his coat and raised it to his nose. His olfactory nerve was now so used to the smell of rotting fish that it didn't smell any different to him but he was aware that there was an aura around him if he stood still for long enough. He picked up a two litre bottle of Old Tom's

Scrumpy and moved down the shop towards the counter. He put his purchases on the counter and looked up at the man serving. He seemed to tower over Kevin owing to the raised platform behind the counter.

'Can I have twenty Sovereign and a packet of rolling papers, please.'

The man turned to get the cigarettes from the cabinet behind him and when he turned back he sniffed a couple of times and wrinkled his nose. Kevin ignored him. He walked up the road and through the front doors of Belvedere Heights. He could hear the sounds of Anthrax, a favourite of Breath's, reverberating through the building. He pulled out his key as he went up the stairs with the purchases from the corner shop. When he entered the flat, Breath was standing at an open window smoking a cigarette. He turned when he heard Kevin coming in.

'Derek's gone, so's Paddy,' Breath said.

'Good,' said Kevin. 'They were just using the place anyway.'

'They couldn't stand the smell any longer.'

'It has its uses then.'

'We gotta do something man.'

'Like what?'

'I dunno.' Breath turned back to the open window then turned back again. 'Derek said it was making his clothes smell.'

'I know,' said Kevin.

Bo came out of the main bedroom yawning. Kevin and Breath said nothing as Bo was grumpy in the mornings and never answered anyway. She went out into the kitchen and they heard the tap run as she filled a glass with water. The next thing they heard was a cough and a splatter. Bo came out of the kitchen wiping her mouth.

'Right, that's it, I've had enough,' she announced.

'What?' said Kevin.

'That smell, it's made me throw up. I can't stand it any longer.'

'Where are you going to go?' Kevin asked.

'I don't know but I can't stay here.'

'I'll sort it,' Kevin said.

'Yeah, well you can tell me when you have,' Bo said and marched back to the bedroom to get her stuff. Breath gave Kevin a sheepish look. Kevin started rolling a joint.

The joint had made Kevin sleepy. He had been up most of the night drinking cider and listening to Slipknot. The marijuana and alcohol had made the music sound particularly special. It had given him a heightened awareness of the sound. In his brain he could hear the bass, drums and lead guitar as separate and distinctive instruments, and appreciate a timbre and quality in the sounds, whereas without the help of mind stimulants, it just sounded like a mash up of guitars and feedback. He had dozed off on the sofa, upset that Bo was leaving, but without an idea of how to prevent it. The flat was quiet when he woke up which felt unusual after the time when it had been full, even if he hadn't known who half the people were. He stood up and looked out into the hall. He looked in the second bedroom and it was empty. He heard a noise coming from the main bedroom. Breath was standing by the bed putting his stuff in a back pack. Kevin looked at him.

'Sorry man,' Breath said. 'I can't take it any longer either. That smell just keeps getting worse.'

'I don't know what to do,' said Kevin his voice going squeaky with emotion, hangover and coming down from the drugs. 'I've tried getting rid of the rubbish.

Breath shrugged.

Kevin went and sat back down on the sofa. He heard the front door close. The flat was now empty except for him. He didn't want any more dope, picked up the cider bottle but it was empty. He lit an ordinary cigarette from the packet on the table. He sat, smoked, stared into space and thought. He crushed the cigarette out in the ashtray and stood up. He sniffed the great coat and felt in the pocket for his keys. Downstairs Kevin went round to the back of the flats where the bins were, took off the great coat, rolled it into a bundle and put it in one of the bins.

The first stop after Kevin had decided to take some positive action was his supplier. He had to walk across town to get there. The house was an end of terrace that looked like it had been moved there from a war zone. The front door had a sheet of metal riveted to it that was dented and scarred. There was a pile of rubbish in the small front yard, topped off with a bicycle that was minus a wheel. He knocked with his fist. The door opened and two suspicious eyes looked out.

'Frank in?' he asked.

'Who wants to know?'

'Oh, come on, it's me, Kev.'

'You buying or selling?'

'Sniffy, it's me Kev, remember?'

'I been told to ask is all, Frank's new rules.' Sniffy said as he opened the door a bit more. Kevin squeezed in and Sniffy did a quick reccy of the street before closing the door. The carpet in the hall was shiny where dirt and grease had packed it down to a smooth surface and Kevin's nose seemed to fizz from some chemical smell that was in the atmosphere. Several dogs could be heard barking somewhere in the house.

'He's in there,' Sniffy nodded towards a door. Kevin went in. Frank, the dealer, was wedged in a large armchair watching a boxing match on the TV and feinting with the blows the fighters were inflicting on each other. He was very large and wore track suit bottoms and an old worn T-shirt. His hair hung in ringlets around his face and his feet were bare. Lying by them a Borzoi dog sat looking at Kevin, a low growl emitting from its throat. Kevin stood waiting for Frank to look up from the TV.

'Hello Kevin me old mate, what can I do for you today? Got some good Afghan black just come in, very mellow.'

'I need some bennies Frank,' Kevin told him.

'Gettin' a job are you?' Frank laughed at his own joke not expecting or getting an answer from Kevin.

'Got something needs doing,' Kevin said eventually.

'Where's the coat?' Frank asked.

'I had to get rid of it,' Kevin said not feeling like going into details.

'Let's see what we can do for you then.' He clicked his fingers and Sniffy who had been standing just in the doorway came forward with a flat attaché case and put it on Frank's lap.

'Let me see now,' said Frank, sorting through the contents of the case that held small plastic bags of substances, all neatly labelled. 'Only the best for my friend Kev. How about these?' Frank held up two sachets.

'How much baby powder they got in them?'

'I'm fuckin' upset you even asked me that,' Frank said.

'How much?' Kevin asked.

'Thirty quid the two, twenty five to you.'

Kevin reached into his back pocket and went to hand the notes to Frank. Frank put a hand up. 'Give it to Sniffy, I don't handle money.'

Kevin handed over the notes to Sniffy who looked at them and nodded to Frank. Kevin put the drugs in his pocket.

'Now fuck off,' Frank said and turned his attention back to the television.

Kevin set off down the road in the direction of the flat. He felt vulnerable without the protective layer of his coat. He went into the corner shop where he had bought cider the night before, picked up a wire basket and went to the display of cleaning materials. After some consideration he selected Domestos, Cillit Bang, Toilet Duck, Febreze, Cream Cleanser, an antibacterial spray, a brush, a sponge and a pack of dish cloths. He took the selection to the till.

'Someone's going to be busy,' the man said.

For the next three hours, with the help of the speed, Kevin cleaned. He scrubbed floors, cleaned tiles, aired beds, sprayed, polished, wiped and disinfected. All the time he worked he was thinking of how when the place was purged of the smell, he would go and find Bo and bring her back. He spent most of the time cleaning in the kitchen knowing that the smell was strongest in there. He played through some of the fastest tracks he knew from the selection of Slayer, Korn, Nirvana Slipknot, Motorhead and Anthrax. Tracks that had driving, galloping beats that spurred him on in a frenzy. When he had finished he stood in the middle of the living room and sniffed the air. The cleaning chemicals had done their job and the atmosphere was redolent with the smell of bleach and chemical flowers.

Kevin left the flat. He was coming down from the speed, shaky from all the effort, and from the fug of cleaning materials he had inhaled. He needed some fresh air and the work had sharpened his appetite. He went to the Sunflowers Café and had their all day breakfast with several cups of tea. A walk along the front, a few ciggies in one of the shelters rounded off with a joint on the beach and Kevin was feeling his old self again, ready to go back and see if his cleaning splurge had done the trick. He opened the front door of the flat and walked into the hall. He didn't even have time for an exploratory sniff; the stench of rotting fish hit him like a wave. The smell of cleaning materials was gone, ousted, wafted away by the stink of fish. Kevin walked around the flat shaking with despair. In the kitchen he reeled backwards from the stench, worse in there than it had ever been. Despair turned to impotent rage and fury, there wasn't even anyone to take it out on; he was up against an unseen enemy. In the corner of the room was a baseball bat left there by one of the previous occupants who had harboured an over reactive drug psychosis. Kevin picked it up, hefted it in his hand and performed a practise swing. A red standby light on the music system winked at Kevin as if mocking him.

Kevin swung the bat down on the top of the system in the general area of the red light. Bits of Perspex splintered, broke and flew off in several directions. He hit it again and some of the casing sprung apart revealing wires, valves and circuit boards. Several more blows demolished the whole system till it was just a pile of broken parts. Kevin fished in his pocket for the keys to the flat, chucked them in the centre of the debris and left.

A PRIVATE VIEW

{ CHAPTER 40 }

'Ray's not happy,' Bob said to Clare, chuckling.

'I couldn't be less interested,' she replied without looking up from the paper she was reading.

'Ray's all right,' Bob said after a pause.

'I don't like him and I don't trust him. Anyway what's he not happy about?'

'He wants to open an amusement arcade on the seafront and needs to buy this property but the guy who owns it won't sell it.'

'My heart bleeds for him.'

'I said I'd help him.'

'What can you do?'

'I might be able to use my influence.'

'I wouldn't get mixed up with it if I were you. He's a gangster. Anyway where is this place he wants to buy, surely there must be other places where he can set up an amusement arcade?'

'Well this place is in a good position. Anywhere else in the town would be more expensive and he might not get the permissions he needs.'

'You still haven't told me where this place is.'

'It's the bit going out of town, down by the tennis courts. It's that gallery place, fish something.'

'Oh, I know.'

Bob stood up. 'Anyway, I said to Ray I'd check it out, so I'm going there now, do you want anything in town?'

'Yes, can you get some Jamie Oliver fresh pasta and some Jamie Oliver Carbonara sauce. Oh and the Jamie Oliver garlic bread.'

'Anything else?' Bob asked. 'Jamie Oliver's trousers, Jamie Oliver's head on a plate?'

'No, just the pasta stuff,' Clare said deciding to ignore the barbs. 'You do want some supper don't you?'

Bob drove into town musing on a wife who did nothing but read cheap fiction and magazines, spent his money on outrageously priced face creams to counteract the effects of drinking expensive white wines, a daughter who was possibly going off the rails and who cheeked him at every opportunity, even Tom was acting a bit sullen since he started puberty and spent all his time playing computer games. It seemed to him that none of his family could be bothered about him except as the provider of income. The only fun he seemed to get was flirting with that Stella at Ray's club. He hadn't actually made a direct pass at her as yet but he thought it would not be long if he kept feeling like a cash dispenser cum punch bag all the time. She certainly behaved like she was up for it, that smile she gave him and the way she leaned forward to chat giving him a good eyeful of cleavage.

Bob was starting to fantasize now he was thinking about her. He pictured her backside as she bent down to the chiller cabinet behind the bar, imagining what her tits would be like and thinking she'd be like a pig in bed, all snuffly and grunting. He had to brake hard at a pedestrian crossing, the tyres squeaking on the road and the family waiting to cross, looking at him accusingly. He waved and mouthed 'sorry'.

Suitably chastised from his lewd thoughts he continued driving sedately until he reached the car park outside The Fish Works Art Gallery. He got out of the car and could smell frying onions and the savoury odour of cooking sausages. He looked over at Toddy's Bacon Crematorium, remembered what he had said to Ray about it and suppressed his appetite.

There are certain character traits to which people will never admit. Being a Philistine about art comes just after not having a sense of humour, being a bad driver and being rubbish at sex. Bob's appreciation of art fell in the 'I know what I like' category, so he felt no trepidation as he approached the entrance to the Fish Works Art Gallery. Ben was sat at the reception desk. It was Saturday and he was alone in the gallery. The classes had finished for the week and Hannah always had Saturdays off. It was usually a good day for trade, there being a mixture of locals and tourists. People came in intermittently. One moment there could be several people milling about, apologising to each other for being in the way, or it would be empty for a while until another lot came in. He had a new canvas on his easel ready to start a painting but knew he might not get a chance to do much today. The painting of Jo, which he had now finished, was proving to be a bit of a problem.

Ben hadn't considered what he might do with the painting

now that he had completed it. It was unlikely to sell at the gallery and came with the added problem that it might be unfair to display it as Jo lived in the town and people could recognise her. He didn't even want to ask her and put her in a difficult position, so had made an arrangement with a London gallery, where he sometimes exhibited, to take the painting. The picture was on the floor facing the wall waiting for Ben to package it ready for delivery.

Bob walked into the gallery. He prided himself on being able to talk to anyone. Canvassing for votes as a councillor brought him in contact with a wide range of people. He knew what things people liked to talk about, how to ask the right questions, to remember names, keep eye contact and look genuinely interested in what they were saying. He would get chatting to Ben, draw him out, see what his hopes and fears were, and find out more of his secrets other than the ones he already knew.

'Morning,' he said cheerfully as he entered.

'Hi,' said Ben looking up.

'Alright if I look around?'

'Of course'

'Nice day for it, been busy?'

'Not bad,' Ben answered.

Bob went up to the nearest picture, a wide beach scene with a huddle of boats just right of centre with ropes leading from their prows and hung with weed. Bob studied it carefully. He liked it. Nothing challenging about that, no geometric faces with both eyes on one side. He stood looking at it as if he were an art critic.

'Is that local?' he said to Ben.

'Could be,' said Ben smiling. 'Sometimes the boats and settings come from different times and places.'

'I see, so you're the artist are you?'

''Fraid so,' said Ben

'I like it,' Bob said.

Ben thanked him. Bob went to study another picture and Ben started to clear the desk.

'You'd do better in a classier part of town wouldn't you?' Bob asked.

'Possibly,' said Ben. 'But I like it here and the rent's cheap. You in business yourself?'

'I dabble,' Bob said.

'You dabble well by the looks of it.' It was easy to tell when someone was reasonably well off. It was usually their complexion and their shoes that told the story. Ben had a suspicion that Bob was here for more than just to look at the pictures. He felt he was being probed. He could probe back just as well. Bob moved to the further part of the gallery away from the entrance. Ben went out to his office and came back with a roll each of bubble wrap and brown paper and proceeded to unroll the bubble wrap across the desk top. The phone rang and Ben picked it up.

'Hello, is that Ben?' a voice asked.

'Speaking.'

'Just thought I'd let you know.' Ben recognised Ken's voice. 'They've gone.'

'That's good,' Ben answered. 'We'll put stage two into action in the next day or two. Did you get a key?'

'Yes, the caretaker sometimes leaves the cupboard open where the keys to the flats are kept, so I borrowed one and got a key cut.'

'Good stuff,' Ben said.

'Freda and I are going to get some sleep now.'

'You do that, see you soon.' Ben put the phone down smiling to himself. He picked up the painting of Jo from the floor and laid it on the bubble wrap, picked up a pair of scissors and cut along until he had a flap that would surround the picture. He folded it over and reached for the cellotape.

Bob came back to the desk from the lower part of the gallery.

'Excellent work,' he said.

'Thanks,' Ben responded.

'Are you in the town guide?' Bob asked.

'No I don't think so.'

'Well you ought to be. It would bring more people down here.

'Are you something to do with it then?'

'Yes, sorry, I'm Bob, Bob Elliot.' He put his hand out to Ben. Ben thought there was something familiar about the name but it was a common enough surname. He put out his hand to shake Bob's and as he did so the unsecured flap of the bubble wrap slid away from the surface of the painting. As they let go of each other's hands both men looked down at the now exposed painting of Jo.

For Bob it took a moment to realise the full impact of the situation. Faced with a picture of his own daughter, fully naked, reclining on a richly patterned rug, seemed to alter reality in his head. All sorts of speculation and imagined scenarios went through his mind as a result of being short on the facts of how everything had arrived at this moment in time. Ben went to pass off the accidental revealing of the painting, not realising how devastating this minor slip of bubble wrap could have on the other man.

'Oops,' he said. 'I meant to stick that down.' Noting the obvious change in the expression of Bob, who at that point was still speechless, Ben put it down to old fashioned prudishness.

'Our model, Jo,' he said by way of explanation. 'Not right for here, sending it up to London.'

'Where did you get that?' Bob's voice was very quiet but his face was beginning to go red.

Ben thought that perhaps he had read Bob's reaction wrong

and he was instead rather taken with the picture.

'It's mine. What I mean to say is I painted it. She's our life model, comes in once a week for our life classes.'

'That,' said Bob, feeling his anger bubbling up through his discomposure, 'is my daughter.'

'Oh,' said Ben, now fully aware of why the other man's mood of friendly bonhomie had changed.

'But you knew?' he said, his voice faltering a little.

'No I did not. Nor did I come in here expecting to find a picture of my daughter disporting herself naked, and to find out that not only has she been taking her clothes off in public but in front of a group of strangers as well.'

'She said...' Ben started.

'I don't care what my daughter said. You, Sir, have taken advantage of a minor.'

'Now look here,' Ben said starting to find the accusations unfair.

'No, you look here.' Bob's voice had risen to a shout. 'I know about you, you've been in trouble with the law before. You are a reprobate and a scoundrel, I am going to report this to the authorities and have you arrested for corrupting a minor.'

'I have a signed...' Ben started but Bob shouted over him. 'I'm going to take that picture as evidence.'

'You are bloody well not. That is my private property and totally above board.'

'Above board?' Bob yelled. 'Grooming a seventeen year old?'

'She's eighteen,' Ben said.

'I know how old my own bloody daughter is. You just wait.' Bob was now wagging his finger at Ben. 'I'm going to the police so they can seize that picture as evidence and arrest you at the same time.'

He stormed out of the gallery.

CONFRONTATION

{ CHAPTER 41 }

Cyril heard the bell of his shop door and looked up quickly. There was a hunted nervous look in his eyes. He was still suffering from the after effects of his encounter with Jo. Nobody had ever tried to catch him out at his game before and, even though he had managed to wrestle the bag and camera from her, he was still nervous that there might be some sort of repercussion from the incident. Now that he had the camera, and therefore the evidence, it would be her word against his if there were any involvements with the law. But who was she? She must have known about him and his game, so she must know one of the other girls he had photographed. His bet was the most recent – Maddy.

Unfortunately, that gave two people's accounts against his

one, and the recent prosecution of a high profile celebrity was uppermost in his mind. He wondered if she might come back with help and demand the bag and camera back. He had by now watched both videos of the session, hers and the one he secretly recorded from the other side of the studio. At the point when they both grab for Jo's bag and she pushes him, the action is right on the edge of the frame but it still catches him sprawling and knocking into the tea trolley. His shame and anger are refreshed by watching the action each time and he had only watched it twice. The card from the camera was safely hidden and the bag and camera wrapped and under the counter.

Cyril looked up to see Justin and breathed a sigh of relief.

'Hello my friend, found Daddy yet have you?'

'I have actually, but that's not what I've come about.'

There was something in Justin's demeanour that told Cyril he was angry. His face was serious and his jaw tight. It wasn't his fault, Cyril thought, if things hadn't worked out between him and Ben.

'I did warn you,' Cyril said.

'I said it wasn't about that. I've come about your model agency scam.'

Cyril now became defensive. 'That is a perfectly legitimate business.'

'What, to trick girls into taking their clothes off with promises of fast tracking their career just so you can film and grope them?'

Cyril was trying to remain calm. Whatever Justin knew it could only be what he must have been told. No evidence had left the shop.

'I don't know where you get your information,' Cyril said, smiling. 'But I think someone might have been exaggerating a little, even telling porkies.'

'You had a Jo Elliot in here the other day,' Justin said.

So that's it, he knew Jo. Cyril felt his mask slipping. He would have liked to have snarled 'bitch' when he heard the name, but he held his calm façade.

'Oh yes, Jo, I think I remember. Not a lot of potential there. I think she got a little bit cross when I told her she didn't have what it takes.'

'And you didn't promise her introductions to magazine editors in return for going topless?'

'Is that what she said,' Cyril scoffed. 'The little minx. She couldn't wait to show her tits off that one.'

Justin was trying hard to control his anger.

'I'm sorry young man,' Cyril continued. 'What you are suggesting amounts to defamation of character and I wish you to leave now.'

'I would like the video camera back please.'

'Oh, so it's yours is it? You and that little bitch cooked this game up between you, did you? How did you two hook up?'

'It's none of your business Cyril.'

'You're a fast worker or was it her?' Cyril reached under the counter and pulled out the bag and camera. 'Neat bit of kit that. Nearly fooled me but I've been around a bit and you've got to be cleverer than that to catch me out.'

Justin unzipped the bag.

'I've taken the card out and destroyed it if that's what you're looking for. I'm not that daft.'

Cyril was beginning to enjoy himself now he thought he knew the score and had the upper hand as well.

'Do you know how much distress you cause these girls when you treat them like that?' Justin said conversationally as he checked the camera in the bag.

'Pfftt,' Cyril scoffed. 'I don't know what you're talking about and neither do you.'

'Madelaine was upset for days.'

'Madelaine, Madelaine.' Cyril pretended he was trying to remember. 'I don't know any Madelaine. There are so many girls. They all come in here with their dreams, thinking they will be in Vogue next week. I can't help it if I have to tell them about the real world. Of course they get upset.'

Justin looked at Cyril long and hard.

'And what did you get out of it?' Cyril continued. 'A shag, a blow job, or a threesome with those two girls, very nice?'

Justin felt like punching Cyril but he had something better for bringing Cyril down. He looked at Cyril and for the first time in that visit he was smiling. He looked at Cyril and then down at the camera. Cyril, camera, Cyril, camera.

'What?' said Cyril, slightly un-nerved. Justin was holding a small antenna that he had pulled out of the camera casing.

'You think you're clever, don't you Cyril? Do you know what that is?'

The colour drained from Cyril's face. He did know what it was.

'The camera,' Justin said. 'Was not only recording your session with Jo, it was sending the images to my laptop as I was sitting in my car around the corner. Jo was exceptionally brave coming in here with that camera and letting you perform your nasty, perverted little scam on her.'

'You're bluffing,' Cyril said, but his voice was wavering.

Justin took his mobile phone out of his pocket and held it up for Cyril, who heard his own voice tinny from the phone's loudspeaker saying 'that's right love, head up' and saw himself bent to the camera on the tripod.

'It's all there, even you grabbing the bag as Jo was trying to escape. You're hair looked nice by the way.'

Cyril all but snarled. 'What are you going to do, blackmail me?'

'Oh no, Cyril, much simpler than that. I'm going to give

you the opportunity to give me all the images you have of Jo and Maddy. I want them wiped from your computer and any other device you have recorded them onto. If for any reason I think you have kept any of these images, this piece of film will be taken to the police, and if they take this place apart they will confiscate every image you have made, to build a case that will take you to court and eventually prison.'

Justin went over to Cyril's window and found the poster advertising the model portfolio. He tore it off the window. 'We will be checking periodically that you are no longer perpetrating this scam; so no more posters and no more ads in the local paper. You will be monitored and the police will be informed if it ever comes to our notice that you are still at it. Now, we've got some work to do deleting those images.'

A BOX OF MAGGOTS

{ CHAPTER 42 }

Ken met Ben and Wilf in the entrance hall of Belvedere Heights. They were back in their uniform of gas fitters in case anyone other than Ken challenged their presence. Wilf was carrying the tool box.

'Bit whiffy, even down here isn't it,' Wilf commented as he sniffed the air in the hall.

'It gets worse as you go up but luckily it hasn't penetrated our flat.'

'Well, this won't take long,' Ben said.

'You must come in and have some tea afterwards,' Ken said.

They went up the stairs and outside the vacated flat Ken produced a key and unlocked the door. They reeled back as the door opened and the smell hit them.

'I don't know how they stuck it for so long,' Ken said. 'I'll wait here if that's all right with you.'

Hands over noses Ben and Wilf entered.

'Well, they left it pretty clean and tidy,' Ben commented.

'I think someone tried to clean up. I can smell bleach but nothing can stand up to that stench.'

Wilf's foot crunched on something and he looked down at a piece of broken plastic. A trail led his eyes to the pile of broken bits that had been the stereo. 'Looks like someone took their frustration out on that,' he said.

Ben shook his head. 'Wanton destruction.'

In the kitchen he jemmied up the floor board where they had put the plastic container of squid guts.

'Oh, Jesus,' he said as he looked down at a writhing mass of maggots.

'Here you are, just put this on it.' Wilf handed him the lid of the container, Ben clipped it on and lifted it out of the floor cavity. 'Job done,' he said.

'Yeah.' Wilf smiled.

They went around opening the windows in the flat and put a couple of air fresheners in strategic places.

'Should clear in a day or two,' Wilf said to Ken as they closed the front door of the flat.

'Thanks guys, we owe you.'

'Don't mention it,' said Ben.

'I'll just go and put this in the truck,' said Wilf. 'I'm sure you don't want me to bring it with me into your place. I'll be back in a minute.'

Wilf put the offending plastic container under a tarpaulin in the back of the van and re-entered the block of flats.

In Ken and Freda's flat it just smelt of furniture polish and cake. Every surface was shiny and neat and the place looked comfortable. Ben looked out of place, still in the overalls and seated in a large armchair holding a delicate bone china cup and saucer.

'These overalls are quite clean,' Wilf told them as he sat down.

'Don't worry about that,' Freda told him. 'Milk?'

'What happens next?' Ben asked.

'We have formed a union,' Ken told them. 'There are still four other flats occupied. Mr and Mrs Reid in flat seventeen have found this solicitor through Citizen's Advice Bureau who charges much more reasonable rates, and she specialises in property law especially cases like this. We have created a fund to cover expenses.

'That covers the fair means but as we know this Ray Collins is not shy about using foul to get his way, so we wait and see what he does next when he finds his noise pollution plan hasn't worked. He would probably be very upset if he found out we had managed to do to his tenants what he has been trying to do to us for the past six months.'

'Well, keep us informed,' Wilf said biting into a piece of Victoria sponge and getting a dab of icing sugar on his nose.

'We've had a whip round and collected this for you two.' Ken pushed an envelope across the coffee table towards Ben. 'We really appreciate it.'

'Thank you, but there's no need for that,' Ben protested pushing the envelope back.

'No, we all agreed, you had the idea and put the plan into action. We think you should have some sort of reward.'

'It's not necessary,' Wilf said.

'Sorry you've got to deal with that charming box of delights now you've removed it from the flat,' Freda said, changing the subject.

'It's actually created some nice fat maggots – they'll be good for fishing,' said Wilf.

Freda wrinkled her nose in disgust.

'The smell should be gone in a couple of days,' said Ben. 'You can go in and close the windows after that.'

Ben and Wilf left, got in the truck and drove back along the seafront. Ben told Wilf about his latest trouble with Jo's father spotting the painting in the gallery.

'You've got a lot on your plate at the moment what with that and the guy who thinks you're his father,' Wilf commented.

'I know,' said Ben. 'What happened to the carefree days?'

'Have you heard from him again?'

'Well he's still around, but things have started to get a bit complicated.' Ben then went on to tell Wilf how he had seen Jo and Justin together.

'Well that might take his mind off the paternity thing for a while. Have you managed to remember anything about it yet?

'Not a thing unfortunately. I've racked my brains until they rattled. What about you?'

'No, 'fraid not. I've drawn a blank there myself.'

'I suppose it will have to be the DNA test eventually,' said Ben. 'I am going to be really pissed off if it turns out I am his dad and I can't even remember the encounter with his mother or what happened.'

'What's he like?' Wilf asked.

'Oh, he's a nice enough chap. I wouldn't mind if it turned out he was my son. I could think of worse characters. He's intelligent, good looking – must be mine.'

'Does he look like you?'

'Actually no. There is very little physical resemblance there.'

'I'd like to meet this chap,' Wilf said.

THE MARIE CELESTE

{ CHAPTER 43 }

'Something must have happened by now,' Ray said to Dave as he parked the Lexus outside Belvedere Heights. 'Last time I came by they had all the windows open and you could hear some terrible noise coming out of there half way down the street.' He waited while Dave struggled to get out of the passenger seat, eventually giving up and strolling over to the front doors to the flats. Dave caught up as Ray pushed the doors open.

'Smells a bit fishy in here; must be somebody's rubbish.' Ray went up two of the flights of stairs, stopped and looked behind him. Dave was half way up the second flight but had stopped and was leaning on the banisters breathing heavily.

'What's happened to the lift?' he asked.

'I put it out of action,' Ray said. 'Pending repair, told everyone it was unsafe. I thought you were supposed to be fit.'

'I am, I am,' puffed Dave continuing his ascent. 'It's just stairs, they kill me.'

They reached the door of the flat that Kevin had recently vacated. Ken had been back and closed the windows. Air fresheners had made the place smell a bit sweeter but there was still an underlying note of rotting fish.

Ray thumped on the door with his fist. There was no answer. He tried again. When there was no response to this he indicated the door to Dave who fumbled with a bunch of keys.

'It's a bit smelly in here as well,' Ray said as they entered the hall of the flat. He walked into the living room.

'Little fucker's done a runner,' he said looking around. His eyes came to rest on the smashed stereo.

'Looks like someone's trashed the stereo,' Dave offered.

'I can see that,' Ray said giving Dave a look. 'But why?'

'Dunno,' said Dave.

Ray wandered through the rooms taking in the furniture still in place, and that it seemed reasonably clean and tidy. 'It's like the Marie Celeste.'

'What's the Marie Celeste?' Dave asked.

'It was a ship that was found in the Southern Ocean, which was...oh never mind. It's fackin' great isn't it. You let someone have somewhere to live free of charge and they just bugger off. We had better check the other flats to see if anyone else has moved out yet.'

Ken answered the door to Ray's knock. Ray had put on his 'most reasonable man in the world' smile which didn't make a lot of difference when he had The Incredible Hulk standing next to him.

'Hello Mr Macmillan,' Ray said. 'Don't suppose you know what happened to the young couple in flat twelve do you?'

'Have they moved out?' said Ken feigning surprise.

'Yes they have.'

'No, sorry, can't help you there.'

'There has also been an act of mindless vandalism carried out in that flat.'

'It hardly concerns me does it?'

'Do you know anything about it?'

'All I know is, there were some very dodgy characters around when that flat was occupied. That and the loud music makes me suspicious that they might have been put there for a reason.'

'I was helping them out,' said Ray. 'A homeless couple needing somewhere to live.'

'Homeless couples don't usually have massive stereos.'

'I would like to know how it got smashed to pieces.'

'Do I look like the sort of person who might carry out an act of vandalism?'

'I'm not accusing you directly.'

'And I don't hire out heavies to do it for me,' Ken said flashing a glance in the direction of Dave.

'OK, OK,' said Ray.

'Anyway why are you so concerned about the stereo, it wouldn't happen to be yours would it?'

'Course not, I just wanted to return it to them.'

'Yeah sure,' said Ken, unable to keep a note of sarcasm out of his voice.

'I don't suppose you know where they've gone?' Ray asked.

'Not the sort of people to leave a forwarding address were they?' Ken said.

'Have you thought anything about that other offer?'

'You mean the flat down Bingley Road?'

'That's the one.'

'It's above a kebab shop,' Ken said.

'I know, nice flat though.'

'Depends what you call nice.'

Grace Poulson sat at the kitchen table making an exquisitely formed roll up. She had Cutter's Choice in a tin and Rizla papers. It was the dexterity of her long fingers and the deft moistening with the tip of her tongue that turned it into a long, slim tube. Bo watched her intrigued. Grace lit the cigarette and picked at a couple of strands of tobacco, revealing the pink pointed tongue again. She blew out a cloud of smoke.

'You just need to take a bit of control, Bo, you can't just drift.' she said.

'I know, but I get depressed.'

The kitchen was a model 1950's fitted job, all yellow Formica with wooden trim and still in good condition, the sort of thing that retro designers would wet their pants over before ripping it out and selling it at an outrageously inflated price. Bo and Grace sat at the matching table and chairs smoking and shooting the breeze. Grace was thin with cropped dark hair. She wore a vest top with battle fatigue trousers and she had a degree in law. Two mugs of tea sat on the table with the ash tray and smoking stuff. The house they were in was originally a hotel, turned into flats by a developer, let out to DHSS customers for a while before falling into disrepair and dereliction. Grace had taken over one of the flats as a legal squat.

'So where's this Kevin now?' Grace asked.

'I dunno, still in the flat I suppose.'

'Anyway, you say you couldn't go on living there?'

Bo looked down at the table. It was the first time anyone had seemed interested in her or her problems. Being very quiet, people tended to ignore her, so it was unusual that someone not only listened but asked her questions as well.

'I could put up with the people,' she told Grace. 'Mostly it didn't matter because we were smoking but in the end it was the smell that got to me. I just couldn't stand it anymore.'

'Didn't someone clear up, try to get rid of it somehow?'

'It was more than that. It wasn't just the flat being dirty. I think it was a bad spirit. I read this book once about possession and one of the symptoms is smell.'

'I don't think that's very likely,' said Grace who was a practical person. Her father had been a banker and made a lot of money in the city buying futures. Grace, her mother and father and two older brothers had lived in a large house in Surrey with considerable wealth. Her two brothers had followed their father's example and taken jobs in the money industry hoping to emulate their father. Her mother, who had never had to work was incapable of making a decision so everything was decided by her father by default. It was a perfect match, her father liked making decisions and her mother didn't. But something about that relationship sowed a seed of discontent in Grace. At her expensive public school she began to hate the obvious wealth and privilege, including her own. She started to affect a left wing bias. It fitted. It made her different. It was rebellion with intelligence. It felt good to support the underdog and piss her father off at the same time. History lessons fed the political stance; the enclosures act, the formation of the trades' unions. But Grace was no dropout and ignoring the fact that it was her father's influence that told her every action had to be informed and intelligently worked out, she studied law and gained a degree. Her passion was the waste of unused empty property above shops in towns, that property companies chose to ignore if their portfolios were making money, set against the fact that there were so many homeless people. Grace worked hard for homeless charities dealing with the legal aspects and working for a fraction of what she could earn in a normal practice. The squat was her own pet project and she took people in who were needy.

'Well you can stay here until things change or get better for you.'

'Thanks,' said Bo looking down at the table again. She found Grace's intenseness slightly unnerving.

'You need a project though,' Grace continued. 'Not necessarily a job but something to do.'

Bo nodded.

KEVIN LOOKS FOR BO

{ CHAPTER 44 }

Kevin stood on the step looking at the old fashioned front door with a sunrise pattern in stained glass at the top. He had rung the door bell and heard the distant chimes of a popular melody sound somewhere in the house.

'What do you want?' the woman said as she answered the door to Kevin. Her tone let him know she was not pleased to see him. She was a large woman in a shapeless dress, and the years of permanently scowling had stamped an impression on her face that meant she looked like she was scowling even on the rare occasions when she wasn't. Today she was scowling.

'Is Bo here?' Kevin asked.

'No she's not.'

'Do you know where she is?'

'No, and if I did I wouldn't tell you.'

'OK,' said Kevin turning away.

'You stay out of her life,' she called after him. 'You're nothing but a bad influence with your drugs and your smelly flat and your 'orrible music.'

'Stick it up your arse,' Kevin muttered.

'What did you say?' she shouted after him.

'I said it's time to cut your grass,' he called back.

'Little fucker,' Bo's mother said.

Kevin made his way back towards the town from the estate where Bo's mother lived. He was sure from the encounter that Bo wasn't there and that her mother wasn't lying. He knew that Bo would have to be desperate before she went home to her mother's constant nagging. Kevin walked down long connecting roads past industrial estates, used car lots and out of town DIY stores. He eventually reached the outskirts of the town and into streets of small shops not really knowing where he was going. Approaching a corner where two roads met, a figure jumped out in front of him.

'Da dahn.' Spig said dramatically.

'Hiya,' Kevin said without stopping.

'Did I make you jump?' Spig asked.

'Nah, I thought it was the Milky Bar Kid.'

'I hate that,' said Spig.

'Yeah?'

'That's what they call me at school.'

'It's the glasses,' said Kevin.

'I know. I saw you from across the park and ran round,' Spig informed him.

'Very clever.'

They walked on for a while without saying anything.

'Where you going?' Spig asked.

'I dunno,' said Kevin.

'Ain't you got the flat anymore?'

'Moved out.'

'I came round a couple of times.'

'Did you?'

'There were a lot of people there.'

'I know.'

'What happened?'

'You don't half ask a lot of questions. Can't you see I'm thinking?'

'You can't see if someone's thinking,' Spig muttered.

He had been pleased to see someone he knew when he spotted Kevin. He had been sitting on a swing in the park feeling bored, now he was feeling disappointed that Kevin didn't seem quite so pleased to see him. They had walked up the seafront, Spig quietly respecting Kevin's request for silence but still wanting to hang around with him. Kevin went and sat in one of the shelters and Spig joined him. He watched Kevin get out a packet of cigarettes and before he had put one in his mouth Spig had struck a match in readiness. Kevin cupped his hand around the offered light.

'Gis one,' said Spig.

Kevin offered the pack and Spig took one. He took a drag and blew out the smoke like a veteran smoker. 'What happened to your coat?'

'I had to get rid of it.'

'Was it that smell, like the same as in the flat?'

'Yeah.'

'That was rank,' Spig observed. 'Is that why you moved out?'

'Yeah.' Kevin gave him a look and Spig realised he had started asking questions again.

Kevin sat with his elbows on his knees smoking and

looking down at the cracks in the concrete.

'I done that Smoky Joe's,' Spig said.

'You what?' Kevin asked turning to look at Spig.

'I done Smoky Joe's, you know, set light to it.'

'Fuckin' 'ell,' Kevin muttered, not sure whether to be impressed or concerned. 'What for?'

Spig shrugged. He wasn't sure himself. He brightened up. 'It was great, like a sodding great fire work. Did you see it?'

'No, I heard about it. Did anyone see you?'

'Course not, it was dark.'

'You're a fuckin' liability, you are,' Kevin said.

Spig beamed, pleased at last he had impressed Kevin. They lapsed into silence again. A dog trotted by, made a detour into the shelter, sniffed Kevin's hand and licked it experimentally. Kevin stroked its head and ear and it trotted on again.

'What's up with you then?' Spig asked risking another question.

'I dunno where Bo has got to.'

'I know where she is,' Spig said.

Kevin looked at him, 'Now he fuckin' tells me.'

'I didn't know you wanted to know.'

'Jesus.' Kevin leant his head against the wall of the shelter.

'I'll show you,' said Spig getting up.

'First of all,' said Grace. 'There is a job rota, cooking, washing up, general maintenance, that sort of thing.'

Kevin was leaning against the door frame, Grace against the kitchen work top. Bo was sitting at the kitchen table, joined now by Spig who was fiddling with Grace's lighter. Kevin didn't say anything.

'Secondly,' continued Grace. 'We all pay our way here. There is no rent but we have to pay household bills which are divided up equally. Oh, and no drugs.'

Kevin looked at the floor to try and hide his smirk.

'I'm serious Kevin,' Grace said.

'Sounds like a squat run by capitalist pigs,' Kevin said.

'No, it's a squat run like a co-operative. There is a difference.' Still looking at Kevin she reached over to the table where Spig was sitting and took the lighter out of his hands and put it in her pocket.

'The only way you can stop here Kevin is if Bo wants you to, as you will be sharing a room. So you two will have to discuss it. Come on Spig.' She tapped him on the shoulder and jerked her head towards the door. 'I want to talk to you.' Spig followed Grace through to the living room casting a sheepish look at Kevin.

SLUT

{ CHAPTER 45 }

Bob got back from the gallery and found Clare and Jo talking in the kitchen. Before either of them could say anything they could tell from Bob's expression that something was wrong.

'Nice to go somewhere in the town and find out my own daughter is a slut.'

'Bob,' Clare protested.

Jo absorbed the shock with confusion not knowing which bit of her life he had found out about. Had a member of staff at the hotel seen her going into Justin's room with him, had Cyril managed to find some twisted way of exacting revenge on her, but that was unlikely as that would mean incriminating himself. More likely it was her activity at the studio and the life modelling he had found out about. Jo decided not to react until she knew more so she looked back at him with her best insolent stare.

'Look at her, butter wouldn't melt in her mouth.'

'What's going on?' Clare asked.

'I'll tell you what's going on,' Bob answered. 'I go to this gallery on a fact finding mission and I am faced with a picture of my own daughter, without a stitch on, laid out on a rug like a pound of sausages in a butcher's shop window.'

Bob had driven back from the gallery in a different mood to the journey there. Frustration had turned to anger and shame. But there was something else in there with this cocktail of emotions, and Bob wasn't sure he wanted to examine it, because this other feeling was a sense of satisfaction that at least he now had something on his daughter that was tangible, something he could actually accuse her of, something with evidence that she would not be able to refute or wriggle out of with her clever words and back chat.

'Can you be more specific?' Clare asked.

Bob puffed out his chest. 'This daughter of yours has been disporting herself to all and sundry, stark naked for all to see at that gallery place under the pretext of 'art'.' Bob made the inverted comma sign with his fingers as if to confirm the point.

Clare turned to Jo, 'Is this true?'

'I have been modelling at that gallery for their life classes, yes' Jo replied.

'Why didn't you tell us?' Clare asked.

'Well I think the answer to that might be apparent from Dad's reaction,' she pointed out.

'People might have seen that - that pornographic picture; people I know,' Bob shouted. 'Business associates, other councillors could go in there and see that photo of you. How does that make you feel?'

'It's a painting not a photograph and it isn't pornography.'

'You didn't think how that might affect me did you?'

'I wasn't counting on you finding out.'

'What made you do it Jo?' Clare asked.

'It was a job for the holidays, it was well paid and contrary to what Dad thinks had nothing to do with sex.'

'What taking your clothes off for money?' Bob retaliated.

'The nude as an art form is a tradition going back centuries,' Jo told him, quoting Ben.

'Yes, so is prostitution.'

'It has nothing to do with prostitution.'

'It's tantamount to that.'

'Well obviously you know more about it than I do.'

'The trouble with you, my girl, is you think you know it all.'

'Look, this argument is not getting us anywhere,' Clare intervened.

'You're right,' said Bob. 'Argument ended. I'll tell you what's happening. You,' he pointed at Jo. 'You're grounded. You are not leaving this house till I say so. And I am going to phone the police and get this guy at the gallery arrested.'

'What for?' Jo said.

'Well, corrupting a minor for a start.'

Jo started to get worried remembering she had lied about her age, duped her mother into signing the form and it could lead to getting Ben into trouble.

'Ben didn't know. I lied to him about my age, it's not his fault.'

'Oh, I see, on first name terms and you're trying to protect him now. I'd like to know what else went on there.'

'Nothing,' said Jo. 'It's your mind. He's a nice bloke.'

'Nice bloke,' Bob exploded. 'You see you're just a kid. You know nothing about Ben Frampton. He's a bad character, and a shifty dodgy reprobate with a criminal past and you get mixed up with him in some seedy business and call him a nice bloke.'

'What did you say his name was?' Clare asked.

'Ben Frampton. You must have heard of him, a thoroughly bad lot, local character, been in prison for fraud, the whole lot. Well, I'll tell you this much, he's gone too far this time, messing with my daughter, he'll be back inside before he can draw another breath.'

'Hold on just a minute,' Clare said. Bob looked at her.

'Let's just calm down and look at this situation rationally.'

'There's nothing to look at, it's a black and white situation.'

'Robert.' Clare looked at him. 'Stop behaving like a herd of bloody elephants. 'Let's consider everything first.'

Bob took a deep breath. He was rather enjoying the patriarchal stamping especially as he was on the moral high ground, but when Clare called him Robert, he knew he had better take notice.

'What do you think will happen if you go to the police?' she asked.

'Well, I suspect they will arrest him and impound that picture as evidence.'

'And what else do you think will happen?'

Jo was looking at her mother knowing that now she was dealing with things a more sensible solution might come about.

'He'll be prosecuted I hope.'

'Yes, I expect all that will happen and of course it will be splashed across the pages of the local paper.' Clare waited for this to sink in. Bob had not thought about this aspect of things.

She continued: 'You know what they're like, they'd fall on this like hungry wolves. Local councillor's daughter, a bit of nudity and scandal, they'll love it. They impound the picture, some clever copper will take a picture of the painting to show his mates, next thing the paper print it which won't matter too much because it will be all over Facebook along with pictures of you, me, Jo and Tom. Remember you've got enemies as well as friends in this town, they'll twist it around and have a field day.'

Bob saw the sense in what Clare was saying. The two things he really didn't want was any scandal in the local paper or any journalists coming sniffing around and poking their nose into his business.

'So what do you suggest we do then?' Bob asked, slightly calmer now.

'I'll go round and see him. I will sort something out and make sure that picture doesn't see the light of day for some time to come, if ever. You, Jo, will not be going to that gallery again.'

'Why not?' said Jo.

'Jesus Christ,' Bob said. 'I offer you a good holiday job in the Council Offices and you would rather go off prancing around in your bloody birthday suit. You're a disgrace. I can't believe you're my bloody daughter sometimes.'

Clare shot him a glance.

'You are grounded,' Bob told Jo. 'For the foreseeable future.'

'That's not fair,' said Jo aware she had arranged to meet Justin, and she certainly wasn't going to tell her parents about that at this moment in time.

FLASH BACK 1996

{ CHAPTER 46 }

Ben stepped back to the edge of the stage to view his work in progress. He was painting the scenery for the Cocklebury Amateur Dramatic Society (CADS) production of Lady Windermere's Fan. The set was lady Windermere's drawing room with tall windows, ornate drapes and William Morris wallpaper. He had been working in between rehearsals and sometimes when they were doing a read through in the stalls, so he knew the cast and the play quite well by now. He had set up a system of ladders and a scaffold contraption on wheels that enabled him to reach to the top of the screen. It was laborious having to get down every now and then to check his progress and make sure the perspective was correct. All the set furniture, a side board, an occasional table, some chairs and a Victorian two- seater sofa had been moved to the centre of the stage away from the backdrop and covered in dust sheets. He was alone in the theatre, opting to stay a bit longer to finish an area he had started, the cast had already gone, leaving Ben to lock up.

'Don't step back any further,' he heard a voice say.

Ben turned and realised he was standing on the edge of the stage. He looked out over the empty seats, shielding his eyes from the lights, and could just make out a figure in the auditorium.

'Sorry, forgot my script.'

'OK,' Ben said. He wasn't sure who it was and turned back to viewing his scenery.

'It's coming along isn't it?' the voice said.

'I think so,' said Ben.

'It's good.'

'Thank you,' Ben replied. 'Who is that?'

'Sorry, it's Lady Windermere,'

'Oh hi Clare.'

'I forgot my script.'

'So you said.'

'Why didn't they just put wallpaper where there is supposed to be wallpaper?' Clare asked.

Ben turned again shielding his eyes. 'Because it wouldn't have looked right with the other things that are painted, like the drapes and stuff.'

'A lot of work for you.'

'I don't mind. Look I can't see you very well with these lights.' Ben was fed up with squinting.

'I'll come up there.' Clare said.

'Dress rehearsal tonight wasn't it? Ben asked, reminded by the fact that Clare's face looked scrubbed from removing the make-up.

'Do I look a mess?' she asked him.

'No, you look fine.' She was wearing a print dress of a thin material that seemed to cling to her.

'How do you do all this?' she waved at the backdrop that Ben was painting. 'It looks so real from out there.'

'Oh I don't know,' said Ben. 'Tricks you learn, how to scale things up. I don't know how you remember all those words.'

'I don't sometimes. Luckily Wilde said some very memorable things so you use them like stepping stones to tell you what comes next.'

'He had some good one-liners, didn't he?'

'They're called epigrams.'

'Sorry, I'm showing my ignorance.'

Clare smiled at him.

'What makes you do it?' Ben asked. 'The acting, I mean. Do you want to be a proper actress?'

'Don't you think I am a proper actress?'

'Professionally, I mean.'

'My husband said I should do something in the community. He thinks it will help him in his ambitions in the local election.'

'Oh yes, he's a councillor isn't he?'

'Not yet, he will be if he gets elected.'

'I see.'

'It's good fun as well, and not as stuffy as joining the WI and all that sort of thing. Where did they get you from?'

'Me? Oh, I'm cheap.'

'I think you're being modest.'

'Not really, you don't make a lot of money out of art.'

'Unless you're Monet, of course.' She said it teasingly and waited for Ben to react.

'You know about that do you?'

'Your reputation goes before you.'

'Seems so,' Ben said and moved towards the back drop picking up his paint brush again.

'Sorry, have I upset you now?' Clare asked

'It's OK, but that's all people seem to know about me.'

'If it's any consolation I think it was very brave of you to come back to live here.'

'That wasn't bravery, it was sheer bloody mindedness. I wasn't going to be run out of town. Perhaps you had better go home, you don't want to ruin your husband's chances by hobnobbing with a jail bird.'

'You are upset aren't you?' She went up to him and put her hand on his arm. 'I'm sorry.'

Ben was used to how people regarded him when they knew about his run in with the law. It ranged from a noticeable dislike to a wary prejudice and in some instances an admiration and respect for his notoriety. It still irked him though.

'It's OK,' Ben said, still not looking at her.

'I don't really care what my husband thinks. Anyway he's not here, and I can hobnob with who I like.'

Ben sat down on the sofa and stretched. 'I am about finished here,' he said.

There was something about this interaction that didn't seem natural, that it hadn't occurred by chance. He realised she was flirting with him, not just by the conversation but the way she was looking at him, a look that scanned his face and made him feel exposed. Was she just having some fun, teasing, playing with him or did she have something more serious in mind?

Clare went and sat down next to him. 'Are you married?'

'No, I tried it once but it wasn't for me.'

Ben had been in situations like this before and there always seemed to be a tipping point, the moment when the unspoken understanding became so apparent that a physical move was required or a stalemate was reached. Clare had given Ben enough indication that a move on his part would be welcomed as she sat down on the sofa next to him, close enough for him to feel the heat of her body, smell whatever cosmetic she had used to remove her stage make-up, mingled with a natural body scent. She was looking directly at him. He leaned over, put his arm around her waist and kissed her. She responded, kissing him back and putting her arm around his neck. He could feel her warm flesh through the thin material of her dress.

'Are the doors locked,' he said fumbling with the top of her dress.

'We can go into my dressing room if you like.'

'No, this is fine.'

'You like doing it under a spotlight?'

'Stop it, and help me with this.'

Clare shook the top of her dress down. 'I shall forget my words if I think of this during the play.'

Ben reached behind her and undid her bra. 'I don't think this bit is in the play.'

Clare leant back against the end of the sofa. She had fine breasts and Ben caressed them and kissed her neck. 'This would shock the good citizens of the town.'

Ben ran his hand up her thigh under the dress. Her flesh was warm. 'I didn't really forget my script. I came back to get to know you better.'

'Job done then,' Ben murmured.

'I was looking at you while we were doing that last read through, I thought you were very attractive.'

Ben slipped his hand between her legs and she moaned softly. She stood up. For a moment Ben thought she might have changed her mind but she let the dress fall away.

'Come on,' she said. 'That's enough foreplay, I want you now,'

Ben stood up and unbuckled the belt of his jeans while Clare slid her knickers down and lay back on the sofa.

Ben didn't hear from Clare for at least a fortnight. He could hardly contact her as she was a married woman. It had been a pleasant episode and Ben thought that if it ended there that was fine. He knew very little about her and rather than agonise too much put it down to the contrariness of the female. She was horny, took a fancy to him and offered him the opportunity of sex. He sighed, women were lucky like that - they would rarely fail in enticing a hapless male. Then one day she turned up at Ben's studio.

'Hi, how's the play going?' Ben asked.

'It starts next week; I've brought you a couple of complimentary tickets.' She handed them to Ben.

'Thanks,' he said.

'You will come, won't you?'

'I don't know whether I can watch you on that sofa with another man.'

'Stop it,' she admonished. 'I presume you enjoyed what happened?'

'Of course.'

'Enough to want to do it again?' She was stood close to him her breast almost touching his arm.

'That would be nice,' Ben told her. 'But this is not the most congenial of places.'

She slapped his arm. 'Not here, not now. I sometimes visit a friend of mine in Suffolk. That's where my husband thinks I'm going anyway. I've booked a hotel for the weekend.' She took a card from her bag. 'It's quite smart; I've booked it in your name for obvious reasons.' She leaned forward. 'I want to make love with you properly, in a bed. I want to spend a whole night with you, not snatching moments in dark corners or fumbling around on sofas, though that was fun. The date is on there, we'll meet on the Friday. Can you do that?'

'Yes, of course.' Ben was still looking at the card with the picture and logo of the hotel on it. Clare reached up and kissed him on the mouth, a breathy, fleshy, urgent kiss as if sealing something. She left leaving Ben a little bewildered, 'God, I must be easy meat' he mused realising Clare must have arranged it all before asking him.

He went and watched the play alone, an empty seat next to him in the stalls. She played it well and Ben couldn't help a private smile when she was seated on the sofa. Just once she caught sight of Ben when she came to the front of the stage and Ben noticed a slight faltering in the delivery of her line as their eyes met. A couple of weekends later they met at the Feather's Hotel. Ben had tried to look a little less Bohemian as the hotel was smart but most of the time was spent in the bedroom without clothes anyway. Ben never worked out whether it was a case of her husband not fulfilling her sexually, if it was a fling she wanted or whether she was infatuated with him. She didn't seem to want to talk about it and Ben, happy with a weekend of wild sex with no strings attached, didn't press her.

She never contacted him again. He saw her once in a car at traffic lights but she didn't see him, and once in a supermarket with a man Ben presumed was her husband so it came as a shock when, after eighteen years, she walked into his gallery. Ben recognised her straight away, she was still attractive.

'Hello stranger, it's been a while,' he said.

'You look good Ben, how are you?'

'Still struggling,' he said cheerfully.

'I hear you are doing very well.'

'It depends who you talk to,' Ben said.

'There is a reason for my visit.'

'You haven't come in to browse then.'

'No. My husband came in the other day and I understand you had words with him.'

Ben, thought back, trying to fit stuff together like a jigsaw.

'Your life model, Jo, the girl you have painted is our daughter, Bob's and my daughter,' she told him

'Shit,' said Ben. 'I had no idea.'

'No of course you didn't. Jo is seventeen.'

'She said she was eighteen.'

'I know, but that's not the main problem here, it's more complicated than that. You see, I got pregnant with her eighteen years ago, does that ring any bells?'

Ben thought for a moment. 'Oh come on,' Ben said. 'You can't be saying..'

'She's your daughter Ben.'

So many synapses fired at once in Ben's brain, he just looked at Clare dumbfounded.

'Are you sure?' he said at last.

Clare gave a humourless laugh, 'Absolutely.'

A lot of questions started to form in Ben's mind.

'What about your husband?'

'The only reason I'm telling you this is because of what has just happened. I said I'd sort it out so he doesn't get the police involved. I couldn't do it without telling you the truth but Bob must never know.'

'Does Jo know?'

'Of course not. Do you think she'd come and do this if she knew you were her father?'

'Sorry, stupid question.'

'My husband is threatening to go to the police to try and get you prosecuted over this. I want to prevent that and try and smooth things over, preserve the status quo, but my husband doesn't quite see it like that. I've spoken to Jo and I know that this was carried out in a respectable manner. Bob doesn't see it like that, he is angry, but I can deal with that side of things. I didn't want you to be put in a corner and then all this stuff might come out about what happened between us.'

'I don't understand,' Ben interrupted. 'How you didn't know about Jo working here.'

'Because she didn't tell me.'

'But you signed the form.'

'What form?'

'We asked Jo to get her parents to sign a form saying they agreed.

'Show me,' Clare said.

Ben went to a drawer in the desk and sorted through some papers. He handed the form to Clare. She took out glasses from her bag and looked at the form.

'The crafty little mare.'

'Is that your signature?' Ben asked.

'Yes it is.' She looked over her glasses at Ben. 'I thought I was signing a form to let her do some sort of sport, rowing or something.'

'You didn't read it then?'

'I couldn't, I didn't have my glasses to hand.'

Ben smiled. 'She's got a spark, Jo, hasn't she? She gets what she wants. I seem to remember someone else like that.'

'It didn't take a lot of encouragement if I remember rightly.'

'What happened after that weekend, did you have a change of heart?'

'You still don't get it do you?'

'Get what?'

'That weekend, the primary purpose was to get pregnant.'

'Really?' said Ben.

'Yes, really. You were good material, good genes, clever, good looking. It was your hands; I remember, that clinched it, sensitive, elegant fingers. And I fancied you, I'm not totally calculating.

'But why?' asked Ben.

Clare sighed. 'I found out Bob was not able to give me children, low sperm count.'

'What, he had a test?'

'No, when nothing happened after a couple of years of marriage, I had a test without telling him. I was OK so I concluded it must be Bob. I knew it would be upsetting for him knowing it was his problem and I didn't want to go through all that IVF treatment. My plan was simpler.'

'So I was just a sperm donor,' Ben said.

'I hope it was more pleasant than having to masturbate into a jar.'

'No contest,' Ben said. 'So he's none the wiser and neither is

Jo then. Did you have any more children after that?'

'I have a son, I mean we have a son.'

'I don't remember a return match,' Ben said.

'I thought it would not be a good idea to involve you again.'

'So how did this little miracle happen?'

'I used to go to a gym. There was a guy there, one of the instructors.'

'Another pleasant weekend then?'

'I thought a different approach was better with hindsight. He was a married man with children and I knew he would be discreet, so we had a liaison until the job was done and then Tom was born.'

'So, a happy family, meat and two veg,' Ben summed up.

'Now you know everything and you could destroy me if you wanted to.'

'I wouldn't do that,' said Ben. 'But we have another problem. One I don't think you are aware of.'

A shadow of concern crossed Clare's face. 'And what's that?'

'Do you know that Jo is seeing someone?'

'Yes I know, but we haven't met him yet.'

'She got to know him here, and the reason he was here is because he thinks I am his father.'

Clare put her hand to her mouth. Ben told her more of the story of Justin concluding: 'So they have to know before it goes any further.'

'She can't know about her past, everything would unravel.'

'I understand that, but I don't know how involved they have become. Do you?'

'No, but I think she's pretty keen on him. If we just forbid it without a reason the attraction will be stronger.'

'That's not an option then. I shall have to talk to Justin; at least I can tell him the score.'

'Just make sure he doesn't let on to Jo.'

'It's not certain yet, that I am Justin's father. We are going to have a DNA test, so that is more imperative than ever now. I shall have to ask him to put things on hold till we know.'

'Will you do that?' Clare asked.

'Yes, I am as keen as you are to get this sorted out.'

'About the picture,' Clare said.

'What about the picture?' Ben replied.

'Bob wants it safely out of sight.'

'It's gone to a gallery in London but I can get it back.'

'That won't appease him. I am going to ask some favours from you, which I know is a tall order as well as asking you to keep quiet about all this.'

'Go on then, fire away.'

'Jo can't work here anymore.'

'No, of course, that's a given.'

'And to make sure the painting doesn't fall into the wrong hands, I would like to buy it.'

'Really?' said Ben. 'Well I never turn down a sale, but it's the first time I've sold a painting unseen.'

'Can you get it back from the gallery?'

'I can ring them and arrange its return. What will you do with it?'

'I'll put it away until she's older.'

'She probably won't want to see it then.'

'Maybe not.' Clare opened her handbag. 'I'll write you a cheque; will three thousand pounds cover it?'

'More than enough,' said Ben. 'Are you sure?'

'I think you should be compensated after my husband's outburst here. I don't think you did anything wrong. Foolish maybe, but not wrong.'

'I've always been foolish,' Ben said with a smile.

Clare wrote the cheque and handed it to Ben. 'And you will deal with things your end won't you?'

'I will. You can rely on me.'

'I'll give you my mobile number. Text me if you need to get in contact or when the painting comes back and I'll ring you.'

'Thanks.'

'Well, now you know everything.'

'Yes,' said Ben. 'This is proving to be an interesting time.' He put his hand out to shake hands with Clare. She took it but drew him towards her, reached up and kissed him.

'I'll be in touch,' she said.

FLASH BACK 1996

REALITY CHECK

{ CHAPTER 47 }

After Clare left, Ben sat at the reception desk in the gallery mulling over the revelation of Jo being his daughter. At least there was no fudging about with this one. No 'don't knows' or 'can't remembers' or the need for a DNA test. So many things had happened that affected his life and the lives of others, Jo and Justin particularly. Was it just coincidence, he thought now, that in his dealings with Jo he had liked her instinctively and had felt a protectiveness towards her? Was that something to do with a genetic connection? He didn't know. He was saddened to think that although he now knew he had a daughter for sure, she would never be able to know that he was her father. Then there was the added problem of the relationship between her and Justin. How serious was that and if it had to be stopped how would it be resolved without telling Jo the real reason? Ben could hear some people outside the gallery.

'Come on, let's go and have a look in here,' he heard a woman's voice say.

'Why?' from a whiny, truculent male adolescent.

'Because it'll be fun.'

'I wanna go on the pier.'

'We can do that later.'

'I wanna go now.'

'Look, it won't take long. You'll like it. You like art don't you?'

'Art's boring.'

They came in, a woman with her two teenage children. The girl, younger, seemed more amenable, the boy sullen.

'Hello,' she said to Ben brightly as if compensating for her son's behaviour. 'Can we just have a look around?'

'Of course,' said Ben.

The mother and daughter chatted amiably while they looked around. The son refused to partake and wandered aimlessly, staring down at the toes of his trainers. Ben reflected on how he would have coped if he had had a conventional family and offspring and concluded 'not very well'. The boy shuffled off to wait outside. Girls seemed easier than boys he thought to himself. The woman and her daughter finished their tour of the gallery. The girl decided to write in the visitor's book as the woman said: 'Thank you you've got some lovely pictures.' Ben thanked her. 'Sorry about him.' She nodded towards the doorway. 'They go through a phase, I expect you know what it's like.' Ben was about to say, 'No I don't actually,' but decided the woman was just being polite and said: 'Oh yes, I do.' The girl gave him a blank stare. After they had gone Ben looked in the visitor's book. The girl had written, 'Bunch of crap'.

Ben turned out the lights, locked the door of the gallery and started off down the promenade. It was a job he wasn't looking forward to, seeing Justin, but it had to be done and he was the only person who could do it. There was slim chance at the back of Ben's mind that Justin was wrong and that Ben was not his father, but until they got the DNA test back he would have to keep away from Jo and if it came back with a positive result, well, it would be up to Justin to deal with it then. It took Ben twenty minutes to walk to the Falkirk Hotel. He was hoping the walk might help him decide how to broach the subject with Justin but as he approached the hotel he realised he was nowhere close to a solution than when he had started out.

Justin was coming down the steps of the hotel as Ben arrived.

'I've been meaning to come and see you,' said Justin.

'I know,' said Ben.

'But I've been busy with other things.'

'I need to talk to you Justin.'

'Have you remembered something?'

'It's not about that.'

'You look very serious, have you changed your mind about the test?'

'No, in fact it is more imperative than ever now.'

Justin frowned as he didn't understand Ben's concern or know the reason for it.

'Can we go somewhere, somewhere quiet?' Ben asked

'You're worrying me now,' said Justin. 'There's a bench over there on the promenade. Will that do?'

They crossed the road and sat down looking out at the sea, still blue and sparkling with light and a swell making the waves break on the shingle, creating a rhythm with the sound and the rattling of the stones as the wave retreated.

'I know about you and Jo.' Ben said.

'Is that was this is about? Is it a problem?'

'There are things you need to know.'

Justin, thinking Ben was going to reveal some flaw in Jo's character said: 'I know all I need to know about Jo.'

'I'm afraid it's not as simple as that. This has come as a shock to me, but whereas the paternity situation with us is still undecided, it seems I am definitely Jo's father.'

Justin looked out at the sea without saying anything at first while he absorbed the knowledge.

'Shit,' he said under his breath. 'When did you, how, what did....? Christ almighty,' he said eventually, unable to form a question.

Ben gave Justin a brief version of the meeting with Bob and of Jo's mother coming to see him.

'You've certainly done the rounds haven't you?'

'That's not fair,' Ben replied. 'It's just one of those weird coincidences. It's better we work this out than start with recriminations.'

'Just my luck isn't it, to go and fall for someone who turns out to be my half-sister?'

'Is it serious?' Ben asked.

'It depends what you mean by serious,' Justin said.

'Is it a sexual relationship? And don't say it's none of my business because it is now.'

'Yes,' said Justin.

'Is there any risk...?'

'No there isn't, we took precautions. It's only happened once but it wasn't just a one night stand. There is a connection.'

After the previous barb Ben felt an implied criticism and did not reply for a moment.

'I'm sorry,' said Justin. 'I didn't mean...'

'It's OK,' said Ben. 'This is too serious to bicker over.'

'I was just on my way to see her as it happens,' Justin told him.

'Good job I caught you then. Were you meeting her somewhere?'

'No, I didn't want to phone, I was going to go around to her house.'

'She is in trouble with her parents at the moment over the modelling at the gallery. This is how all this came out'

They were silent for a moment.

'You need to put things with Jo on hold,' Ben said.

'I realise that,' Justin replied.

'And because she can't know the reason it won't be easy.'

'I think I know that too. What a bloody mess we get ourselves into.'

'Have you got the DNA kit?' Ben asked.

'Yes, it's in my room.'

'Well, that's the first step.'

'It's sod's law isn't it, that it's going to be positive.'

Up in the hotel room Justin laid out the kit and read the instructions.

'We have to swab the inside of our mouths with these and put them into these two separate tubes.'

'How long does it take?' Ben asked.

Justin looked at the instructions. 'Three weeks,' he said.

'Shit,' said Ben.

'But you can pay extra and have it fast tracked, five days.'

'Let's do that then,' said Ben. 'What are you going to do if Jo contacts you?'

'I don't know,' said Justin. 'I can hardly say can you wait five days and I'll tell you then if we can go on seeing each other.'

'Five days is not long, can you just avoid her until then?'

'That's what I was thinking. I may have to change hotels.'

'What will you do then? I mean if it's positive?'

Justin thought for a while before answering. 'I suppose I shall just have to tell her I've had a change of heart and if she thinks I'm just a complete bastard, I shall have to live with that.'

'You could tell her you've decided to go back to your girlfriend.'

'Doesn't make a lot of difference either way does it?

KEVIN CORNERED

{ CHAPTER 48 }

The hallway outside the squat was dark. Only the electricity in the flat was on. Kevin had been out to have a smoke of his own choice as Grace had banned all illegal drugs from coming in. As Kevin fumbled with his key he was aware of a presence. For all his bulk Dave was light on his feet and Kevin didn't hear him move out of the shadows to stand next to him. Dave's body could absorb light, sound and radio waves.

'Who's that?' Kevin said.

'Hello Kev,' Ray was stood the other side of Kevin. 'Aren't you going to invite us in?'

'What do you want?'

'We want to have a little chat.'

The door opened. Bo had heard the sound of the key in the lock. Ray and Dave followed Kevin into the flat closely before the door could shut on them. Bo looked at them dumbly knowing they weren't good news.

'This is cosy,' Ray commented. 'Where can we have our little tête-à-tête then?'

Kevin went into the kitchen and they all followed. Ray looked around.

'Very nice, shabby chic, I like it.' Then his manner changed with a more menacing tone.

'What was wrong with the other place then? Not fashionable enough for you?'

'It smelt bad,' Kevin said.

'Well whose fault was that then? You had your girl-friend there. Didn't she do any housework?'

Grace came into the room looking concerned. 'What's going on here and who are you?'

'Nice to meet you too,' Ray said.

'I'd like to know what you're doing here.' Grace said to Ray her eyes flicking nervously in the direction of Dave every now and then, who was standing just inside the door.

'We're mates, aren't we Kev?' He looked at Grace, 'We like to keep any eye on him, make sure he's all right.' Kevin was standing by the sink. He didn't answer.

'So Kev,' Ray said ignoring Grace once more. 'We have a broken agreement and a very broken sound system, how did that happen?'

'I dunno,' said Kevin.

'We weren't the only ones there,' Bo pointed out in a bid to try and stick up for Kevin.

'What is the set up here?' Ray asked. 'Happy families or something?' He turned to Grace.

'Are you the mum?'

'Look, would you say what you have to say and then leave please.' Grace said.

'And what are you going to do if we don't? Call the police?' Ray asked.

A silence hung in the air.

'No, I thought not,' Ray sneered.

Grace had summed up the situation and who Ray and Dave were from their manner, the conversation so far and the bits that Bo had told her about.

'So Kevin,' Ray sat down at the table, Dave remained standing. 'You're in deep shit really aren't you?'

'Why?' said Kevin.

'Well apart from letting me down personally and damage to property, there is still the little business of dealing drugs to my chef.'

'But I'm clean,' Kevin protested.

'Are you accusing Kevin of a criminal offence?' Grace asked.

'Listen Lesbos, this is none of your business so butt out.'

'What did you call me?' Grace asked; her voice level and calm.

'Come on, it was a joke.' Ray was wrong footed by the steel in Grace's voice.

'What did you call me?' Grace asked again. Even Dave was useless in a situation like this.

'Well look at you,' Ray said, his voice wavering because he was on unfamiliar ground.

'So you are inferring that I am a lesbian from the way I dress.

'No offence,' Ray said. 'Look, I've got business with Kevin. Private business.'

'If you are conducting business here and making insults about me, insults made up of opinions based on ignorance and shoddy stereotyping, it is my business.'

Ray stood up. 'Fackin' 'ell, I've had enough of this. We'll go and talk about this somewhere else. Come on Kevin.'

Kevin didn't move.

'Dave,' Ray said.

Dave made a move towards Kevin.

'Don't you dare start any rough stuff in this house,' Grace said, moving to block Dave's path towards Kevin. Dave who was used to handling drunks of both sexes found Grace's determined look and stance more intimidating than anything he had dealt with up to now, and cast a pleading look at Ray.

'Come on, let's get out of here,' Ray said to Dave, conceding defeat. He turned to Kevin. 'I haven't finished with you yet, you owe me. I want to see you down at the club very soon so we can sort this out otherwise it will be the worst for you. I've still got you on CCTV selling your waccy baccy to my chef. Remember that.'

FLASHBACK 1982

{ CHAPTER 49 }

Ben unlocked the doors to the studio and opened them both wide. Light was already flooding in from the glass panels in the roof. The studio was a lock up, one of several in a yard at the back of a row of shops. The other trades were motor mechanic, a joiner and a bicycle repair shop with some of the units just used for storage. Before Ben took it over it had been used by a printmaker who had since retired, and some of the alterations he had made such as the glass roof panels made it an ideal studio. Ben kept the doors open in summer partly for the extra light but also because it made him feel less isolated. The rent was cheap; the only draw-back was being stuck in an obscure position where the public rarely ventured. One of the hotels and an 'interiors' shop in the town displayed his work, but Ben still had to supplement his income by doing odd jobs, deck chair attendant being one of them. The day before was the picnic on the beach with Janet and Rose. They had arranged to meet again the next day but as Janet and Rose had a day trip booked it was agreed they would get together again in the evening when they got back.

It had rained in the night. A lorry backed into the yard splashing rain water from the puddles in the rutted surface. The driver, revving the engine with the effort, filled the space with carbon monoxide and Ben pulled one of the doors across more in protest than the fact it might make any difference. One of the mechanics came out to help the lorry driver. Ben nodded to him then went back inside and put the kettle on. The space in the studio could have been made bigger but was an untidy mess with all the stuff needed for the making of pictures: stacks of canvasses, some bare, some started, some discarded for various reasons, a wooden bureau with flat shallow drawers for paper. A tailor's dummy stood in the corner dressed in a military jacket. There were several easels, work tops littered with jars of brushes, pencils and markers, also tubes of paint, squeezed, twisted and distorted sitting next to palettes with their own abstract designs. Ben set two easels side by side and manoeuvered a large canvas from the back of the studio so it sat across the two easels. He angled it to catch the best light coming down from the sky light. The canvas had been under painted in a dreamy wash of sap green and lemon yellow.

'Left hand down a bit, OK OK, come on, come on, whoa, that's it.'

Ben liked the community feel of the yard. They would sit outside in deck chairs during breaks in the summer, a mixture of different, down to earth characters; the retired man who did up bicycles he retrieved from the local tip, an antique dealer who used one of the units to store spare stock. There was a tradition of help and support and a closing of ranks against petty government officials inspecting for tax dodges and flouting of health and safety rules.

Ben squeezed burnt umber and pthalo green onto his palette and thought about Rose. She was unlike the usual holidaying girls, she seemed more sophisticated and he knew she could be fiery. She was also very pretty and Ben was looking forward to their date that evening, hoping perhaps they could split up from Wilf and Janet later on, with the chance of taking things further. So far they had only kissed but she had kissed him back with urgency that Ben understood from experience. Still sharp in his memory was the act of stroking sun cream onto her back and long limbs and how she had sighed from the touch of his hands. A sigh that held a promise he was eager to call in. He poured some turps into a shallow dish and started thinning the paint on his palette.

A shadow passed across the canvas as Ben went to apply the brush to it. He looked up. There was a man standing in the doorway of the studio.

'Mr. Frampton?' He was quite a large man and his face was red with a slight sheen of perspiration on it. He wore a nylon shirt, an ill-fitting jacket and a tie that looked like it was strangling him.

'That's me,' said Ben.

'Detective Inspector Morrison,' the man said and as an afterthought reached into his inside pocket and brought out what Ben presumed was identification. It could have been his Co-op membership card for all Ben knew, never having seen a policeman's identification before now.

'How can I help?' Ben asked thinking that it would be about one of the break-ins some of the units had had recently.

'It's about your business partner, Hamish McKintyre.'

Ben looked at the police inspector and frowned. 'Hamish is a customer, not a business partner.'

'A technicality perhaps.'

Ben didn't answer.

'So this is where it all happens is it? We had a job tracking you down,' DI Morrison said and ambled further into Ben's studio with his hands in his pockets. He looked at the long canvas going across two easels. 'So what's this going to be then?'

'A Monet,' said Ben.

DI Morrison looked at Ben a bit startled. 'So you admit to painting forgeries then?'

'Forgeries?' said Ben. 'I'm painting a picture in the style of Monet for Mr McKintyre as it happens, because he can't afford the real thing at several million pounds each. If there was anything illegal in that then you would have to arrest every art student in the British Isles.'

'Oh no, nothing illegal in that as such. It's when you sign them 'Monet' and put them up for auction; that is when it becomes illegal.'

Ben suddenly felt a creeping dread that things were taking a turn that did not look good for him. There was an indication that Morrison was trying to trap him with words so Ben took a deep breath to try and keep his cool.

'I don't sign them,' Ben said.

Morrison wandered around till he was standing behind the painting. 'Why on earth would you want to paint on old canvasses?' he said looking around the side of the canvas at Ben with his eyebrows raised in inquiry. It was starting to look bad for Ben and he knew it.

'Mr McKintyre supplied them saying they were old paintings that came from his aunt's house and I might as well use them.'

'And he had a lot of these did he?'

'Looks like it doesn't it?'

'Enough to do the other Monets, Cezannes and Goggins?'

'Gaugins,' Ben corrected him.

'Don't get clever with me,' Morrison said suddenly looking stern. 'Did it never occur to you that he seemed to be ordering a lot of paintings even for a private collector?'

'He said he had friends who admired them and he was giving them away as gifts.'

'Really, and how much was he paying you for these copies?'

'Depending on size, about two hundred pounds for a medium size painting and up to four hundred and fifty for one this size.'

Morrison scoffed. 'And the rest went in your Swiss bank account I assume.'

'I don't have a Swiss bank account,' said Ben.

'Come on Mr Frampton, you had a good thing going here. You painted the pictures and McKintyre shipped them to America and sold them at auction. Your share if it was a fifty fifty split would have been several thousands of pounds.'

Ben realised that if the bit about McKintyre selling them in America was true, things did not look good for him but he held on to the fact that DI Morrison could be bluffing.

'That is such a pile of horseshit Inspector. Loads of people copy the masters or paint in the style of a particular one of them.'

'The difference is Mr Frampton,' Morrison was now pointing his finger at Ben. 'They don't sign them.'

'Neither did I,' said Ben.

'Well, that is funny isn't it, because the ones we retrieved from Mr McKintyre's house were signed and so were the ones that had already been sold in America. It was all going nicely until one of them was bought by a museum and someone spotted it as a fake. And don't even attempt to explain it away because Mr McKintyre is already in custody, and has already made a full statement.'

'But I...'

'I am arresting you for fraud and we will continue this little conversation down at the station.'

'What now?' said Ben.

'Yes now. I have a car waiting out on the street with two uniformed officers in it so don't try anything stupid.'

'Can I at least make a phone call?'

'You can when you get to the station. I advise that one of them is to a solicitor who should be present when we next interview you. If you lock up here and don't attempt anything I won't handcuff you.'

Ben closed the doors and locked them.

'Benjamin Oliver Frampton, I am charging you with fraudulently passing off your work as somebody else's with the express purpose of

increasing the value and thereby profiting illegally from the sale of said work,' DI Morrison said to Ben at the police station. 'You can make two telephone calls, one to a next of kin to explain where you are and the other to a solicitor. If you do not know of a solicitor one will be appointed to you.'

'I don't really have next of kin,' Ben said.

DI Morrison looked at him.

'My Mother's dead and I don't see my Father. I have no idea where he is even.'

'All alone in the world are you?' Morrison said.

'Can I get bail?'

'You can but you'll have to get somebody to put up security.'

'The only person I know is at work.'

'Well ring them at work then.' Morrison pushed the phone over to him.

'I can't.'

'Why not?'

'Because he is about five miles off shore in a fishing boat.'

'You'll have to ring him later then.'

'Look, I'm supposed to be seeing someone tonight and if I don't turn up they will wonder where I am.'

'Well ring them then.'

'I don't know how to get hold of her, we've only just met.'

A smile spread across Morrison's face. 'I'm sure she will understand.'

Ben banged on the desk in front of him with the flat of his hand. 'You don't give a shit do you?'

'Frankly no,' said Morrison. He turned to the uniformed officer stood behind him.

'Take him down to the cells Williams.'

PC Williams gestured to Ben to go first, with an over polite gesture that stank of sarcasm.

They went along a corridor and down some steps with Williams following closely behind. They came to a row of steel doors. Ben stopped when he heard Williams stop and a bunch of keys rattled as he selected one and opened the door of a cell. Williams leant against the wall next to the door looking at Ben. It was a world weary expectant look and Ben couldn't fathom whether there was some procedure that had to take place prior to being locked up or if he should just go into the cell. He returned Williams' look. 'Those doors at the end of the corridor open out onto the yard,' he said to Ben.

Ben looked at him confused. There were double exit doors at the end of the corridor, the sort you pushed the bars down to open.

'So?' Ben said.

'The yard gates are open during the day.'

Ben found this turn of events extraordinary. 'Are you offering me the chance to escape?' he asked.

'Come on, thicky, don't take too long to make up your mind.'

Ben weighed up the odds in microseconds. Escaping would make him look guilty but he already looked guilty. There would be a court case and possibly prison. If he acted quickly Wilf could get him across the channel. Would they bother to come after him for a minor crime? He would not be able to return but then again prison would be tough.

'OK, thanks,' he said and walked towards the doors thinking that Williams might be playing a trick on him and suddenly grab him.

'Well we can't let it look like I just let you go, can we?'

'What do you want me to do?' Ben asked.

Williams pointed at his own face. 'At least make it look like I tried to stop you.'

Ben hadn't been in any sort of fight since he left school and the idea of hitting somebody even with provocation was alien to him. Williams was suggesting that Ben punch him and punch him hard enough to make a mark. The alternative was to just go meekly into the cell where Williams was standing. He thought again of the consequences of being prosecuted, of Rose waiting for him, angry at being stood up.

'What?' said Ben. 'You want me to hit you? Why are you doing this?'

'Let's just say I think you are innocent.'

What did this pudding of a policeman know about Ben and the charge over him? Did he care about the due process of law? Did he have some sort of moral agenda of his own?

The punch Ben aimed at Williams' chin was half-hearted and probably not hard enough to leave a mark, and even though he was expecting it there was still a look of surprise on Williams' face as Ben's fist connected. He put his hand up to his face, then after a brief pause he said. 'Well go on then.'

Ben half ran down the remaining length of the corridor and pushed down on the bars of the double doors. Nothing happened. He went to turn around but before he got that far something like a battering ram hit him. His head bounced between Williams' buttoned uniform jacket and the door, and as the first punch of many landed on his face, his legs concertinaed and he sprawled across the floor. Williams stood over him grinning.

'Christ, people are dumb,' he said. 'They fall for it every time.' Then he grabbed Ben's collar and dragged him towards the cells.

STUPID STUPID STUPID

{ CHAPTER 50 }

Jo looked at the screen of her mobile phone. 'Stupid, stupid, stupid,' she said to it. She was sitting on her bed and thinking about how events had conspired into placing her in this position: found out, grounded, her father stamping around like an elephant on steroids and her mother tight lipped and upset. Then there was Justin. He hadn't phoned and although she wanted to speak to him felt she couldn't phone him and risk looking too eager. He was probably thinking the same thing – that's what was stupid. Then again perhaps he didn't want to see her again and all he had been after all along was a shag and if she hadn't spotted that before then she was stupid. There was a soft knock on her door.

FISH FARCE

'Yes,' she shouted, hoping it wasn't her father come to remonstrate about morality again or her mum for more tearful discussions. Tom put his head around the door. Jo looked up then back down at the screen on her phone. Tom came and sat next to her on the bed. He sat there for a minute then leant his head against her arm.

'I didn't tell on you,' he said.

'I know you didn't,' Jo replied and put her arm around him.

'Everyone's in a bad mood,' he complained. 'And going around as if I wasn't there.'

'Think yourself lucky,' Jo answered.

'Is it because of that job where you took your clothes off?' Tom asked.

'That's about it, yeah,' said Jo.

'I don't think it was all that bad,' Tom said.

'Thanks,' she gave his shoulders a squeeze.

'Dad said you've got a boyfriend.'

'Did he?'

'Dad said he's old enough to be your father. Does that mean he's as old as Dad?'

'No, he's exaggerating; he's only a bit older than me.'

'And Dad said he's only after one thing, is that true?'

'I don't know yet.'

'Why don't you ask him?'

'It's not that simple.'

'Yes, but if you tell him you haven't got it, like if it was the Staff of Ra in the Indiana Jones movie, then he wouldn't be after you if you haven't got it, would he?'

'Maybe I have got something as valuable as the Staff of Ra.' Jo smiled

'Can't you just tell him you haven't got it then?'

Jo worked out the possible problems of explaining to Tom his misconception of the situation and realising what a monstrous task it was, settled on simplicity.

'Justin is a really nice person, he's fun and interesting and I think you would really like him.'

'When can I meet him?'

'Oh, I don't know,' said Jo letting go of Tom and laying back on the bed, still looking at her phone and willing it to ring.

'Do you think he'd like to play Zombie Warriors?'

'I expect so,' said Jo who was not really listening.

Tom stood up. He didn't really understand how grown-ups could get so moody about stupid things.

He paused at the door. 'Can I ask you something?'

'Go on then,' Jo said.

'Have you done sex with him yet?'

Jo tore her gaze away from the screen of the phone and looked at Tom, not sure how to answer so direct a question.

'No of course not,' she said, but she had gone very red.

THE PLAN

{ CHAPTER 51 }

Kevin was on washing up duty. He had filled the bowl in the sink and squirted a good third of the bottle of Peach and Cranberry washing up liquid into it. The action of the water coming out of the tap had created a cloud of bubbles that now threatened to overflow the sink and was engulfing the taps. Kevin batted away some of the foam to find the tap and turn it off. He plunged his hands in the water and screamed. It was near boiling and he jumped away from the sink, alternately, flapping his hands in the air and squeezing them between his thighs to try and allay the pain. When it had subsided he located the cold tap and turned it on. More bubbles appeared and when Kevin was satisfied with the temperature of the water he started on the stack of plates, mugs and cutlery piled on the draining board.

The pile of washing-up looked to Kevin like Mount Impossible and several times he laid his elbows on the edge of the sink, lowered his head and sighed. Each time he did tackle it the repetitive action of circular motion of brush on plate could only be relieved by looking out of the window and into the street below. This sent Kevin into a reverie where random thoughts floated and collided, and a plate could take a full five minutes of rhythmic washing and the pile of dirty dishes never seemed to diminish.

Grace came into the kitchen and Kevin, hearing her, broke off from his day dreaming to look more industrious. Grace spotted the large cloud of bubbles around the sink area.

'Are you rinsing Kevin?' she asked.

'Er yes,' Kevin lied.

Grace leant against the sink. 'Who were those guys?' she asked.

Kevin told her about the club and Ray and Dave the bouncer.

'How did you get mixed up with them?'

Kevin described how he had come to be at the club and how, bizarrely, it had turned into an offer of a free flat. Kevin had never really bothered too much about why one moment he was being threatened with police intervention for selling drugs and the next being offered a flat rent free.

Grace, who had offered her services to the tenants of Belvedere Heights, now squared the circle with the information Kevin was giving her.

'You realise now why this Ray character let you use the flat then?'

'Not really,' Kevin said.

Grace sighed. It wasn't really worth labouring the point with Kevin.

'And how did Edward Spigott fit into all this?' she asked instead.

'Spig?' said Kevin grinning. 'He's just there isn't he? He just turns up.'

'I think Edward has some serious issues,' Grace said.

'Yeah,' Kevin said. 'He.....' Kevin stopped, thinking it wasn't wise to tell Grace about Spig's propensity for starting fires. Grace always got serious about certain things and wanted to deal with situations. Kevin couldn't understand this, he just accepted things. If he told Breath about anything like that he would just laugh in his gormless way about it. That was the difference.

'He what?' Grace asked.

'Nuffin,' Kevin replied. He had other reasons for keeping quiet about Spig and his pyromania.

He had recently been back to see Ray at the club, fearing the threat Ray had made about going to the police, not realising it had been a bluff. He had not been looking forward to going back to the club remembering his last visit there with the ever present likelihood of violence from the formidably built Dave. He had been accompanied to Ray's office by Dave. Ray seemed obsessed by the destruction of the music system that Kevin had destroyed. It was not as if it had been an up to date one or particularly new. Kevin had just thought it was part of the furniture like the sofa and the kitchen table, but the idea had been to impress on Kevin the fact that he owed him big time. Ray had told Dave to leave them when he put to Kevin a proposition that seemed totally unconnected with the flat, dealing drugs or the destruction of the sound system, but as Kevin never understood how his dealings with Ray connected he didn't let it worry him.

'I've got a little job for you,' Ray said. 'And if you do this for me we're square, quits, OK?'

'What is it?' Kevin asked, forever wary of Ray.

'When you do this you'll be working on your own. Nothing comes back to me. If you get caught you keep your mouth shut about who got you to do it.'

'Yeah, but what is it you want me to do?'

'You know the art gallery down by the tennis courts and the fish shop.'

'What Dean's Plaice?'

'Not the fish shop, the art gallery.'

'Oh yeah.'

'It's called 'Fish Works'.'

'Yeah, the fish shop.'

'No, the art gallery, Jesus.'

'Yeah, yeah, I know.'

'It's going to meet with a little accident.'

'Is it?'

'Yes,' said Ray. 'And you're going to make it happen.'

'Am I?'

'Yes, it's going to burn down. I want you to cause a fire at the art gallery.'

'What for?' asked Kevin.

'The owner is a friend of mine and he wants to burn it down for the insurance.'

'Oh, right.' An idea was forming in Kevin's mind.

'Nobody gets hurt; the place is empty at night. You get a rag and a bit of petrol, soak the rag, light it and stick it through the letter box. Make sure nobody sees you. It'll be like that place on the seafront that went up in flames the other night.'

'Yeah,' said Kevin.

'So, what are you going to do?'

'I am going to cause a fire at the art gallery and burn it down.'

'How are you going to do it?' Ray asked, making sure Kevin got it right.

'Get an oily rag, put it through the letter box and light it.'

'Light it first then put it through the letter box.'

'Yeah, OK.'

'And you tell no one, got it?'

'Yeah,' said Kevin. 'But...'

'But what?' Ray said.

'It's a lot to ask just for a broken sound system.'

Ray looked at him.

'It's a risk, innit?' said Kevin.

'So you want some money as well do you?'

Kevin started to feel nervous that Ray was going to get nasty. Ray took a key from his pocket that seemed to be on a long chain and opened a drawer in his desk. He took out a wad of notes, licked his thumb and counted out several from the top. 'Two hundred pounds do you then?'

Kevin nodded. Ray handed him the cash.

'Right, now listen,' Ray said. 'No slip-ups and no blabbing, got it?'

'I'm taking Bo down to the Job Centre,' Grace said.

Kevin, who had still not finished the washing up, was sporting two rings of foam around each elbow so it looked like he was wearing puffed sleeves. He looked at Bo and Grace standing by the entrance to the kitchen.

'Cool,' Kevin said even though he thought it was the least cool thing he had ever heard.

The front door closed and Kevin went back to the washing-up. He groaned, the pile seemed to have got bigger if anything. What's happening, he thought, I'm washing up, Bo's getting a job, where did the glory days go, getting stoned on the beach?

The doorbell rang and Kevin dried his hands on his jeans and made his way to answer it. He opened it a crack.

'Hello,' a voice said.

'Yay Spig,' Kevin said opening the door wide. Spig was

surprised by the response he got from Kevin as all he got usually was a grunt.

'Not here, is she?' Spig asked, looking around him as he came into the hall.

'Who?' Kevin asked.

'Grace.'

'No, why?'

'She doesn't half go on,' Spig said wrinkling his nose.

'Oh yeah,' said Kevin grinning. 'I know what you mean.'

'Says she wants to take me to Social Services and all that lark. What are you doing?'

'Just chilling,' said Kevin.

'What's that then?' Spig pointed to the suds on Kevin's arms.

'Oh, and doin' a bit of washing up.'

Spig looked at him astonished.

'Yeah, well,' said Kevin. 'It's gotta be done.'

Spig sat down at the kitchen table. 'Got a ciggy,' he said.

Kevin pushed a packet of cigarettes and his lighter over to him. Spig lit up, took a drag, and blew the smoke out through his nose. Kevin took the lighter from Spig and lit it looking at Spig through the flame.

'Remember Smoky Joe's?' Kevin said.

Spig looked at him, a smile spreading across his face at the memory.

'Wanna do another one like that?' Kevin said already knowing the answer.

A FEW WHISKIES

{ CHAPTER 52 }

'I didn't think I had any children,' Ben said to the barman. 'Now it turns out I've actually got two. Life's weird like that isn't it?'

'It sure is,' said the barman. He was looking at Ben's unfocused eyes until Ben looked down at the bar for his glass. He went to pick it up and missed. 'Whoops,' he said and got it on the next attempt.

'So you see,' he continued. 'Er, where was I?'

'You've got two children,' the barman reminded him, hoping this wasn't going to be a long rambling maudlin, cod philosophical monologue with unconnected tangents about the unthankful task of being a parent, the ungrateful nature of teenagers, how he had wished he had followed his dream instead of settling down with someone like Gladys who now looked like her mother and watched soaps all day.

'Yes, you see, I didn't know about either of them. One moment you're just happily living your life and the next moment along comes this guy and says 'Hello, do you remember something that happened thirty years ago?' And you know what? I don't, why should I? I mean thirty years is a long time. Then he wants some sort of test but he doesn't look a bit like me, then he starts going with this girl and her mother comes along and says 'Hey, do you remember me? We had a fling a while back and guess what? You have a daughter.' So this guy who claims he's my son can't go with her because they might be half siblings then her dad comes along and wants to sue me and then the mother comes back and buys the painting off me. I can't tell her I'm her dad and the boy can't tell her why he can't see her anymore and the whole thing is a bit of conandum, comumdrum corrundum....'

'I think it's time you went home, do you want me to get you a taxi?' the barman asked.

'I'm absolutely fine thank you,' Ben replied and drained his glass.

He had left the Falkirk Hotel and Justin a couple of hours earlier and gone into the first hotel where he could get a drink, and ordered half a lager as if he needed to swill his mouth out after swabbing it with the cotton stick for the DNA test. Being in a hotel with drink reminded Ben of a drinking game he and some of his friends had indulged in when he was younger and more reckless. The idea of the game was to try and get along the seafront from west to east and have half a pint in every establishment along the way. At the smarter end some places would not serve them or were residents only but as they got further east and more inebriated the places were not so fussy. They used to get extremely drunk and would argue the next day, through head-thumping hangovers, how far they had got and in which of the posher establishments they had managed to get served. There were never any winners but that wasn't the point.

Whether it was the memory of this or the complex situations arising around him to do with his possible progeny he was not sure, but after visiting several of the hotels and bars along the front, he had lost count of how many halves he had had. He only knew that at some point he had switched to whisky owing to the fact that he could only take so much beer into his body without feeling bloated. It was usually at this point he stopped drinking but tonight the numbing effect of the alcohol had been welcome, allowing relief from the ramifications of all the things that had happened over the last few days.

Once outside the bar he stood against the railings, looking out over the sea and watching the mesmeric effect of the waves curling around the barnacled posts of the pier supports. He made his way east holding onto the rail for its steadying effect. He thought of going to see Wendy. He wanted to talk, to tell someone about Jo, this girl he was now rather pleased to know was his daughter. He could tell Wendy, even though he was sworn to secrecy. Everyone always thought they could tell just one other person even the darkest secret. Telling Wendy might help even though she would not be able to come up with a solution – there wasn't a solution, he just wanted to unload all this emotional baggage.

The street lights got fewer, the railings came to an end as Ben stumbled past the beach huts. He knew all their names: Ma's Bar, Pizza Hut, Love Shack, Sea la Vie. Wendy wouldn't want to see him in this state and anyway it was late and she had probably gone to bed. Wilf wouldn't take kindly to be woken either if he was getting up with the tide to go fishing.

Suddenly Ben felt desperately tired, and as he approached the gallery realised that all he wanted to do was to fall onto the sofa in his office and crash out into oblivion. He fumbled with his keys and opened the door closing it behind him and locking it again. He didn't want to put any lights on, his eyes had got used to the dark and he didn't want to be blinded. Besides, he thought, he knew his way around everything without requiring any light.

He banged his leg into the corner of the reception desk. 'Shit,' he muttered, and put his hand out knocking sideways the canvas on the easel. He located the wall and kept his fingertips in contact with it as he navigated the short corridor to his office. He walked into the door, bashing his head and knee at the same time. Once through the door Ben put his hand out tentatively to locate the arm of the sofa. He sank down into the cushions, just managing to remove his shoes before laying down full length. Within thirty seconds he was snoring.

THE NIGHTMARE

{ CHAPTER 53 }

The dream always started in the same way, and even in the dream Wilf knows how it will end, but still has to go through every part, unable to stop the passage of events that lead to the conclusion. It starts with a calm sea, early morning with a mist swirling over the surface of the water. Wilf is in his boat and it is drifting, no engine sound, it is quiet. He sees something floating. He doesn't have to turn the wheel because the boat is drifting towards it; either that or it is drifting towards him. It reminds him of the beginning of the 'Arena' programme with the bottle floating on the sea, and he can even hear the dreamy Brian Eno music as the thing gets nearer and nearer. But it is not a bottle, it's a body. Every detail is clear and as the dream progresses Wilf knows he is approaching its ghastly climax. The body is lying in the water face down. It is bloated from being submerged for some time and the clothes are stretched tight over the flesh because of it. The body is male with thick matted hair on the back of the head, a shirt that is torn and jeans. Through the torn shirt he can see the pale, white flesh, puckered with a strange greenish tinge.

Wilf knows what he must do. As the body reaches the side of the boat he reaches for his gaff hook and manages to get it under the belt of the man's jeans. He knows he will never get the body into the boat without having to handle it. The flesh feels tight and slippery and a creeping horror comes over him that if he is not careful it might split. He holds the body against the side of the boat. He is leaning over and struggling. He cannot lift it, and the only way he might get it into the boat is by rolling it. This is the point he dreads, he knows what is going to happen but he can't stop the dream. The body turns as he starts to roll it and as the front comes into view he sees that the man has no face. Where his face should be there is just a hole, an empty crater, dark and fissured with bits of jagged bone and threads of white tattered flesh still attached to it.

It is now that Wilf wakes up, his heart thumping and his skin damp with sweat. This is no nightmare made up in Wilf's mind, and not something remembered from a horror film, this scenario was real and happened to Wilf years ago, the shock so great it appears in his dreams at times of stress, the image forever burnt into his brain ready to surface, magnificent in its detail and horror.

The man had been a local amateur fisherman, known to Wilf which made it worse. He had been caught out at sea in a thick mist and mown down by a ferry as big and impersonal as a block of flats. No one on the ferry was aware of the accident as the man's boat was crushed and splintered, the man flailing and falling into the water, caught in the undertow of the massive ship and drawn inexorably into the churning blades of the propeller that sliced his face off and left him for the salt water and fishes to deal with, until Wilf happened along.

Wilf got out of bed. It was no good trying to get back to sleep after the nightmare. He knew that from experience. He looked out of the bedroom windows. The moon lit the sea in its shadowy, colourless way, the troughs between the waves dark and the surf a ghostly white.

He got dressed. He knew why he had had the nightmare again. What was it they said, he thought to himself – 'a friend is someone you can call on at four in the morning' and then conversely 'a friend is someone who doesn't call you at four in the morning.' Wendy had rung Wilf that evening to ask if he had seen Ben and if he also thought Ben was troubled. Perhaps he couldn't sleep either. She was worried about him. He had not been to see her for several days and she knew he had things on his mind. Uppermost had been the paternity issue with Justin but there were other things he had said he couldn't talk about. Usually if Ben wasn't at the gallery or at Wendy's, he was with Wilf. But Wilf hadn't seen him.

It was chilly as Wilf walked through the scrub and dunes towards town, his way lit by the moon. He felt better striding out, the sound and rhythm of the sea to his left. He wanted to get his thoughts in order and clear before he spoke to Ben. Of course, Ben didn't remember the events of over thirty years earlier but Wilf did. Wilf remembered it as clear as yesterday but then, he hadn't been arrested and beaten up in a police cell by a thug of a policeman and suffered concussion.

Wilf reached the part of the seafront where the shingle turned to concrete and where the promenade started. He wasn't sure what to do, wake Ben up now or sit and wait till the sun came up and knock at a more reasonable hour. He could see the tennis courts in the distance.

By the time he was level with them Wilf had broken into a run, all the concerns about when to contact Ben gone. He smelled smoke at first, just a whiff in the air, and then as he got nearer and the smell stronger he could see a glow in the windows of the gallery. Stupid son of a bitch, Wilf thought, thinking Ben had dropped a cigarette carelessly in the gallery. Wilf thundered on the door with both fists calling Ben's name. He kicked at the bottom of the door and then tried his shoulder against it, half aware that these things only work in movies. He could feel the heat through the door and hear its ominous rumble. Thoughts of ringing the fire brigade were quickly dismissed as action was required now if Ben was inside.

He looked around him. Lying on the shingle at the top of the beach was a large chunk of driftwood. He remembered helping Ben to lug it up from the shoreline for an idea he had of making it into a plinth for a sculpture. It must have been a piece of a groyne at one time. It was about three feet long and had two massive bolts through it. He remembered they joked that it was Frankenstein's monster driftwood. Wilf could barely lift it on his own but he manhandled it to the door managing to get it into a horizontal position for long enough to crash the end into the door by the lock. The door splintered and swung inwards. The rush of oxygen into the building created a burst of flame that rolled towards Wilf as he dropped the battering ram. He staggered backwards.

Thick smoke stung his eyes and scorched his throat choking him. Wilf knew he had to go in low as smoke and heat rose. He crouched down and moved forwards hoping he would still be able to get through. Flames were crackling all around him but there was no light owing to the smoke. Wilf knew the layout of the gallery and navigated the desk tripping on the fallen easel the Ben had knocked down earlier. The heat was unbearable but as he got past the main reception area and into the corridor it eased a bit but the smoke was still thick, and by now his lungs were heaving, his eyes seared by it and next to useless. The door of the office was open and Wilf felt for Ben on the sofa just inside the door. He shook him and shouted his name several times but there was no response. The smoke must have already got to him and Wilf realised he was going to have to manhandle him out of danger, if it wasn't already too late and there was no time to try and ascertain that now.

There was no way he was going to be able to lift him, Ben was no light weight. Wilf realised he could only drag him. He started rolling Ben towards him to get him onto the floor and visions of the corpse at the side of the boat came back to him. He tried getting his arms under Ben's arm pits, but being a dead weight and not helped by the sweat running down Wilf's arms, he kept slipping back out his grasp. Wilf felt the agonising frustration of not being able to move him and knowing that time was running out.

'Come on, come on, you stupid bastard, I'm not going to let you die like this.' He grabbed hold of Ben's belt and the scruff of his shirt and managed to start dragging him into the corridor. He could feel the heat intensifying and searing his back as if his clothes were on fire. Suddenly there was a crashing noise behind him and Wilf turned. A portion of the roof had caved in. Flames shot into the night sky and pulsed outwards, pushed by the sections and joists of the roof coming down. A tongue of flame caught Wilf's hair and it crackled like a torch before Wilf rubbed both hands over it to smother it. He didn't feel any pain, that would come later, but the path to the main door was now cut off. He grabbed Ben's ankles and started dragging him back towards the office.

The window in the office was now the only option but getting a dead weight over the sill and out of the building was going to be next to impossible. Now the roof had caved in there was more material to feed the flames and they were roaring towards the office. He managed to get Ben back there and kicked the door shut. Fat lot of good that will do he thought, fire doors were not something they had thought to invest in. He dragged Ben over to the window. The flames were eating through the door and the partition wall was already buckling and bulging. He managed to get the window open but spluttering with the smoke he had no time to appreciate the sweet cool air. With one last superhuman effort he got his arms under Ben's torso, laced his fingers together and heaved upwards. He managed to get Ben's head and shoulders over the sill but still not enough to stop him slipping back while he repositioned his hands. He struggled, crying with the frustration and the effort of nearly being there but still with the prospect of failure. Then he realised Ben was moving with no effort from him, and in the gloom of the night outside he was able to make out the uniformed figures of firemen in their navy jackets and yellow helmets. Hands were taking over from him pulling the inert figure of Ben out of the building. With the relief that he no longer had to struggle, Wilf's legs crumpled and he lost consciousness.

BUGGER OFF THEN

{ CHAPTER 54 }

Jo stood looking at the smoking remains of the Fish Works Art Gallery. The windows were blown out, the roof collapsed, the door caved in. Blackened fragments of glass lay on the concrete outside. Jo had escaped from home risking further punishment for breaking her curfew, but she couldn't just sit at home wondering what was going on with Justin.

After much agonising she had eventually phoned him, in fact she had phoned him several times and each time he had declined to take the call. Wondering what was going on she had sent him a simple text to ask him where he was. She had thought about it a long time to make sure it sounded light hearted with no trace of angst or desperation. Nothing came back. Had he gone home? She thought back to the girl friend, the one he said he'd broken up with, or was that just a ploy? If it was all over, she thought, she would rather know why than not know at all.

In the end she decided to do her usual jog along the seafront and stop off at the Falkirk Hotel just to see if he was there. Finding the Fish Works Art Gallery as a burnt out ruin was a major surprise. As she stood and stared, a man walking his dog slowed down to look also.

'Bloody kids,' he said.

'How do you know it was kids?' Jo asked, annoyed at the bigoted statement.

'Stands to reason doesn't it? Someone did that snack bar on the seafront a little while ago. Either that or an insurance job.'

'Was anyone hurt?' Jo asked.

'I doubt it,' the man said. 'It happened last night. The place would have been empty.'

'S'pose so,' said Jo and carried on jogging. She felt sorry for Ben and sorry that a disaster should befall him. She liked Ben, he was different to most adults. He didn't talk down to her or treat her differently just because she was a teenager. The life modelling job was over anyway, and wondering if Justin knew about it, took her thoughts back to why she was jogging along the seafront with the express purpose of going to see him.

She plodded on. It was hot. It had been a long dry summer but the heat was beginning to pall, and unlike the reaction of people when the first warm days start, they were now getting irritable and tetchy. Everywhere was dry and desiccated, refuse stank, litter skidded along the concrete of the esplanade blown by an onshore breeze. An empty can rattled across the shingle as Jo drew nearer to the Falkirk. She sat on one of the seafront benches to get her breath back, thinking of a scenario where there might have been some misunderstanding and everything was fine, but she scoffed at her Mills and Boon, wishful thinking, although still secretly hoping it could be true. She didn't want to come across as angry and make some sort of heavy scene. If it was all over she would pretend she was not bothered. Perhaps it would be easier if he had already left, even if she might then never know the reason behind him just taking off.

She went through the entrance doors of the hotel and up to the reception desk. There was a youngish guy behind the desk in a white shirt and black waistcoat. He had short, spiky gelled hair and Jo reckoned he was the same age as her possibly even younger.

'Is Mr Danbury still staying here?' she asked.

'I'll have a look,' he replied. His fingers scampered across a keyboard out of Jo's line of vision as he studied a screen. 'Checked out a little while ago,' he said.

Jo couldn't help her spirits wilting. 'OK, thanks,' she said.

The young man grinned thinking he could read the situation.

'What?' Jo said to him.

'Nothing,' he said, his grin wiped in a moment. 'He's only just gone, he might still be in the car park.'

Jo looked around her.

'Through there,' he said.

Jo went through a rear door and past a store room. She could hear the clatter of the kitchen somewhere. Around the corner was the hotel's small car park. Justin had the rear door of his car open and was putting stuff onto the back seat. All resolve about being cool was forgotten seeing him getting ready to leave without having contacted her. She leaned against the corner of the building watching him. He stowed a bag and stood there as if making sure he had everything. A couple of yards away four elderly people were getting out of a Ford Mondeo, the two men helping the ladies out of the back seats. Jo took no notice of them.

'See you then,' she called out to Justin.

He spun round. 'Jo.'

'Oh, you remember.' She hated the sarcasm in her voice.

From the Ford Mondeo, a foot sensibly shod, although narrower than the puffed ankle above it, hovered over the tarmac. A white permed head moved back and forth trying to get momentum to move the body from the seat as one of the men pulled on her arm to help. She looked like a bird trying to extricate itself from a tight shell.

'I was going to contact you.' Justin said.

'Really,' Jo replied. 'When, a month, a year?'

Eventually the woman stood, smoothing her clothes down with her hands as if they were ruffled feathers. She moved towards the entrance wincing at each step and passing close to Jo.

'Look Jo, it's really complicated.' Justin was annoyed that he couldn't tell her the truth. He didn't know what was worse, leaving without a word or lying. Now he was caught he would have to lie.

'Which bit is complicated,' Jo asked. 'Fucking me or fucking off?'

The woman's head swivelled. 'Well really,' she said.

'It's not what you think. There are things I need to do,' Justin said seemingly oblivious of the four spectators to their exchange. 'I have to go home for a bit.'

'Back to Amy is it?'

'Something like that. I need to see her, sort things out.' It was too tempting to resist, an easy excuse, still a letdown but not as stark as saying he had just changed his mind.

Jo absorbed the impact. 'Why didn't you tell me,' she said. 'I would have understood.' Her anger was fading. If sentiment took its place she was done for and the last thing she wanted to do was cry, that would be too pathetic for words. Justin looked at her. Everything he wanted to say he couldn't.

'I didn't know where to start,' he said, moving towards her.

'I suppose it was a fair trade,' she said. 'You helped me and got a shag as a reward. Bit like the way Cyril operates really.'

The other three other occupants of the car, who by now were following the first woman, had decided to ignore the lovers tiff and walked by them towards the entrance as if nothing was going on.

'Please,' Justin said. 'Don't say that.' Even though she sounded angry he could see tears in her eyelashes.

'Go on. Just bugger off,' she said.

He went to try and put his arms around her but she pushed him away. 'What's the point?' she said. 'Just go.'

Justin shrugged, annoyed that she had fended him off. He hated leaving on such a bad note but it was unavoidable.

'Look, I have to sort something out. I will get back to you.'

'What? String me along in case it doesn't work out with your girlfriend.'

'It's more complicated than that; you wouldn't understand.'

'I think I understand perfectly,' she shot back and turned to go. 'Have a nice life.'

'Don't be angry,' he said.

'I can't help it,' Jo said.

Justin watched her go feeling despair at not being able to handle the situation better. Eventually he got into his car and turned the ignition.

IN THE HOSPITAL

{ CHAPTER 55 }

Ben could hear his mother's voice. She wasn't calling, it was as if she was just chatting to someone in the next room. His throat was sore and his eyes swollen and scratchy and he was stuck somewhere. Stuck and not knowing where he was. He struggled but it felt like he was wading through treacle. He was in some kind of labyrinth, corridors went off in several directions with rooms dotted along each one, containing a memory of childhood. He could hear his mother's voice coming from one of them.

Was this a dream? Or had he died and this was some form of purgatory, having to relive his life like they said you did, and to do it by entering each room in turn. Some of the doors were locked. Some opened but there was nothing in them, just an overpowering sense of nostalgia like smelling the inside of a school satchel and being back at school in an instant. Some held a tantalising glimpse of a forgotten episode, a single thing like the veranda of a house, a dog splashing in a stream, a girl's skirt riding up her thighs, all with their separate stories but with the rest behind a veil and out of reach.

Over all this was his Mother's voice, calm and chatty. He pictured her, red lipstick, curled hair and the inevitable cigarette. He felt a sensation of rising, reaching somewhere, moving towards the voice. He struggled to speak, his mouth and throat were glued, his tongue stuck to the roof of his mouth. He tried to open his eyes and it was like scraping a toothbrush over his eyeballs. Misty, crystalised light got through the slits he managed to open. He saw movement, smelt a mixture of shepherd's pie and carbolic. He worked the muscles of his mouth, tried to work up some spit from his saliva glands. Eventually he was able to say: 'Mum?'

'I'm not your Mum,' the nurse said.

'Where am I?' Ben managed.

'You're in 'orspital,' she replied.

'What happened?'

'You were in a fire,' she said, and as an afterthought: 'I think.'

'I'll tell the doctor you've come round'

'Can I have some water please?' Ben asked.

The nurse picked up a plastic beaker, like a child's cup, with a straw, and held it for Ben. He lifted his head off the pillow and sucked through the straw. He felt pain at the act of swallowing from his chemically attacked throat and winced.

'Thanks,' he said, his head sinking back into the pillows. He closed his eyes.

IN THE HOSPITAL

More time passed slipping in and out of strange states of half dreaming and of random thoughts, coalescing and creating bizarre situations before fading. How much time passed he did not know and when he opened the slits in his eyes again there was a tall ruddy man standing next to his bed. He reminded Ben of a farmer he had once known. Only the stethoscope, that badge of medical authority, informed Ben he was a doctor.

'How do you feel?' the doctor asked.

'Worse than I look, I think.'

The doctor smiled. 'Do you have soreness in your throat and airways?'

'Yes,' Ben replied.

'Feel dizziness and nausea?'

'Oh yes.'

'Pains in the chest?'

'Yes, worst hangover I've ever had.'

The doctor laughed. 'Yes, we did find a little bit of blood in your alcohol. It probably didn't help. Nasty business smoke inhalation, never know what's in it.'

'I thought smoke was smoke,' Ben said.

'Unfortunately it's not that simple, there's a lot of carbon monoxide in it which is not only toxic, it starves the body of oxygen. Then there are other poisonous gases depending on what is burning, cyanide, that sort of thing. We have to run a few tests and it will be a chance to get over the hangover.'

'What actually happened doctor?' Ben asked.

'From what I gather from police and the ambulance team you were asleep when the fire started and someone rescued you. Apparently he risked his life otherwise you would be in the mortuary instead of hospital.'

'Where is he now?'

'He's in the burns unit. He suffered some injuries from the

fire as well as smoke inhalation.

'Who was it? I'll need to thank him.'

'I don't know his name. You'll get to see him in time.'

'Where was the fire?

'I don't know, they don't tell us much about how people ended up here. Somewhere on the seafront I think.'

Ben slept some more. He had assumed it was the gallery but at the present moment he couldn't care less. The clatter and bustle of the ward meant he slipped in and out of sleep, mixing dreams with reality. He felt pressure on his forehead and opened his eyes. Wendy stood there looking down at him having kissed his forehead.

'You silly boy. What have you been doing?'

Ben tried to smile, pleased to see a friendly face. 'Getting drunk mostly.'

'And setting fire to yourself.'

'Not intentionally.'

'Well you made a good job of it.'

'How bad is it?'

'The gallery? It's gone. Well, one end is still standing, with a few pictures still on it, but badly damaged. I'm afraid all the work that was in there is gone. Some bits in the office didn't burn but again they are smoke damaged. Oil based paints, so I am reliably informed by the firemen, are highly combustible. They think you must have been working and left a cigarette burning.'

'I was in no fit state to work.'

'They are sending in fire investigators.'

'I suppose they suspect insurance fraud.'

'Was it insured?' Wendy asked.

'Wilf insured the building.'

'Had you insured the contents?'

'What do you think?' Ben risked another grin. 'Does Wilf

know what's happened?'

'I should think so, it was Wilf who pulled you out of the fire.'

'Wilf?' Ben said lifting his head off the pillow and wincing. 'I didn't know it was Wilf. What was he doing there?'

'No one knows yet. He's in a pretty bad way. But he may have come to find you because I rang him earlier to ask whether he'd seen you.'

'Why?' Ben asked.

'Because I was worried about you.'

'Oh,' was all Ben could say.

'I know you've had a lot of things on your plate recently. I was concerned.'

'Yes, of course. Thanks. I didn't realise.' Ben didn't like to think of someone worrying about him. He felt awkward about it but touched at the same time.

'I'll go and see Wilf now and let you know how he is.' Wendy said.

CITIZEN'S ARREST

{ CHAPTER 56 }

Jo ran as if physical effort could overcome, or even blot, out the anger and hurt she was feeling from her encounter with Justin. At least she hadn't cried, that was something, but all resolve to pretend she didn't care had gone the moment the first sarcastic comment had tripped off her tongue. So that was it. He would go now and she would go through the process of trying to forget him. She didn't regret losing her virginity with him, the time was right and it had been her decision. After all, she had given him the most obvious come-on, dropping her towel in front of him. Perhaps he was just being polite. She had offered herself on a plate so to speak, she could hardly complain. It was just that it seemed so right,

right at the time and right that it was Justin. What peeved her was the fact that her reading of Justin and the situation had been so off beam. Lesson learnt.

She breathed to the rhythm of her silent padding, and the beating of her heart, which seemed to calm her. She had not run for days, not since her father had first grounded her, and it felt good to be doing something physical again. She ran faster and for longer than normal pushing herself harder and harder, partly because of the need for exercise and partly to try and expunge her emotions. She ran past the hotels, past the flats, past the roads that terminated at the seafront and led back to different parts of the town, past the war memorial, past the statue of Lord Something or Other whose family had owned most of the town since Regency times, although he didn't look very happy about it, past the entrance to the pier with the rock and candy floss stalls, past the fish and chip shops, down as far as the sailing club where the dinghies were parked on the beach and the halyards on the masts tapped out a rhythm that sounded eerie even on a summer's day.

She stopped and leant on the railings. Sweat ran down her face, down the valley of her spine to the small of her back and down her legs. There was a shelter, one of the old double ones with back to back seats separated by a partition of frosted glass. The side looking out to sea was occupied so Jo went and sat the other side that looked out across the road and into a park beyond. She felt the buzz that the run had given her and she waited while her breathing slowed. There was a corner broken off and missing in one of the panes of glass in the partition and Jo could hear a rumble of voices from the other side. As she leaned back she could hear the voices more clearly. At first she didn't take a lot of notice then something she heard made her listen more intently.

'You won't tell anyone, will you Kev?' The voice sounded frightened.

'Not likely to am I? You're sure no one saw you?'

'Course I am.'

'And you haven't told no-one?'

'Not stupid am I?'

'Christ,' Kevin breathed. 'Let's just hope they go on thinking the fire was an accident.'

'I just did what you said and you said the place would be empty.'

Jo realised now that they must be talking about the gallery. She leaned her head back against the glass trying to catch more.

'Is he all right?' Spig asked.

'Course he's not all right, he's in hospital.'

'How do you know?'

'I heard it on the news.'

'I'm frightened,' said Spig.

'Just keep a low profile. They don't suspect arson at the moment; they think it might have been an accident.'

Jo had no idea who they were but they were obviously talking about the fire at the art gallery, and contrary to what the guy with the dog had said earlier when she first went past it someone had been hurt. The thought that it might be Ben, and that she should find out how he was, came second to the fact that she might have stumbled on the only real evidence of the perpetrators. She got up and jogged a little way back up the seafront from the direction she had come and then walked casually back to get a look at the characters in the shelter. They took no notice of her and as she drew level with them they stood up. Jo slowed her pace, and as they were about to move on, she decided to follow them. All that she knew about them was the snippet of conversation she had overheard, what they looked like, and that one of them was called Kev. It wasn't a lot of evidence to go on but it might just be the only bit of evidence that proved the fire was not accidental. Following them could just give her more information such as where they lived.

Kevin and Spig crossed the road and Jo followed casually at a distance. At a junction with a road going into the town they parted company. Kevin carried on along the seafront and Spig took the road inland. Jo made a quick decision, she had a name for the older one so decided to follow the younger one who looked a bit like the Milky Bar Kid. He walked hunched over with his hands in his pockets. It was a long road of terraced houses and Jo hung back hoping it wasn't obvious that she was following him. He turned a corner at a junction and spotted Jo out of the corner of his eye.

Half way down the next road Spig glanced over his shoulder. The girl was still following him. He wasn't sure if she was actually following him or whether she just happened to be going the same way, but in his heightened state of nervousness, paranoia got the better of him and he started to run, slowly at first, as if he was just in a hurry to get somewhere. After a few yards he flicked another glance over his shoulder. That confirmed it, she was running too.

Spig panicked. They were running down a street of houses and Spig knew there was an alley a few yards away coming up on his left. He put on a spurt of speed and as he came level with it he turned quickly and ran even faster down the cinder track. Jo realised at this point that she had to decide what she was going to do if she caught him. Now he knew he was being pursued he was hardly going to lead her to his home address. He was unlikely to offer up any information and making some sort of citizen's arrest was out of the question. But she wasn't about to give up the chase yet.

Spig came to the end of the alley where it joined another suburban road. He crossed it, and knowing all the alleys as well as he did, shot down another back alley behind some houses. He knew this led nowhere but he had a plan. Reaching a fence at the end he jumped and caught the top of it with both hands, swung one leg over the top and dropped into the garden the other side. Luckily there was no one to see him and he was hoping that this ploy might shake off his pursuer. The jump had made him lose his balance and he ended up sprawled in a patch of cabbages. He righted himself and ran across the garden to a gate at the far end of it. This joined another alley that ran behind the houses and next to some industrial units cordoned by a fence of metal palings topped with barbed spikes.

He crouched down to see if he was still being followed and through the branches of bushes growing by the gate saw that the girl was climbing the fence to continue following him. Panicking that he had failed to lose her, Spig set off again. Further along the fence there was a gap left from a break-in and was, as yet, unrepaired. Spig managed to squeeze through the gap into a yard littered with crash damaged vehicles. Jo emerged onto the path, having also tiptoed through some stranger's vegetable patch, following the obvious footprints of her quarry in the soft earth. She stood and looked down the straight path that led off into the distance, with no sign of the kid. There was no way he could have got to the end so he must have somehow made a detour or was hiding somewhere. Jo started a slow run looking to her right and left as she went along.

There was a ditch on the left, overgrown with nettles and brambles, separating the back gardens of the houses from the industrial estate. If he was amongst that lot, thought Jo, she was never going to find him but the density of it made it unlikely he was in there. A bit further on Jo stopped and looked around again, then spotted the gap in the fence. She bent down, angled her shoulders, and managed to wriggle through. She ended up standing by an Audi TT with a badly crumpled front wing. It was a Sunday so there was nobody about.

Spig, using the few minutes advantage, had spotted a Mercedes with a half open boot which gave him an idea. He climbed in and pulled the lid down making sure he didn't close it entirely. The spring action of the boot lid meant he had to hold it in position. Jo walked slowly between the cars looking for any sign of movement, and in the silence, with her senses alerted, she considered the fragility of these machines and how easily damaged they were, from a scrape down one wing to a mess of twisted metal of some of the worst ones; they looked like soft drink cans that had been crushed in someone's fist and thrown aside.

How many fatalities did it represent, thought Jo, how many people hospitalised? She reached the end of the row and on a sudden thought crouched down and looked under the cars but apart from wheels and the odd bit of dangling trim there was nothing. Obviously he had escaped, he had outwitted her, so all she had to go on was that she knew what he looked like and had heard his admission of guilt. She wandered back along the line of cars and stopped by the Mercedes. At least she could identify him if it came to it. Still deep in thought, pondering her next move, she sat on the boot of the Mercedes and heard it click shut.

Spig froze. He knew this meant trouble. He couldn't open it from the inside. If he didn't give away his hiding place now while his pursuer was still there, he could be stuck until Monday morning when the garage opened again. A creeping sense of fear came over him that it might be air tight. He panicked and hammered on the inside of the lid.

'Let me out, let me out,' he yelled.

Jo jumped up, looked down at the boot lid and grinned. The situation, the lead up to it, and what had just happened became clear in a flash. By pure chance she had her opponent in check mate.

'Who's in there?' she shouted at the car boot.

'Me,' the voice called back.

'Who's me?'

There was silence.

'Are you the kid I was chasing?'

'Yes.'

'What's your name?'

Silence.

'OK, I'm going home now, see ya.'

Spig kicked and punched the boot lid. 'Let me out.'

'What's your name?' Jo asked again.

Spig thought hard and thought of the kid at school he hated most. 'Keith Turnbull,' he said.

'Did you set light to the art gallery?' she asked.

'No I didn't, let me out, I can't breathe.'

Jo felt under the rim of the boot lid for the catch, tried to open it and realised it was locked. She went around to the driver's door but that was locked also. She tried all the doors without luck. She called through the lid. 'It's all locked I'm afraid, are you OK?'

'Yes,' a doleful voice replied.

'Can you breathe?'

There was a pause. 'Yes, just get me out.'

'I'll have to call for help.' Suddenly it dawned on Jo that perhaps she had made the perfect citizen's arrest albeit unwittingly. She took out her phone and dialled 999.

WHAT FOOLS WE ARE

{ CHAPTER 57 }

Wendy had brought Ben in some pyjamas, slippers and a dressing gown. They were all new, purchased from Marks and Spencer. Ben didn't own any of these items and had originally been loaned a pair of baggy and somewhat threadbare pyjamas by the hospital. Ben looked up as Wendy placed the new purchases on the bed, still in their plastic packaging.

'I was getting rather attached to these,' he said, peering at Wendy through the least painful eye.

'I think it might be the other way around,' Wendy replied. 'You may want to change before they get too attached to you.'

'Thanks,' said Ben. 'I appreciate it. At least I can go outside for a smoke now.'

'I thought you'd have had enough of that by now.'

'Not quite the same. How's Wilf?'

'Not too bad. The burns were first degree with a few patches of second degree. Smoke inhalation as well. He's getting better, same as you, but it will take a bit longer.'

'Did he tell you what happened? I mean why he was there when the fire started?'

'Yes he did.'

'And?'

'He wants to tell you himself.'

'OK,' said Ben, wondering why the mystery. 'They're going to let me go home tomorrow.'

'I know, I spoke to the sister, she's worried you've got nowhere to go.'

'Yes, there is that. I was going to...'

'I told her you were coming to stay with me.'

'Thanks,' said Ben. 'It'll be temporary.'

'It needn't be.'

Ben looked at her. Wendy sat down. They rarely talked about their relationship. On one hand they were happy with the loose arrangement they had of friendship, going out together, having dinner and Ben staying over now and again. It suited both of them so they didn't think about it too much. On the other hand neither of them was sure if the other was afraid to commit themselves any further. The problem also lay in Ben's lack of funds. They were both aware that if Ben moved in to the B&B permanently he would be living under Wendy's roof. He didn't want to presume this was OK, and Wendy was aware of a male pride issue if she were to suggest it. The most recent events made them understand they couldn't avoid the issue any longer.

'I don't want to be some sort of kept man,' Ben protested.

'Don't be so bloody old fashioned, and besides you've lost

everything Ben.'

'There wasn't much to lose.'

'You had a business.'

'And a few canvasses and paint, it doesn't amount to much does it?'

'I am not being completely unselfish here, I've had an idea.' Wendy said. 'We can put the art classes on at the B&B.'

Ben frowned. 'Are you sure that will work?'

'Of course it will work. It's the perfect set up. You continue the art classes with the locals and people who still want to attend, and I can advertise painting weekends and holidays all in. We have the room to do it and it could increase the revenue of the B&B.'

'It could work,' Ben said. 'As long as it benefits you as well. I wouldn't like to think you were doing it just for me.'

'Of course it will benefit me. As I said it could bring more people to stay and I'll have a resident maintenance man.'

Ben smiled.

'Is it a deal then?' Wendy put out her hand. Ben shook it, 'It's a deal'

Ben went down in the lift dressed in his new pyjamas and dressing gown. He felt strange and thought he must also look it except quite a lot of men seemed to be shuffling around dressed similarly. He had never been in hospital before and it seemed odd at first. Nobody took any notice of him so he realised he couldn't look any odder than anyone else. At the desk of the burns unit he was directed to the bed occupied by Wilf. He was half propped up on the pillows, his head wrapped in a bandage and his eyes were closed. Ben looked down at him, unsure if he was sleeping. Wilf opened an eye and looked Ben up and down as best he could.

'You look like an advertisement in a mail order catalogue.' Wilf said.

'I'll have you know these are made from the finest Chinese silk flown from Hong Kong.'

'Marks and Spencer?' Wilf enquired.

'Yeah,' said Ben. 'Wendy got them for me.'

'Ah, the lovely Wendy.'

'She wants to take me in, like a stray dog.'

'Why not?'

'I don't want people feeling sorry for me.'

'You've got a funny way of going about it.'

'I came to see how you were. I hear you're up for some sort of bravery award.'

'Don't talk daft,' Wilf said. 'It'll cost you a few beers when we get out of here.'

'How come you got it worse than me?'

'Because you were lying down and I was standing up, which in the circumstances was just as well.'

Ben sat down on the chair next to the bed. 'How much longer are you going to be in here for?'

'Not sure, but the nurse who comes in and puts the ointment on each day is very nice so I'm in no hurry.'

'What's going to happen to the building?'

'I don't know,' Wilf replied. 'It depends what the fire investigators come up with.'

'Do you think it was arson?' Ben asked.

'I don't know, could have been anything. Current rumour says it was either me doing it for the insurance, an accident, either random or caused by you or arson. Remember Smoky Joe's going up a fortnight ago. Bit of a coincidence wasn't it?'

'What about the solicitor's letter you got, do you think there's a connection?'

'I don't know,' Wilf answered. 'No doubt the investigators will follow that one up.'

'It does beg the question, what were you doing there at three in the morning?'

Wilf thought for a moment. 'I came to tell you something.'

'At three in the morning?'

'It was important.'

Flash back 1982

Wilf peered at himself in the bathroom mirror. He combed his hair for the third time. Then picked up a pair of scissors from the glass shelf in front of him and snipped a couple of stray hairs from his moustache. There was an urgent knocking on the door.

'How much longer are you going to be in there?'

'Shan't be long,' he called back.

He took his favourite shirt from the hanger behind the door and put it on. It was pale blue with tiny white stars on it and was one of those shirts that just seemed to make him feel good. He tucked it into the waist band of his trousers and exited the bathroom in a cloud of Brut. His sister Marge was leaning against the wall opposite.

'Stone the crows,' she mocked looking him up and down. 'Who's the victim tonight then?'

Wilf went to his room, put on his watch and picked up his wallet. 'Bye, Mum,' he called out as he left the house, but didn't wait for an answer.

Ben and Wilf had arranged to meet up with Rose and Janet on the following evening after the picnic on the beach. Ben and Rose had seemed inseparable on the day of the picnic so it was unspoken but understood that Wilf would pair up with Janet. Secretly he found Rose more attractive, but it was no big deal; the girls were on holiday, it was a bit of fun and they would probably go home and never hear from each other again. Wilf turned the corner into the yard where Ben's studio was. It was strangely quiet and the door was closed. If Ben was there it would usually be open. Wilf rapped on one of the glass panels and called out. There was no answer. He walked a circle with his hands in his pockets and tried again. Still no answer.

'Looking for Ben?' a voice said. It was one of the mechanics working

late in the unit opposite.

'Yeah, have you seen him?'

'He was in earlier.' The guy was frowning. 'Someone came to see him, a guy in a suit, looked sort of official. Ben locked up and went off with him. He hasn't been back.'

Wilf was frowning now. 'That's odd,' he said.

'Is it important?' the guy said.

'How important is a date with two beautiful girls?'

The guy grinned. 'I'll get me coat, only joking, I expect he's gone to get spruced up.'

'I expect so, thanks anyway.'

'Have good time,' the guy called out as Wilf made to leave.

'I intend to.'

'You'll have them both to yourself if he doesn't turn up.'

'Yeah.' Wilf laughed.

Wilf called at the flat where Ben had a room but there was no answer there either. He walked away wondering what had happened to him. At least he knew where they were meeting so he still had a chance to meet up with them later.

Wilf arrived at the Smuggler's Den a bit earlier than arranged and before Rose and Janet got there. He got himself half a lager and sat down. After twenty minutes the girls arrived, cheerful, bright and fizzing with enthusiasm. Wilf stood up to greet them. Rose looked around.

'Yeah, sorry, I can't find Ben.' He explained to them about going to the studio concluding. 'I expect he got held up somewhere. He knows where we are, he'll probably turn up later.'

Rose who had looked a little crestfallen when she saw Ben was not there, brightened up. Wilf got them both drinks, lemon top lager shandies.

Ben was not going to turn up later. Ben was in a police cell, one eye closed and puffed up, blood down his shirt from his nose and a split lip, lying on the plank bed occasionally retching into a bucket, thanks to the over zealous policeman who had kicked him several times in the guts.

Two hours passed and still no sign of Ben. Wilf was embarrassed and Rose became more morose as the minutes ticked by.

'I'll get some more drinks,' Wilf said. 'Same again?'

'I'll have a vodka and tonic,' Rose said.

Wilf brought the drinks back carrying a couple of menus under his arm. 'Food's not bad here do you want something to eat?'

'I'm not hungry,' said Rose. Wilf and Janet looked at each other.

'Well, I'm having something,' Janet declared. 'I'm starving.'

Wilf and Janet ordered and when it came Rose occasionally took a chip from Wilf's plate. She drained her vodka and tonic and stood up. 'Another drink anyone?' They declined and Rose went to the bar and came back with another vodka and tonic.

After they had finished eating and the plates were cleared the atmosphere between the three became even gloomier. Wilf was trying hard to be light hearted and entertaining but he was struggling.

'Well, I feel like a bit of a gooseberry,' Rose said. 'I think I'll go back to the chalet.

'Oh, don't go,' Janet said. 'You're not being a gooseberry is she Wilf?'

'No, not at all,' said Wilf, and he meant it. He didn't want to see Rose go off in her present mood and they all realised now that it was unlikely Ben was going to turn up.

'Look, there's a club in town. We can go dancing, how about that? I don't mind dancing with two girls.'

Janet jumped at the chance to escape the gloomy atmosphere. 'Come on Rose it'll be fun.'

'OK,' she said, but without enthusiasm.

The club was a disco with a bar, crowded with young holiday makers and locals. Upbeat danceable pop songs played while flashing lights and strobes lit the people, the tables and the bar. Dark corners were spasmodically illuminated revealing couples and groups. They found a table and sat down. Rose seemed to brighten up with the atmosphere of the club. 'Right, who's having a cocktail,' she asked.

'You two go and have a dance and I'll get us all a cocktail.'

'I'd rather have a lager,' Wilf said.

'You're having a cocktail, no argument,' she said. 'This is our last night and we are going to enjoy it, Ben or no Ben.'

Wilf was no dancer but he could jig around to the music capably enough.

'She's changed her tune,' Janet confided in Wilf as they were dancing.

'Well, she might do better here than at the pub,' Wilf replied.

They got back to the table to find three brightly coloured drinks festooned with bits of fruit and paper umbrellas.

'Suits you,' said Rose as they sipped the cocktails and she sussed that Wilf was feeling self-conscious sipping through a straw. 'All you need now is a Hawaiian shirt.'

'I like this shirt.' Wilf said and they laughed.

Janet leaned towards Rose. 'Don't look now but there's a bloke over there looking this way. This could be your date.'

Wilf glanced towards the bar. There was a young man standing there, one elbow propped on the bar, looking in their direction. He had dark hair that fell over his forehead and he was wearing a white shirt that glowed iridescent in the ultra violet of the disco lights.

'Here he comes,' said Janet.

The young man walked over to their table and looked at Janet. 'Would you like to dance?'

Janet hesitated, because she had thought he was definitely going to ask Rose, and flashed a look at Wilf. The young man sensing some problem said to Wilf, 'Is that all right mate?'

Wilf nodded to the young man and then to Janet. She stood up and they went to the dance floor.

'Come on then,' Wilf said to Rose holding out his hand. 'Let's join them.'

The number was a bubbly pop song with a drum rhythm you couldn't help but want to dance to and Wilf saw Rose smiling as they moved to the music opposite each other, the alcohol doing its timeless job. Exhausted after three songs Rose and Wilf sat down.

'I'm sorry,' Rose said.

'What for?' Wilf asked.

She slumped back in her seat. 'Oh you know. Everything. Ben not turning up. He obviously didn't want to see me again.'

'Hardly your fault, I'm sure there's a good reason for Ben not turning up.'

'And for being miserable, and now that guy's got your girl, it hasn't worked out very well for you has it?'

'I think it's worked out very well,' said Wilf, and before he had thought about it very much they were kissing. He knew she was drunk, he knew she was doing it in some way to compensate for being stood up, and he knew he was taking advantage of the situation.

It was getting late. The DJ played Heart of Glass by Blondie and Wilf and Rose went back to the dance floor. Janet was still dancing with the guy in the white shirt. They were entwined, kissing and barely moving. Wilf held Rose close to him and pressed against her. She responded, pulling him tighter to her, both of them lost in the moment with the music. Janet interrupted. I'm going back to Paul's she told them looking flushed and excited. Looking at the way Wilf and Rose were dancing she didn't feel the slightest qualm. In fact she was pleased with the way it had turned out. Although she liked Wilf she did not find him attractive so to see that he and Rose seemed to be hitting it off solved two problems in one go.

Wilf felt the chill night air cool his body through his damp shirt as he walked with Rose past the entrance to the pier. A man was locking the gates for the night. Their fingers were entwined and they swung their arms as they walked.

'I wonder what the hell happened to Ben,' Wilf said.

Rose stopped. 'Shh,' she said putting a finger to his lips and pressing herself against him as if they were still in the club. 'It doesn't matter, it all turned out alright in the end. Aren't you pleased or would you rather be with Janet?' He could hear a slowness in her speech that told him she was a little drunk.

'No, of course not,' Wilf protested.

They reached the door of the chalet. Rose fumbled for the key and opened the door. She turned and they kissed. It could have been a good night kiss but they both knew it wasn't.

'What about Janet?' Wilf asked as they stepped inside.

'I don't think she'll be back any time soon, do you?' Rose said closing the door behind them.

'So that was it, you see,' said Wilf. 'I knew as soon as you showed me the photograph and told me about Justin, that what happened that night had not just gone away.'

'And that was the night I was arrested?' Ben asked.

'And that bastard copper beat you up.'

'I have no recollection of the lead up to that.'

'Of course not, you were concussed. When you told me about Justin it all came flooding back to me. The fact you couldn't remember anything was a relief. I thought he would eventually draw a blank and go away again. And then the more I thought about it, I mean that he might be my son, the more intrigued I became, but to do anything would mean I would have to explain what happened that night. Then he got mixed up with that girl and I realised I had to come clean.'

'The DNA test would have solved their problems.'

'I know,' said Wilf.

'So you could have kept quiet.'

'It wasn't just that,' Wilf said.

Neither of them spoke for a while and Ben knew they were heading for murky waters.

'Two reasons,' said Wilf, then fell silent again.

Ben waited realising Wilf was having difficulty dredging something up.

'I felt guilty about what happened.'

'Pah,' said Ben dismissively. 'It's too long ago. If it makes you feel any better I would have done the same in your shoes.'

'No,' said Wilf. 'I don't think you would have. I took advantage of you not being there, I took advantage of her, she was unhappy thinking she had been stood up and she had drunk more than she probably would have done in normal circumstances.'

'You don't know that,' Ben said.

'No, but the whole episode makes me feel bad.'

'What happened after that night?' Ben asked.

'Janet came back in the early hours and I left the chalet. The next morning they were gone. We never exchanged telephone numbers or addresses. I presume she could have found me if she had wanted to but obviously she didn't. All I knew was her first name and that she came from Surrey.'

'You have nothing to be ashamed of Wilf. That sort of thing happens all the time. If she didn't get hold of you to tell you she was pregnant what else could you do?'

Neither of them spoke for a while. He knew Wilf had more to say. It all made sense now. He remembered being beaten up in the police cell. The policeman said Ben had tried to escape. The events leading up to it had been blotted from his memory. It solved the mystery and Ben could understand Wilf's predicament. He had been telling the truth when he said it didn't matter. How could he be angry or jealous when he could not remember anything about Rose or Janet?

'You said there were two things.'

Wilf was quiet for a while arranging his thoughts. Eventually he spoke:

'When Eileen left it was simpler to say she had left me for someone else. It was more complicated than that.'

Ben waited, he wanted to give Wilf some breathing space.

'She wanted a baby and it wasn't happening. She thought I

was to blame.'

'Couldn't you have had a test?' Ben asked.

'You didn't know Eileen did you? A test might have proved something she didn't want to know. It was easier to blame me. I thought she might be right for a time, I mean I had no evidence to the contrary then, did I?'

Wilf looked at Ben and Ben knew he was struggling. 'Do you want to stop now?'

'You might as well know the rest,' Wilf said. 'She had several relationships after she left me and none of them resulted in the thing she desired most. She went downhill, depression, pills.' He paused trying to keep his voice level. 'The pills cured the depression – along with half a bottle of vodka.' He stopped.

'I'm sorry, I didn't know,' Ben said.

'There was no point in telling anyone, it was my own problem and Eileen's of course. It didn't occur to me at first that I wanted children as well. I was too wrapped up worrying about Eileen. Later on, after Eileen had gone, quite a bit of time after she'd gone, I sort of thought about it a bit more so when you told me about Justin, I thought, well yeah, maybe he is mine, and do you know what? I felt happy about it. It was a shock when you showed me that photograph, seeing Rose again after all those years.'

Ben had stood up and wandered over to the window to ease the tension created by Wilf's obvious distress. There was a pause before Wilf said: 'On her birthday I visit her grave.'

'That's nice,' said Ben immediately regretting the clumsiness of his response.

'I can't go on the date she died – it's too much.'

'I can understand that,' Ben said.

'I put a fish on her grave when I go.'

'A fish?' Ben turned around unable to keep the note of consternation out of his voice.

Wilf looked pained. 'I don't do flowers.'

'I see.'

'They don't mean anything to me. Anyway Eileen hated dead flowers and all they do is die. I see them on other graves.'

Ben turned back to looking out of the window. He watched as two ambulance men took a stretchered figure out of the ambulance with a drip attached. It swayed with the motion and he could see the haste in their movements like it was a silent film he was observing.

'I don't expect it stays there long,' Wilf continued. 'Foxes or something will take it in the night. I'm not stupid; it's just something – an offering.'

Ben turned back to face the room. 'I think Eileen would have understood.'

Wilf looked up at Ben. 'What bloody fools we are, eh?'

GET YOURSELF ON TWITTER!

{ CHAPTER 58 }

Bob and Clare Elliot sat at the table in their conservatory. It was Sunday morning and Bob was reading The Sunday Times while Clare thumbed idly through the colour supplement. There was coffee on the table and Bob took a sip from his cup now and then and a bite out of some toast that had long gone cold. The sun was just rising above the shrubs in the garden allowing fringes of light through the windows. Bob seemed engrossed in something in the paper, and Clare looked up at him occasionally from the magazine she wasn't really reading. She had told him she had visited Ben at the gallery, although most of what she reported was a fabrication. She invented a scene where she had been angry with him and threatened that unless he forfeited the picture she would go to the police. She had called on her acting skills, that were by now just a memory, to sound convincing. Bob had been partly satisfied with the solution although he thought Ben was getting off lightly, and after the most recent events Clare was concerned.

'So, you know the gallery burnt down then don't you?' she said.

'Yes, I did,' Bob replied without taking his eyes from the paper.

'The man who owned it was inside it at the time you know?'

'Yes I know.' Bob bit in to a piece of toast. 'But he got out.'

'It was lucky someone was passing.'

'Lucky for him, yes.'

Clare was getting frustrated at Bob's nonchalance. He was either pretending or he didn't understand the full impact of what had happened.

'You do realise that if you had gone to the police you might have been a suspect?'

Bob put the paper on the table and looked at Clare. 'But we didn't, so it's OK.'

'You don't seem very concerned. The guy could have died.'

'Frankly I'm not that bothered.'

'He was still a human being.'

'Clare, he is a rogue and a waster who took advantage of our daughter. It would have been rough justice and no great loss.'

Clare looked at Bob for a while suppressing the desire to defend Ben more vociferously, but at the same time realising it might give something away or at least seem odd.

'Please tell me you had nothing to do with that fire Bob.'

'Christ Almighty Clare, what do you think I am? Of course I didn't. I wouldn't do a thing like that.'

'It's just that you're in cahoots with that Ray from the club and you told me yourself he was trying to get that land to develop it.'

'I told Ray I would not be involved in any rough stuff or

anything illegal.'

'Still, do you think he might have been responsible in some way for it?'

'No. He may be a bit of a gangster but he wouldn't stoop that low. I think that Frampton fellow got off lightly. I still think we should have gone to the police.'

'It wouldn't have done any good if you had,' Clare told him.

'Don't be daft, she was under eighteen, he would have been prosecuted for corruption of a minor.'

'He had a signed form of parental consent.'

'Forged, like his paintings I suspect.'

'No, I signed it.' She didn't have to tell Bob this and the evidence would be gone by now anyway, but she felt the need to try and exonerate Ben in some way. Bob looked at her.

'What the hell were you thinking of?'

'I didn't know what I was signing. I didn't have my glasses to hand when she asked me.'

'Oh very clever.'

'Doesn't matter now anyway.'

Bob grunted. Clare had not told him that she had paid for the painting and he hadn't asked, assuming that to avoid any legal investigation Ben had arranged for Clare to have the painting when it came back from the London gallery.

'Look,' said Clare. 'The painting is coming here, so no one need ever see it. The gallery has gone. Nothing untoward happened to Jo, she was not interfered with or corrupted in any way. Aren't you satisfied with that?'

'You don't know she wasn't corrupted, and besides we still have the problem of an errant daughter, who lies, connives, does exactly as she pleases and has no respect for me.'

'Don't be so hard on her. Jo's OK, just cut her a bit of slack.'

'And what about this boyfriend, some older guy, I don't like the sound of that.'

'You don't have to worry about that, it's all over.'

'How do you know?'

'Because she told me.'

'Why does she tell you all these things and not me, don't I matter or something?'

'Why do you think she doesn't tell you these things? It's because you always start flying off the handle at her for what she might do. Of course she's not going to tell you anything.'

'I am her father.'

'I know, but it doesn't work like that. The more truth you accept from people without condemning them the more they will open up to you.'

'I don't understand all that psychology stuff.'

'It's only human nature.'

Clare heard movement from upstairs

'Anyway shush, we don't want her knowing we were discussing her.'

Bob picked up the paper again.

'Morning everyone,' Jo said as she bounced down the stairs and into the kitchen. 'Where's Tom?'

'Still in bed I expect,' Clare said.

'Lazy little oik.' Jo responded. She helped herself to juice from the fridge. Her hair was fluffy from blow drying and she was wearing a blue and white striped top, white shorts and Crocs.

'Morning Papa,' she said, kissing him on the top of his head.

'Someone's very chipper this morning,' Clare remarked.

'I'm going out today,' Jo said. The curfew had been lifted a few days previously by Bob on insistence from Clare, seeing as she flouted it anyway and it was pointless trying to enforce it when sometimes both her and Bob were out at the same time.

'Where are you going?'

'Maddy rang me up; we're going for a day's sailing on

Elmore's Dad's yacht.'

Bob looked up. 'Who's in charge?' he asked.

'Don't worry Father; his dad's going to captain,'

'Good, and make sure you wear a life jacket.'

'Yes Dad.' Jo looked at her mother and raised her eyes. Clare smiled.

'You know about the gallery then?' Jo said, busying herself with cereal and milk.

'Terrible business, very sad,' said Clare.

'It was his own fault,' Bob said. 'Apparently he was drunk.'

'Who told you that?' Jo asked, sitting down at the table.

'I was talking to a guy from the fire brigade, he said they could have set light to his breath there was so much whisky on it.'

Jo waited until she had finished her mouthful of cereal. 'Actually it was torched,' she said conversationally.

'What do you know about it?' Bob asked.

'Apparently,' Jo continued, ignoring her father's question, 'it was an eleven year old boy, pyromaniac. He put a petrol soaked rag through the letter box and dropped a match in. He's confessed to it and to the seafood hut on the seafront a couple of weeks ago.'

'I didn't know any of this,' Bob said.

Jo waggled her smart phone at him. 'You want to get yourself on Twitter. You're so out of touch Dad.'

'Sounds like gossip to me,' he said.

'You'll see,' Jo replied.

THE MAN IN THE LONG BLACK COAT

{ CHAPTER 59 }

The first days that gave an indication summer might end brought a chill that blew in off the sea. Collars were turned up, and coats and jumpers appeared as people went about their various jobs and concerns around the town. The doors of high street shops that had welcomed customers by being open wide, remained closed as the breeze chilled the ankles of the shop assistants. In the high street of Cocklebury-on-Sea there were few independent shops. All that sat between Starbucks and Boots and Smiths were mainly charity shops. For a fraction of the cost of shopping in the chain stores you could indulge in a little retail therapy for things you didn't really need; the modern alternative to hunting and gathering.

A nice Capodimonte figurine of a shepherdess holding a lamb, now that would look nice on the sideboard along with the other ones; have you read that Dan Brown? Look only fifty pee; that handbag is only two pounds fifty, I know I've got twelve handbags but you can't pass up an offer like that. Rails of clothes smelling slightly musty; they're not second hand, they're pre-loved. Men's shoes looking sadder than lost dogs and gaping like cadavers, creaky creases across the brows. DVDs of Only Fools and Horses and Bergerac stand next to the vinyl LPs, singles and CDs.

Dealers do the odd circuit now and again looking for minor treasures the staff had missed. You can spot them, they always turn the china over. They can usually sniff out the good stuff. The car booters also come around looking for stuff that will turn a few pence profit but they usually cruise around on a Sunday picking up what people leave outside the front door after a loft clear out.

Kevin had checked them all out from Mind to Scope. Mornings were better as they were busier, filled with pensioners with nothing better to do. He checked the rails of men's coats, leather blousons, tweed jackets, suit jackets, dinner jackets. He found what he wanted in The British Heart Foundation, long, black with wide lapels and cinched in at the back with a belt. He looked at the viscose lining and read the label on the pocket, Burton – and best of all it didn't smell of fish. Twelve pounds, not that the price made any difference, Kevin wasn't going to pay for it. Kevin looked over at the assistant at the till. She had a pile of CDs she was sorting through.

'Never 'eard of 'alf this stuff,' she said to no one in particular, although the door behind her was open and two other volunteers were sorting through a mountain of old clothes. She kept up her monologue regardless of the fact that perhaps no one was listening to her.

'They're just plain silly some of these names. I mean why would you want to call a group The Killers, it's not very nice is it? This one's called Throbbing Gristle, I don't know.'

A woman brought a blouse to the counter. The assistant pushed the pile of CDs to one side.

'Oh, that's nice,' she told her. 'You'll look nice in that one. Do you want a bag? Two pounds fifty please. I was going to buy that one meself but I couldn't get into it. Fit you though. I could do with losing a bit of weight, but you know what it's like.'

The lady shopper smiled.

'Fran, Fran. The till's locked on me again.'

A woman appeared from the back room, pressed a button and the till drawer sprung open.

'I can never understand all this new-fangled stuff, buttons all the time, buttons, buttons.

Thanks love.'

She went back to her CDs screwing up her nose in disgust at most of them. 'Prefab Sprout, what a stupid name; oh here we go, Jim Reeves, that's more like it. Phil Collins, I like 'im. Ooh look, hits of the sixties.'

She opened the CD case and placed the disc into a small machine on the counter.

'Let's 'ave a bit of music, cheer ourselves up.'

The first piano notes came out of the tinny speaker followed by the Tra-la-la introduction.

The woman at the counter started moving her arms in a slow locomotion as she sang along with the words, moving her hips in a grotesque parody of something like the twist and looking like a stack of gently gyrating tyres.

'You can all sing along if you like, come on,' and she started singing along with Neil Sedaka.

'Ooh, happy birthday sweet sixteen.'

Some of the other browsers started to look embarrassed

and Kevin was hoping this wasn't going to empty the shop as he would be less noticeable with other shoppers in there. Her enthusiasm tailed off as no one seemed to be taking up her offer of a sing-song. She stopped as a man came to the counter with a pile of paperback books.

'That lot will keep you out of mischief for a bit then,' she said as she took the money. Kevin chose his moment. He took the coat off its hanger and put it on. Positioning himself at an angle with the mirror so he could see the till, he waited until the woman turned her back to put the money in it and slipped out of the shop. He had done this many times before. He wasn't surprised that the staff never caught him; they were too slow to catch a tortoise. Even if he had the money he wouldn't pay out of principle as they were still run by capitalist pigs who pocketed the money anyway. He only just had enough money left for a bit of dope he was going to score next from a mate. The rest of his benefit Grace had taken after she had totted up everyone's contribution to the squat and added on to Kevin's share, the money he had borrowed from Bo.

He walked quickly down several interconnecting streets to get as far away as possible in case he had been spotted. He heard a squeal of tyres and a police car pulled sharply into the kerb just in front of him blocking his path. A uniformed officer got out of the passenger door.

'Hello Kevin.'

'The coat's mine, I've had it for ages,' Kevin said.

'It's not about the coat Kevin.'

'I'm clean, I haven't got any dope.' He held out his arms as if prepared to be searched.

'It's not about the drugs either Kevin.'

The other officer was getting out of the driving seat.

'What do you want then?' he asked.

'Do you know a kid called Edward Spiggot?'

BARBECUED LOBSTER

{ CHAPTER 60 }

Ben's battered cool box had survived the fire and it clanked with its contents as he trotted up the steps to Wilf's hut on the beach. He had walked past the remains of the gallery and even though there was nothing really to see except the charred remnants, the bare, blackened walls and the police tape cordoning it off, he still stopped and looked for a while. The Tupelo Honey had already been winched up onto the beach and Wilf's converted pot- bellied stove was sending out a heat haze that rippled the view of the sea beyond. Ben couldn't see Wilf but could hear him rummaging around in the hut and swearing under his breath.

'Son of a bitch.'

'What have you lost?' Ben called out, more to let Wilf know he was there than to find out what he was looking for. Wilf emerged carrying a murderous looking cook's knife and a two inch thick piece of oak chopping board, scarred and rutted with use.

'Where did you get those?' Ben asked, knowing the answer more or less.

'The knife came up in a net one day and I found the board washed up on the beach on the same day. I don't know whether they had ever met before but they're good friends now.'

Ben smiled. 'Beer?' he said, putting down the cool box.

'I thought you'd never ask,' Wilf replied, placing the board and knife on the rickety table next to the stove.

'Good day?' Ben asked knocking the tops off two bottles and handing one to Wilf.

'I'm making the most of it,' Wilf replied. 'There won't be too many more.' It was a freak September day. Although the weather had started to cool, the day had been warm and mellow with calm seas and barely a ripple of wind.

Wilf removed some damp sacking from the top of a flat plastic fish box stamped with Cocklebury-on-Sea on the side. Underneath were two glistening blue black lobsters. Wilf picked one up holding it by the body just behind the head. The claws of the animal reached back and over its body but couldn't get the angle to attack its captor. Wilf placed it on the oak board and picked up the knife. He placed the blade of the knife at a central point along the lobster's back and with one action cleaved it in two.

Ben winced. 'Christ, doesn't that hurt?'

'Only if you get your finger in the way,' Wilf replied. He did the same with the other one and placed them cut side up on the griddle of the stove. He cut several slices of butter from a pack and laid them over the lobsters. Where the butter stuck out over the edge of the shell, it melted, dripped and turned to smoke on the coals, drifting across and allowing Ben to smell the sweet nutty odour of burnt butter.

'You've seen Justin then?' Ben asked.

'Yeah,' Wilf said. 'He came over to the house for a chat after you spoke to him.'

'Yes, he'd just got the DNA test back as negative so he was already aware of that side of things. I think when I told him the full story he was relieved that I could tie up the loose ends for him, that his search had not been in vain, and that there was no blood relationship between him and Jo. Are you going to have a DNA test?'

'No, we were both pretty certain that the events as I remembered them proved things fairly conclusively.'

'Can't have been easy for him finding out he was the result of a holiday romance.'

'Romance?' said Wilf.

'You know what I mean,' Ben replied.

'His mother went to bed with me after one too many drinks because she thought she had been stood up.'

'Is that what you told Justin?'

'Of course not.' Wilf moved the lobster halves slightly with the tongs. The translucent flesh was beginning to turn white and the shells a brilliant red where they weren't charred with the heat 'Anyway he already knew the facts, it was just an identity mix up.'

'Are you going to keep in touch?'

'We said we'd have a pint now and again.'

'Did he patch it up with Jo?'

Wilf laughed. 'Tried to, she blew him out. Said he'd had his chance and she was going out with a local lad. His dad's got a yacht down at the marina apparently.'

'After all that,' Ben said.

'It's how it goes, isn't it?' Wilf put two halves of lobster on a chipped plate and handed it to Ben.

'There's some bread in that box,' he said, pointing with the tongs.

'What happened to the painting?' Wilf asked. 'Did you get it back?'

Ben smiled. 'It was delivered the day of the fire so unfortunately it perished along with everything else. Probably just as well.'

They picked out the chunks of creamy white lobster flesh dripping with golden butter from the shells and mopped up the juices on their plates with the bread.

'Why's that?' Wilf asked, unaware of the complete story. Ben had thought it wise not to tell anyone the bit about Jo's mother and his involvement with her. The cheque Clare had given had been in a drawer in the office so that too was gone and Ben had let Clare know.

'It just draws a line under the whole thing and her dad will be pleased as well.'

Wilf nodded. 'You've got some money coming to you shortly,' he said.

Ben looked up. 'What for? You don't owe me anything.'

'Insurance,' Wilf said through a mouthful of lobster and bread.

'What insurance? I wasn't insured.'

'No, but I was.'

'Yeah, but that's building insurance surely.'

'Last time I renewed the insurance,' Wilf said, 'I shopped around a bit and got this package that included contents for the same price I was already paying just for the building. So I thought I bet that idiot hasn't got any contents insurance so I went for the package. You didn't have any insurance did you?'

'You know me well enough to know the answer to that.'

'You need to make a list of what you lost; paint, easels, canvasses. You can only get cost price for stock, but I argued with the loss adjusters that the finished paintings would have to include something for the work that went into them rather than just the paint and canvas.'

'Well it's certainly unexpected.'

'Also loss of business. I think it will be quite a good sum.'

'What's going to happen to the premises now?'

'No point in rebuilding it – it was only an old net shed anyway. I expect I shall sell the land.'

'So the insurance company is OK about everything then?'

'Oh yes, it was definitely arson. The police picked up this kid, eleven year old. He did Smoky Joe's on the seafront. Apparently he has a history, suspended from school for setting light to the science lab. Problems at home. He'd been put up to it by an older lad, local dopehead. The police leant on him a bit and he said he'd been paid by the owner of that night club RayJays. The police investigation also turned up the fact that he was the one who had the solicitor's letter sent to me offering to buy the land. So he's in deep shit and unless he has a good lawyer he'll be doing a stretch. The kid said he would never have done it if he'd known there was somebody in there.'

'That's comforting,' Ben said.

Wilf chucked the lobster shells onto the shingle so the gulls would clear up for them and took another beer from the box. 'Cheers,' he said to Ben.

The End

Printed in Great Britain
by Amazon

27015077R00223